Welcome to Land of Fright™!

Land of Fright™ is a world of spine-tingling short horror stories filled with the strange, the eerie, and the weird. The **Land of Fright**™ tales encompass the vast expanse of time and space. In the **Land of Fright™** series of books you will visit the world of the Past in Ancient Rome, Medieval England, the old West, World War II, and other eras yet to be explored. You will find many tales that exist right here in the Present, tales filled with modern lives that have taken a turn down a darker path. You will travel into the Future to tour strange new worlds and interact with alien societies, or to just take a disturbing peek at what tomorrow may bring.

Each **Land of Fright**™ story exists in its own territory (which we like to call a **terrorstory**.) Some of the story realms you visit will intrigue you. Some of them may unsettle you. Some of them may even titillate and amuse you. We hope many of them will give you delicious chills along your journey as you meet up with zombies, werewolves, immortals, warlocks, secret agents, and a crazed voodoo queen.

First, we need to check your ID. **Land of Fright**™ is intended for mature audiences. You will experience adult language, graphic violence, and some explicit sex. Ready to enter? Good. We'll take that ticket now. **Land of Fright**™ awaits. You can pass through the dark gates and—Step Into Fear!

Readers Love Land of Fright™!

"This is the first story I've read by this author and it blew me away! A gripping tale that kept me wondering until the end. Images from this will, I fear, haunt me at unexpected moments for many months to come. Readers, be warned! :)" – Amazon review for **Dung Beetles (Land of Fright™ #27 – in Collection III)**

"Some truly original stories. At last, a great collection of unique and different stories. Whilst this is billed as horror, the author managed to steer away from senseless violence and gratuitous gore and instead with artful story telling inspires you to use your own imagination. A great collection. Already looking for other collections… especially loved Kill the Queen (God Save the Queen)." – Amazon UK review for **Land of Fright™ Collection I**

"This was a great story. Even though it was short I still connected with the main character and was rooting for her. Once I read the twist I cheered her on. This was an enjoyable short story." – Amazon review for **Snowflakes (Land of Fright™ #3 – in Collection I)**

"Love the freaky tales from the Land of Fright. This one is particularly nasty and dark. A tale of double revenge unfolds in a graveyard where a perceived business betrayal causes the perceiver to enact an insidious plan to impose the ultimate suffering on his partner. The suffering takes an unexpected turn that I did not see coming." – Amazon review for **Cemetery Dance (Land of Fright™ #49 – in Collection V)**

"I absolutely loved the heck out of this story. The whole story was bizarre, and the end? Well, it was perfect!" – Amazon review for **The Throw-Aways (Land of Fright™ #31 – in Collection IV)**

"I like the idea of a malevolent dimension that finds a way to reach into our world... this was an entertaining read and can be read at lunch or as a palate cleanser between longer stories." – Amazon review for **Sparklers (Land of Fright™ #15 – in Collection II)**

"I enjoyed this quite a bit, but then I enjoy anything set in Pompeii. A horror story is a first, though, and well done. I'm become a fan of the author and so far have enjoyed several of his stories." – Amazon review for **Ghosts of Pompeii (Land of Fright™ #14 – in Collection II)**

"Fantastic science fiction short that has a surprising plot twist, great aliens, cool future tech and occurs in a remote lived-in future mining colony on a distant planet. This short hit all the marks I look for in science fiction stories. The alien creatures are truly alien and attack with a mindless ruthlessness. The desperate colonists defend themselves in a uniquely futuristic way. This work nails the art of the short story. Recommended." – Amazon review for **Out of Ink (Land of Fright™ #26 – in Collection III)**

"I am a fan of the Land of Fright series and have found the horror found in the stories diverse and delightfully bizarre. This tale amp's up the gritty to 11. The barbarian warrior king in this short story is a well written, fearsome, crude and believable beast of a man. This story is not for those offended by sex or violence. I was immersed and found it great escapism, exactly what I look for in recreational reading."- Amazon review for **The King Who Owned The World (Land of Fright™ #50 – in Collection V)**

"Varied stories with widely different themes and cunning plot twists. This writer shows a lot of imagination. Enjoyed every page." – Amazon UK review for **Land of Fright™ – Collection I)**

"Perfect bite size weirdness. Land of Fright does it again with this Zone like short that has two creative plot twists that really caught me off guard. I know comparing this type of work to the Twilight Zone is overdone but it really is a high compliment that denotes original, well conceived and delightfully weird short fiction. Recommended." – Amazon review for **Flipbook (Land of Fright™ #19 – in Collection II)**

"An enjoyable story; refreshingly told from the point of view of the cat...definitely good suspense." – Amazon review for **Pharaoh's Cat (Land of Fright™ #30 – in Collection III)**

"A fun thrill-ride into the Mexican jungle, and another great Land of Fright tale. Not enough people have written horror stories or novels about Aztec sacrifices." -Amazon review for **Virgin Sacrifice (Land of Fright™ #42 – in Collection V)**

"This short has a cool premise and was very effective at quickly transporting me to the sands of the coliseum in ancient Rome. The images of dead and dying gladiators are detailed and vivid. There is a malevolent force that very much likes its job and is not about to give it up, ever. Recommended." – Amazon review for **Hammer of Charon (Land of Fright™ #29 - in Collection III)**

"The thing I like about the Land of Fright series of short stories is that they are so diverse yet share a common weird, unusual and original vibe. From horror to science fiction they are all powerful despite of their brevity. Another great addition to the Land of Fright festival of the odd." - Amazon review for **Snowflakes (Land of Fright™ #3 – in Collection I)**

Welcome to the
Land of Fright™
A World of Spine-Tingling Stories filled with the Strange, the Eerie, and the Weird

Land of Fright™

Collection VI

JACK O'DONNELL

DEDICATION

To everyone who likes taking a trip into the Land of Fright™ with me!

LAND OF FRIGHT™ COLLECTION VI CONTENTS

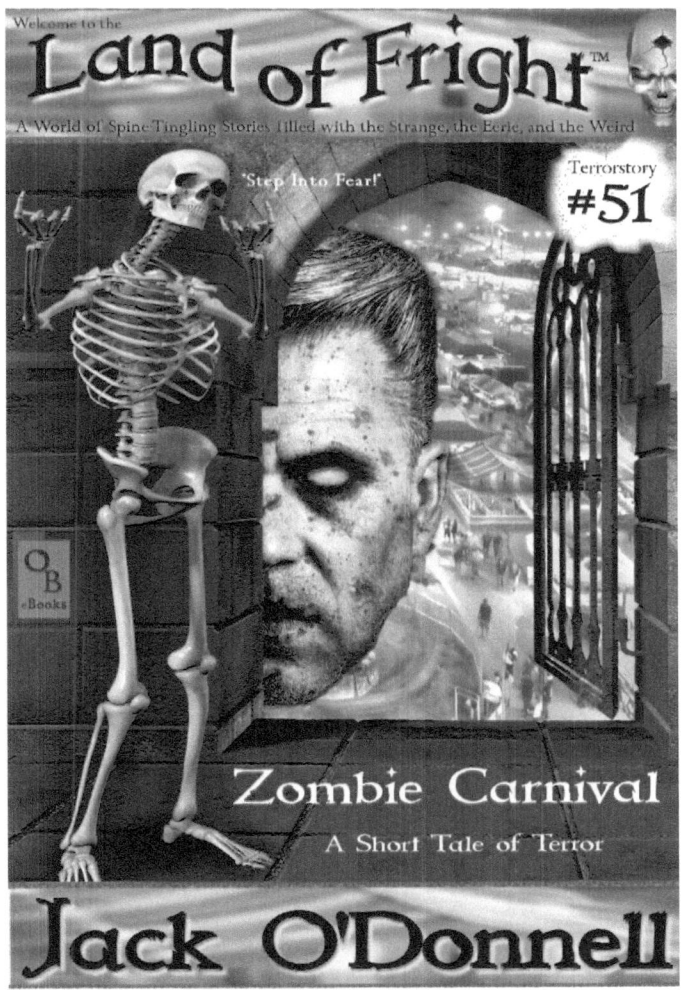

TERRORSTORY #51
ZOMBIE CARNIVAL

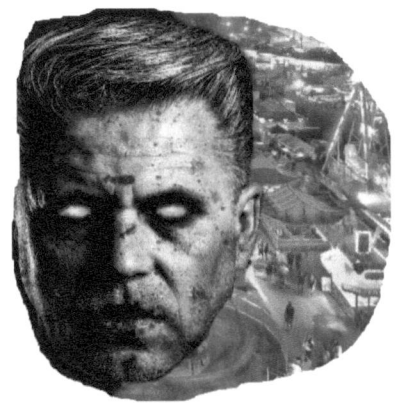

Robbie Sinclair was the one who saw the carnival first.

Robbie was kind of a dick. But that went with the territory. He was a football player for the Monroe Mustangs, and all the jocks at his high school had over-inflated egos. But Robbie was a little different from all the others. He was a kicker, so he never felt like he achieved the true star status he thought he was entitled to. Hell, his damn foot had been directly responsible for three of their five wins this season, but the rest of the offense kept getting all the praise. Robbie was a good-looking kid with close-cropped

3

black hair and a strong square jaw, so he had a lot of female admirers, but the girls he really wanted kept gravitating towards the quarterback, the running backs, and the linebackers, not to him.

He wasn't too keen on studying, but he managed to get through three grades of high school with a B-average. He wasn't an idiot; he just really didn't give a shit. Besides, his teachers had it out for him, always marking points off his papers or tests for asinine reasons. So Robbie didn't just have a chip on his shoulder; he had a full bag of Lays decked out on his upper neck and back.

Robbie saw the carnival loom up out of the fog as he stared out the passenger side window. "Check it out. Check it out. What the hell is that?"

Carly Lewis glanced over from the driver's seat and immediately saw the bright lights, the neon flashes. She was a voluptuous blonde with a pert nose and softly rounded chin. And Robbie would fully admit that her very large breasts were a hugely positive addition to her personality. Despite the fall chill in the air, Carly was only wearing a white blouse and no jacket, unlike Robbie who was wearing his varsity football jacket. She was the kind of person who could wear shorts when it was fifty degrees; she just enjoyed the cold and much preferred being cool than being too warm. "It's a carnival." Her face lit up. She loved carnivals. The rides, the games, the cotton candy, the sights, the sounds, the smells. She loved everything about them. "That looks awesome!"

Nelson Torino leaned forward in the back seat, looking past his current girl Shirley (oh shit, what the hell was her last name?) to get a glance out the window. He was a backup wide receiver on the football team. He had good hands, but he was the slowest of the bunch, so he didn't get a lot of playing time. He was the skinny white boy of the otherwise all black receiving corps.

"What time is it?" Shirley asked from her seat next to Nelson.

Nelson glanced down at his phone. "It's only nine-thirty."

"I need to be home by midnight," Shirley said.

Nelson frowned. Shirley (was it Palmer? No. Maybe Pamphilis; she did have a darker tone to her skin than the rest of them so maybe she was Greek or something) could be a real downer. Her attitude was as ancient as her name. Who the hell named their kid Shirley anymore? The expression fuddy duddy popped into his head. Nelson had no idea where it came from, and he wasn't sure what it even meant, but that's what Shirley felt like sometimes. A real fuddy duddy. Her thick-rimmed black glasses didn't help her out, either. She did look like a throwback to the 1950's. At least she had a nice rack and showed plenty of cleavage. She never wore a bra, either, which really drove Nelson wild because her nipples always seemed to be erect. Always. They always poked out of the fabric of whatever she was wearing. He also couldn't help but notice that Carly never seemed to be wearing a bra either. He wondered if the two purposely did that just to tease and torment him and Robbie.

Carly waved her hand at Shirley. "Pshaww. Plenty of time. Let's check it out." Carly had grown up with Shirley, who lived a few houses down from her on the same block. It wasn't that she particularly liked Shirley; it was more like she felt better about herself whenever Shirley was around. And she liked to feel good about herself, so she and Shirley did a lot of things together. Shirley had flat drab brown hair, kind of a big nose, and those really ugly glasses, so Carly knew it made her look that much prettier to any boys who might be around when Shirley was with her.

"Hells yeah," Robbie said.

"I don't have any money," Shirley said.

"I got you covered," Robbie said. Robbie was rich, too. Well, at least his parents were and they never hesitated to give Robbie a generous cash handout whenever he asked. His sense of entitlement was another layer that added to his general level of dickness. And he never missed an opportunity to let everyone else know how rich he was.

Nelson cleared his throat. "I'm tapped out, too."

Robbie frowned. "Damn, you two are perfect for each other. The poor princess and the penniless pauper."

Carly giggled.

"I'll pay you back," Nelson said.

"You know what?" Robbie said. "You don't have to. I'm feeling fucking generous today." He reached into his pocket and pulled out a thick wad of bills. He peeled off two hundred dollar bills and handed them back to Nelson. "My treat. You don't have to pay me back. It's cool."

"You sure?" Nelson asked, taking the offered bills.

"Yeah. No sweat. Plenty more where that came from."

"Thanks, man," Nelson said. He handed a hundred to Shirley, but she waved it away. "You hold on to it," she said.

Carly glanced over to Robbie. "I like a guy with a

thick wad." She reached over and playfully rubbed at his crotch.

Robbie glanced down at Carly's hand on his crotch. He beamed her a huge smile. "Now *that's* what I'm talkin' about!" He looked back out at the carnival. "Let's have us some fucking fun, people!"

They stood outside the car in the parking lot, staring up at the neon sign. The sign read: *ombie Carnival.* The metal borders encasing the neon letters were rusted, giving the large sign a hint of bloody stains decorating its edges.

"Ombie carnival," Nelson said, repeating what he saw on the sign. "Never heard of it."

Then a Z crackled and burst to light. The big letter hadn't been visible before, but it must have been there and they just hadn't seen it.

They all stared at the sign. Their smiles grew, but Shirley's not as much as the others. She pushed her glasses back up her nose and pulled her unbuttoned pink sweater jacket a little tighter around herself.

"No way." Robbie stared at the sign with obvious delight. "Zombie Carnival. Are you kidding me? That is fucking awesome!"

Carly pushed at Robbie's shoulder. "Hey, check that guy out."

Robbie and the others turned to follow Carly's pointing fingers. A man dressed in ragged, ripped clothes stumbled through the parking lot three rows of cars back. It wasn't even a stumble; it was definitely an undead shuffle, an oddly stiff movement they had all seen hundreds of times in zombie movies and on TV shows. He lurched and stuttered, moving with herky-jerky motions. The zombie man paused, as if suddenly sensing their presence. He slowly turned his head towards them. His face was an ashen gray, his hair wildly tousled in total disarray. Several ragged rips in his face marred his flesh. His eyes were dull and glassy, yet somehow showed an eerie life within them.

"Man, that is legit," Robbie said. "He looks awesome."

Just then, a bit of dark bile oozed out of the man's mouth and pooled down over his dry-cracked lips and chin.

"That's disgusting," Shirley said.

Robbie clapped his hands, his smile growing even wider. "That is awesome!" He grabbed Carly's hand and pulled her towards the ticket booth near the front gate. "Come on, let's go."

Shirley continued to stare at the shuffling zombie man.

Nelson touched Shirley's shoulder and she started, fighting back a gasp. "Holy shit," Nelson said. "We're not even inside the carnival yet."

Shirley said nothing.

"Come on, we should stick together." He headed towards the ticket booth, then paused and went back to take Shirley's reluctant hand, dragging her along with him.

Robbie stepped up to the ticket booth. It reminded him of the old outhouse on Mr. Gaffin's farm. It was a tiny structure made out of decaying wood, barely deep enough to hold the body of the ticket seller. The old man sat on a stool, patiently waiting for Robbie's order. The old man had deeply sunken eyes, gaunt cheeks, and a thick head of bone-white hair that didn't seem to fit the rest of his appearance at all. Robbie thought it might be a wig. He wondered why the guy would even bother wearing a wig, but it wasn't important at all so the question just went away. "Three adults and one scaredy cat," Robbie said to the old man. Robbie looked at Carly and she giggled.

"That'll be eighty five dollars," the old man said.

"Eighty five?" Nelson asked. That didn't divide up right between four people. Tax, maybe?

The old man wordlessly pointed to a hand-scrawled price list, drawn in chalk on a nearby slab of wood. It read: *Adults - $20, Children - $20, Scaredy Cats - $25, Infants Admitted Free.*

"Are you serious?" Nelson asked.

"I don't make up the prices. I just collect the money," the old man said, making no effort to hide the boredom he felt for Nelson's question. "You want to go to the carnival, or not?"

"Hell yeah, we do." Robbie handed him a hundred dollar bill. "Keep the change. Buy yourself a brush."

The old man wordlessly took the offered money and handed Robbie four tickets. Robbie stared down at the tickets in his hand. The tickets looked aged, battered and worn around the edges. Robbie handed out a ticket to each of the others, making certain Shirley was the recipient of the ticket marked *Scaredy Cat*, giving her a smirk as he handed it to her.

Shirley just took the ticket with an even expression, not giving him the satisfaction of reacting to it.

"Come on, let's go." Robbie said and led them

towards the gated opening nearby. The entire carnival was surrounded by a high chain-link fence and the entrance was a small opening manned by two people. Well, one of them looked like a person; the man sitting on a stool near a small table that held a bowl filled with ripped-in-half ticket stubs was a grizzled old man with a shadowy, scruffy layer of bristles covering his cheeks, chin, and neck. His oily black hair was matted down to his head, awkwardly flattened over the obvious receding hairline starting to overpower his skull. The other person near the entrance had a chain around her neck and she did the zombie shuffle back and forth near the entrance. She was wearing ripped fishnet stockings, a ripped leather jacket unzipped to her navel. She had jet black hair and her mouth was covered in smeared lipstick that gave her lips the appearance of a bloody frown.

Robbie approached the ticket taker and his zombie pet.

"Tickets, please," the ticket taker said. He held out his bony-fingered hand palm up.

Robbie and Carly handed the ticket taker their tickets. The man put the tickets to his mouth, bit them in half, spit out the half in his mouth into the bowl on the table next to him, and handed the tickets back towards Robbie. "Umm, you can keep them," Robbie said and he and Carly moved past the gated entrance into the carnival grounds.

Shirley handed her ticket to the ticket taker and he stared at her *Scaredy Cat* ticket for a moment. Then, he looked up at her and gave her the eeriest, creepiest smile she had ever seen. To Shirley, it was the look of a sadistic murderer about to flay a helpless victim knowing that he was going to get away with what he was doing and there was no one going to stop him. The ticket taker bit the ticket in half, spit out the torn half into the bowl, and handed the ticket back to Shirley. Shirley just stared at the offered half-ticket.

Suddenly, the zombie pet twisted and turned her torso. "I gotta take a damn piss," she growled.

The ticket taker turned sharply to the zombie woman. "Damn it, Sally Mae, you ain't supposed to talk." His words came out in a sharp hiss. "You is spoilin' it. You is a zombie."

"I don't care." The woman zombie pet named Sally Mae scrunched up, twisting and turning her body. "I gotta go."

The ticket taker snatched at Nelson's offered ticket and impatiently waved him on, throwing Shirley's half ticket and Nelson's full ticket into the bowl.

Once they were all inside the fence together, Robbie frowned at the ticket taker and the zombie pet woman. "Man, that is so lame. They just ruined it for me."

"Like you really thought they were real zombies?" Nelson asked.

"I was caught up in the moment, yeah."

Carly grabbed Robbie's arm and tugged him closer to her. "Win me a prize, Robbie."

Robbie flashed back to when he was eight. The carnival was the shit. The kaleidoscope of colors, the flaring lights, the smell of carnival food, popcorn and cotton candy and corn dogs. The rattle of the roller coaster. The spinning blasts of red as the tilt-a-whirl cabs went round and round. Was this not heaven on Earth? And all those prizes. Just out of reach. Just one more ring toss, one more toss of the ball, one more blast from his water gun in the derby race would've shattered the balloon before everybody else's balloon burst. Always so close to winning a big prize. Always so damn close. But he never did. He never won a damn thing. And the wave of disappointment flooded back into him. The imaginary remembered love of the carnival was replaced by that lingering disappointment, a disappointment that turned to frustration, a frustration that turned to anger, an anger that turned to hate. He hated the carnival. It was just a big fucking teasing slut, flashing him her tits but never letting him get any. But he never stopped wanting. Even if she was a slut, he couldn't look away because she was still so fucking hot. Robbie gritted his teeth and clenched his fingers into a fist. Okay, sure, he had won a bunch of shitty little consolation prizes, but never the big one. Never the grand prize. Tonight he was going to win a big prize even if it fucking killed him. He released his fist, forcing himself to relax.

"And what do I get if I do?" Robbie asked Carly, a blatant smirk smearing across his lips.

"Oh, you know what you get," Carly purred.

Robbie looked up at the scintillating, sparkling lights that filled up the midway. "One prize coming up." He paused. "Amongst other things coming up." Robbie leered at the group. Carly giggled. Nelson rolled his eyes at Shirley. Shirley pushed her glasses back up the bridge of her nose.

"Whoa. Check this out!" Robbie said. "Damn, look at that shit."

They were standing before a game booth. A large wheel slowly spun round and round in the booth, about a dozen feet deep into the booth. It was very similar to a balloon toss game where participants tossed darts at under-inflated balloons trying to pop them. Except instead of balloons being thumbtacked to the rotating board for this game, severed zombie heads were attached to the spinning wheel. The objective of the game was to sink a dart into the eye of a zombie head.

All of the zombie heads were *alive* in the sense that their lips moved, their mouths contorted, their facial muscles twitched, and their eyes darted from side to side. They should have made no breathing sounds because they had no lungs in which to inhale or exhale air, but somehow weird grunts and groans seem to come out of their mouths.

Nelson looked up to the crude hand-painted wooden sign that hung above the booth. *Pop An Eyeball*. And in smaller letters beneath that it read: *Every Pop Wins A Prize*. "That's fucking sick," he said, but still smiled and gave a slight laugh.

Shirley said nothing. She leaned into Nelson and clutched at his arm, pulling herself closer to him, as if using him as a shield against the grotesque scene before them.

Robbie looked to the carny manning the booth. He had expected to see some greasy, dirty looking man with two missing front teeth and ragged unkempt hair. Or maybe some morbidly obese woman sipping on a diet coke. But instead he saw a smartly dressed man in a finely-tailored three-piece suit. The man's face was clean-shaven, his hair smartly combed. He immediately reminded Robbie of an undertaker. Had he known what was going to happen to the group, Robbie would have taken that feeling much more seriously, but at the time the carny man's appearance was simply an amusing addition to the whole weird atmosphere of the zombie carnival.

"Ready to play?" the carny man asked.

"Hells yeah," Robbie said.

"Three darts, five bucks," the carny man said as he held out his clean, finely-manicured fingers, showing three fingers, then five, then flipped his hand over to display his empty palm.

Robbie pulled out his wad of bills, flipped through them, and handed the carny man a twenty.

"Excellent," the smartly dressed carny man said. "Twelve darts, it is." He folded the twenty dollar bill neatly in half and slid it into the pocket of his smoothly pressed pants.

"I just wanted three," Robbie said.

"I don't give change," the carny man said. The carny man set twelve rust-tipped darts down on the low platform in front of Robbie. Then, he added a thirteenth dart to the mix. "For luck," he said to Robbie with a warm smile.

"I just wanted three," Robbie repeated.

"Oh, don't argue, Robbie," Carly said. "Just play."

Robbie gave the carny man an unhappy glare. The carny man gave him nothing but a flat expression in return.

"Win me a prize, Robbie," Carly said. She tugged on his arm, pressing her breasts firmly and deliberately against him.

Robbie looked down at Carly and she smiled coyly. He bent his head down and gave her a quick kiss.

Nelson glanced over to his left, looking at several stacked rows of wooden shelves within the game booth. There were grossly deformed teddy bears lining one shelf, some with their limbs completely torn off, others with their stuffing guts spilling out over their rotund bellies. There were glistening smears of red at the edges where their limbs were missing, and more smears of red streaked the stuffing guts. Beneath the row of tormented and tortured teddy bears, there lay a smattering of what looked like rusted farm implements, a sickle, the tongs of a pitchfork, a severely rusted hammer. Nelson frowned. What kind of shit prizes were those?

Robbie picked up his first dart and gave it a toss. He wasn't even close. There were nine zombie heads on the spinning board and his first dart sailed uselessly past the edge of the board, missing everything.

"Aren't you supposed to aim for the heads?" Shirley wondered, eagerly grabbing at the opportunity to get at least one dig in on Robbie.

"Oh, real funny, Shirley," Robbie said. He thrust a rusted-tip dart towards her. "Here, you try."

Shirley looked at the offered dart, but did not take it.

"Yeah, I didn't think so," Robbie said. He turned back to face the spinning board and tossed the second dart. This time he at least hit the board, but he missed one of the zombie heads by about two inches.

On the sixth dart, Robbie hit a zombie head. The dart sunk into the zombie's forehead with a soft plopping noise and stayed there. The zombie's mouth stopped moving and its eyes went still.

"Dang, dude," Nelson said. "You killed it." He laughed.

Robbie looked over to the carny man. "Do I get something for that?"

"My unabashed enthusiasm for your expert throwing skills," the carny man said dryly.

"You should probably stick to kicking field goals," Shirley muttered.

"Whoa, zing," Nelson said and laughed.

Robbie frowned at Shirley and grabbed another dart, reaching down to snatch it angrily from the counter ledge before him. He looked at Nelson. "Your gal pal is really starting to piss me off with her smart mouth."

Robbie missed hitting any heads on his next four tries, then sunk another dart into a zombie head, this one sinking into the zombie's cheek. The zombie's eyes went askew as it constantly tried to look at the sharp implement sticking out of its face but not quite able to see it fully.

Carly grabbed Robbie's arm and squeezed. "Come on, Robbie. You can do it," Carly said. "This one's for the win. Right between the ol' goalposts. You've done it a hundred times." She rubbed at his crotch. "Do it for me."

Robbie picked up the twelfth dart from the counter. "Now I'm feeling inspired," he said with a grin. He aimed and threw the dart. The dart sank into the spinning board squarely between two zombie heads as he again missed. "Fuck!"

"Last one," the carny man said. "Make it count."

"Want me to try?" Nelson asked.

"Fuck, go ahead. I suck. I don't care." Robbie waved his hand disgustedly at the last remaining dart on the counter. He looked away from Carly, not wanting to see her disappointed face.

Nelson grabbed the last dart and rolled it between his fingers. He looked at the rotating board, at the slowly spinning zombie heads. He took a deep breath and rolled his shoulders. "Knock," he said, simulating a commander ordering his bowmen to get their arrows in place. He raised the dart and made a mock throw, sizing up the board, the speed of the rotation, the placement of the severed zombie heads, the location of the zombie eyes. He zoned in on one particularly bulging eye, watching it go round and round, gauging its speed, judging its location. "Loose," he said, and then he let the dart fly with a confident flick of his wrist. The sharp-tipped projectile soared forward, rotating smoothly in the air as it flew. Then a satisfying splat filled the booth as the dart hit home, plunging directly into the center of the bulging eye. Pus and goo and some residual blood erupted out of the punctured eye, sending a stream of rotting gunk oozing down the zombie's cheek, then down onto its forehead as the head turned upside down as the rotating game board continued to spin.

"We've got a winner!" the carny man shouted. He seemed genuinely pleased.

Nelson pumped his fist. "Yes!"

Shirley frowned at the oozing eye as the spinning board went slowly round and round. "That's disgusting." The zombie's other eye stared directly at her and for a moment she thought she saw some shimmering sign of life emanating from behind the eye. She nervously looked away.

The carny man made a wide sweeping gesture with his arm, pointing to the shelves filled with the odd prizes. "Anything from the top row," he said.

Nelson looked at the rows of shelves that contained the prizes, then looked at Shirley, then back to the prizes on the shelves. He turned to look at

Robbie. "No, man, it was your money, your darts," Nelson said to Robbie. "I just helped you. You pick."

Robbie looked at Nelson, hesitated a moment. "You sure?"

"Yeah, man. Go ahead." Nelson waved his hand toward the prizes.

Robbie turned away from his friend to look at the prize shelves. He studied the prizes for a moment, and then pointed to a teddy bear with red-stained fluff spilling out of its belly. "That one, with its guts hanging out."

The carny man nodded. He grabbed the mutilated teddy bear and handed it to Robbie. "You have chosen—" The carny man paused before he released his grip on the bear. "—wisely." He grinned a very self-satisfied grin.

Robbie took the mutilated teddy bear from the carny man and immediately handed the prize bear over to Carly. "Here you go, baby," Robbie said. Carly squealed with delight and hugged the bear tightly to her chest. But then she immediately squealed with a different tone in her voice; this second squeal was more of a squeal of disgust than a squeal of delight. She pushed the teddy bear away from her, throwing it to the ground. "It's all wet! Yuck!"

"Oh, shit," Nelson said.

Robbie quickly glanced aside at Nelson, then turned back to look at Carly. The front of her white blouse was smeared with a glistening red stain. He quickly looked over at the carny man. "That's not... is it?"

The carny man's expression remained flat and emotionless.

Robbie looked back to Carly. Her nipples were hard for some reason, and their tips poked at the now red and wet fabric of her blouse. Usually, anything of that nature excited Robbie, but he just couldn't get past the gross red stain all over his girlfriend's clothes.

Carly stared down at the red smear bloodying her chest with a scowl. "Man, that's fucking gross," she said. She looked up at the carny man with an irate glare. "Not cool, dude. Not cool."

Shirley suddenly grabbed at Nelson's arm, pulling him close to her. Nelson looked curiously at her, then followed her gaze down to the discarded teddy bear. A mass of white maggots tumbled out of the mutilated teddy bear's belly, squirming and wriggling madly. "Oh, fuck, that's sick," Nelson said.

Robbie and Carly immediately saw the writhing blob of larvae and both their faces took on nearly the same exact expression of disgust.

Carly immediately fumbled at the buttons on her blouse, eventually ripping and tearing at them to get the blouse off of herself and away from her skin. She threw the blouse down at the monstrous teddy bear, covering the mauled mass with more of a lucky throw than any skill. The cloth shifted slightly as the maggots continued to squirm beneath it. Carly rubbed frantically at her arms, making sure no maggots were crawling on her flesh.

Everyone stared at the blood-soaked blouse, at the lump underneath it, at the subtle but grotesque movements of the maggots shifting beneath the fabric.

Everyone except the carny man. He found a sudden keen interest in Carly's ample breasts. She wore no bra, so her large breasts were quite visible in the twinkling glow of the neon lights that burned brightly nearby.

Carly felt the carny man's gaze on her and turned to see the man ogling her breasts. She turned fully to face him and thrust her chest towards him. "Why don't you take a picture? It lasts longer."

The carny man grinned and raised a Polaroid camera that somehow was now in his hand. He pointed the camera at Carly and clicked a button. A flash popped in a bright hot white burst of light and the camera spit out a blurry undeveloped picture.

"You son of a bitch," Robbie said, snarling as he reached into the booth to snatch the picture from the end of the camera where it had popped out. He looked at the picture, but it was still blurry, still slowly developing so the image it contained wasn't clear yet.

Shirley took off her sweater jacket and wordlessly handed it towards Carly. Carly shook her head and waved the offered sweater away. "Sorry, I don't do pink. Ever." Nonplussed, Shirley put the sweater back on.

Nelson did his best not to stare at Carly's breasts, but every few seconds he failed miserably.

"Jesus," Robbie muttered, the word barely audible, but the stress in his voice very apparent. He held up the now-developed picture to the group. The picture showed Shirley frozen in a shriek of terror, her terrified face filling the tiny square.

"What the fuck?" Carly said. "I didn't hear her scream." She looked at Shirley. "Did you make that face? Did you just scream like that?"

Shirley shook her head.

"She will," the carny man said. "She will."

Shirley froze for just the briefest of moments, her

eyes widening slightly, then she immediately clutched at Nelson, hiding even further behind him, trying to make herself invisible to the carny man's darkly gleaming eyes.

Carly glared at the carny man. "Fuck you." Carly snatched the picture from Robbie's hand and ripped it into a dozen pieces, then let the torn fragments drip down out of her fingers while she stared at the carny man with a smug satisfied face.

The carny man looked back at her with a flatly indifferent expression, then his gaze went blatantly down to her bare breasts.

They continued moving through the carnival. Carly was now wearing Robbie's jacket, but she hadn't bothered to zip it all the way up so her breasts were still prominent and quite visible. Nelson tried his best not to find the ideal angle to get a look at Carly's big nipples but he kept failing. Shirley kept very close to Nelson, holding on to his arm. More park patrons milled about the zombie carnival grounds now, various different groups visible in the near distance. Sounds of screams and nervous laughter flittered in from various directions, the screams far more audible and lengthier than the laughter.

They walked past a baseball target game that was named **Zombie Bath**. A large glass-walled enclosure was set up at the front of the game booth on the left side of the booth. Inside the enclosure was a seat attached to a trigger, and atop the seat stood a zombie. The zombie's feet moved but he stayed in place because he wore a metal neck collar that was tightly chained to the trigger apparatus. The bullseye target set up a few dozen yards into the booth was a big red X carved into the severed head of a zombie that was attached to a metal arm. If a player hit the target, that would trigger the seat in the large glass enclosure to collapse and the occupant of the seat would plunge into the liquid below. Usually, that liquid was just water. But not for this game.

A group of teenagers were gathered around the game booth, laughing and giggling at the zombie standing on the seat within the glass enclosure. "Dummy don't even know how to sit," one of them said and they all laughed. A boy paid for three balls and started throwing them at the target. He missed his first throw, but cleanly nailed the target on his second throw, hitting the bullseye on the severed zombie head with a solid thwack to its skull. The metal collar on the zombie opened as the seat in the glass enclosure collapsed and the zombie plunged into the liquid below, the liquid coming up to its waist. A burst of steam erupted out of the liquid and then the zombie's skin started to boil, and then started to melt. The zombie slammed up against the glass in the enclosure, flailing its arms uselessly against the clear barrier, its mouth opening and closing spasmodically. Layers of putrified skin sloughed off the zombie, oozing along its arms and chest to drop into the acidic liquid where it then seemed to sizzle and continue to melt. Slowly, ever so slowly, the zombie seemed to shrink, sinking lower and lower into the liquid.

One of the boys moved right up to the glass enclosure and thrust his face towards the zombie. "I'm melting," he said in a very bad imitation of the wicked witch from the Wizard of Oz. "I'm melting."

"Damn," Robbie said, his voice low. "These effects are fucking unbelievable."

They turned and continued on, moving through the carnival.

A black zombie cat suddenly staggered across their path in what looked like a drunken stumble. It would have been funny except for the gooey strands of intestines that trailed behind the animal. Its two back legs kept tripping over the intestines that dangled out of its slashed belly. The black zombie cat paused and turned to look at the group, its one good bloodshot eye facing directly at Shirley; its other eye dangled out of its socket. Its black fur was matted with filth, and a smattering smear of mud and bits of twigs and leaves was painted across its back. A clump of pink cotton candy was stuck to its fur near its butt. The cat meowed; it was a sad gurgling mewling sound that barely had any energy to it.

"Ha, one scaredy cat talking to another," Robbie said. He grinned a churlish grin at Shirley.

Shirley ignored Robbie's little quip. She frowned at the cat. "That's so mean," she said. "That poor cat."

And then the cat was gone, disappearing into the shadows of a nearby game booth.

"Poor us," Carly said.

The others looked at her curiously.

"A black zombie cat just crossed our path," Carly said. "That can't lead to anything good.

The sign above the game booth read **"River of Blood"** painted in red letters on a battered, rough-edged piece of what looked like driftwood.

"Three bucks a pluck." Carly looked at the tattered

canvas sign that was held in place by a knife on one of the inner walls of the booth, reading it aloud. "Every pluck wins a prize."

The four of them stood before this twisted variation of the Pluck-A-Duck carnival game. Usually, the game involved a tub of flowing water filled with little yellow rubber duckies moving along a soft current, gently bobbing up and down as they moved around the long cylindrical metal tub. The contestant would pick up a duck, grabbing it as it sailed along in the current, and show the carny worker the number on the bottom of the duck. The carny would grab a prize from the prize bin that matched the number on the duck and hand it to the lucky winner.

But this game involved what looked like a tub filled with flowing blood. It certainly wasn't water. The edges of the tub were clearly stained with a reddish liquid. And this game didn't involve little yellow rubber duckies either. Instead, pale severed fingers moved along the current, all of them positioned knuckles and fingernails up.

"That's disgusting," Shirley said.

"Yeah, you said that already," Robbie said.

"I'll go first," Carly said.

"Of course you will," Shirley muttered, but loud enough for everyone to obviously hear.

"Unless, of course, little miss scaredy cat wants to participate," Carly said. Carly made a broad sweeping gesture towards the blood river filled with the floating severed fingers.

Shirley shook her head. "I'm not touching that."

Robbie put his hand comfortingly around Nelson's shoulder. "I bet you get that a lot."

Nelson reached behind his head and grabbed a

handful of Robbie's shirt. He lifted Robbie's arm up off his shoulder and deliberately moved it against Robbie's side, pressing it against Robbie's body. "Not as much as you'd think." He moved up to Shirley and pulled her to him, giving her a deep kiss. He cupped her ass and pulled her tight against his groin, grinding a little bit into her. Shirley broke off the kiss and put her hand on Nelson's chest. "Nelson, please," she whispered as she adjusted her glasses.

"Dude, you got her begging!" Robbie said. "Nice work!"

Several carny zombies lumbered past, making odd noises. The group watched them for a moment.

"If they're zombies, aren't they supposed to try to eat us?" Carly asked as she watched the carny zombies stumble away. A shoe fell off the foot of one of the passing zombies, but the zombie paid the lost piece of apparel no heed and continued shuffle-stumbling forward.

"They's jus' decoration," a female voice said.

Carly turned to see the River of Blood carny worker looking at her. She hadn't noticed her before. The woman looked like some really bad B-movie version of an African explorer. She had on khaki shorts, a sweat-stained khaki shirt. The pith hat atop her head was cocked askew, and her dirty blonde hair stuck out wildly in all directions. Her face was smeared with dirt, and what could also have been streaks of blood.

"The real zombies come later," the carny woman added. "You gonna play? If not, move along. You's holdin' up the line." The blonde carny woman jerked her head, motioning over Carly's shoulder.

Carly glanced behind her to see no one standing

there besides Robbie, Nelson, and Shirley. She turned back to the carny woman. "They're with me."

The woman cocked her head slightly. "Are they?" she asked. She cocked her head even more, and her matted, dirty blonde hair dangled down from her head like pieces of shredded snake skin. "Are they really?" The pith hat should have fallen off her head at this point because of the extreme angle of her head, but somehow it stayed fixed in place atop her wild blonde hair.

Carly frowned at her. She turned to Robbie. "Gimme three dollars."

Robbie gave her the money and Carly handed the bills to the carny woman. The carny woman grabbed the bills, snatching at them with her grubby, filthy fingers. "Three bucks. One pluck." She sneered at Carly. "And one dumb fuck."

Carly took aggressive, threatening steps toward the carny woman, but Robbie's warning hand on her arm slowed her down. "She's just playing her part."

Carly glared at the carny woman, then sniffed indignantly at her and turned her attention back to the game. She moved closer to the elongated metal tub that contained the river of blood. She stared down at the floating fingers, watching them slowly move past her in the slight current. There were a few pinkies and a rare thumb amidst the flotsam and jetsam of ring fingers, index fingers, and middle fingers. It was hard to believe the entire tub was filled with blood, but the liquid certainly looked convincing, and it certainly had a distinct coppery odor to it that wasn't the smell of any water. She watched a pinkie finger appear from around the corner of the tub and move closer. Or maybe it wasn't a pinkie? Maybe it was a kid's finger.

Carly shuddered inwardly at the thought. This was really creepy. Cool, but also definitely creep-city. *Just grab one. Don't be a Shirley.*

Carly reached down for a fat index finger floating in the middle of the river of blood. That's when a hand erupted out of the blood river and grabbed her wrist! Carly shrieked; her hand opened and the severed finger plopped back into the river. Shirley shrieked and threw her hands up over her mouth, the expression on her face looking remarkably similar to the expression that had been captured on the Polaroid photo taken earlier by the Pop An Eyeball carny man. Robbie took a few startled steps back very quickly. "Fuck!" Nelson just stared, his eyes wide.

The carny woman slapped her thigh and hooted out a huge hooting laugh, a massive grin taking up nearly her entire face. "Got you, you dumb cunt!"

Carly tried to pull her wrist free of the blood-soaked hand gripping her wrist, wrenching and twisting her shoulder, but the hand wouldn't let go. "Let go, motherfucker!"

Robbie surged forward and grabbed at the fingers, prying them away from Carly's wrist. "Let go, you fuck!

The bloody fingers released their hold and the hand sunk slowly back down into the water like a wrecked ship slowly sinking to its doom.

Robbie pulled Carly away from the tub. "You okay?"

Carly fought to calm her panting breath. "Yeah. Scared the shit out of me."

"Yeah, you and me both." Robbie glanced down at Carly's wrist to see blood sliding down over the back of her hand and dripping off the tips of her fingers.

"Shit, did it cut you?"

Carly looked up at him, still somewhat in a dazed state of shock. "What?"

"There's blood all over your hand." Robbie raised his hand to point at hers, then quickly saw the blood staining his own hand. "Shit." Robbie looked over to Nelson and Shirley. "You got anything to wipe this off with?"

They didn't answer. Shirley just stared at Carly's bloody hand.

Robbie snapped his bloodied fingers at Nelson and Shirley, his wet fingers barely making any sound. "Hey, boneheads. You got anything to wipe this off with? Go find some napkins or something."

Shirley finally came back to her senses. "We need to find a bathroom or something. Wash it off."

Robbie nodded. "Yeah, yeah."

"We passed some port-a-potties back there." Nelson pointed back to his left. "There's probably some kind of sink near them."

"Hey, you dumb bitch!" the carny woman shouted after them as they headed away. "Don't you want your prize?"

All six of the port-a-potties were marked Occupied, every door indicator showing the reddish color that meant someone was inside using it. There was a small sink near the port-a-potties and Robbie helped Carly rinse off her arm, then washed off his hands. They were all relieved to learn she hadn't been cut; all the blood had come from the river and the hand that had grabbed her.

Carly looked up at the port-a-potties. "I really

gotta go," she said.

"Now?" Robbie asked.

"Yeah. If you must know, I nearly shit myself, too," Carly said. "That fucking hand scared the crap out of me."

Robbie laughed. "Me, too." He shook his head. "Damn, that fucking got me good. I almost screamed as loud as Nelson."

Nelson frowned. "Hey, I didn't scream."

"Yeah, right. I heard you scream like a little girl."

Nelson shook his head. "Wasn't me."

Carly stepped closer to one of the occupied port-a-potties. "We've been out here for like ten minutes and no one has come out of any of those. You really think someone's in them?"

"Just knock," Shirley said.

Carly glanced at her, but said nothing. She moved even closer to the port-a-potty, tilting her head towards the green plastic door, listening. She quickly pulled back. "Oh, man, someone's grunting and groaning in there."

Robbie nodded his head. "I do that sometimes. Especially if it's a big one and it's stuck."

Carly smacked Robbie in the chest. "That's gross."

"Yeah, but man does it feel good when it finally comes out."

Carly twisted up her nose. "Okay, really. Stop. That's disgusting."

"Isn't that scaredy cat's line?" Robbie asked. "You trying to steal Shirley's thunder?"

"Hey," Nelson said, interrupting Robbie and Carly. "That one is green. Try that one."

They all turned to stare at the second port-a-potty on the right that Nelson was pointing at. The door latch indicator was now indeed green.

"Did anyone see anybody come out?" Robbie asked.

"Go check," Carly said, nudging Robbie forward with a shoulder shove.

Robbie hesitated for a moment, but then moved towards the port-a-potty. He reached the portable toilet and just stared at it for a moment, not moving.

"You know there's a zombie in there, right?" Nelson said to him. None of the others had moved any closer, so they were all still a few yards away from the big plastic toilet box.

Carly danced an I-gotta-pee dance, twisting and contorting her waist, crossing her legs. "Come on, Robbie, check it."

Robbie hesitated for another moment, staring at the green door latch. He reached down slowly, then quickly grabbed at the latch and flung the door open.

Nelson was right.

A zombie surged forward out of the port-a-potty, snarling and growling, reaching for Robbie with outstretched decaying fingers.

"Fuuuck!" Robbie jerked backwards and fell to the ground. He pushed backwards, doing a crab walk as fast as he could until he bumped into Nelson and stopped. He felt a wet warmth spreading across his groin and glanced down there to see that he had pissed himself. "Man, that fucker slobbered on me." He quickly got to his feet and hurried over to the portable hand washing station that was situated near the port-a-potties. He quickly filled his cupped hands with water and hurriedly splashed the liquid over his crotch area.

The zombie continued to clutch at the air, snarling

and gurgling as its decaying fingers grabbed at nothing. They quickly realized the zombie was chained to the back port-a-potty wall so it couldn't even get fully out of the plastic toilet box. Its filthy, tattered pants were around its ankles and its decaying penis flopped about as it lurched. The zombie's hands continued to grab at the empty air before it with curved fingers. Nelson stared at the undead man. The make-up was incredible. The guy really did look like a zombie. His eye sockets looked like they went three inches into his skull. He had patches of hair missing on his head, as if he had been in an earlier fight and someone had ripped out a few handfuls of his hair. His skin was mottled and gray, streaked with dirt and blood, and what Nelson hoped wasn't shit but it sure looked like it. And the guy certainly smelled like a zombie, too. The stench was overpowering and Nelson had to fight back a gag.

Carly noticed all the door latches were now suddenly green. She frowned. She knew damn well that no one had come out of any of the other port-a-potties. They were all probably filled with a zombie waiting to jump out. She squirmed and contorted her legs. She really had to go! She couldn't wait any longer. She hurried behind one of the port-a-potties, quickly yanked her jeans and panties down and squatted. An ecstasy-inducing stream of urine flowed out of her, softly splashing against the grassy ground.

The dirt area where the urine hit stirred slightly. But it wasn't just because of the liquid striking it. It was a motion caused by something moving underneath the ground.

Carly continued to relieve herself, sighing softly at the release of all the pressure that had been

31

threatening to burst out of her.

The dirt stirred more vigorously now, clumps of earth and grass being pushed aside as whatever was causing the motion was starting to pick up its game.

Carly shifted slightly as her urine flow continued to stream out of her.

The hand that erupted out of the ground grabbed a handful of her pubic hair, and one of the mud-streaked fingers slid up into her.

To say that Carly screamed at the top of her lungs would be an understatement. She screamed at the top of them, in the middle of them, and at the bottom of her lungs. She let out the loudest scream that had ever been heard in that county. She leaped at least three feet into the air, jumping higher than she had ever jumped before in her life. She could feel some of her pubic hairs being ripped out of her body as she leaped away from the wildly clutching fingers; it was a far worse feeling than any bikini waxing she had ever had. Pain seared through her, lighting up her entire body with bolts of agony.

Robbie raced around the port-a-potties to see Carly. She still had her jeans and panties pulled down to her ankles and she was fidgeting and crying and shaking. The insides of her thighs were wet, glistening in the blazing dazzle of neon lights that seemed to be burning everywhere on the carnival grounds now. Robbie hurried over to her. That's when he saw the hand jutting out of the ground, clutching and groping at the air with its filthy mud-and-blood stained fingers. He moved over to the hand and stomped on it repeatedly, driving his foot down hard again and again. The satisfying crunch of bone sounded. Or was that metal? Or plastic? It was probably some kind of animatronic hand, Robbie thought as he bashed at it with his foot. The grisly looking fingers continued to weave and flutter, but much more weakly now.

"I want to go home," Carly said, fighting back tears.

Robbie looked over to her and he felt his heart breaking. Carly was not prone to tears. He couldn't remember a time of ever seeing her cry, not even at the movies. Her pants were still down around her ankles, her golden yellow patch of pubic hair visible, the inside of her thighs clearly wet. She hugged her arms about herself, as if trying to fight off a deep chill. He had never seen Carly look so vulnerable in his life. He looked up to see Nelson and Shirley just staring at her. He hurried up to Carly, blocking her from their view. "Pull your pants up," he said to her softly.

She glanced at him quizzically, as if in a total daze.

Robbie bent down and grabbed at the edge of her jeans. "Pull your pants up."

Carly glanced down to see her lower body nakedness. "Fuck," she said, coming out of her daze. She nudged Robbie aside and snatched at her panties and jeans, awkwardly fumbling with them until she finally got them back on. "Take me home, Robbie. Now!"

Robbie held up his hands, trying to defend himself from her very sharp tone. "Okay, okay." He looked at her with a soft expression. "You okay?"

"No, I'm not okay. I want to go home." She wiped angrily at the oncoming flood of tears that threatened at the corners of her eyes. "Now."

"Okay," Robbie said. "Okay."

They studied the large stone building directly in their path. It had the facade of a classic museum with rough-hewn stone walls and no windows. Two thick stone columns marked the entryway that led to a heavy wooden door laced with metal strips. Metal fences barred any movement to either side of the building. The only way forward was to go through it. They stared at the sign above the door quietly for a long time: **Hall of Murdering Mirrors.**

"So are we going in?" Carly asked. "If we have to go through there to get out, then let's just fucking go through it."

No one answered Carly right away.

"You sure this is the way out?" Nelson asked.

"I'm positive," Shirley said. "This is the way we came."

Nelson frowned. "Well, I'm positive this wasn't here before, so this can't be the way we came."

Just a few yards behind them, zombie carnival workers lumbered past, making grotesque noises.

Nelson shouted at the zombie workers. "Hey, is this the way out?"

The zombie carnival workers ignored his shout and continued shuffle-stumbling on.

"Let's go back. There's gotta be a different way," Nelson said.

"I am not walking back through all that shit," Carly said. She squeezed Robbie's shoulder. "Let's just fucking go."

"Sure." Robbie finally said. He glanced up at the stone building. "It looks cool."

Carly frowned, not giving a rat's ass about any coolness right about now.

"I don't see any ticket taker," Shirley said as she

glanced around the area.

"Fuck it," Robbie said. "Let's just walk right in."

And so they did.

Robbie and Carly had turned left when Nelson and Shirley had turned right and they quickly found themselves alone in the Hall of Murdering Mirrors. The reflections of themselves in the mirrors had completely disoriented them. The couples had shouted at each other, trying to direct each other to come back together, but somehow they just moved farther and farther apart until the couples were completely separated within the gloomy confines of the twisting and turning mirrored corridors.

As Robbie and Carly moved through the maze of mirrors, Robbie caught glimpses of Carly's breasts in the mirrors as her loose jacket fluttered with her movements. He grabbed her hand and pulled her to a stop, pulling her closer to him.

She looked up at him quizzically and he gave her a look she knew well. "Not now, Robbie, come on. Seriously? We need to get out of here. I just want to go home."

"You know what would be hot?" he asked.

She cocked her head slightly. "Are you serious? You've got to be kidding me."

Robbie continued, as if she hadn't said a word in protest. "Watching ourselves fuck in all these mirrors," he said. "'Member that time in Vegas? That room with the mirrors on the ceiling? I still jerk off to that night."

"You jerk off?" Carly said. "Don't I give you enough?"

"You tellin' me you don't play with yourself?"

Carly shook her head. "I don't. I save it all for you."

Robbie looked at her. "Really? Damn, that is fucking hot." He grabbed her tighter and kissed her hard.

Carly moaned and pressed herself tighter against him. Then she pulled away and pushed back against his chest, but without much effort.

"You feeling better now?" Robbie asked gently.

"A little," she said. "That fucking hand…" Her voice trailed off. "I think it ripped out some of my pubes."

"Are you serious?"

"Yeah."

"Fuck." Robbie looked at her, his gaze gentle. "Does it hurt?"

"A little. It's feeling better now."

"I'm sorry. We don't have to. All these mirrors are just so cool. And you keep flashing me your boobs…"

Carly pursed her lips at him.

"Yeah, forget it. We don't have to." Robbie looked away from her, but couldn't get away from seeing her face in all the reflections that surrounded them.

"No, it's okay," Carly said. She was quiet for a moment, then reached out and touched his hand. "I want your fingers on me now. I want to remember *you* touching me. Not…"

"You sure?"

"Yeah. It's okay. Kiss me again."

Robbie kissed her. He put his hand beneath the jacket and cupped Carly's breast, squeezing her warm flesh in his fingers. Her nipple was pointed and erect against his palm. He pulled back from the kiss and watched himself squeeze Carly's breast from a dozen different angles in the mirrors that surrounded them. He looked up at Carly to see her doing the same thing; she glanced at his hand on her breast, moving her gaze from mirror to mirror. Even though the light in the Hall of Murdering Mirrors was gloomy and murky, a pale light coming from somewhere illuminated them in a soft glow.

"You know Nelson and Shirley might see us," Robbie said.

"I know," Carly said. She slid the varsity jacket off her shoulders and let the piece of clothing fall to the floor. Robbie bent down and took one of her nipples in his mouth, sucking on the hardened nub, teasing it with flickering licks of his tongue. Her large breasts shifted slightly as she took in a deep breath and let out a delighted whispered moan.

Robbie slid his hand down lower, going into her pants.

"Go easy," she whispered. She unbuttoned her jeans to give him easier access.

They enjoyed themselves for a little while before things got real crazy.

The mirror turned Shirley into a killer.

Shirley stood transfixed as the reflection of herself took on a life of its own within the mirror world. A sadistic grin appeared on her reflection's face and suddenly a glinting butcher knife appeared in her reflection's hand.

Nelson stood next to Shirley in the dimly lit corridor, disturbed and fascinated by what he saw happening to her reflection in the mirror before them, unable to look away from the macabre sight.

And then the mirror-Shirley turned to the mirror-Nelson and thrust the butcher knife straight into his chest. Nelson gasped and instinctively grabbed at his chest, but it was only the mirror-Nelson who was getting the brunt of mirror-Shirley's wrath.

Shirley turned away sharply from the mirror and buried her face in Nelson's shoulder. Nelson put his arm around her, and as he did so he happened to glance down and saw a bloody butcher's knife in Shirley's hand. "Shit!" He immediately stepped away from her and pushed her sharply away from him, shoving her hard enough to send her stumbling down to the hallway floor.

"Nelson!" Shirley cried out, clearly startled by his violent shove. She looked up at him with a shocked, hurt expression. Her glasses were slightly askew on her face, awkwardly dangling off the side of her nose.

Nelson froze for a moment. He stared down at her. The butcher knife was no longer in her hand. "I'm sorry. I'm sorry. I thought I saw..." He reached down to pick her up, but instead of grabbing Shirley's hand he smacked his head into a mirror. The surface of the mirror cracked, sending spiderwebbing lines racing through the glass. A deep furrow formed on his forehead. "What the fuck?"

"Nelson!" Shirley called out, reaching a hand up towards him.

Nelson again reached out towards her outstretched hand. Again, he struck a mirror, his hand cracking against the smooth surface. He turned to his left and saw another Shirley reaching up to him, and then another Shirley slightly askew from that Shirley, and then another Shirley slightly distant from that Shirley, and another and another. Everywhere he looked a different Shirley was on the ground raising her hand up towards him, all of them with their glasses sadly askew on their faces. "Nelson!" all the Shirleys cried out in unison, the multiple voices echoing through the air.

Nelson took a step forward and banged into a mirror, again cracking the reflective glass. He turned to his right and banged into another mirror. "Shirley!" He spun in every direction, facing dozens of reflections of himself, all of them wearing the same mask of fear that he felt contorting his facial features.

Suddenly, the mirrors shimmered. It was just a flash of a shaking movement, causing all of the reflections to take on a blurred edge for a brief moment. And then the reflective images cleared and came back to focus. All of the reflections were no longer a mirror image of himself. Each reflection was slightly different, but they all had one thing in common. They were all zombified abominations of himself. One zombified-Nelson didn't have a right arm. Another zombified-Nelson didn't have a jaw. A third zombified-Nelson had a deep and dark scarred eye socket where its left eye should have been. Another had deep grooves slashed across its chest as if a lawn rake had been savagely ripped across its upper body.

"Shirley!" he cried out. But Shirley was gone; not even a mirror-image of her was visible now.

Nelson spun about, trying to take in all the grotesque zombie versions of himself, trying to comprehend what was happening to him. When one of the zombified Nelsons reached out and grabbed hold of his arm, Nelson realized they weren't reflections at all. They were real. And they were coming for him.

Robbie watched Carly take him in and out of her mouth in a dozen different mirrors from a dozen different angles. She was kneeling on the floor, his varsity jacket bunched up beneath her knees to give her a comfortable cushion. The warmth of her mouth and the soft touches of her fingers on his scrotum were intoxicating. He closed his eyes, enjoying the oral pleasure his girl was giving him.

When he opened his eyes back up in a few seconds, the mirror images around him were all different. Some of the mirror-Robbies now looked like they had been transformed into zombies. Their bodies were no longer tight and muscular; they all had mottled grey skin, with bits of decayed flesh dangling off their faces and arms.

And some of the mirror-Carlys were now mirror-zombie-Carlys, their flesh no longer supple and smooth and pink. They were also covered in a layer of mottled grey flesh, their bodies in a grotesque state of decay. One of the mirror-zombie-Carlys only had one breast, the other breast being completely gnawed away.

Several mirror-zombie-Robbies moved around a mirror-Carly, forming a circle about her. They all had their undead appendages in their hands, stroking them obscenely as they moved closer to the mirror-Carly. One of them pulled its mottled grey penis right out of its body with a vigorous upward stroke. The mirror-zombie-Robbie kept making the stroking motions even though its penis was no longer attached to its body.

Robbie looked away to see a mirror-zombie-Robbie eating a mirror-Carly out. Literally. Its face was between her legs and he could see the mirror-zombie-Robbie's jaws working and he knew the undead bestial image of himself was chewing its way through the mirror-Carly's reproductive organs.

Robbie glanced down into a nearby mirror, seeing a mirror-Carly take a mirror-zombie-Robbie's decaying member into her mouth… and start chewing on it. His face filled with alarm and he quickly glanced down at his own member, which now hung down flaccid and limp near Carly's cheek. She no longer was paying attention to his cock. She, too, was riveted by the perverse tableau of scenes playing out all around them.

Robbie reached down to Carly, grabbing her under her arm, and lifted her up to him. "Let's get out of here," he said, his voice barely above a whisper.

"Yeah, let's," Carly agreed.

They both continued to stare at the perverse sexual scenes filling the mirrors all around them, their clothes forgotten at their feet for now. All around them, horrible scenes played themselves out, an overwhelming mixture of zombie on zombie, human on human, zombie on human, human on zombie interactions that were impossible to keep track of. "Oh my God," Robbie muttered. "Oh my God." His breath started to come in shorter and shorter gasps.

Robbie and Carly started to turn, clutching at each other, rotating their naked bodies, looking for a way out of this monstrous maze of murderous mirrors. The images in the mirrors started to turn along with their movements, started to rotate, moving faster and faster. Robbie and Carly clutched at each other as everything around them began to spin even faster and faster. The images in the mirrors circled them, moving yet faster and faster around them until everything around them was just a blur of streaking colors. The force of the violently spinning motion pulled them away from each other. Robbie snaked out his hand and clutched at Carly's wrist, trying to keep her close to him as the dizzying spinning motion threatened to push them farther and farther apart.

"Robbie!" Carly shouted, her eyes begging him not to let go of her.

Robbie struggled to maintain his grip on Carly's wrist but the force of the spinning motion was just too great and he lost his grip on her.

"Make it stop!" Carly screamed and closed her eyes tight.

Shirley had no idea where she was. One moment she had been on the floor in the Hall of Murdering Mirrors reaching out towards Nelson, and the next moment she was lying in a loose pile of straw. She slowly sat up and straightened her glasses. A candle burned on a small wooden table nearby, illuminating only her immediate surroundings. The area beyond that was dark. "Nelson?"

There was no reply.

"Robbie? Carly? You guys out there?"

No reply.

She fought back a nearly uncontrollable urge to start crying. She just wanted to go home. What the hell was happening? Did somebody drug her?

A rustling sound from the darkness nearly made

her wet herself.

"Who's there?" She craned her neck slightly forward, trying to see into the inky blackness beyond the pool of light the tiny candle threw out from its little flame. She wasn't prone to cursing, but at this moment she didn't really care. She was too scared to care. "Who the fuck is out there?"

When the seven snarling zombie dogs crept forward out of the darkness she didn't bother to try and stop her body from reacting; a warm stream of urine flooded her crotch and spread along her inner thighs. The light from the candle seemed to grow stronger, the pool of light growing wider and deeper to accommodate the presence of the undead beasts.

The dogs stopped a few feet away from the edge of the straw. Each dog sat back on its haunches and stared at her. All of them were Dobermans of some sort, all of them with ugly yellow gleaming eyes, all of them with partially decayed mouths that revealed sharp, jagged-edged teeth. They were positioned in staggered rows, with two in the front row, three in the middle row, and two more in the back row. They just continued to stare at her, as motionless as statues. Their mouths didn't move. Their eyes didn't move. They just sat as still as stone.

Shirley stared back. What the fuck? Just thinking the curse word somehow made her feel more emboldened. "What the fuck?" she suddenly shouted at the dogs. She leaned forward, raising her voice. "What the fuck!"

The dogs didn't even blink.

"Make it stop!" Carly screamed again.

She opened her eyes to see that she was no longer in the Hall of Murdering Mirrors. She was still spinning fast, even faster than they had been moving in the Hall of Murdering Mirrors. She tried to move her arms but realized that she couldn't. Some force was pinning her down, pressing her back up against a hard surface. She tried to lift her head, but she wasn't able to move that either.

Her surroundings came back more into focus. She saw other people, or least other human bodies. She wasn't sure if they were people or not.

And then she realized where she was. She was on a Graviton-type ride. It was a huge cylindrical ride with a wide circular opening in the middle. People lined up with their backs planted flat against the cylinder's wall, facing the wide opening, forming a full circle of riders. One side of the circle of riders could see the other side. The ride then started to spin slowly, and picked up speed as it went along, spinning faster and faster. Soon, it was spinning so fast that the g-forces kept the riders pinned up against the wall and they could barely move.

Carly couldn't move her head because of the extreme g-forces keeping her naked body pinned to the wall, but she could move her eyes. She tilted her gaze upwards to see several ooze-drooling zombies staring down into the ride from a viewer's deck above the spinning cylinder. A metal railing circled the deck, keeping viewers safe from falling into the ride. But these viewers weren't sensible human beings. One of the zombies dumbly reached out its arms, as if trying to grab at the riders spinning madly a few yards below it. It reached its arms out further and further, and then went tumbling over the metal railing into the ride. The terrific forces of the spinning ride ripped the zombie's body apart, sending its appendages hurtling in all directions, smashing into the wall. And into other riders. The zombie's ripped-out arm splattered against the wall right near one of Carly's legs. She felt liquid and bits of bones spatter across her naked legs.

Another zombie in the viewing area above groped mindlessly downward, reaching, stretching. Then, it too fell over the railing and into the ride, and the g-forces tore its decay-ravaged body into a dozen pieces. Its ripped-off head headed straight for Carly, rotating round and round as it sailed through the air. Carly's eyes widened as the severed head soared straight towards her, its rotted face getting larger and larger in her vision as it neared.

The dogs wouldn't let Shirley leave. The moment she neared the edge of the straw, the dogs came out of their statue-like state and started snarling and growling and barking, drooling blood out from between their very pointed, very sharp teeth. When she receded back away from the edge of the straw, the dogs immediately became stony and still. Some droplets of blood fell from their mouths, but other than that they showed no signs of movement, no signs of life at all. Eventually the blood stopped dripping down from their mouths and then there was no movement from the zombie dogs at all.

It took her awhile to notice the pile of dog collars sitting in a corner. They were somewhat hidden in shadow, but she caught a reflective glare from one of the diamond-shaped studs that encircled one of the collars and that drew her attention to them. She moved over to them and picked one of them up. It was more of a large ring than a collar because there was no buckle to it, no latching mechanism; it was just a solid circle of firm leather adorned with diamond-shaped studs aligned about two inches apart along the circumference of the collar ring.

She stared at the leather ring in her hand, then looked at the dogs sitting motionless in their staged rows. She looked down at the ring again, then back at the dogs. "You gotta be fucking kidding me," she muttered.

Robbie now found himself on a ride of some sort. His world was spinning. Whirling. Tilting. The surroundings were a dizzying blur of colored streaks, flashes of forms. He was sitting on a plastic-coated foam seat, his legs clamped into place by a long metal bar that ran the length of the compartment he was seated in. The world spun dizzyingly around him.

"Stop!" Robbie screamed. "Stop!"

Robbie felt his stomach lurch, felt the bile rise up hot and scratchy in his throat. He grabbed the metal bar across his legs as if holding on for dear life.

He continued to spin and tilt and whirl, the movements growing more intense, more violent. His head banged back and forth.

"Stop!" Robbie screamed. "Make it stop!"

And then the ride abruptly slowed, and then stopped. The metal bar across his legs clicked and then slowly raised up away from him. Robbie stumbled out of the compartment, falling to the slanted floor of the ride. He quickly got up, wobbling as he moved, doing his best not to fall down again as he took a simple step. His head felt like it was still spinning, but his body wasn't.

He glanced over towards another of the ride's seating compartments and saw just the lower halves of two bodies still clamped down in place by the metal bar; the upper portion of their bodies were nowhere to be seen. The back seat of the ride was smeared with blood and what looked like strings of intestines.

Robbie staggered off the ride, his face pale and ashen. He gripped a metal railing, bent over and vomited. He wiped his mouth with the back of his hand, his head still hanging down. The ride's sign flashed hotly down at him from high above his head: **Twirl and Hurl**.

Robbie vomited again, then spit out a few sour bits from his mouth with disgusted vigor. He glanced up, looking for Carly.

But she was nowhere to be seen.

Shirley missed her first three tosses. The first toss hit one of the closer zombie-Doberman-dogs in the front row on the side of its body and bounced off; the hard leather ring rolled across the floor before tipping over onto its side a few yards away. The second toss landed between the first and second row of dogs, missing all of them completely. The third toss nearly was a ringer, but it hit the closest dog on the left side of the top of its head and bounced off. The ring stopped a few feet away from the edge of the straw and toppled onto its side. Shirley was pretty confident she could grab it and still stay on the straw, but she hadn't felt the need to try that yet.

Shirley glanced at the remaining rings. She had about a dozen left. She had no idea if ringing a dog's head would even do anything, but she was out of ideas. And even if she did ring a dog's head was there a particular dog she was supposed to choose? They all looked the same to her. Sure they had slightly different markings, different snout sizes, different ear lengths, different shades of coloring in their fur, but for the most part they looked pretty similar. They were all grossly disgusting, decaying undead Dobermans.

Shirley grabbed another ring and moved closer to the dogs, careful to stay away from the edge of the straw, but still moving herself a little bit closer. The hard leather felt cool in her hand. She made a few mock throws, flipping her wrist towards the closest dog, but keeping a firm grip on the ring, channeling her inner Nelson. And then she let loose, flipping her wrist, releasing her grip on the leather ring. The ring wobbled a bit in flight, but then successfully encircled the dog's head and came to rest on its shoulders. She did it! She got one.

The diamond studs flared up for a brief moment as the collar shrunk and tightened around the dog's neck, encircling the animal's throat. Then the little diamond lights on the collar went dark, and so did the dog's eyes. They just emptied of whatever force was still inside them. Its fur also changed, appearing to harden and solidify.

Shirley stared at the beast. It now really was a statue. She was pretty sure of that. She didn't think it would move anymore. She stared at the ring on the floor just a few feet beyond the edge of the straw. One way to find out. She edged closer to the ring, keeping her gaze mostly on the dogs but also keeping the ring in the bottom of her vision. She reached the edge of the straw and quickly reached out to snatch at the fallen ring. The remaining dogs started barking and snarling and growling wildly, all six of them except for the one she had successfully ensnared with the leather ring collar. The dog she had collared had not moved at all. She quickly moved back deeper onto the straw and the dogs returned to their motionless state.

She counted the remaining leather rings. There were nine, plus the one in her hand. She had ten left. She looked back at the dogs. Six dogs left and nine rings. The odds were not in her favor.

"Have you seen my girlfriend?" Robbie asked.

"Is she naked like you?" a girl with curly brown hair asked. She was standing amidst a group of five other girls. All of them were dressed in dark clothes and black makeup.

The group of girls laughed along with the girl with the curly brown hair.

Robbie glanced down at his nakedness, then scowled an irritated scowl at them. "You have to help me find her."

"Umm, no, we don't." The group of girls moved on, continuing to laugh.

"Carly!" Robbie shouted. "Carly!"

Robbie saw a male figure a few yards in the distant gloom and he hurried over to him. The man was facing away from him. Robbie reached the guy and grabbed at his shoulder, violently spinning him around. "You have to help—" His voice died off as he saw that the man was a zombie. The zombie snarled at him with blood-drenched lips curled up to reveal blood-streaked teeth. The zombie lunged at him and tried to bite him. Robbie reacted instinctively. He locked his fingers together and swung his double-fist straight at the side of the zombie's head. The zombie's brittle decaying skull cracked and its brains oozed out as it dropped to the ground like a discarded beer can.

Robbie stared at the downed zombie for a moment. And then he looked closer at the zombie's pants.

Shirley stared at her empty hands. She looked up at the five statuesque dogs she had successfully collared with a few lucky throws. And then she looked at the two remaining dogs that did not have collars rung around their necks.

She peered into the darkness, trying to see where all her missed rings had gone, but not one of them was visible. She thought she might have seen the edge of one of the rings off to the far right, but she couldn't be sure. Nothing was visible beyond the throw of the candle's dim light.

And then she bolted from the safety of the straw, charging forward, sprinting towards the deep darkness that lay beyond the candlelight's throw. The two uncollared dogs immediately came to life, snarling and growling. Shirley raced past the first statuesque dog that she had collared and turned into stone earlier. The two uncollared zombie dogs started barking and drooling thick rivulets of blood as they sprang into motion, zeroing in on Shirley.

Shirley glanced about frantically for one of the rings, but still did not see one. She heard the dogs quickly approaching. Her heart pounded in her chest, in her ears, and she hesitated as a hot heavy growl made her glance over her shoulder. And then she tripped over one of the missing rings, stumbling on the hard leather, but she was able to keep her balance. She glanced down and one of the diamond-shaped studs glinted faintly back at her as if giving her a sadistic wink.

Shirley snatched at the fallen ring and raised the leather collar as one of the zombie dogs moved quickly towards her, the beast snarling and snapping and drooling blood as it began to move into position to lunge at her throat. The second zombie Doberman also quickly neared, growling a savage growl, its yellow eyes gleaming with a savage fury. Shirley stared with wide, frightened eyes at the approaching undead Dobermans.

And then she did the only thing she could think of.

❦

Robbie, now dressed in the zombie man's pants, staggered and ran, and walked, and sprinted and stumbled through the carnival grounds, shouting for Carly. "Carly!"

Then he ran some more, stumbled in his bare feet, turned and twisted, and staggered some more and shouted for Nelson. "Nelson!"

He found himself amidst a slew of small carnival tents and he poked his head inside each one as he passed by it, shouting for Carly or Nelson. And then soon he was even shouting for Shirley.

He reached another tent and shoved his head inside, shouting, "Shir—" and then his shout cut off abruptly. He moved fully into the tent.

Inside the tent, Robbie stared at Shirley; she was now a permanent fixture in Zombie Carnival. She was frozen in an odd position, as if caught by a freeze ray in mid-stride. Her head was craned backwards, her frozen gaze fixated on some spot nearby lower to the ground. Some kind of weird collar decorated with diamonds was around her neck, her raised hand still gripping the collar. There were several statues of dogs positioned nearby, all of them frozen in a sitting position. They each had the same kind of collar encircling their necks that was also around Shirley's neck.

Robbie moved closer to Shirley and reached his hand out towards her, but stopped short before he touched her. He glanced down to see the black zombie cat they had seen earlier curled up between the stone Shirley's legs. "Jesus, Shirley..." Robbie said. The black zombie cat purred a grotesque purr that sounded more like the dying, rasping breath coming from the lungs of an emphysema-laden smoker. It licked at the eyeball dangling down out of its eye socket, trying to clean the blood off the orb as best it could.

In the distance, the sound of two dogs barking wildly overpowered the sound of the cat's eerie purring, but then the barking sounds faded off farther into the distance.

Robbie exited the tent.

"Carly!" Robbie shouted, spinning and turning,

trying to take in his surroundings with a clear head as he moved through the carnival. He tripped over his own exhausted bare feet and nearly fell to the ground, but managed to keep his balance.

He stumbled forward, moving past a group of people playing a basketball toss game. Except they weren't trying to throw basketballs into the basket; they were trying to make a basket with severed zombie heads.

"Damn, fucker almost bit my fingers off," a young man said as he held a severed zombie head in his hands. He rotated the head so the zombie's face was pointing away from him. The young man suddenly pivoted his body and lowered the severed zombie head down, putting the chomping teeth near his friend's crotch. His friend leaped back, slapping at the severed head, knocking it out of the young man's hand. "Damn fool!" his friend snapped at the young man.

The severed zombie head rolled up to Robbie and stopped a few inches from his bare feet. Robbie stared down at the severed head. The zombie's eyes focused directly on him. "I'm too dead for this shit," the zombie head said.

Robbie reacted instinctively, rearing his bare right foot back, driving it forward, lifting it. He hit the severed head square in its rotting face with the side of his foot, sending it sailing up into the air straight towards a large blood-stained basket in the upper reaches of the rear of the game booth.

Robbie stumbled on, ignoring the pain in his bare foot, not even bothering to watch as the kicked head landing squarely into the basket. Neon lights blazed all around him, filling the night sky with glowing slashes of colored light. Zombies and carnival patrons blurred in his mind, everyone becoming a mindless stumbling caricature of a human. "Carly!" he shouted.

Exhaustion started to overtake Robbie. He just needed to rest. Just for a few minutes. The side of his bare foot ached where he had struck the zombie head. The area around him now was dark, all sense of where he was on the carnival grounds long since vanished. He stumbled a few more steps in the murky darkness and then his hand suddenly came to rest on a stool of some sort. He fumbled at the stool, managing to sit himself down upon it. He was about to take a relaxing breath when super-hot bright lights burst into the air behind him.

He slowly swiveled on the stool, shielding his eyes for a moment as he turned towards the source of the bright lights. As his eyes adjusted to the brightness, he slowly lowered his hand to see that he was seated at a game booth, occupying seat number four in a line of eight seats. He stared at the seat number indicator sign in front of him. Seat number four. That was his jersey number. Not that it mattered, but his brain registered that as a mild curiosity as he looked at it.

He looked down to see that a gun of some sort rested in a holster before him. A thick tube was attached to the bottom of the gun, the tube stained blood-red. The other end of the tube wasn't visible as the tube disappeared into the ground below the gun. Robbie glanced up at the severed zombie head sitting on a pole about a half a dozen feet away from him. The zombie's eyes were closed, its dried, cracked lips pressed shut. Its skin was mottled and gray, severely wrinkled; it had the textured appearance of old parchment, very old and very dry. Robbie glanced down to his left at the slots numbered one, two, and three. Each one had a very similar severed zombie head sitting on a pole, their eyes closed and their lips sealed as well. Robbie glanced right at slots numbered five through eight and saw the same type of severed zombie heads attached to poles.

"Step right up folks. The Dinner Bell Dash is about to start!"

Robbie looked up to see a fat man dressed in a chef's outfit, complete with a dazzling white apron and a pristine white chef's hat atop his rotund head. He stood just past slot eight, shouting and waving at other park patrons as they walked past. "We just need a few more participants and we can start the race! Come on over and take a seat and grab a gun! It's time to start blasting and dashing!"

Two girls appeared from the gloom behind Robbie and took up seats in rows six and seven. He looked over at them, but they were too interested in the game to give him any heed, intently studying the guns as they stared at the shooting devices holstered before them.

"This is the grand prize race, folks!" the fat chef shouted. "You do not want to miss this one!"

Robbie looked up past the zombie heads. Deeper in the game booth, to his left, a group of eight zombies stood lined up in a row. Each zombie had a thickly corded rope tied tightly around its neck. The ropes were attached to some kind of slot system set up in the ceiling of the game booth. The zombies tried to move forward but the ropes around their necks held them back. The zombies wore an odd assortment of various bibs, some attached by being tied around their necks; one of the bibs was attached by a knife stuck into the upper chest of a zombie at the far end of the line, and another zombie had rusted nails pinning a plastic lobster bib to its throat. Their arms flailed impotently in front of them, grabbing nothing but empty air. Robbie could hear them make grunting noises as they struggled to move forward.

To the far right in the game booth, some figure stood hidden in the dark. Robbie couldn't tell for sure if it was another zombie or not because the figure was draped in a thick veil of shadow. But he was pretty sure it wasn't a zombie because this figure made more of a sad whimpering sound than an animalistic grunting noise.

An elderly man and his aging wife took up seats in slot one and two, they too just looming up out of the darkness to join the game.

"Get ready to race!" the fat chef shouted. "Grab your guns and get ready!"

The elderly man and his wife giggled as they handled their weapons. The young girls on Robbie's right looked like serious contenders; they grabbed their guns and studied them judiciously, whispering in low tones as they turned them over in their hands.

Robbie just stared, his mind numb, his body awash with fatigue and pain. He wasn't quite sure what was going on anymore.

"Listen for the bell!" the fat chef shouted. "When it dings, it's dinner time!"

Robbie realized he hadn't even picked up his gun yet, so he hurriedly snatched at it and readied himself, aiming at the zombie head in front of him.

Ding! "Dinner time!" the fat chef shrieked.

The eyes of the severed zombie head in front of Robbie sprang open wide at the sound of the bell. Robbie pulled the trigger and sent a strong thin spray of blood (he knew it was blood and not just colored water) straight at the zombie head. His aim was off and the spray hit the zombie's cheek, splashing in all directions. The zombie's mouth opened and closed with no discernible pattern, smacking its lips in a grossly exaggerated gesture of someone gleefully licking their chops before a big meal. Robbie adjusted his aim and successfully sent a mouthful of blood straight between the zombie's open lips.

The zombie in slot number four lurched forward, the rope moving down a notch in the slot where the rope was attached.

Robbie chanced a glance away from the zombie head and looked up deeper into the booth. He saw that his zombie in slot four was slightly ahead of the others, but the zombie in slot seven was not too far behind. He looked back down at the zombie head and concentrated on his aim, keeping the stream of blood flowing into the zombie's open mouth.

Robbie's zombie racer was three-quarters of the way along the race track with a healthy lead when his zombie head sputtered and gagged. It choked out a mouthful of blood, closing its lips between its fitful bursts. "No!" Robbie shouted.

The zombie racer in slot four slowed, then came to a dead stop.

Robbie glanced to his right and saw the girls feverishly concentrating on their aim. He looked up into the booth to see zombies in slot six and slot seven move even with his racer in slot four. Even the zombies in slot one and two were gaining on his zombie in slot four.

Robbie cursed and kept shooting the stream of blood at his zombie's mouth, trying to force blood into the zombie's throat.

The zombie in slot seven moved ahead of his zombie and he heard one of the girls triumphantly shout her satisfaction at passing him.

The fat chef watched the proceedings with wry amusement from his position near the finish line.

Robbie felt his palm get sweaty and his hand started to shake as he gripped the gun ever tighter. He gripped the gun with both hands to steady his aim and continued to fire.

And then the zombie in slot one passed his zombie. The muscles in Robbie's neck tightened up, squeezing at his shoulder blades. It was a sensation he was very familiar with. It was the same kind of tension and fear he felt before every field goal kick in every game he ever played. The tightness and ache actually calmed him, cleared his head in a way that forced him to put all his focus on the task at hand.

Robbie turned his gun to his right and sprayed the two girls with a thick wall of red liquid, moving his arm rapidly up and down and side to side to create a wide swathing curtain of blood. The girls spluttered and sputtered as blood hit them from head to toe, squirting into their noses and their mouths before they had a chance to protect themselves. They instantly dropped their guns and shrieked, throwing their hands up by their heads to protect their faces.

Robbie turned the gun to his left and fired, not even bothering to look where he was aiming. He heard the old woman cry out.

He returned his aim to the zombie head before

him, zeroing in on its open mouth, sending a bullseye blast of blood straight between its open lips.

The zombie in slot four surged forward.

One of the girls to Robbie's right took an angry, threatening step towards him, her teeth clenched, her face smeared with blood; he saw her out of the corner of his eye. Without looking away from the severed zombie head gulping the stream of blood he was sending its way, Robbie quickly jerked his wrist to the right and sent another blasting barrage of blood into the girl's face. The blood hit the girl square in the face, surprising her, making her stumble, and actually knocked her down; she hit the dusty ground with a loud grunt. Robbie turned his hand back and quickly re-centered his aim, continuing to fill the zombie's mouth with blood. The girl's friend hurried over to her fallen companion, crouching down next to her.

"Oh, that was rich!" the fat chef exclaimed.

The zombie in slot four moved forward. The finish line was in reach. Only two more steps. It only needed to stumble forward two more times to cross the finish line. Robbie kept his aim true, spraying a smooth red stream into the severed zombie head's mouth. The rope tied around the zombie's neck slackened and the zombie lurched forward another step. Then the rope grew taut around the zombie's neck, digging into its throat as the zombie tried to keep moving. Only one more slot to go!

Robbie didn't see the old man's fist swinging towards his head until the last moment. But he did see it and he reacted quickly, ducking under the blow. The old man grunted as he missed, the violence of his swing knocking him off balance; he missed his intended target and only swung his tightly curled fingers through the empty air instead.

Robbie's aim shifted slightly as he ducked away from the old man's punch, and he sprayed blood into the zombie's unblinking eyes. He quickly corrected his aim and sent more blood into the zombie's mouth.

Ding! Ding! Ding!

"We have a winner!" the fat chef shouted, his smile wide and bright and genuine.

Robbie looked over to see that his zombie in slot four had crossed the finish line first. He grinned darkly.

"It's Dinner Time!" the fat chef shouted. He moved into the deep shadows of the booth and pulled out the whimpering figure that Robbie had seen earlier before the race had started.

It was Nelson. He recognized him immediately even though part of his face looked like it had been chewed away.

Robbie didn't even have time to say his name before the zombie from slot four made quick work of Nelson, chomping down on his neck, pulling him down out of sight into the shadows. Obscene chewing and gnawing noises floated out of the darkness.

"You win!" the fat chef shouted. "You get to choose." The fat chef held up what looked like a laminated menu in one hand, and a torn piece of parchment in the other. He raised up the parchment. "You can take the map that will lead you out of here." He lowered the parchment and raised up his right hand. "Or you can pick the Chef's Selection from the menu."

Suddenly, Nelson rose up out of the darkness, his

face covered in blood and wracked in a tortured grimace, his arms streaked with blood and dirt. He clawed and scratched at the Chef, trying to get any kind of hold, any kind of grip he could to escape the ravenous zombie from slot four who was in the middle of eating him. His fingers snatched at the parchment, ripping the map from the Chef's hand in his desperate grabbing attempts to find some escape. The zombie from slot four reared up out of the darkness and sunk its teeth into Nelson's neck, pulling him back down into the darkness. The gnawing, chewing sounds resumed. Everything had happened so fast that Robbie had no time to react.

The fat chef stared amusedly at his empty left hand for a moment. He looked to the menu and gave it a slight shake towards Robbie. "Chef's Selection it is." The fat chef set the menu down and snapped his chubby fingers. He rubbed his big belly, studying Robbie with his black beady eyes.

Another carny dressed in a chef's uniform disappeared for a moment behind the game booth, then came back out clutching a brown leather leash in his hand. The leash was taut, leading back into the darkness behind the booth. The carny tugged on the leash, pulling a shape into the gaudy neon lights. The shape shuffled forward, stumbling awkwardly as it came out into the light. The zombie's stare was vacant, its eyes now just reflective orbs buried in its skull. Its mouth hung slightly open, as if frozen in a slack-jawed expression. Its naked body was streaked with blood and dirt; its cheekbone looked like it had been smashed in with a hammer or some other heavy blunt object.

He had found Carly.

All around Robbie, the carny workers clapped and cheered and whistled. The elegantly dressed man from the Pop An Eyeball game was there, and the dirty blonde from the River of Blood game, and the ticket taker and his zombie pet. They all cheered with delirious glee. Robbie vaguely registered that the young girls and the old man and his wife seemed to have vanished, and he wondered for a brief flashing moment whether they had even really been there at all.

Robbie took the offered leash. And then he joined in the triumphant celebration, whooping it up, gleefully swinging his hand around in the air as his eyes gleamed with madness. "I won. I finally won the Grand Prize!"

The thing that used to be Carly stared at the naked torso of the meal standing before her, her undead eyes burning with an unholy hunger.

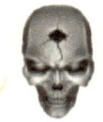

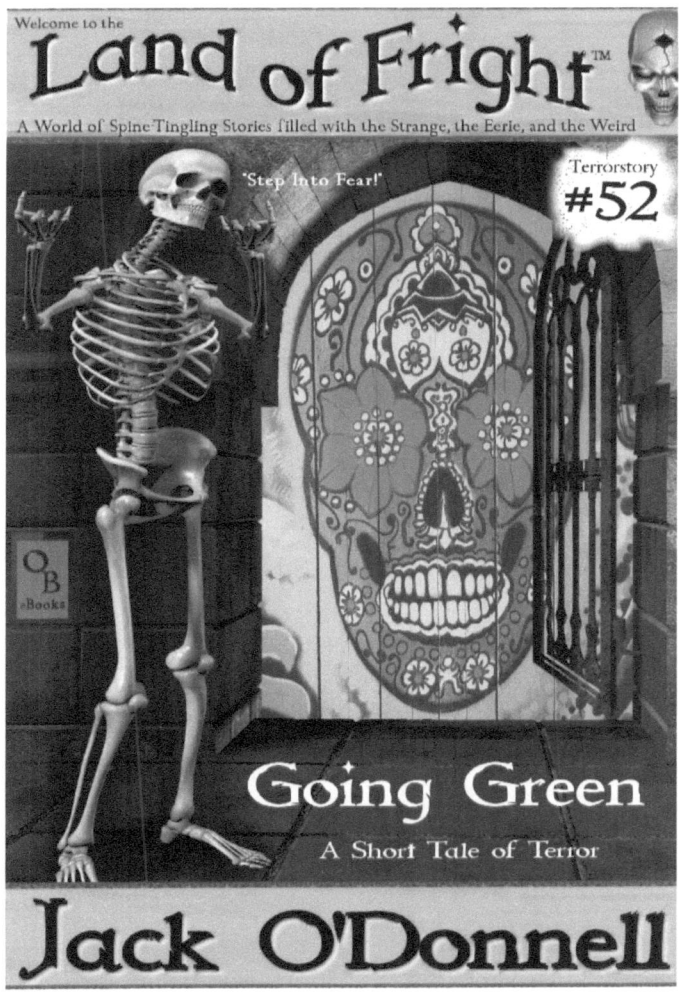

Welcome to the
Land of Fright™
A World of Spine-Tingling Stories filled with the Strange, the Eerie, and the Weird

"Step Into Fear!"

Terrorstory
#52

Going Green

A Short Tale of Terror

Jack O'Donnell

TERRORSTORY #52
GOING GREEN

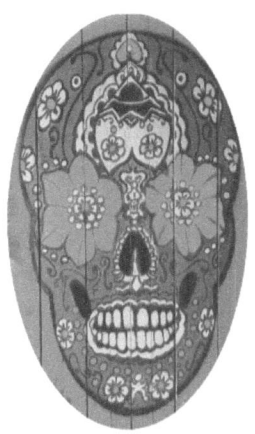

Ginny St. Clair grunted with a satisfied sigh as she heard the satisfying plop of her turd hit the surface of the water in the toilet. The annoying pain was gone from her stomach, the discomfort pushed out along with the prize she hoped awaited her. She hoped the formula was right this time. She had been working on it for months, trying new combinations of swamp water, alligator bile, mixing it with shreds of the bald cypress trees that grew tall in the dark, murky waters of the New Orleans swamp that surrounded her home. She fervently hoped that topping it off with sacrificial blood and a new set of voodoo incantations she had recently discovered in her grandmother's scribbled writings would do the trick. The final concoction had been quite foul to the taste, bitter with a sour tang that assaulted her taste buds on every swallow, but she had managed to get the full brothy brew down her throat this time without gagging it up. And then it had sat in her stomach like a lump, mingling with her own accursed fluids, the voodoo powers within her dark soul adding the final bit of unholy energy to the mixture.

She rose up off the toilet, her large flabby breasts bouncing off her naked stomach as she stood up. She turned and glanced down into the toilet bowl. The large feces log sat at the bottom of the bowl, the water otherwise relatively clear with only a hint of murkiness. She reached into the cool water and grabbed the fresh turd. She turned and glanced around the small bathroom, looking for the bowl she could have sworn she had set down nearby in anticipation of this moment, but the bowl was nowhere to be found. She uttered a curse and moved out of the bathroom, the turd cupped in her hand.

She found a cereal bowl on the kitchen table, gave it a quick rinse in the sink to wash out the bits of corn flakes residue still in the bowl, then dropped the feces into the bowl. She quickly poked and prodded at the feces, looking for the prize she so fervently hoped it contained. At first she felt nothing but soft squishiness, but then her fingers pinched around something solid and a dark hope blossomed in her dark thoughts like the beautiful thorns that erupted on a rose's stem. She pulled the object out of the feces and raised it up to look closer at it. She quickly moved back to the sink and rinsed the object off, clearing the slick residue from its surface. She held the small object up again, the filtered sunlight coming in from the heavily scratched window off to the right of the kitchen sink glinting off its hardened surface. It was a seed, its husk a dark brown color with a hint of green veins criss-crossing its surface. A seed she had created within her own body. The green veins seemed to pulse with just a hint of unearthly, unholy life, the movement barely discernible but visible if you watched the green veins long enough. A seed ready for planting.

She set the seed down on a nearby plate, right next to the half-eaten blueberry waffle on the plate. She shushed away a baby alligator that was crawling on the counter near her plate, waving at the small animal with quick jerks of her heavily wrinkled and weathered hand, forcing the scaly animal to jump down to the floor with an annoyed, angry hiss. She hurried back to the feces in the bowl, digging her fingers into the moist brown lump, hoping to find more buried treasure within. The time to make a move was ripe. Those cunts in L.A. were threatening to find a new supplier. It was downright humiliating listening to them talk about moving their business to someone else. No one threatened the Voodoo Queen like that. No one.

"Do you really need to be doing that while I'm standing here?" Tim asked, staring at the old naked woman with poorly disguised disgust. Tim Leihstall was tall and thin, with red blotches dotting his cheeks and chin. Even though he was in his mid-twenties, he never could seem to get rid of his teen acne. His black hair always seemed to be coated with a thin layer of grease no matter how much he washed it. He wanted to look away from the naked old woman, but there was something about Ginny that kept him entranced. Everyone said Ginny was the original voodoo queen of the swamps. Stories pegged her to be over three hundred and twenty years old. Voodoo was keeping her alive, they said. Alligator blood, secret plants that only grew deep in the bayou, swamp water from the heart of the swamp. All those things. She put them together in some concoction that kept her alive. She sure did have skin that looked like it could have been on an alligator. Thick and coarse and tough. Her flesh still had the color of deeply tanned human flesh, but if you looked close enough you'd swear you could see a hint of that deep alligator green color in the millions of wrinkles that rippled through her flesh. No one knew why she decided to deal in illegal drugs, but the whole operation seemed to get her off and she thrived on it.

Ginny looked up to see Tim watching her. "You just like looking at my bald little cunny," Ginny said and chortled a most unpleasant laugh. She resumed digging in the bowl and came up with another seed. She held it high, admiring it.

"Jesus, at least wash your hands," Tim said, wrinkling his nose.

Ginny looked at her hand, then raised it close to her nose to give it a sniff. "This brings life. I don't know why everyone is so disgusted by it."

"That's just nasty," Tim said.

"I think you may change your mind after you see what it will help bring about."

Tim squinted curiously.

"You'll see. Bring me one of them dirt blocks."

Ginny pointed to a pile of compressed, tightly packed bricks of dirt sitting on a nearby table. Next to the darker colored bricks sat other bricks of a more whitish hue; these were bricks of compressed cocaine.

Tim handed Ginny a brick of dirt. Ginny took the seed she had just extracted from her feces and pressed it into the dirt, pushing the seed deep into the brick with her long slender finger. She pinched the dirt over the seed, closing up the hole she had just made.

"Gimme your hand." Ginny reached out her brown-stained fingers towards Tim, wiggling them impatiently.

Tim made a foul face, and kept his hands down at his sides.

"Give me your fucking hand, Tim. Now."

There was no denying the authoritative command in Ginny's voice. Tim reluctantly raised his hand to Ginny. Ginny snatched his wrist and tugged his hand over the brick of dirt. She moved her one long, sharply pointed fingernail over Tim's forefinger, cutting his flesh, drawing blood.

"Fuck!" Tim yelped.

He moved to pull his arm away but Ginny held his hand firmly in place over the dirt brick. "Hold fucking still." Ginny squeezed at his finger, sending a stronger flow of blood dripping down onto the dirt. The dirt brick quickly absorbed the blood. After a few more moments, after a few more drops of fresh red blood plopped onto the dirt, Ginny released her tight grip on Tim's hand.

Tim yanked his hand away from Ginny and put his finger in his mouth, sucking at the wound. But then a look of horror and disgust filled his face and he spit his finger out of his mouth, sputtering and spurting and spitting. "God damn it, Ginny." He quickly moved to the sink and spit into the basin. He flipped the faucet on and threw water into his mouth, leaning over the basin, spitting and splashing, working hard to get the foul taste out of his mouth.

Ginny chortled her awful chortle. She shuffled her naked body back to the bowl of feces, eagerly looking for more seeds.

"You gave a coke-head five suitcases full of powder to take from New Orleans to L.A.? Doesn't that seem like a bad idea to you?" Harry asked.

Tim shook his head. "Ex coke-head. If he doesn't make it there with all five suitcases intact and untouched, then he doesn't get his money."

"And the money we are paying him is worth more than the coke he is carrying?" Harry asked. Harry Orsen was Tim's friend from high school. Harry had been laid off from his factory job a few months ago, a victim of automation, and Tim had managed to get him a job in Ginny's organization. Harry also had some remnants of his horrid teen acne, but his skin was more dotted with old scars than the brighter red blemishes that afflicted Tim. He kept his brown hair short and tight against his head.

Tim frowned. "Of course not."

Harry just stared at him. And continued to stare at him until Tim had a revelation.

"You don't think—" Tim started to say before Harry cut him off with a raised finger.

Harry shook his head. "No, *you* don't think."

"Jonesy wouldn't rip us off." Tim paused. "And he

wouldn't dare rip Ginny off."

"*I* would rip you off for that kind of money."

Tim looked at him. "No you wouldn't."

"Okay, I wouldn't," Harry said. "But come on, Tim. Jonesy isn't the most reliable mule you've ever worked with."

Tim was quiet for a moment. "No," he finally said. "I don't think Jonesy would rip me off. He'd be too scared to. That's why I sent him and not Ramsey. Besides, Tank is watching over him."

"Hmm," Harry said.

"What's that little hmm supposed to mean? Tank's reliable, ain't he?"

"I don't know. A trunk full of powdered bravery can do things to a man."

Tim couldn't contain himself any longer and fully busted out a big fat smile and a smothered snort.

"What's so damn funny?"

"He ain't just carryin' coke," Tim said.

"He ain't just carryin' coke?" Harry looked at Tim curiously. "What the hell else is he carrying then?"

"A little bit of bayou hoodoo voodoo for those fuckers in La La Land."

"From Ginny?"

Tim nodded. "Yep. Ginny's sick of those fuckers messing with her. They just didn't listen, so they're gonna feel some good ol' New Orleans wrath." Tim paused. "I don't know exactly what's going on, or what's in them, but Ginny was all worked up over it. She..." he started to tell Harry about what he had seen Ginny do in her house on the edges of the swamp, but then thought better about reliving it and closed his mouth, trying very hard not to remember that he had put his Ginny-shit-stained finger into his mouth. He glanced down at his bandaged finger, then looked back up at Harry. "Never seen that old broad so excited in my life. She kept babbling on about finally perfecting something she's been working on." He shrugged, wiping at his lips with his fingers. "I don't know. Once she starts babblin' about all that voodoo stuff, I stop listening. Kind of freaks me out. Important thing is she's gonna be sending those L.A. fucks a pretty serious message."

Harry rubbed at his forehead. "Ho, boy. And Jonesy don't know?"

"Nope. He thinks he's just carryin' coke."

Harry nodded. "Good. Cause I think he'd squeal like a church mouse if he knew he was carrying some voodoo shit. That sissy boy don't like surprises. Timid as a tea mouse."

Tim nodded.

"And there's no way he can open them?" Harry asked.

Tim shook his head. "They're made of metal and all locked up. Ginny already sent the keys to those fucks in LA, so Jonesy don't even have them."

"We can do this, Jonesy."

Jonesy continued to stare with disbelief at the big man. Gerlach Tank. Even his name made him sound like a big plodding beast. Tank had a deep barrel chest, massive arms, a thick bull neck, and thunder thighs. But not thunder thighs because they were fat; his legs were all powerful muscle. Tank was supposed to be the muscle behind the operation, and here the big German was trying to be the brains. "Ain't you supposed to be watching me and making sure *I* don't steal the coke?" Jonesy asked.

"I'm done with that voodoo witch. I can't work for her anymore," Tank said, shaking his head.

"Come on, Tank, she ain't so bad."

Tank continued to shake his head. "She's bad, Jonesy." He paused. "I've seen her... do things..." he said and then paused again. "And those stories Tim tells..." He stopped talking, and Jonesy wasn't sure but he could have sworn he might have seen the big man actually shudder.

Lorenzo Jones, aka Jonesy, looked away from Tank to stare at the five metal suitcases that were laying on the motel room bed. Five shiny silver boxes filled with coke. He brushed his long blond hair away from his blue eyes. He was a thin man, with a very feminine face, a face you could even call beautiful. "How do we even get the coke out? The suitcases are locked and we don't have the keys. Those bitches in L.A. have the keys."

"We don't have to actually open them. We can just drill holes in them and shake the coke out."

Jonesy was quiet for a moment. "You think so?"

Tank nodded. "I know so. I already tried it."

Jonesy stared at the suitcases. He frowned. "When the hell did you do that?"

"Not on those. I bought one just like it on eBay."

"And?"

"And I drilled right through it," Tank said. "Had to find the right bit, and put a little muscle behind it, but I put a hole in it."

"You realize all this talk of holes and drilling is getting me hot, right?"

Tank smiled at Jonesy. "Come and get some."

Jonesy was pretty confident no one suspected he and Tank were fucking. They barely acknowledged each other when anyone else was around. It was all kind of exciting and they were both getting off on the secrecy of the whole thing. And when they did find themselves alone together, it was nothing but fireworks. Jonesy liked to dress up for Tank and prance around him in a pretty dress until Tank couldn't take it anymore. He would throw Jonesy to the bed, hike up his frilly dress, and fuck the living shit out of him.

Tonight in the motel room had been no exception.

Jonesy lazily stroked Tank's massive chest as he lay next to him. "So how would we get rid of it?"

"Just a little bit at a time. Just enough to pay our bills and keep us going. If we do actually do this, we can't draw attention to ourselves by trying to sell the whole load at once."

"I don't know, Tank. Is it worth it?" Jonesy asked. He moved onto his side, keeping his hand on Tank's chest. "She'll come looking for us. We're talking millions of dollars. Nobody just lets that go. We'd be looking over our shoulders forever."

"We work for drug dealers and transport coke. We *need* to be looking over our shoulders forever. What difference does it make? This way, we work for ourselves, not for them."

Jonesy shook his head. "I don't know."

"Texas is a big state," Tank said.

Jonesy let a soft frown slide down onto his lips. "Lots of pretty cowboys in Texas."

"Aw, come on, Jonesy. None as pretty as you," Tank said.

"You're just saying that to get into my pants

again."

"Is it working?"

"Yes."

⋙ ⋘

"I keep thinking you are joking about this, but you aren't," Jonesy said. "You're serious."

Tank remained quiet.

"Why? What did she do to get you so spooked?"

"Jonesy— " he stopped and looked away, his expression almost sheepish.

"What? Tell me."

"I don't want you to think I might be crazy," Tank said.

"Look at us. You're Charles Atlas and I'm the ninety eight pound weakling you kick sand on at the beach. You're supposed to be beating me to a pulp, not fucking me to a pulp." Jonesy reached up and put his hand on Tank's shoulder. "We're both crazy." He swiped a few strands of his blond hair away from his eyes and smiled at Tank.

Tank put his beefy hand atop of Jonesy's, squeezing his slender fingers. He pulled his hand away and was quiet for a moment longer before speaking. "I'm not sure if she's human, Jonesy."

Jonesy frowned. "What do you mean?"

"I keep hearing things."

"Like what?"

"You know how old she is?" Tank asked.

Jonesy shook his head.

"Someone said she's over three hundred years old."

"Come on, Tank. That's not possible."

Tank nodded. "Exactly. Not *humanly* possible."

Jonesy was quiet.

"It's that swamp she lives in," Tank said. "Something in there is keeping her alive."

"Something in the bayou is keeping her alive?" The frown on Jonesy's face deepened. "You're talking voodoo again here, right?"

Tank didn't answer. "I can't do it anymore, Jonesy. I can't go near her anymore. Those eyes... They see right into me and scare the shit out of me... I can't do it." Tank stared down at the dingy carpeting on the motel room floor. "She's gonna know that I want to get away from her. She's gonna know I want to betray her. She's gonna see right into me and she's just gonna know." He slowly shook his head from side to side. "She's gonna know." Tank raised up his head to look at his friend. "And she isn't going to be happy about it."

The tears pooling in the corners of Tank's eyes nearly broke Jonesy's heart.

"You boys need to help me find them suitcases," Ginny said.

Tim frowned. "Jonesy's driving them to L.A. and Tank is chaperoning him to make sure he gets there. We're gonna fly in and meet them there."

Ginny shook her head. "No, he ain't heading for the city of angels. In fact, I think they's acting like little devils."

Tim's frown deepened. They were in Ginny's office, inside the small building situated on the edge of the marshy swamp near Ginny's house. An old wooden table hewn from swamp trees filled a corner of the room, surrounded by several handcrafted chairs; all of the furniture was weathered and scarred by time.

Ginny held up her phone. A tiny map filled the screen. Five red dots blinked on the map. "They's stopped. They ain't moved for a whole day. Somethin's wrong."

"You bugged them suitcases with GPS trackers?" Tim asked.

"You think I'm gonna let that much coke go without keepin' track of it?" Ginny asked.

Tim shook his head. He looked back at the tiny map on Ginny's phone. "Looks like they're still close. Maybe half a day away."

Ginny nodded. "You didn't tell him what else was in them suitcases, did you?"

Tim shook his head. "Of course not. I don't even know what else you put in there. Just them seeds and the coke, but I have no idea what they is for."

"What exactly is this *else* that's in the suitcases?" Harry asked. His voice was a bit hesitant, but his curiosity overpowered any trepidation he felt.

Ginny stared at the two young men and a grim smile slithered onto her lips. "We're going green, boys," Ginny said.

The dark coldness in Ginny's stare made Harry physically shudder. Tim's entire body trembled as if the words Ginny had just uttered carried with them a frigid blast of arctic air.

"There's no going back if we do this," Jonesy said.

Tank nodded. He clutched the drill in his beefy hand, staring down at the silver suitcase on the bed.

"She'll come after us. And it's not like you don't

stand out in a crowd. Me, I can hide. You, not so much."

Tank paused and looked over at Jonesy. "You wouldn't abandon me, would you, Jonesy?" There was an obvious earnestness to his question.

"And skip out on all that beefcake? Never."

Tank stared at Jonesy with a tender sweetness. "Jonesy, I—"

"Ahh, shut up, you big oaf, and let's steal some coke."

Tank stared at the power drill in his hand. He pressed the power button and the drill bit whirled and whirred, filling the motel room with its grating sound.

Jonesy felt his teeth set on edge. The sound of the drill was just like the grinding, grating sound that filled a dentist's office. He hated the dentist's office. He hadn't set foot in one for over ten years. Receding gum line be damned.

Tank took his finger off the drill's trigger and the whirring sound faded away. He looked at the metal case sitting on the motel bed. He thought about where to drill the hole, thinking of the most discrete place to put the hole, but then he realized it didn't matter at all where he put the hole. There was nothing discrete about what they were doing at all. He took another drink of his beer. They had been sitting and thinking and pacing and thinking and sitting for hours after they had twisted the caps off their beers; their drinks had been ice cold when he first put the drill bit into the drill, but now the beer was warm.

"Fuck it." Tank depressed the drill trigger and brought the tip straight down onto the side of the metal case. The hard metal of the case resisted the drill at first so he pressed down firmer on it, putting his weight behind it, his muscles bulging behind the effort. Then, the drill bit caught and started eating into the case, penetrating its metal surface.

Jonesy half expected a cloud of white dust to explode up into Tank's face any second. But that didn't happen.

Something else did.

Tank pushed the drill in as far as it would go, gave the drill a twist and a turn, trying to widen the hole a bit, then withdrew the drill bit. He let go of the trigger and stared at the drill bit as it came to a stop. The bit was still clean, not a trace of any white powder on it whatsoever.

Jonesy frowned. He stared at the drill bit. A hint of what looked like dirt stained the bit, but he figured it was just some kind of residue from the suitcase. "Maybe it's not long enough. Maybe it didn't reach the coke bags."

Tank turned away from the metal case to set the drill down on the table next to the bed. When he turned back to the metal case, he leaped away from it, nearly stumbling over the corner of the bed frame.

A greenish tendril, somewhat snake-like, oozed out of the small hole he had just made in the case. The green stringy object started to take on a more solid form, thickening, turning a deep green color, becoming like a vine twisting in the air as it rose upward.

Jonesy just stared at it. He had no idea what to make of it. He had never seen anything like it. But then he realized with a growing chill that he *had* seen something like it. In the bayous of New Orleans near where he grew up. And he had seen such vines hanging from the swamp trees near Ginny's place.

The greenish entity widened at its tip, thickened, looking like a cobra flaring out its hood. There was the odd semblance of a face within the flared hood. A face that had an uncanny resemblance to the face of Ginny St. Clair.

The green vine shot towards Tank like a cobra striking at its prey, and encircled the big man's neck like a hangman's noose.

Jonesy bolted for the motel room door.

Jonesy tightened his grip on the steering wheel, then angrily wiped the tears away from his cheeks. The torrent of shame continued to roll down his face in warm streaks of wetness. *I left him! I left Tank alone to die!* He curled his fingers tighter, digging his painted nails into the steering wheel. *You can't just leave him there.*

He double checked his speed against the sixty five miles per hour speed limit sign that breezed past him on the right side of the highway. He was doing sixty seven. Maybe I should start speeding, Jonesy thought. *Maybe I should hit eighty, then ninety, then just crash into an overpass, smash myself into smithereens against the cement wall.* But he knew he couldn't do it. He didn't have the guts to do it.

Jonesy again angrily wiped the tears away from his cheeks. He knew calling the police, or even an ambulance, was out of the question, but he knew in his heart that he couldn't just leave Tank's body in that room. *Maybe he's not dead? No, he's dead. I just know he's dead.* He thought of the odd green tendril, the green vine, the smell of swamp it gave off. The face of Ginny St. Clair. A nervous fear filled him at the thought of the old woman, but another voice tried to bolster his courage. *You can't just leave him there. Jesus, Jonesy, stop being such a coward your whole life.*

Jonesy mustered all the courage he had left and headed back towards the motel.

Jonesy reached for the motel room door, but then stopped when he heard voices. Voices were coming from inside the room. He couldn't make out what they were saying, but there were definitely people in the room. He put his ear closer to the door, but still couldn't discern the words. He looked down at the floor of the motel landing, seeing the small crack at the bottom of the door. He bent down, then moved to his knees, listening. He moved to a prone position, putting his ear closer to the crack.

"You okay there, buddy?"

Jonesy looked up to see a man holding an ice bucket standing a few feet away, staring down at him.

Jonesy quickly moved back up to his feet. "Yes, I'm okay," he said, brushing off his pants, looking away from the frowning face of the man.

Suddenly, the motel room door opened and Ginny stood at the threshold. She smiled warmly at Jonesy. "Jonesy!" she exclaimed with an even larger smile. "We were wondering where you were. Come in, come in." Ginny grabbed Jonesy's arm and pulled him into the room with surprising strength, slamming the motel room door shut behind them.

Jonesy stared with frightened fascination at the

body of Gerlach Tank sitting on the motel room bed. "Is he… still alive?" Jonesy asked.

Tank sat on the bed, leaning back up against the headboard. His eyes were open, staring, his muscular legs stretched out fully before his body on the bed. His big hands rested in his lap. The four other suitcases were scattered all across the room, all of them still closed. Tim and Harry were busy collecting them. One of the bedside tables was overturned, one of its legs cracked in half. The TV was on the floor, its screen shattered. The lamp lay on the carpeting underneath the motel room window, somehow its bulb still intact.

"Yes," Ginny said. "Well, yes and no," she corrected herself quickly, but didn't elaborate. She stared down at the body of the big man on the bed. A tiny wisp of a green tendril extended out of his mouth. Ginny reached down and pushed the green tendril back down into his mouth and pressed Tank's lips closed, as if she were pushing a sprouting plant stem back down into the soil and pinching the dirt tightly closed over it.

Jonesy looked closer at Tank's eyes. They looked slightly bloodshot, but the veiny strings in his eyes had more of a greenish hue to them than a reddish color. Then the eyes blinked and Jonesy took a startled step back, fighting back a gasp.

"Hi, Jonesy," Tank said.

"Jesus," Jonesy gasped.

"Why did you leave me?" Tank asked. There was an honest earnestness to his question.

Jonesy stared numbly at Tank for a long moment. "Shit, Tank. What the hell happened?"

Tank stared up at Jonesy with a forlorn expression

masking his face. A green ooze of a tear slipped out of his eye and slowly trailed down his cheek. "Why, Jonesy? Why? You left me to die alone."

Jonesy was quiet for a moment. He stared down at the drill-damaged suitcase near the foot of the bed, then glanced slowly up at Tank, his face filled with sadness, self-loathing, and a hint of fear. "I'm a coward, Tank. You know that. I'm a chicken shit." Jonesy looked at Ginny. "What the hell did you do to him? What was in that fucking suitcase?"

"He's gone green," Ginny said and chortled gleefully. She stared at the silver suitcases that Tim and Harry had placed on the bed, then fixated on the small jagged hole the drill had bored into the suitcase nearest the foot of the bed. She looked up at Jonesy. "You want to explain to me why there is a hole in one of my suitcases?"

Jonesy forced himself to turn away from Tank's stare. He looked at Tim and Harry, who were now standing guard near the motel room door, but they just gave him blank looks. He was in deep shit and he knew it. "I—" he started to speak, but then stopped. His mind immediately started to race, his thoughts coming in a tumbling, jumbling barrage of self-preservation scenarios. His heartbeat surged and he felt a layer of slick sweat push through his skin to bead up on his flesh. What the fuck had happened to Tank? He looked drugged. Was he under some kind of voodoo spell? He was certain he had been returning to the motel to find a dead man. Was Tank really Tank anymore? Was he under Ginny's spell now? Was he even human? Did he still owe him his loyalty? "The guy is huge," Jonesy blurted. He pointed a shaking finger at Tank. "There was no way

I could stop him." He immediately regretted his weasel-like outburst, but once the words came out of his lips he knew he couldn't take them back.

Ginny just stared at Jonesy, her expression flat.

"He was gonna kill me, Ginny, I swear it." A lifetime of lying helped this lie come easily. "He said he was scared of you and couldn't take working for you no more. He wanted to get out," Jonesy said, purposefully avoiding looking anywhere near Tank.

"The devil made you do it, eh?" Ginny was quiet for a moment. "Interesting," she finally said. "And I suppose you were coming to warn me?" Ginny asked.

Jonesy tilted his head up and down, the movement a gross exaggeration of a nod. "Yeah. Sure. Sure I was."

Ginny looked closer at Jonesy, squinting at him, the wrinkles in her flesh deepening, revealing a hint of the legendary green hidden beneath their dark folds. "You scared of me?"

"No," Jonesy said, but then immediately corrected himself. "Yes. Shit, Ginny, everybody's kind of scared of you."

Ginny looked over to Tim and Harry. "Tim, you scared of me?"

"Are you kidding me?" Tim asked rhetorically. "Hell yeah I'm scared of you."

"You ever think of stealing from me?" Ginny asked, moving her gaze from Tim to Harry.

Tim shook his head. "No. I ain't crazy."

"No, ma'am," Harry said.

Ginny looked over to Tank. "Guess he wasn't scared enough. I'm gonna have to work a little harder on that with the rest of you."

Tim and Harry didn't say anything.

Jonesy shook his head back and forth. "No you don't. No you don't.

"Now what?" Tim asked. "What do you want to do with him?"

Ginny looked at Jonesy. "Jonesy's going to finish what he started and deliver the coke," Ginny told him. "Right, Jonesy? Our friends in L.A. are waiting."

Jonesy bobbed his head up and down. "Yeah, yeah, sure."

"Tank will escort you." She paused. "To keep you safe. Me and the boys here will be right behind you."

Jonesy nodded numbly. "Yeah, sure, Ginny, sure."

Ginny turned to Jonesy. "In a way, I guess I should thank you. I was gonna test the vines on those cunts in L.A. first, but testin' it on Tank is a much better idea. Now I can use him."

"What... what did you do to him?" Jonesy asked.

Ginny glanced at Tank then looked back to Jonesy. "I told you. He's gone green." She smiled and cackled, revealing her browning teeth.

Jonesy didn't smile back.

≈⊰⧉⊱≈

The Matriarch fingered the necklace of keys that dangled around her neck. She was a portly Mexican woman with short black hair and a serious face that made every other serious face in the room look like a happy clown's smile. Her dress was somber, a deep brown that nearly covered her from head to toe. She stared down at the brown suitcase that rested on the table before her and try to smile a dark smile but her lips only moved from a downturned state to a flat line; she didn't have the muscle memory to raise her lips any higher.

"Are… they… already in there?" Consuela asked. She was a pretty Hispanic woman with straight black hair that fell past her shoulders. She stood on the opposite side of the table, glancing furtively at the brown suitcase, but never letting her gaze linger on it for too long. They were in the Matriarch's study, the walls lined with enormous bookshelves, large statues and a few large paintings.

The Matriarch nodded. "That voodoo bruja bitch won't know what hit her." The Matriarch smiled her even-lipped grim smile. "And then the word will spread. Disrespect me and you'll pay the ultimate price."

"Are they… strong enough to take them down?" Consuela asked.

"Have you ever seen a pack of jackals take down a lion?" the Matriarch asked. She looked at the brown suitcase. "They may be small, but they are viciously savage."

Consuela made the sign of the cross, moving her arm up and down and side to side. "I don't like this black magic, Mama. I don't like it at all."

"We're going brown, my little chica," the Matriarch said. And then she laughed and that sound frightened Consuela more than she had ever been frightened before, especially because her mother's lips still refused to turn upwards into any resemblance of a smile even as she laughed. The young Hispanic woman made the sign of the cross again, this time moving her arm up and down and side to side with a quicker flurry of motion.

Jonesy gripped the steering wheel with both hands,

staring out at the open country road stretching off into the distance. A truck passed by on the other side of the wide median that separated the traffic, but other than that the road before them was empty of other vehicles.

Tank sat quietly beside him in the passenger seat of the car. The big man was fascinated with his hands, turning them over and over again as he studied them.

"You... okay, Tank?" Jonesy asked. He purposely avoided looking in Tank's direction.

"It's... weird," Tank said, keeping his gaze on his hands. "I can... feel it... like it's growing inside me."

Jonesy didn't say anything. He chanced a quick glance at Tank out of the corner of his eye, but then quickly looked away when he saw the vine-like tentacles extending out of the ends of Tank's fingers.

"It feels like they're coiled up inside me, ready to shoot out," Tank said.

Jonesy suddenly felt something touch his cheek, felt something slide up and down his skin. He batted at whatever was touching him, but missed it. The feeling on his flesh quickly returned, as something cool and moist pressed against his cheek.

"Don't you like it, Jonesy?" Tank asked.

Jonesy glanced up into the rearview mirror and saw a green tendril moving slowly back and forth across his cheek. He turned a startled glance to Tank, looking at him straight on. A long vine-like tendril had extended out of one of Tank's fingers, reaching across the seat to touch his face. "Shit, Tank! What the fuck is that?" Jonesy quickly turned back to look out the windshield at the flat road ahead, his fingers tightening on the steering wheel.

"I don't know," Tank said, his words coming out

in a slow, dreamy manner. "It's just part of me now."

"That is fucked up," Jonesy said. "That is some fucked up voodoo shit for sure."

"Yeah," Tank said. "Hey, we got any water? I'm really thirsty."

Jonesy and Tank entered the abandoned warehouse, both of them clutching a silver suitcase in either hand. Four Mexican women clutched submachine guns, two on either side of the warehouse entrance. Their brightly colored flowery dresses seem incredibly incongruent with the dull grey metal slabs of steel that comprised the structure of the warehouse.

A solitary folding table was set up in the middle of the warehouse, with five more Mexican women standing behind it. Four of them were armed, they too dressed in vibrant flowery dresses. The one standing closest to the table was not armed. She was obviously the matriarch of this gang. She was a portly Mexican woman with short black hair and a serious face. Her dress was a much more somber deep brown that nearly covered her from head to toe. A large brown suitcase, most likely filled with the money for the transaction, was situated on the table before her.

Jonesy heard two of the Mexican women who had been flanking the entrance walking up behind them, but he didn't bother to look; he knew they were there.

Jonesy and Tank reached the table and put the four suitcases atop it.

"What the fuck is this?" the Matriarch asked. She fingered the necklace of five keys that dangled atop her large breasts.

"It's all here," Jonesy said. He forced the nervous high pitch out of his voice. "We just consolidated."

"Consolidated?" The Matriarch frowned as she repeated the word. "What the fuck is that?"

"We combined them." Jonesy pointed to the four locked silver suitcases. "It all fit into four suitcases."

The Matriarch shook her head. "I don't like this shit. I don't like fucking last minute changes. Last minute changes makes me want to shoot your fucking dicks off."

Two of the women immediately aimed their AK-47's at the crotches of the two men.

Jonesy threw up his hands. "Whoa, whoa." He pointed to the suitcases. "It's all there. If it's not, then you don't give us the money." He quickly pulled his hands back down to his side when he felt the slight quiver in his fingers threatening to expose the nervous trepidation tingling his spine.

"If it's not all there, I *will* blow your dicks off," the Matriarch assured him.

Jonesy motioned again to the suitcases with a toss of his head. "You got the keys. Open 'em up." He felt a hint of moisture starting to line his brow.

The Matriarch raised her left hand and snapped her fingers. "Consuela."

One of the women holding an AK-47 moved quickly forward, shouldering the sub-machine gun with its strap. She gingerly removed the necklace of keys from the Matriarch's neck and stepped up to the table.

Jonesy took a slight step back away from the table.

Tank glanced at him with a flat expression on his face, but he said nothing. The veins in his eyes pulsed ever so slightly, the green tint only visible if you looked close enough.

The woman the Matriarch called Consuela tried a key, but it didn't fit.

Jonesy took another small shuffling step back. One ball of sweat beaded on his forehead, but didn't fall.

Consuela moved on to the next key and successfully inserted it into the suitcase lock.

Jonesy took another step back, but the hard tip of a gun barrel pressing against his spine stopped his backward progress.

Consuela flipped the latches and opened up the silver suitcase.

Jonesy felt his entire body tense up.

Consuela reached down into the suitcase and raised up a block of coke tightly packed into a brick-like form.

Jonesy felt the tension ooze out of his shoulder blades. His knees felt wobbly, but he forced himself to stay standing tall.

"Test it," the Matriarch said.

One of the Mexican women armed with an AK-47 walked back to a white limousine that was parked a few dozen yards away inside the vast warehouse and opened up the car door. She motioned sharply towards the interior of the limo and three people quickly scurried out. Three women emerged, all sharply dressed, two young Mexican women in dark pantsuits and a young Mexican woman in a cream-colored pantsuit. But what was unnerving about these three women was their faces. All three of them had their faces painted in skeletal white patterns, as if they were dressed up for a Day of the Dead celebration. They moved up to the table.

The young woman in the cream pantsuit produced

what looked like a cosmetic case, but it also served as a portable coke snorting station with its smooth mirrored surface and tiny snorting tube tucked neatly into a groove. Consuela cut a small slit into the coke brick with a tiny switchblade, scooped some of the white powder onto the edge of the blade, then dumped it on the woman's waiting mirror.

The woman in the cream pantsuit snorted a line. She wiped at her nose and smiled. She looked like a grinning skull.

"What's with the face paint?" Jonesy asked.

"We celebrate death in my world just as much as we celebrate life," the Matriarch said. "Today, we celebrate *your* death."

"What the fuck does that mean?" Jonesy asked.

The Matriarch shrugged. "We all die."

A deep frown creased Jonesy's brow. No wonder Ginny wanted to teach this smug bitch a lesson.

One of the young women in the dark pantsuits produced a chemical analysis kit and quickly tested the composition of the product with the assistance of the other woman in the dark pantsuit. She, too, looked up and nodded with a hint of a smile on her skeletal-decorated face.

"Check the rest," the Matriarch said.

Consuela nodded. She picked the right key on the first try for the next suitcase and the silver latch on the suitcase clicked. She reached into the suitcase and pulled out a brick of coke. Or so she thought.

As Consuela raised her switchblade and moved it towards the coke brick, the Matriarch pointed to the brown suitcase resting on the table next to the silver suitcases. "Aren't you going to check the money?"

Jonesy grabbed the brown suitcase and flipped it

around so the two latches faced him. He flipped up one of the latches.

"I have a question," one of the women holding an AK-47 said.

The Matriarch looked at her, clearly annoyed that she even spoke.

Jonesy paused before opening the second latch, looking curiously at the Matriarch and her soldier.

"How could they..." the soldier woman paused and then continued, "...*consolidate* the product if we have the keys?"

Consuela continued on with what she was doing as the woman spoke. She slit a hole in the coke brick and—

—the green tendrils struck quickly, exploding up out of the brick like tightly-wound springs uncoiling, whipping towards anyone on the wrong side of the table. The Matriarch, the five women with AK-47s, the three coke testers, all were targets of the green lengths of whipping, curling vine-like tendrils. Every one of them came under attack from the thrashing frenzy of the green swamp vines as if they were all under assault simultaneously from a nine-armed octopus. Two of the women with AK-47s managed to fire off a few shots, but they were quickly overwhelmed by the attacking tentacles and their guns went silent. A tentacle-vine encircled the Matriarch's neck and started to squeeze. Another vine-like tentacle wrapped around a soldier's wrist and squeezed, cutting off the flow of blood to her hand, forcing her to drop her AK-47. Another tentacle encircled a soldier's thigh and thrust her high into the air, shaking her violently. Another tentacle penetrated a woman soldier's mouth, sliding hard and fast down her throat, choking her.

The two women directly behind Jonesy and Tank bolted forward, guns at the ready, but neither one knew what to shoot at in the wild frenzy of motion so their weapons stayed silent. Tank turned and grabbed one of the women with the vine-like tentacles that exploded out of each of his fingers, gripping the woman twice around each arm and twice around each leg. Another tentacle like appendage wrapped tightly around her throat. The final vine-tentacle went around her waist. Tank lifted her up high, raising her up above his head, his tentacle-appendages holding her tightly. And then he ripped her apart, tearing her arms out of her sockets, ripping her legs from her waist, decapitating her head from her body. A showering rain of red poured down onto Tank and he relished the blood rain, bathing in its life-giving power, absorbing the life fluid into his skin.

Jonesy ducked under the onslaught of blood, throwing his hands up over his head in a futile effort to block the torrent of red from splashing all over him. "Holy fuck, Tank!" he said as he fell to his knees.

The second woman managed to keep her grip on her weapon even as she was drenched by the deluge of blood. She turned the AK-47 to aim it directly at Tank's chest, and pulled the trigger. But a green tendril had slid into the barrel, a long shoot emerging from the end of Tank's index finger, just as she fired and the weapon backfired into her face, sending splintering hot shards of metal spearing through her flesh and bone.

Tank howled in pain as he withdrew his now-shredded tentacle finger. A dark greenish-red ooze poured from the end of the ragged wound.

The second woman lost her grip on her weapon and the AK-47 clattered to the cement floor. But that didn't matter as another thick tendril of green vine emanating from Tank's finger wrapped around her throat and started to squeeze tight.

Jonesy heard more gunfire erupt nearby, the pinging of bullets echoing in the cavernous space as they struck the ground, the support beams, the walls. Glass shattered in the distance as a bullet blew through a window pane. But the gunfire was short-lived and the echoing pings soon faded. The screams, however, did not fade so quickly.

When Jonesy finally looked out from behind the shield of his crossed arms, the warehouse was eerily quiet. He glanced down at his arms and legs to see that he was covered in blood. "Jesus..." He slowly rose to his feet. He felt a large presence looming over him and he looked to his right to see Tank towering over him. Tank had been a big man before, but now he was huge. He seemed to have grown an extra foot or two and his wide chest was now even wider, more expansive. His thick arms and legs were now even thicker, the bulges more pronounced. Even his head seemed...larger. *He's a fathead*, Jonesy thought and nearly laughed with the insane madness of it all.

Tank turned his head down to stare at Jonesy. "Hi, Jonesy," he said.

"Jesus, Tank. What the fuck just happened?"

"We won," he said and looked up to survey the carnage.

Jonesy followed his gaze. There was blood and

body parts everywhere. The skull-painted head of one of the coke-testing Mexican women rested on the warehouse floor just a few feet away. Other bloodied and battered bodies lay on the floor near the table, which was somehow miraculously still upright. The four suitcases rested atop the table, along with the brown suitcase, still unopened.

Ginny strode into the warehouse, walking with the unsteady gait of a woman well into her golden years. "Well, this is a fine mess," she said and chortled. Tim and Harry flanked her, both brandishing guns. She paused near a pool of blood, then bent down to slide her finger through the red liquid. She raised her blood-smeared finger up to her nose and gave it a sniff, and then a quick lick. "This'll do." She quickly held out her other arm, motioning for one of the boys to help her back up to a standing position. Tim hurried over to her and grabbed her wrinkled arm, helping her to straighten back up. She motioned to all the blood. "Soak this all up. We can use it."

Harry frowned, but Tim understood Ginny's desire for more fresh blood as he glanced at Tank. He nudged Harry and they quickly moved back outside to get their supplies.

Tank looked down at Ginny as she approached him. "I don't think I can move, Ginny," he said.

Ginny glanced down to see that somehow Tank's shoes had burst. The vines had erupted out of his toes and had driven themselves into the concrete floor somehow. And then Ginny realized quickly that they weren't vines; they were roots. Fucking Tank had taken root in the goddamn warehouse. Ginny patted Tank on his large midsection. "Guess you won't be trying to run away from me no more, eh Tank?"

Tank shook his big head. "No, ma'am. I guess not." Tank raised up one of his vine-like appendages and displayed the severed head of the Matriarch to Ginny. "This is for you." The Matriarch's eyes were closed, her frown deep. Streaks of blood smeared her decapitated head.

"Oh, Tank. That's so sweet." Ginny chortled her awful chortle.

Tank looked at Ginny. "What happened to me?" The blood that had coated his exposed flesh from ripping the Mexican woman apart above his head was now mostly gone, absorbed into his skin. His clothes were still damp with redness, but the fabric was slowly drying as the blood on them was slowly absorbed by his body. Only a few stray streaks of red marred his skin.

She smiled at him, looking him up and down. "That's some strong voodoo shit going on right there," she said. "It's gonna be okay, Tank. Jonesy's gonna feed you, right Jonesy?" She paused then corrected herself. "I mean water you. Right, Jonesy?" Ginny turned to look at Jonesy.

Jonesy didn't answer. He was too busy running out the door with the brown suitcase clutched in his hand, leaving a bloody trail as he raced through the warehouse.

"Stop him, Tank," Ginny ordered, her voice calm.

A tendril vine shot out from Tank's finger and ensnared one of Jonesy's ankles, tripping him up. Jonesy went down hard, splashing into a pool of blood, sliding through the dark red liquid, smearing the concrete floor with a wide trail of crimson. The brown suitcase flew out of his hands and hit the wall near the door. The force of the impact dislodged the second latch on the brown suitcase and it flipped open with a soft click.

Jonesy stared from his prone position in the pool of blood at the contents of the suitcase. It wasn't full of money. It wasn't full of stacks of beautiful greenbacks. It was filled with something brown. Something brown and breathing with ragged breaths. Something alive. Something very much alive.

Jonesy rose up quickly, slipping once in the blood, but managing to get to his feet.

Ginny whipped her head back towards the severed head of the Matriarch, feeling a chilling pull from the dead woman. The Matriarch's eyes were now open, her lips upturned into a tight smile. "Fucking bruja bitch," Ginny muttered angrily. The Matriarch had been a bruja, a Mexican witch, and she had cast her black magic upon them. Fucking bruja bitch.

The tiny creatures that erupted out of the suitcase were a nightmare whirlwind of savage teeth and vicious claws. There were three of them, each one of them with grotesquely distorted human faces, each one of their hideous faces painted in a horrific skull-like pattern, each one of them a disturbed version of the three coke testers who had their faces painted skeletal-white in a similar fashion. They were duendes. Beliefs about duendes varied from region to region in Spain and Mexico – some believed they were the souls of infants who died before they could be baptized, others simply portrayed them as malevolent, naughty spirits that hide in a person's home and wreak havoc. But these were true duendes, the malformed monstrosities arisen from aborted fetuses.

The first duende launched itself at Jonesy and struck him right in the chest, sinking its claws deep into his flesh. It didn't hesitate and bit through his shirt to take out a chunk of skin meat along with the fabric of his shirt. It swallowed the piece of Jonesy's flesh quickly and went back in for more. Jonesy shrieked an ear-splitting shriek as pain ripped through him. A geyser of blood spurted into the air as the duende punctured arteries and veins. He wasn't going green. He was going red. Blood red.

Tank went into action, shooting his vine-fingers at the duende, urgently trying to grab it and choke the unholy life out of it. He grabbed the duende that was atop Jonesy and ripped it away from him. He hurled the little beast against the warehouse wall. The duende splattered into a mashed pulp of guts and intestines and blood and whatever else its demonic innards contained. It slid down the wall to lay lifeless on the warehouse floor.

Tim and Harry chose the wrong time to re-enter the warehouse, mops and buckets in hand. The second duende leaped at Tim, going straight for his exposed throat. Tim reacted with an instinctive twisting of his body as the tiny dark shape leaped towards him, turning his body so the duende struck him in the shoulder. The duende sunk its teeth deep into Tim's flesh, rending and tearing at his shoulder meat. Tim screamed in pain and alarm. He swatted at the duende with the bucket he held in his opposite hand, cracking the plastic bucket futilely against the back of the grotesque little beast chewing on him.

Harry was frozen in place, temporarily shocked by the attack. He stood motionless, watching, mop and bucket in hand.

The duende spit out a mouthful of Tim's skin and muscles and veins and went back in for another bite, snarling savagely as it gnashed its teeth deeper into Tim's shoulder and upper back.

Tim spun about madly, trying to whack the duende off his shoulder with the bucket. Then, a green tendril wrapped itself about the duende and yanked roughly, ripping the beast away from Tim. The duende took another mouthful of Tim with it as it was violently torn away from him. Tank whipped the little beast against a support beam, smashing the duende into a flattened pulp.

The third duende charged straight at Ginny, leaping straight for her weathered face, its sharp claws outstretched, its sharp teeth exposed within a snarling mask of rage. But a green vine grabbed it out of the air, pulling it away from Ginny, snatching it away from the voodoo queen just as the duende's claws were a millimeter away from reaching Ginny's aged flesh. The duende snarled a high-pitched whine as Tank whipped it about in the air. He raised it up high, then brought it smashing down with terrific force against the concrete floor, flattening the duende into a pancake mass of blood and bone and bile.

A moment of quiet settled over the warehouse.

Tim was laid out on the floor, blood spurting profusely from the ragged bites in his shoulder. He gasped and gurgled and then went still.

Harry still stood frozen, unable to move.

Ginny turned to look at Jonesy. He had his hands clamped down over his breast, desperately trying to stop the blood oozing out of his chest. She shuffled over to him, maneuvering around pools of blood to get to him. She stood over him, staring down at him. His face was pale, growing more and more ashen with each passing moment. Ginny looked over to Tank, who was rooted to the warehouse floor a few yards away. "He don't look so good, Tank. Is he worth saving?"

Tank nodded. "I love him. He's a sad, scared little man. I need to protect him."

"Plant your seed in him," Ginny said. "You have that power now. It's inside you."

Tank stared down at his hand for a moment, flexing his fingers. A tiny wisp of a green tendril extended out of his index finger; it wiggled and waved as if it were caught in a soft breeze. Then a much longer and thicker tendril extended out from Tank's middle finger. Tank moved his vine-like digit behind Jonesy and the thick green tendril slid down inside Jonesy's pants. Jonesy wiggled his butt and let out a soft exclamation.

"I didn't mean that way." Ginny pointed to her mouth, but then shrugged. "Whatever floats your boat. I'll never understand you two twisted fucks."

Tank slid into Jonesy and deposited his seed into him.

Jonesy moaned as the voodoo vine power infiltrated his body, penetrating him, spreading wide. Tiny green veins criss-crossed themselves over his wound, sealing the gash in his chest. Jonesy coughed, spitting up a few last remnants of blood, but then some of the color started to return to his face, the pale ashen tone fading away to be replaced by a more vibrant fleshy color, with just a hint of green. "Tank..." Jonesy started to say, but then let his voice trail away. He looked away from his big friend.

"You don't have to be scared anymore," Tank said softly to Jonesy. "I'll protect you."

A tear squeezed out of Jonesy's eye and trailed

down his face, the color of the tear shining with a hint of a ghostly green sheen.

"Aww, you two gay fucks are gonna make me cry next," Ginny said. "And some people think I don't have a heart." She looked away at Harry, who still stood motionless in the doorway, mop and bucket still in hand. "God damn it, boy," Ginny shouted at Harry. "Soak up that blood! Don't let it go to waste."

Harry looked up dumbly at Ginny. He still didn't move.

Ginny pointed at the blood pooling around Tim's body. "Soak it up! We're gonna need it." She glanced around the warehouse, taking in all the carnage, the ripped apart Mexican women, the smashed duendes, the rivers of blood flowing everywhere. "We're gonna need as much as we can get."

Harry hesitantly set his bucket down on the ground. He gripped the mop with both hands, staring down at the ever widening sea of crimson spreading out from Tim's dead body. And then he started to soak up the red liquid, swishing the mop through Tim's blood.

Tank looked down to Ginny. "Now what?"

Ginny was quiet for a moment. She looked up at Tank, glanced at Jonesy, then looked back to Tank. "You boys know why they decided to make money green?" Ginny asked. She stared at Tank, at his green tendril fingers, at the greenish veins now more and more visible as they pulsed beneath his skin. His skin was starting to take on a more roughly textured look, as if the bald cypress tree bark was starting to make its presence known within his epidermal layers.

No one answered.

"Because green ink was plentiful and durable and

the color green was associated with stability. That's what we need, boys. Durability and stability. We're gonna bring some fucking stability into this business. Now we play hard and we play fast. Those fucking micks in Queens are next. Then those dagos in Chicago. Wait until they get a load of you Germinator brothers." She thumbed a wagging digit at Tank and Jonesy. "And wait until they get a load of what I'm gonna do with my little gator pals." She rubbed her belly. "I'm brewing up a batch just for them. We're gonna go green in a big way." And then she laughed and laughed and laughed, her chortling guffaws echoing in the warehouse.

Harry was too busy soaking up Tim's blood to partake in the mirth, but Tank and Jonesy finally joined in with Ginny and laughed along with her.

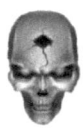

TERRORSTORY #53
MESSAGE IN A BOTTLE

"A modern day message in a bottle," Shawnna Yurovich said. She was a redheaded Russian beauty, her luxurious long hair flowing down well past her shoulders. She wore a tight green one-piece bathing suit that really did bring out the green of her eyes, and the full swell of her ample bosom.

Brad Connors shook the bottle. The tiny rectangular black object within the glass bottle flitted from side to side, rattling as it struck the sides of the glass. The glass was dirty and severely scratched, but the small object inside was still visible. The top of the bottle was sealed with a crude blob of wax atop a cork that sealed the mouth of the bottle. It may have been a crude seal, but it was definitely effective. The interior of the bottle was bone-dry.

"It looks like an SD card," Shawnna said.

Brad frowned at her. He was tall, muscular, his black hair cut short and neat. A few days of stubble darkened his face. He wore jean shorts and a white tank top. A hint of sunburn colored his shoulders.

Shawnna pointed to the SD card in the bottle. "It's probably got a message on it."

"It looks like the SD card Reggie uses in his Nikon," Charise Simpson said. "Come on, open it up." She was a petite blonde, her hair curly and short. She wore a skimpy two-piece bathing suit that barely covered anything, but her flat chest and flat buttocks didn't give her much to cover anyway.

They were sitting on the beach of the private island Charise's parents had purchased a few years ago. It was off the coast of St. Lucia. The sands were white and clean and just plain luscious underfoot. Tropical trees swayed softly in the warm breeze. Beyond the trees and the beach, the ocean was calm, tranquil and a cool green-blue that just begged to be stared at.

Brad started to pick at the seal that covered the top of the bottle. It was a thick coating of red wax. He quickly grew tired of the effort. He handed the bottle to Shawnna. "Here, use those claws of yours to peel it off."

Shawnna took the bottle and started scraping at the wax with her long nails. She made quick work of the wax, but couldn't budge the thick cork stopper that was shoved tightly into the mouth of the bottle. She held the bottle out toward Charise. "We need a knife. Maybe Carlos can open it."

Charise took the bottle and looked toward the bar that was situated near the edge of the beach closest to the house. The bar was empty. "He's not there yet. It's too early for his shift."

"You mean too late," Brad said, then finished off the last swig of his daiquiri. "We've been up for, what, twenty-six hours now?" He set the glass back down in the sand. He took the bottle from Charise and stood up, wiping sand off his shorts with his free hand. "There's gotta be a knife in there somewhere." He headed for the bar, stumbling awkwardly as he moved tipsily across the shifting sand. The others got up and followed him towards the bar.

Brad thought about the bottle. Shawnna had spotted it first. It was just lying in the sand, obviously pushed in during high tide. It got caught in the sand and the weak tide couldn't pull it back out into the ocean. He wondered where it had come from. There were no obvious markings on the bottle. It looked like it used to have some kind of writing on it, or maybe some kind of label, but it was long washed off. Now it was just a very scratched up bottle. It had clearly journeyed through some rough waters. He was still impressed by how dry the inside was. The wax seal and the cork stopper had not allowed a single drop of water into the bottle. The bottle was thick, too, the glass obviously very strong. There were scratches all over it, but no cracks. Where had it come from? And what the hell was on that SD card?

It was kind of silly and childish, but he was damn curious. It was kind of fun. He had seen stuff like this in movies and on TV, had read about it, but he had never really seen an actual message in a bottle himself.

He felt a little giddy. He knew that was probably more from the peach daiquiris than anything, but the pleasant alcoholic sensation making his brain buzz only made this mysterious bottle that much more intriguing and exciting.

The videos and pictures they saw on the SD card dampened that enthusiasm and filled them with absolute terror, but that didn't happen until later.

Brad found a sharp, curved knife behind the bar and managed to dig the cork out from the bottle. He tipped the bottle over and dumped the SD card into his open palm. He set the now empty bottle down on the bar. Behind him, unnoticed by the group, several bottles that looked very similar to the bottle he had just set down on the bar top lined the shelves. He lifted the small memory card up and stared at it.

"Let's check it out," Charise said. "Stick it in your phone or something."

"It won't fit. I've got a card reader on my laptop," Brad said. "It's back in my room." He paused. "Oh, shit. No, it's in Reggie's room. We hard-wired them together to play Starcraft. I left it there yesterday."

"Well go get it," Charise said.

"Reggie's still sleeping. He's a fucking bear if he doesn't get his beauty sleep."

"Then don't wake him up, shit," Charise said. "Come on, go get it. I want to see what's on that thing."

Brad nodded. "Yeah, me too." He handed the SD card to Charise. "Be right back." He headed off towards his bungalow.

Shawnna coughed loudly as Brad started to move away. "Umm, excuse me?"

Brad paused, a momentary flash of angry annoyance crossing his features. He pushed that aggravated tightness out of his face before he stopped and spun back to face Shawnna.

"You forgetting something?" Shawnna asked, an exaggerated pout on her lips.

Brad shuffled over to her through the sand and gave her a quick kiss on her lips.

Shawnna pulled back from the kiss and flicked her fingers towards the bungalows. "Go on, go."

Brad scooted off, trudging through the shifting sand, disappearing around a growth of tropical trees that flanked their bungalows.

Charise smiled at Shawnna. "You guys seem to be doing better. For a while there, I wasn't so sure about you two."

Shawnna nodded. "Yeah, it's going good. Almost getting downright cozy."

"Whoa. Cozy? That's a dangerous place to be with a man."

"Nah, it's good. Feels nice," Shawnna said. "I'm finally getting him to behave like I want him to behave." She grinned.

"Don't tell me you're cuddling now."

"Only after he cums twice."

"What about you?" Charise asked.

"I lose track after about ten."

"For real? He still makes you cum that hard? I though he wasn't that big."

"He's not." Shawnna softly shook her head, then shrugged with a crafty smile. "He knows what buttons to push. Or I should say rub in a slow circular motion with just the right amount of pressure on the left side."

"I'll say." Charise paused. "Ten fucking times?"

"At least."

"Can I borrow him sometime maybe?" Charise asked.

Shawnna shook her head. "Not a chance."

"Can I at least watch?" Charise wondered.

Shawnna froze for a moment, as if seriously considering it. Then she shrugged. "Hey, I can't stop you from catching a peek."

Brad crept stealthily into Reggie's room, careful not to wake his friend sleeping on the bed in the bungalow only a few feet away from where he walked. Beneath his feet, beneath the crystal clear glass that comprised the floor of the overwater bungalow, brightly colored tropical fish swam about, moving in and out of the softly swaying plants and the outcroppings of coral.

His bare foot hit something and he reached down to pick up a sock. A portion of the sock was unnaturally stiff and Brad immediately suspected why. Reggie had probably jerked off into it. He made a disgusted face and let the sock drop from his fingers. He glanced around the room, looking for his laptop. Numerous empty beer bottles, half-eaten snacks, and a half-smoked joint were piled up on a glass table near the middle of the room. He turned to look to his right and accidentally bumped into a small side table, jarring the tablet that was resting on the table, the movement bringing the tablet's screen to life.

A picture of a blonde woman filled the screen and Brad looked closer. It was a picture of a petite blonde woman on her knees with a black cock in her mouth. He cursed Reggie for being a sloppy, drunken fool. He knew Reggie had an obsession with blondes, but it was pretty damn stupid of him to leave such an obvious picture so easily seen by anyone. He had most likely been too wasted to make any proper judgement calls. He had probably jerked off and passed out.

Then Brad looked closer at the picture, his slightly inebriated mind absorbing what he was seeing. It was Charise! With a black cock in her mouth. Was that Reggie's cock? If so, damn that boy was a grower. He had seen Reggie's dick inadvertently here and there throughout their years of being friends and it didn't seem all that big, but he had never seen it standing at full attention. He looked closer at the picture. Damn, that boy was a beast. He didn't know Reggie and Charise had hooked up. He wondered if Shawnna knew. She had been trying to steer them together for months, but didn't seem to be having any luck playing cupid.

Then Brad looked closer at the picture and suddenly realized it was a fake. It was a Photoshopped forgery. He could see some of the erase lines and some of the coloring just didn't match up cleanly. He cursed Reggie even louder in his head. The damned fool. If Charise saw this, she would be pissed as hell. And Shawnna would be pissed to high heaven; she would probably be even more pissed than Charise.

He tapped the power button on the tablet, turning the screen off. He thought about waking Reggie and letting him have it, but the damn fool would probably be too fucking groggy to get any sense out of for fifteen minutes. And the girls were waiting for him. He spotted his laptop on the desk near the window, grabbed it, and scurried silently out of Reggie's room.

Brad appeared around the trees, walking briskly back over to the two young ladies. He set his laptop down on the bar. Charise handed him the SD card and he fed the tiny disk into the card reader slot on his laptop.

The contents loaded automatically and an image filled the screen.

"Hey, that's the same tattoo I have!" Charise said. "Motherfucking copycat."

It was a small tattoo on what appeared to be a woman's ankle. It was a tattoo of a rose, the red color bright and vibrant, the petals etched into the woman's flesh with exquisite detail.

"She put it in the same damn place as me," Charise added. "Shit."

And then the camera moved up the woman's bare leg, reaching her knee, the camera operator moving slowly, lingering, teasing the promise of more and more flesh. The camera continued to move up the woman's leg, revealing the woman's naked thigh. And then it kept moving right up between the woman's legs, showing her cleanly shaven folds. A small golden ring was hooked into the folds of one of her labia.

"Uh, Charise," Shawnna said. "Does that pussy belong to the slut who I think it belongs to?"

In a rare moment of silence, Charise was

speechless.

Charise reached over Brad and slammed the laptop closed, nearly crushing Brad's fingers. "Who's the sick fuck spying on me?" She glared at Brad. "You? Reggie, that fucking pervert?"

Brad looked at her. "That was... you?"

"Unless I got an evil twin in an alternative universe." Charise stared at him. "What the fuck? You guys really think it's funny to spy on me?"

"It wasn't me," Brad said, shaking his head in denial.

Charise glowered at him. "Fucking Reggie."

Brad hesitated a moment, thinking of the picture he had just seen on Reggie's tablet, but then he decided he had to protect his friend. "I don't think it was Reggie, either."

Charise's glower deepened. "Nice little time delay on the defense."

"Come on, that's not Reggie. That's not his style," Brad said, his further defense of his friend coming out in another automatic response. But maybe it was Reggie's style. Maybe there was a side to Reggie he wasn't aware of. His thoughts again flashed to the picture of Charise with the black cock in her mouth.

Charise pointed sharply at the closed laptop. "Then explain that."

Brad looked at the laptop, then looked back to Charise. "I can't."

"We should see what else is on there," Shawnna said.

Charise shook her head. "Oh, no. Give me that fucking disk." She held out her hand.

"Maybe it was Carlos," Shawnna said. "Or one of the other employees." She looked at Charise. "Hell, you said there's only about ten other people on this whole island."

"Great, we came out here to escape civilization, and now we have to deal with a fucking peeping tom." Charise glowered at them.

"Do you sleep naked?" Brad asked.

Charise frowned deeply at him. "What kind of fucked up question is that?"

Shawnna frowned at Brad as well, curiously awaiting his reply.

Brad pointed to the closed laptop. "It looked like that woman... you... were naked on a bed. When was the last time you were naked on your bed here?"

Charise was about to give him a nasty retort, but then she closed her mouth. Her eyes shifted away from them. "Wait a minute. I was never naked on the bed." She paused, then looked at the closed laptop. "What the fuck...?" She pointed at the laptop. "Let's see it again."

"Maybe it's not even you," Shawnna said.

But it was.

"Look," Brad said. "People can do all sorts of shit with video these days. And audio, too. They can fake almost anything now. They can manipulate your face and your lips and put words in your mouth that you didn't even speak."

Charise was visibly shaken. She sat in a wicker chair, her legs curled up, her head hanging down. Bright sunlight streamed in from a window nearby, the warm tropical light filling the room with a golden glow.

They were in another one of the island's over-the-water bungalows. The floor beneath them in this bungalow was also made of clear thick glass, giving them a view of the coral and the vibrant sea life flourishing just beneath their bungalow. Several colorful tropical fish swam by. Vegetation swayed gently back and forth in the current beneath the glass floor.

Reggie was with them now, sitting at the desk in the corner of the bungalow. He looked tired, his face haggard, his nappy hair in disarray. He was dark-skinned and muscular; he was not as big and buff as Brad, but he was still toned and defined. He watched the video on the SD card play out. When the video reached the part that showed the golden-ringed pussy, Reggie paused the video and looked away. He turned to look at Brad and Shawnna. "Look, I know you guys are trying to get us to hook up, but isn't this a bit heavy-handed?" He purposely avoided looking in Charise's direction.

"Just keep watching," Brad said.

Reggie looked at him, then shifted his gaze over to Charise. He had never seen her be so quiet before. "This okay with you?" he asked her, his voice soft.

Charise didn't look up, but she did answer. "Yeah, go ahead."

Reggie turned back to the laptop and resumed the video.

The camera lingered on the smooth, golden-ringed pussy for a long moment, then continued its journey up the woman's body, moving over her flat stomach, then reaching her small bare breasts. The camera lingered on her breasts for a time, moving from one nipple to the other, then it continued upward.

The edge of the knife came into view on the video next.

"What the fuck?" Reggie said. He turned around to look at the others.

"Just keep watching," Brad said.

Reggie turned back to the laptop screen. The camera followed the edge of the knife, the blade catching a ray of light and glinting hotly as the camera moved along its silvery length. The tip of the blade was pressed against the woman's neck, not with enough force to draw blood, but with just enough pressure to press the skin inward where steel met flesh. Whomever was holding the blade was not visible, so the identity of the assailant was still unknown.

The gagged mouth came into view next, the white cloth firmly entrenched in the woman's mouth, the fabric tight across her lips; it looked like a sock was wrapped tightly about her head.

"What the hell am I watching?" Reggie asked, this time keeping his gaze glued on the screen.

No one answered.

Reggie kept watching.

When Charise's wide, fear-stoked eyes came into view, Reggie hit pause on the video. "Okay, seriously, what the fuck?" He turned to face the others. "Why am I watching this? What the fuck is this?"

"We found a bottle washed up on the beach this morning," Brad said. "There was an SD card inside it." He pointed to the laptop. "That's what's on it."

Reggie frowned. "This is a joke, right?" Reggie said. "You guys prankin' me?"

"It's no joke," Charise said. She finally looked up. "It's no joke and it's freakin' me the fuck out."

Reggie looked at her, then back to Brad. "Who made it? What the hell is it?"

Brad shook his head. "We don't know." He looked at Reggie. "You didn't make it, did you?"

Reggie scrunched his face into a deep frown. "What? No. Why the hell would I make something like that?"

Brad held up his hands defensively. "I know. I know. Just asking. Part of me was hoping you'd say yes. Because otherwise I don't know what the fuck is going on." Brad paused. "And that's freakin' me the fuck out, too."

"Maybe you were drugged," Shawnna said to Charise.

Charise shook her head. "I still think I would've remembered something like that, don't you?"

"So you are saying that never happened? What's on that video never happened?" Reggie asked.

"I just had my...ring...put in two days before we left to come here," Charise said. "And we've been here two days. That means it would've been made in the last four days. I think I would've remembered that even if I had been drugged to the gills."

"She was with me pretty much the whole time in those two days before we left," Shawnna said. "Shopping and packing and getting ready for the trip. And we've been together practically the entire time since we got to the island."

"So who the hell made it and when?" Reggie asked.

"It was definitely made in one of the bungalows. You can tell by the bed and the surroundings," Brad said.

"I'm really trying hard to understand this, but I

can't," Reggie said. "This doesn't make any sense."

"None of us understand," Brad said.

⋯⋯⋅✦⋅⋯⋯

"Can you get through?" Shawnna asked.

Charise shook her head and tossed her phone down onto a side table near the couch. "Nope. I told you. No wireless, no internet when we're out here. That's the whole point. To get away and unplug."

"So now what? We just have to wait until next week until the boat comes to get us?"

"Pretty much," Charise said. She looked very unhappy.

"What about a plane?" Shawnna asked. Doesn't your dad like have a dozen of them?"

Charise shook her head. "They can't land. The runway is under construction. They won't be done for a month or two."

"Figures."

Charise nodded. "Yeah."

"Come on, someone's just playing a trick on us," Shawnna said. "It probably really is Brad and Reggie just fucking with us. You know how much Reggie likes to dick around with his photographs." She sat down on the couch next to Charise and put her arm around her. The two girls were alone in the bungalow.

"Yeah, maybe," Charise said. Her sad face remained.

"Oh, come on. Nothing crazy's gonna happen to us," Shawnna said. "Buck up, kiddo."

"Guys!" Reggie's voice boomed loud.

They looked up to see Reggie burst into the room. He was breathless, his face covered in a sheen of

118

sweat, his chest heaving. "You gotta see this! We found another bottle," he managed to gasp out. He raised up the bottle he held in his hand and shook it; the SD card trapped inside the bottle jangled as it bounced off the glass.

Reggie didn't wait for any response. He abruptly turned and raced back out of the room.

Charise turned to look at Shawnna. "You were saying?"

Shawnna looked away from the screen on Reggie's laptop, burying her face in Brad's shoulder.

Brad could not take his gaze away from the screen. He could not stop watching the video. He could not stop watching the images of himself covered in blood crawling across the sand. Near the end of the short clip, it appeared as if his bloodied hand was reaching up towards something, but the video ended before anything was revealed. "I don't know about anybody else," Brad said. "But I'm about to lose my fucking mind." He ran his fingers through his hair. "I really need to get some better sleep."

No one said a word.

"It looks like you're reaching for something," Reggie said.

"Probably a peach daiquiri," Charise quipped a very inappropriate quip. "I can see the bar in the background.

"I'm naked, covered in blood, crawling in the sand," Brad said. "Who gives a fuck what I'm reaching for?"

Reggie suddenly jabbed at the pause button and

rewound the video a few seconds. He watched in silence for a moment, then rewound the scene and played it again. He bolted up from his chair and ran outside.

The others just watched him, completely baffled by his behavior.

Reggie returned moments later and replayed the few seconds he had watched earlier. He sat back in his chair and exhaled deeply, running his fingers across his face.

"What?" Brad asked. "What is it?"

Reggie pointed to the screen. "Look, there, off to the left. There are three trees, ficus trees, I think." He waved his hand. "It doesn't matter what they are."

"So?" Shawnna said.

"So, look where they are," Reggie replied. "Right next to the bar outside."

The others waited for him to continue, still perplexed.

"There's only one tree near our bar in that area," Reggie said.

Brad squinted at Reggie. "*Our* bar?"

Shawnna just frowned.

"*Our* bar," Reggie confirmed. "There was something about these videos that kept nagging at me. Something didn't seem right." He pointed to the paused image on the screen. "That's not our bar. That's not the bar on this island."

Charise looked closer at the screen, then looked at Reggie, a dawning realization starting to come into her expression.

Reggie noticed the look of understanding come on Charise's face and nodded to her. "Crazy, right? I mean, this island *is* in the Bermuda Triangle."

"Whoa, whoa," Brad said. "What are you saying here?"

Reggie pointed to the image on the screen again. "That's not from our... world. Not from our universe."

"Maybe we're seeing parts of the multiverse," Charise said.

Everyone slowly turned to stare at Charise, all of them taken aback by her comment, all of them surprised that she was even capable of uttering such a sentence.

Charise stared back at them. "Reggie isn't the only geek among us."

"The multiverse?" Brad asked.

Charise nodded. "Other universes. Some scientists think our universe is just one of an infinite number of universes. So there's a universe where the dinosaurs never went extinct. There's a universe where the Nazis won World War Two. There's a universe where nuclear war devastated Earth. There's a universe where the Fast and Furious movies ended after three sequels."

Reggie grinned. "Damn, that would be crazy if we are right." Reggie was quiet for a moment, clearly thinking of the possibility Charise had just laid out.

"So in some... parallel universe there's a version of me getting all battered and bloody right here on this beach?" Brad asked.

Reggie nodded. "That's the theory. An infinite number of universes with infinite scenarios being played out."

"So the bottle we found with the SD card isn't showing something in the future?" Shawnna asked. "It's something that already happened in this other...

universe?" She paused. "I can't believe I am actually asking this question."

"Time and space could be twisted and distorted. It could be from the future, from the past." Reggie shrugged. "No one's really sure how it all works. It's just hypothetical theories."

"How did the bottle get here? Into our universe?" Shawnna asked.

"You do realize how crazy this all sounds, right?" Brad said.

Just then, a dark shadowy shape passed across the doorway outside, the thick shade shielding whoever it was, preventing any quick identification.

"Who was that?" Shawnna asked, grabbing nervously at Brad's arm.

Brad hurried over to the door and glanced up the walkway outside their bungalow, looking in the direction the shadow had been moving.

It was Carlos, the bartender who manned the bar on the beach.

"Hey, Carlos," Brad shouted after him. "What are you doing?"

The man paused and turned to face Brad. A chill raced up Brad's spine. It was Carlos, but it wasn't the Carlos they had met earlier. This Carlos was pale and gaunt, his cheeks hollow, his eyes sunken. He looked exhausted, as if he hadn't slept for days. But despite the man's fatigue, his face took on the surprised expression of a deer caught in the glaring headlights of an approaching semi-truck. He stared at Brad with widening eyes, then turned and bolted away, leaping off the walkway, disappearing into the thick trees that flanked the sandy path.

Brad only vaguely realized later that the man had

been holding a camera in his hand.

"You're sure it was Carlos?" Reggie asked.

"It was Carlos, but it wasn't Carlos," Brad said. He ran his fingers through his hair. "Dude, I'm losing it. This is all just too fucking crazy for me. I really need to get some more sleep."

Reggie ignored his whining rant. "And you're sure he was holding a camera."

"I wouldn't swear it in court, but yeah, I'm pretty sure I saw him holding a camera," Brad said.

"Where did he go?"

Brad waved his hand. "I don't know. He just took off."

"We need to find him," Reggie said.

Brad suddenly raised a pointed finger. "Wait a minute. Wait a minute." He pointed to the laptop. "Play that video we took when we first got here. The first time we were at the bar. The first time we met Carlos."

Reggie only paused for a second, looking at Brad curiously, but then did as his friend requested. He scrolled through a list of videos, found the one Brad was talking about and clicked on it to play it:

Carlos Medellin was a swarthy man, muscular and handsome, looking far different than the emaciated version of him Brad had seen on the trail. His hair was black, sleek like a raven's wing. He had a rounded chin, with a hint of a cleft visible. As Brad watched the video clip he remembered that both Shawnna and Charise thought he was a good looking guy. Maybe too good looking. They had suspicions that he might be gay, but they never really discussed it or never let on that they had their doubts about his heterosexuality. It didn't matter one whit to them. Carlos was a super nice guy. And damn if he didn't make super delicious booze-laden cocktails.

Carlos poured a peach daiquiri into the glass in front of Brad, and slid a fresh slice of peach over the rim.

"Thanks, Carlos," Brad said, reading the man's name off his embroidered shirt. "So what's there to do on this island?" Brad asked, then took a sip from his drink. He smiled appreciatively at the beverage. "Man, that's tasty."

"Swim. Snorkel. Lounge on the beach. That's the big one," Carlos said. "Lots of lounging goes on here."

"I like lounging," Reggie said, his voice coming from off screen as he was the one filming the scene. "I can handle lots of lounging."

"Just stay away from the grotto on the west side of the island," Carlos cautioned. "It's full of poisonous snakes and poisonous frogs. And there's some nasty fish that swim in there. I'm not sure exactly what they are, but they've got some nasty stingers. They'll put you down for weeks if they sting you."

Brad raised his glass to Carlos. "Thanks for the tip."

Brad reached down and clicked a button on Reggie's laptop, pausing the video.

Reggie frowned at him. "What does that have to do with finding Carlos?"

"I don't know. Nothing. Maybe everything," Brad said. He looked at Reggie. "The grotto. I don't know why I know this, but I'm pretty damn sure we need to find that grotto. There's more to Carlos's warning than meets the eye."

Reggie was quiet for a moment. "What, you think he has some kind of hideout there or something?"

"I don't know. That grotto keeps popping up in my head." He shook his head. "I don't know why, but it just does. There's something going on there."

Reggie was quiet, clearly thinking. "The grotto," he muttered. He was quiet for a moment longer, still absorbed in thought, and then he nodded. He looked up at Brad. "You're right. I don't know how I know that either, but I'm pretty sure you're right. Let's get the girls and go check it out. This whole island adventure is so fucking bizarre and inexplicable right about now that nothing surprises me."

But the body they found on the trail did surprise Reggie, and everyone else.

They came upon the body as they headed towards the grotto on the west side of the island. It was Shawnna's body. Or at least someone who looked nearly identical to Shawnna, except this Shawnna was pregnant. Very pregnant and very dead. She was laying on the ground just off the sandy path that wound through the thick growth of tropical bushes and large overhanging trees. Her throat had been slit, leaving a wide gaping gash in her neck. Fat tropical flies flitted about her body, buzzing, landing to feed for a moment or lay eggs, then flying off. Maggots wriggled and crawled along this dead Shawnna's face, some entering her mouth, some exiting. Blood stained the sand, the crimson liquid mostly dried but a few patches still glistened with wetness.

Shawnna buried her face in Brad's shoulder, stifling a cry.

"What the fuck?" Brad said.

No one else muttered a word.

"What the fuck?" Brad said again.

Charise and Reggie exchanged nervous glances. "What the hell is going on, Reggie?" Charise asked, her voice barely making it above a whisper.

Reggie shook his head, staying mute.

Suddenly, a dark shape burst out of the undergrowth, startling them. The shape belonged to a man, a man holding a knife stained with drying blood. He was facing away from them, so they couldn't see his face. The man charged up the sandy path away from them, heading in the direction of the grotto.

Brad stared in shock at the fleeing man. He recognized the man's shirt and his pants. They were identical to the clothes he owned. "What the fuck?" he said yet again.

"Come on, we need to follow him," Reggie said, his voice full of urgency. He darted up the sandy path, moving quickly in the direction the man with the knife had fled.

The others stayed close behind Reggie, trailing his movements.

They quickly lost sight of the knife-wielding man.

"You see which way he went?" Reggie asked. "Shit." He scanned their surroundings, but could see no signs of movement beyond some colorful birds flitting about in the trees that overhung the sandy path. Off to their left, hidden by thick growths of tropical trees that lined the path, sounds of the ocean tumbling onto the beach were just barely audible.

Charise shook her head.

Brad didn't respond. He still looked a little shell-shocked, trying hard to absorb what was happening to them.

Shawnna just held tightly onto Brad's hand, also saying nothing. She just shook her head.

"Shit," Reggie said again. "Anybody get a good look at him?"

The girls shook their heads.

"Brad?" Reggie prompted. "You get a good look at him?"

"I…" Brad started to say, but didn't finish his thought. He had recognized the knife-wielding man but he was too overwhelmed to admit what he had seen to the others. It was all too bizarre, all just too damn fucking weird. He finally shook his head. "No, not really."

"Fuck," Reggie said. He looked again at their surroundings, thinking. Finally, he said, "Let's go find that grotto. I'm with Brad on that one. I can't get it out of my head either now. Something's going on there and we need to find out what."

The grotto was facing the ocean, most likely carved out by centuries of ocean waves pounding against the stone, but there were enough rocks clustered together on the eastern side of the cave to create an area that could be traversed with a little care.

The entrance to the grotto was wide enough to allow all four of them to enter side-by side and plenty of sunlight was able to get into the wide space.

The four of them stood near the end of the sandy path. They all were wearing shorts and t-shirts, their feet covered in lightweight beach shoes. Behind them, the thick underbrush and high tropical trees were visible. Before them, to their left, the ocean stretched out to the horizon and the rocky shoreline began. The grotto was up ahead and off to their right. From their vantage point, they could see that there was a flat expanse of earth along the right side of the grotto that they could walk on, giving them entrance to the deeper cave area within. A large pool of ocean water filled the rest of the cave. They could see part of a shimmering light floating above the water deeper within the grotto.

"What is that?" Shawnna asked. "Do you all see that weird light?"

"Yeah, I see it," Reggie said. "I have no idea what that is."

"It's a rip in space-time," Charise muttered. "A tear in the multiverse."

Reggie looked at her. "Seriously?"

Charise shrugged. "Just a guess."

"You guys are way too calm about all this," Brad said. "I am freaking out in my head. I think I'm going to lose it. I almost feel fucking dizzy."

"I have to pee," Charise announced. She danced in place, twisting and turning her body. "I gotta pee."

"Jesus, just hold it," Reggie said, clearly exasperated.

"I can't. I'm gonna piss myself." Charise headed into the bushes just before the sandy path ended and the rocky outcroppings began.

"No! Stop right there!" Reggie shouted, his voice strongly vehement.

Charise frowned at him, continuing to squirm and twist her legs.

"We do *not* split up," Reggie said. "I don't care if you have to take a shit. We do not split up. We do not let each other out of sight. There's too much weird fucking shit going on right now."

Brad nodded his head, more to himself than to the others.

"I have to go," Charise said. "Right now."

Reggie nodded at the path. "Just go."

"Right here?"

"Yes."

Charise pulled her shorts down and relieved herself on the path, darkening the sand. She looked up at Reggie with an angry face as she pulled her pants back up. "There, you happy? You got another free peek."

"I have to go, too," Reggie said. He turned to face the bushes and unzipped his jean shorts.

"Oh, no," Charise said. "You're not getting off that easily." She stomped over to Reggie.

Reggie looked over his shoulder at her as she approached. "You want to hold it?"

"Yes," Charise said as she reached him. "Yes, I do."

Reggie released his fingers from his cock and raised his hand away from his penis. "Go ahead. Be my guest."

Charise reached down and grabbed his cock.

"Just don't aim at my shoes, okay?" Reggie said.

"How come it's getting longer?" Charise said.

"Okay, seriously?" Reggie said. He pushed her hand away from his penis. He urinated into the bushes, then zipped himself back up.

Reggie and Charise turned back to the path to see Shawnna staring at them both with annoyance and a little bit of disgusted contempt. "Are you two finished being idiots?"

Reggie and Charise looked at her, then turned to look at each other. "Probably not," Reggie said. "I doubt it," Charise said at the same time. Reggie reached out and squeezed Charise's hand. She smiled back at him. Then she looked closer at their joined hands, and pulled hers away from him, wiping her fingers on her shorts.

"*Now* you two are deciding to hook up?" Shawnna said. "There's a dead... copy... of me back on the path and you two are deciding to flirt? You've got to be fucking kidding me."

Reggie looked sheepish and glanced away from her.

Brad thrust his finger towards the grotto. "Are we going in or what?"

Reggie nodded. "We're going in. Carlos warned us about poisonous snakes and poisonous frogs. He was probably lying just to keep us away from here, but keep an eye out anyway."

They headed towards the grotto's entrance.

The shimmering orb of light they had seen earlier from outside was still there when they entered the grotto. It just hung above the water, shimmering and twinkling. They could all hear a slight humming coming from the rift, as if some unknown energy source was giving it power.

"Maybe it's some kind of optical illusion," Brad said. "A trick of the light coming in from outside and reflecting off the water."

Brad picked up a rock, but Reggie quickly grabbed his wrist before he could even raise his arm. "I don't think that's a good idea," Reggie said.

Brad hesitated for a moment, then dropped the rock.

The rift was positioned about ten feet from the edge of the water, so they couldn't get right up to it unless they jumped into the pool and swam to it.

A wave flowed in from the ocean, splashing and spraying water everywhere. A portion of the splashing water hit the rift, but did not come out the other side. It was as if the water was absorbed by the rift like it was some cosmic sponge; the water entered the rift and disappeared.

Then an image appeared within the orb, figures, a man and a woman. A man with a knife towering over a woman. A very angry man towering over a cowering scared pregnant woman. "You stupid possessive bitch!" the man snarled. "You got pregnant just to trap me!" He brought the knife down on her pregnant belly, stabbing her viciously.

Reggie and Charise stared in horror at the scene, watched with wide eyed growing terror as a man who looked remarkably like Brad stabbed a woman who looked remarkably like Shawnna.

Shawnna looked away, turning to bury her face in Brad's shoulder again, but then stopped short. She looked at Brad, then turned completely away from him.

Brad had raised his arm, offering her room to come to him, but then he slowly lowered his arm as Shawnna turned away from him.

The image within the orb shimmered and shifted. It now showed the image of Reggie fucking Charise. She was tied down to a bed, her arms and legs spread-eagled. "You like that?" the Reggie-image asked, grunting heavily as he thrust into the Charise-image. "Stop it, Reggie," the Charise-image begged. "Stop it." The Reggie-image continued to thrust, sweat dripping down his face. "You wanted some black cock, didn't you? Well here you go," he said and thrust harder.

The image shifted, changed. Then it show a Charise-image again being fucked, but this time by a Brad-image. She was on her stomach, with a naked Brad-image atop her. The Brad-image had his hand beneath her, touching her clit, rubbing it as he slid in and out of her. "Oh my God," the Charise-image gasped. "I'm cumming again." "Seven," the Brad-image whispered into her ear. "Yes," the Charise-image gasped. "Yes, fuck me. Make me cum again."

The image again shifted. Now it revealed a Shawnna-image holding a gun. A Reggie-image lay dead at her feet, a bullet hole in his forehead. The Shawnna-image waved the gun at the Brad-image who stood before her holding his hands up defensively. "You want to be with Reggie so much, you can join him in Hell!" The Shawnna-image fired. The Brad-image fell back, clutching at his now-bleeding chest. The Shawnna-image suddenly stopped moving. She turned to stare out at the four of them, as if sensing their presence.

"Fuck," Brad muttered. "Does she see us like we

see her?"

The Shawnna-image raised the gun and fired.

The bullet pinged off a rock just behind Brad's head, showering him with tiny shards of splintered stone. "Shit!" Brad threw his hands up defensively.

The Shawnna-image pulled the trigger again, but the image faded away and the bullet never made it out of the orb.

The four of them fled from the grotto.

Brad hyperventilated. "I'm not doing so good, guys. I can't slow my brain down." He panted and gasped. He was laying down on Reggie's bed, his hand over his eyes. "What is going on? What is going on?"

"Charise was right," Reggie said. "I think it's some kind of rip. A rip in space-time."

"Are you fucking kidding me?" Brad said. He scowled a deep scowl. His breathing was still shallow, desperate.

Reggie shook his head.

"A fucking rip in space-time?" Brad asked. He stared up at the ceiling. He shook his head and turned away from the others to face the wall of the bungalow. He curled up into a fetal position.

"I'm just guessing. I have no idea what it is," Reggie said.

"It's a rip in the multiverse," Charise said. "We saw some of the possibilities of a million different universes being played out."

They all were careful not to sit too close to each other, all of them clearly apprehensive of each other after viewing the disturbing images in the grotto. Outside the bungalow window, the sun was setting, the last rays of the sun turning a deep orange on the horizon.

Reggie nodded, as if accepting that as an obvious conclusion. He sat quietly for a moment, thinking, "That's not what worries me the most," Reggie said.

"We found a rip in the fucking fabric of space and time, and that's not what worries you the most?" Brad asked, still facing away from them. He grunted out a laughing snort. He slowly started to rock back and forth, still curled up into a tight ball.

"Yeah, that is supremely fucked up and I'm still trying to wrap my head around it," Reggie said. "But what worries me the most is that bullet Shawnna—" he paused to glance at Shawnna who sat in a nearby chair fidgeting nervously. "That *other* Shawnna shot out of her gun. It passed over from whatever universe she exists in, into our universe."

"So?" Shawnna asked. She bit nervously at her nails. It was a habit she had thought she had licked eight years ago, but apparently not.

"So if the bullet can pass over, what else can pass over? Or to be more precise, *who* else can pass over?" Reggie paused. "We've already seen someone who looks like Carlos but isn't Carlos. We saw a dead Shawnna that wasn't our Shawnna. And the more I think about it, the more I'm pretty sure that was some other Brad we saw on the path with the knife. Right, Brad? He had the same clothes on as you, didn't he?"

Brad didn't answer.

"So you're thinking it might be some kind of bridge?" Charise said to Reggie. "A bridge that spans the multiverses?"

Reggie looked away from Brad's back and nodded at Charise. "And I'm thinking those messages in the bottles were from someone on... the other side... from some other multiverse trying to warn us."

"Or just trying to fuck with us," Charise said. "They could be doing that just to get their rocks off on it."

Reggie opened his mouth as if to counter Charise, but then pressed his lips together. He knew she was right. They were all capable of doing darker, uglier things. The scenes they had watched playing out within the multiverse rift in the grotto were proof of that.

"So now what?" Shawnna asked. "Now what the fuck do we do? As far as we know, according to your little multi-fucking-verse theory, there's now a bunch of psychotic versions of ourselves running loose on this fucking island and we have no way of getting off it."

Reggie was quiet for a long moment. "We do not let ourselves out of each other's sight for one second. I mean it. Not one fucking second."

"Yeah, you said that already," Charise said.

"No, I mean it," Reggie said. "Think about it," he said and purposely waited for them to catch on to where he was going with his argument. He looked at Charise. "You and I can be some crafty fucks if we want to be. We're smart. What if one of our... other selves... decides they want to stay in this multiverse. What if they decide they want to take our place?"

"Okay, now you are even freaking me out," Charise said.

"I'm freaking myself out," Reggie said. He was quiet for a moment, staring at the colorful tropical fish that swam past beneath the glass floor of the bungalow in the last fading light of the day, staring at the distinct markings on them. "Give me your hand," he suddenly said to Charise.

Charise squinted at him, not doing as he asked.

"Seriously, give me your hand," Reggie said, thrusting his own hand out towards her.

Charise just frowned at him.

"Damn it," Reggie said. He grabbed a half-smoked joint from an ashtray on the table nearby, snatched at a lighter on the table, and lit the end of the joint. He didn't bring the joint to his lips to take a toke. Instead, he brought the red-hot tip down on the back of his hand, burning a mark into his flesh. He winced as the pain seared through his hand, but he did not cry out. He held his burned hand up to Charise. "There, now you know it's me."

Charise stared at the burn mark on Reggie's hand, then looked up to his face. She nodded at him and held out her hand to him. Reggie proceeded to burn a sear mark onto the back of Charise's hand. Charise wasn't shy about yelping in pain as he did so. "Fuck that hurts!"

Shawnna didn't hesitate. She immediately held out her hand to Reggie and let him put a burning sear tattoo into her flesh. She didn't cry out, or even flinch. She turned to look at Brad. "Brad, give him your hand."

Brad slowly rolled over in the bed to look dazedly at her. "What? What are you guys doing?"

"Marking ourselves," Shawnna said. She raised her burned hand up to show Brad.

Brad frowned at the reddening circle on her skin. "Why didn't you just use a sharpie or something? I've got one in my bag."

Shawnna wiped away his question with an impatient wave. "Just give Reggie your hand."

A howling shriek from outside their room drew their attention. It was the awful caterwauling of wild beasts.

Reggie quickly moved to the door, peering outside.

"Reggie, stick together!" Charise shouted at him. She quickly moved to the door to join Reggie, peering over him.

Up in the trees, hundreds of bats fluttered through the foliage, shrieking and screeching as they raced through the high branches. They were hoary bats, their coats dense and dark brown, with white tips on the ends of the hairs that gave the species its hoary appearance for which it was named. Their bodies were covered in fur except for the undersides of their leathery wings.

"Didn't know this island had bats," Charise muttered. "Daddy's gonna get an earful from me about that."

"Well, it does now," Reggie said. "Maybe somebody sent them through the rip."

One of the bats suddenly veered from its path, turning away from all the others, almost as if the creature had just heard them speak. It zeroed in on their bungalow, diving down straight at them, its wings flapping faster and faster. Then another bat turned towards the bungalow, then another and another and another. Within seconds, dozens of bats were descending down towards their bungalow door at an ever-increasing speed, their leathery wings whipping up and down.

The first bat drew closer, snarling as it neared,

revealing tiny sharp teeth behind its sneering lips.

"Shit!" Reggie exclaimed. "Don't let them bite you. Bats are full of fucking rabies." He moved backward, knocking into Charise, propelling them both back deeper into the bungalow. Charise caught her leg on the edge of a chair and went down. Reggie tripped on her falling body and he went down as well, landing hard on Charise's chest. She grunted with a sharp exhale as Reggie fell on her.

The first bat swooped into the room, sweeping through the air where Reggie and Charise would have been standing had they not fallen down. The other bats quickly exploded into the room, filling the bungalow with their squeaks and squeals and the rushing sounds of their flapping wings.

Reggie yanked Charise to her feet, trying his best to shield them both with his free hand, raising his arm protectively over them. "Get to the grotto!" he shouted at Shawnna and Brad. "We have to stop this!" He pulled Charise toward the bungalow door and they had no choice but to race out of the room to flee the crazed frenzied flyers.

"Damn it, Reggie," Charise scolded. "You were the one who said we needed to stick together no matter what."

Reggie nodded his head. "I know, I know. I'm sorry. All those bats freaked me out." He visibly shuddered. "My cousin died of rabies."

They moved down the sandy path, heading towards the grotto. It was dark now, the path gloomy and murky, illuminated by the few sporadic light poles that lined the path every few dozen yards.

Charise glanced back down the path, trying to peer through the murkiness. "Where are they?" Charise muttered, her voice impatient and tight. She looked back to Reggie. "We should go back."

Reggie shook his head. "Let's get to the grotto. They'll meet us there."

"What if they don't?"

"They will." He grabbed Charise's wrist and pulled her behind him.

Charise resisted. "We don't even know if they heard you. We need to stick together."

Reggie paused. Charise was right. "Shit." He released his grip on her wrist. "Okay, let's go back."

They turned back in the direction of the bungalow area to see a man wielding a very long, very nasty-looking knife, blocking their way. His shape was shadowed, nearly invisible in the dark light of the night. The sheen of white smiling teeth appeared.

"It's me," Reggie gasped, his voice barely audible.

"What?" Charise asked.

But Reggie didn't answer. He had no need to answer as his statement was clarified by the emergence of a man who looked just like him, even down to the clothes he was wearing. The Reggie-doppelgänger stepped out of the shadows, revealing himself. "Hard to see us darkies in the night, ain't it?"

"What… how…?" Reggie asked, his mouth staying agape as his words trailed off.

"Who? What? Why? When? How?" the Reggie-doppelgänger said, nodding his head. "They're all good questions."

"How did you get here?" Reggie asked.

"Please," the Reggie-doppelgänger said. "You

know how I got here. I came through the rift. I took the exit ramp out of my universe and got on to the entry ramp into yours." He paused. "Well, it's not just yours anymore since I'm in it, too. It's ours." He paused again. His face turned more ominous, his eyes filling with dark intent. "Well, pretty soon it's going to be just mine." He raised up his index finger and wagged it. "Only one Reggie per universe. That's my new rule."

"Why?" Charise asked. "Why did you come here?"

"Oh, Charise," the Reggie-doppelgänger said, sadly shaking his head. "For you. I came here for you. Isn't that obvious?"

"Me? Why me?"

"I lost Charise, my Charise in my... world. She drowned out in the ocean." The Reggie-doppelgänger pointed in the direction of the ocean. "She got a cramp in her leg when she was out snorkeling by herself. She was too far out to make it back. It was a stupid horrible accident. I'll never make that mistake again. I won't make the same mistake of letting you roam free." He looked at Charise with dark intent. "Your cage is waiting."

Charise frowned. "My cage?"

The Reggie-doppelgänger nodded. "That's where dirty little sex slaves live. In cages. I built a new one just for you near the grotto. It's rather crude, but it'll do. That's where you'll live. I'll come and feed you black cock when you're hungry."

Charise was quiet for a moment, and then she just laughed. It was a deep, hearty laugh.

Both Reggies frowned at her.

"You picked the wrong universe," Charise finally said, fighting back her laughter. "I'm gay. I've got the lesbian hots for Shawnna."

Both Reggies looked at her in surprise.

"You do?" Reggie asked.

Charise scowled at him with knitted brows. "No, I don't, you dumb ass."

Realization came onto Reggie's face and then his face contorted into an expression of embarrassed stupidity. "Oh, shit. Sorry."

"Nice try," the Reggie-doppelgänger said. "I might have even believed you if you had played it out right." He shrugged. "But no matter. I still want you," he said to Charise. "It doesn't really matter what you want." He turned to face Reggie squarely. "And now you have to die." The Reggie-doppelgänger brandished the knife before him, pointing the sharp tip at Reggie. "This'll be like jerking off, but way better."

"Look out!" Reggie shouted, looking over the Reggie-doppelgänger's shoulder. "He's got a knife!"

The Reggie-doppelgänger turned, taking the bait, and Reggie struck, leaping forward, slamming his fist down hard on the Reggie-doppelgänger's wrist, knocking the blade out of his hand.

The two Reggies tussled, punching and pounding and beating on each other. They tumbled to the ground, lashing out with fists and elbows and knees, their bodies entwined in a very deadly duel. Sand sprayed up all around them as they battled on the ground.

Charise lurched forward and grabbed the fallen knife. She waved the knife in front of her, watching the two Reggies fight, but she didn't know who to stab. Then she saw the back of the Reggie-doppelgänger's hand, saw the lack of a burn mark, and she struck, sinking the blade in deep into the Reggie-doppelgänger's side. The Reggie-doppelgänger arched his body, screaming out in pain as the knife slashed into him. Charise cried out with frightened alarm as warm blood pooled over her fingers, but she was determined to finish the job. She stabbed again and again and again, sending blood splashing over all three of them.

Finally, after what seemed like a hundred stabbing slashes, the Reggie-doppelgänger went limp and laid still on the ground.

Reggie pushed himself away from the dead doppelgänger, panting heavily.

Charise was breathing just as hard, her breath coming in and out in quick little bursts. She bent over, clutching at her side, fighting to get her breathing under control. "So does this mean you have a thing for me?" Charise asked as she looked sideways at Reggie who was still laying on the sandy path.

Reggie opened his mouth to say something, but then closed it. He looked away from her.

"Hey, it's cool. I like you," Charise said. She straightened up and pointed to the dead Reggie-doppelgänger with the blood-stained knife. "You aren't that obsessive though, are you?" She looked at the red-streaked knife, thought about dropping it, but then re-gripped it in her fingers and clutched it tight.

Reggie didn't answer. He thought of the pictures of Charise he had created on his tablet, and the thought of where his behavior might lead terrified him.

Charise looked at him curiously. "You got something to tell me, Reggie?" she asked. "Your silence isn't giving me confidence."

"Oh my God!"

Charise looked up to see Shawnna standing on the path, staring down in horror at the dead Reggie-doppelgänger, her hands over her openly shocked mouth. "I killed him," Charise said. Her voice was surprisingly calm. "He was here for me," she added. "He said he came through that fucking portal in the grotto looking for me. Can you believe that shit?"

Shawnna looked at Charise, then the dead doppelgänger, then at Reggie.

Reggie nodded. "He was… obsessed with Charise. He… it… I don't know what the fuck to call him. He wanted to kill me and take my place."

"Fuck," Shawnna said.

"Yeah," Charise agreed.

"What if there's another one?" Shawnna asked.

"What?" Reggie said.

Shawnna pointed at the dead doppelgänger. "What if there's another one… here? What if another… Reggie crossed over?"

"Oh, fuck," Charise said. "She's right. What if two of them crossed over. Or a dozen? Or a fucking hundred?"

"Talk about a gangbang from Hell," Reggie muttered.

"That's not even fucking funny, Reggie," Charise said. "Not funny at all."

Reggie looked sheepish. "Sorry."

"We need to shut that shit down," Charise said. "We need to close that fucking portal and we need to do it now."

"Yeah, but how?" Shawnna asked.

"We need to nuke the fucking thing," Charise said. "Great, but what are we going to *really* do?"

143

Shawnna asked.

No one had an immediate answer. Reggie stared curiously at the dead version of himself laying on the sand; he was finding it difficult to look away, but then he forced himself to look up. "Where's Brad?" he suddenly asked as he glanced around the area and realized Shawnna was alone.

Shawnna shook her head. "I don't know. All those fucking bats were everywhere and we got separated. I heard you shout meet at the grotto, so that's where I was headed."

Reggie nodded. "Okay, hopefully he's heading there."

"How do we shut that portal down?" Charise asked. "Come on, think."

They thought.

Reggie glanced at the dead doppelgänger again, his face growing more troubled the longer he stared at the corpse. It was an odd feeling to stare at a dead version of yourself and Reggie was caught up in the bizarre weirdness of it all.

A possible answer came to Shawnna and her face lit up. "We can't nuke it, but maybe we can still blow it up."

Charise looked at her curiously.

"You said they were working on the runway, right? Building it? Expanding it, or something?"

"Yeah," Charise said.

"So they're construction guys," Shawnna said. "They must have some kind of dynamite around, some explosive shit to clear the land, right?"

Charise nodded, her enthusiasm growing. "Yeah, yeah."

Reggie tore his gaze away from the corpse, forcing

himself to concentrate on what they needed to do next, his excitement growing as well. "Yeah, good idea. They can help us."

Charise shook her head, putting a damper on their enthusiasm. "Most of them left on the boat that brought us in." She looked at them, a twinge of guilt flashing across her features. "I told my dad we wanted some real privacy for a while."

"Great," Shawnna muttered.

"They'll be back in a few days," Charise said, trying to rekindle their enthusiasm.

"We can't wait a few days. We need to blow that fucking grotto up now," Reggie said. "We need to bury that fucking portal under tons of rock. Nobody's gonna move through a ton of rock. Even if the portal is still there, nobody's gonna be able to use it if we can bury it."

Charise nodded. "Let's go see what we can find," Charise said, immediately starting to head towards the runway that was on the far eastern side of the island.

"Wait a minute," Shawnna said. "What about Brad? What about us all sticking together? Which we've done a miserable job of, by the way."

"We don't know where he is," Reggie said.

"He's probably at the grotto," Shawnna said.

They all stood motionless, indecisive as to which direction to go.

"Fuck. We can't just leave him," Charise said.

"We need to shut that fucking thing down. Sooner rather than later," Reggie said. "Fuck." Reggie looked towards the grotto, then looked towards the opposite side of the island. He looked at Charise and Shawnna. "We need to shut that portal down. If we don't, who knows who else might come through it."

"If they haven't already," Charise added.

No one said anything to that.

"Has anybody tried calling out? Calling for help? I can't get any signal," Shawnna said. "I tried calling Brad, but no signal."

"You won't get anything," Charise said. "I told you. No internet out here."

Carlos and three Carlos-doppelgängers stepped out of the darkness. "Say hello to my little friends," Carlos said in his worst Al Pacino-Scarface imitation, nodding his head at his look-alike companions.

"You've got to be shitting me," Reggie said as he stared at the four men before them.

"We heard you talking," Carlos said. "You've been to the grotto. I told you to stay away. I gave you fair warning. We can't let you destroy it."

Two of the Carlos-doppelgängers kissed.

"We're having way too much fun," Carlos said. "We finally found someone we could really love."

One of the Carlos-doppelgängers held a thick bottle in his hand, a bottle half-filled with wine, a bottle that had a strong resemblance to the bottle they had found washed up on the beach.

Charise looked at the bottle. "You're the one putting those messages in the bottles."

Carlos shook his head. "No. One of you must be doing it. Or one of your other selves. Someone from another multiverse, I suppose." He shrugged. "It's a clever idea, though. I wish we had thought of it."

"We're blowing it up," Charise said.

Carlos produced a switchblade, clicking it to reveal the long blade hidden within the case. "No, you're not."

The three Carlos-doppelgängers also drew out

switchblades, all three of them clicking the buttons at exactly the same time as if in some hellishly choreographed dance, revealing the deadly sharp blades.

A bullet took Carlos down. One moment he was glaring at Charise with scowling eyes, and the next moment he no longer had a face. The bullet penetrated the back of his skull and erupted out of the front of his head, blowing his eyes and nose completely away from his face. The exiting bullet whizzed past Charise's head, just missing her; a wet shred of flesh struck Charise in the face and she quickly wiped it away.

A second bullet hit one of the Carlos-doppelgängers in the back, knocking him forward. The third bullet brought the doppelgänger down to his knees and he pitched forward to lay dead on the sandy path.

The remaining two Carlos-doppelgängers spun to face their attacker.

Reggie grabbed both Charise and Shawnna by their wrists, yanking them down, pulling them towards the shelter of nearby brush.

Brad strode out of the darkness, clutching the gun he held with both hands. He took a second Carlos-doppelgänger down with a shot to his heart. The third Carlos-doppelgänger made a move as if to surrender, starting to raise his hands above his head. Brad shot him in the face, sending him toppling to the ground in a dead heap.

Everything was quiet for a long moment.

Brad surveyed the carnage for a brief moment, then turned to scan the direction where he had seen the others last. "Guys, come out."

Shawnna didn't hesitate. She moved out of the brush and came up to Brad.

Brad's face lit up into a beaming smile. "Shawnna!" He grabbed her and hugged her, then pulled back to give her a long, full kiss on the lips before pulling her back into a deep embrace. He again drew back and looked at her. He put his hand to her cheek, gently, lovingly, caressing it. "You okay?" he asked. A burn mark was visible on the back of his hand. Shawnna nodded, turning her head to fully allow Brad's fingers to caress her.

Reggie and Charise cautiously crept out of the undergrowth.

Brad looked over to them as they moved up to him and Shawnna. "I was following them," he said, motioning to Carlos's body. "I heard them say they were going to kill you." He looked at the gun he still held in his hand, then looked up at Reggie.

"It's okay," Reggie said. "You did the right thing." Reggie looked at the gun. "Where the hell did you get that?"

Brad hesitated, but only for a brief second. "Carlos had it hidden by the bar," he said. "I saw it there the first time we met him." He shrugged. "Lucky it was loaded."

Reggie looked curiously at him, but said nothing.

"We need to blow that shit up," Charise said. "This is getting way the fuck out of hand."

Brad looked curiously at Charise, then Reggie.

"We're gonna blow up the grotto," Reggie said. "Get some dynamite from the construction guys working on the runway."

"Nice," Brad said. "Good idea."

"Let's go," Charise said. She paused to pick up a

fallen switchblade.

Reggie scooped up another dropped switchblade and moved after Charise.

"Come on," Brad said to Shawnna. "Let's go." He again reached up to touch Shawnna's face.

Shawnna reached up and took his hand into hers. She noticed the burn mark on the back of his hand and looked at him curiously. "Where did you get that?" she asked.

Brad squinted a confused squint at her. "Reggie gave it to me." He grabbed her hand and looked at the burn mark on the back of it. "Just like yours." He raised her hand and gently kissed her knuckles.

Shawnna hesitated a moment, then smiled softly at him.

"Now let's go blow up the grotto," Brad said. "We don't need any more crazies crossing over into our world."

"You sure this will work?" Brad asked.

Reggie stared at the remote triggering device in his hand. "One way to find out." Reggie depressed the trigger.

The explosion was immediate. A thunderous boom sounded out and the ground beneath their feet shook. Within seconds, the grotto was gone, buried under tons of rock.

"Good riddance," Charise muttered.

"So now what?" Reggie asked. "We've got a whole bunch of dead bodies we can't rationally account for.

We blew up part of your dad's island. I don't think he's gonna be too pleased with us." Reggie and Charise were in Reggie's bungalow. Warm sunlight bathed the room in a pleasant glow. Reggie was at the window, resting his arms on the window ledge, staring out into the vast ocean beyond.

"Yeah, well, I'm not too pleased with him, either. He's gonna get an earful from me when he shows up." Charise joined him at the window, standing close to him, their bodies touching.

Reggie laughed. "You really gonna blame this all on him?"

"Works like a charm every time."

Reggie shook his head. He turned away from the ocean view and moved back into the room. Suddenly, a bottle floated into view beneath the clear glass floor of their over-the-water-bungalow, drifting lazily amongst the softly swaying plants and slow moving tropical fish. Reggie stopped in his tracks and stared down at the bottle. Charise joined him, again standing very close to him, their bodies touching. They both just stared at the bottle for a moment, saying nothing.

Charise looked up at Reggie. "Netflix and chill?"

Reggie looked curiously at her. He grabbed his tablet from the small table and flipped it on. The simulated image of Charise sucking his cock filled the screen. Reggie quickly turned the tablet off, glancing over his shoulder to see if Charise had seen it, but she was again staring down at the bottle, watching it float past. "No internet," he said. "I don't have any movies downloaded, either." He set the tablet down and looked at Charise. "How 'bout we just chill?"

Charise smiled and reached for him. "And lots of it."

—◆◇◆—

"Did all that really happen?" Shawnna asked Brad. "Did you really shoot those... those Carlos-things?" She had her head in his lap as he gently stroked her hair. They were back in their bungalow, resting on their bed. A warm glow of sunlight filtered through the window, casting golden beams onto the see-thru glass floor. Tropical fish swam lazily past in the warm waters below their floor. "I mean, what the hell was that... thing... that portal? It doesn't make any sense. A rip in the multiverse? You gotta be kidding me."

Brad didn't answer. He stared lovingly down into her beautiful green eyes. He gently cupped her face and gave it a gentle caress.

Shawnna moaned and closed her eyes, enjoying Brad's touch.

Part of a dark shape appeared in the water below the clear glass floor, part of what looked like a head, a head with black hair cut short and neat. Brad froze for a moment as he watched the head appear, then part of an arm, then a clothed shoulder. It was most definitely a body. A body wearing a very familiar set of clothes. A set of clothes that he himself owned.

Shawnna reached her hand up and cupped it behind Brad's neck, pulling him down closer to her, parting her lips for his kiss. Brad kissed her, but kept his eyes open, watching more of the body float into view. The body's left hand appeared, a hand with no discernible burn mark on it. Then the right hand of the corpse appeared, it too lacking a burn mark.

The corpse floated out of view and Brad turned his full attention to Shawnna, kissing her fully, deeply, passionately, lovingly on the lips. "I'm so glad I found you," Brad whispered as he pulled back from the kiss. "I love you," he said.

"Oh, Brad," Shawnna said. "I love you, too." She wrapped her arms around his neck and kissed him deeply.

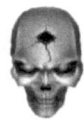

TERRORSTORY #54
THE CHASE

They could see the red eyes in the distance; they were only visible for brief flashes, looking like twinkling pinpoint spots of glowing blood that were gone as soon as they appeared. The wagon bumped and jumped and thumped as it sped down the dark dirt road. They knew what was chasing them, but they weren't sure how many were chasing them. Eleanor insisted she had seen three sets of red eyes, but Anne thought she might have seen four. It didn't matter how many; one set of glowing red eyes belonging to a werewolf chasing them was one too many. They all knew that.

The two horses pulling the wagon knew the pursuing beasts were getting closer, too. They snorted and huffed and there were clear notes of fear in the shrill blasts of hot air that burst out of their nostrils. They no longer ran in smooth unison. Their rhythm was disrupted and each horse strode at its own frantic pace, making for quite a jolting, jarring ride.

Bellamy had to clutch at the wagon's wooden side rails to prevent himself from being ejected from the speeding wagon, curling his arm tightly around the top rail like a drowning man clutching at a loose piece of flotsam. "They're getting closer," Bellamy said. He was a tall, slender man with a hawkish nose. There wasn't any nervous anxiety in his voice. Bellamy never seemed to get nervous about anything. Not about his wedding. Not about his initiation into the Gentlemen's Smoker's Club. Not about his meeting with the Queen. They're getting closer. Looks like it might rain. I'll take two lumps with my tea, thank you very much. He might as well have been reading the ingredients to a recipe aloud. "We'll never outrun them."

There were four of them in the wagon, five if you included the driver sitting on his high perch at the front of the wagon. The wagon was filled with straw that scratched and poked at them with every shifting of their bodies. The smell of manure was there; it was faint but it was there like a soft bubble of stench that arced over the entire back of the wagon. No one had the inclination to scoff at the indignation of riding in the back of a farmer's wagon. There had been no time to find a deluxe coach when they had fled the estate.

Oliver rose up slightly and leaned up towards the driver, keeping his hand on a railing to steady himself as the wagon bucked and tossed. Oliver was a portly man with a rotund face. A blossoming red flush colored his cheeks. His wig was still atop his head, but slightly askew. His ruddy cheeks, labored breathing and crooked wig gave him the disheveled look of a frazzled man. The driver, a young boy whose name he did not know, kept his gaze riveted on the dark road ahead. Towering dark trees flashed by all around them. Luckily for them, the night was filled with a radiant glow cast from the full moon high above that at least gave them some visibility into their surroundings. The tall trees and branches overhanging high above the road created deep pockets of black amidst the pale yellowish glow of the moon's wan light. "Can they go any faster?" Oliver asked.

The boy shook his head. "We're too heavy." He didn't take his gaze from the dark road ahead. "Are they getting closer?"

"Yes," Oliver said.

The young boy snapped the reins, but that made no difference in the horses' speed; they were running for their very lives already.

"What did he say?" Eleanor asked as Oliver shifted back down to a sitting position.

The wagon suddenly jumped and thudded as one of the wheels hit a large rock. Eleanor was propelled a good two feet in the air from the violent jostling. She emitted a little squeaking shriek, but managed to grab a railing and hold on. Her bottom thudded back down to the wagon floor and she gave a sharp grunt.

"Are you okay?" Oliver asked.

Eleanor nodded. "I bit my cheek." She ran her tongue around in her mouth, then looked back to Oliver. "What did he say?"

Bellamy shifted closer to them. Oliver met his gaze. "The driver says we are too heavy," Oliver said. "We won't be able to outrun them."

"Look!" Anne shouted. She thrust a pointing finger back down the dark road.

One pair of glowing red eyes blazed brightly for a brief moment, and then darkness filled in the area where the orbs had just been.

"They're closer!" Anne shouted. "We have to go faster!"

Bellamy glanced at his wife. The fear in Anne's voice tightened his jaw. Her timidity often grated on his nerves, and now it made him curl his fingers into a tight fist.

"Bellamy, make him go faster," Anne said.

"We're too heavy," Oliver said. "We can't go any faster."

The wagon charged on, the motion keeping their bodies bumping and shifting; it was impossible to sit still.

Bellamy glanced at the others in the wagon. One of them had to *leave* the wagon, he realized. But who? Bellamy looked at the pasty white pale face of his wife with a flat expression. If weight was a factor then the choice really was obvious. Anne was easily the heaviest of the group, her weight brought on by a life of luxury and pampering and fine meals and indulgent dining. They could lighten the wagon's load by a good few hundred pounds if she were to... fall overboard.

The party had been a trap. None of them had suspected a thing. A new wealthy family had invited them all to attend a grand gathering on their estate. The four of them had dressed in their finest clothes, donned their powdered wigs. Bellamy and Oliver polished their buckled shoes. Anne had brought her finest fan, the one Bellamy had purchased for her in the orient. Eleanor had dabbed herself with her finest perfume.

Their hosts were the Klaus family, newly arrived from Germany. The source of their wealth was unknown, but it was clearly apparent from the size of their estate that the amount of their fortunes was vast. The Klaus family. Bellamy froze for a moment as he said their name again in his head. The Klaus. He respelled it phonetically in his head. The Claws. He finally got the obvious joke and bit back a bitter laugh.

Tales of monstrous beasts were popular in the theaters so when the first werewolf made its appearance at the party, none of the guests were the wiser. They all thought it was part of a delightful show. Oliver was the one who had noticed the hint of strangeness first. The blood on the wall. It was just a slight smear and it could have easily been mistaken for some spilled meat sauce splashed onto the wall by a drunk guest, but Oliver knew his blood. His father was a mortician so he was used to seeing blood in all manners of variety. He recognized it immediately and something triggered an alarm in him because one moment Bellamy had been enjoying his second glass of champagne and the next moment Oliver was grabbing the glass from his hand and tugging him into a secluded alcove to whisper urgent warnings to him.

"We need to leave," Oliver said, his voice nearly a hiss.

Bellamy squinted dumbly at him.

"There is something afoot here, Bellamy," Oliver said. "Something dark and sinister."

"Something dark and sinister?" Bellamy echoed. "That's being rather melodramatic, even for you, dear Oliver."

"There's blood on the wall. And it is fresh."

"Blood, you say?"

Oliver nodded. "And a foul, fetid odor assaulted me when that beast neared. Either the man hasn't had a bath in ten years, or it was the smell of dank animal fur."

"It was probably the costume. It may just need a good cleaning."

"That was no costume, Bellamy."

Bellamy was aghast at the implications of Oliver's words. "That's absurd, Oliver. You are telling me that was no man covered in fur that we saw?"

Oliver looked hard at Bellamy. "That was no man." He glanced back over his shoulder, back towards the sounds of the party. "We must find our ladies and be gone from this place." He grabbed Bellamy's shoulder and squeezed. "Now."

Bellamy chanced a glanced at Eleanor. She was barely visible within the cloud-like expanse of her blue dress as she sat on the floor of the jostling wagon. Her ample bosom was on display, as always, her chest thrust out to expose her generous cleavage. He had sampled those breasts on numerous occasions. Their indiscretions had ended months before he and Anne had wed, but he still felt an occasional twitch in his groin when he looked at her. He was pretty certain neither Anne nor Oliver suspected their illicit trysts. The image of her shaved sleekness came to his mind and he forced it away. Now was not the time to fantasize about the smoothness of her pink cunny. It was time to decide who of the women would have to go first. His wife or the wife of his good friend. Eleanor was a good thirty or forty pounds lighter than Anne, so she wouldn't lighten their load as much as his wife's sudden departure would.

The screams coming from the Klaus estate were terrifying in their intensity. The shrillness of them had penetrated them to their very souls. They had just exited the house, all of them giving full heed to Oliver's warning of impending danger, when the screaming started. It was as though someone had just viciously pulled on the tails of a thousand cats. The terrible cacophony of death cries filled the night sky like a swarm of sonic bats. They saw a row of finely ornate carriages sitting off to the side of the driveway as they bolted from the house, but no drivers were visible. The carriage drivers were all inside getting drinks and refreshment while their employers partied with the Klaus family.

Oliver spotted a wagon slowly pulling away from the house on a side road, its open back mostly empty except for loose piles of straw. "There!" he shouted, pointing at the departing wagon.

They raced for the wagon. Anne stumbled and fell, crying out Bellamy's name as she went down. Bellamy moved to his wife and his face grew tightly strained with the effort to lift the weight of her body and get her back on her feet. Bellamy and Oliver then helped Anne and Eleanor along with firm hands on elbows, practically lifting them off their feet to propel them forward because the hooped petticoats they wore under their dresses made any quick movement nearly impossible.

Bellamy looked at Oliver. They had both left their frock coats and their three-cornered hats back at the party, so both of them were wearing only their waistcoats over their linen shirts. His breeches were stained with dirt and grime from his scramble into the wagon and his stockings had a large tear on his left knee. A spot of blood dotted his left knee where his skin had been scraped by the rough-cut wooden floor of the wagon. His shoes were still buckled, they too covered with mud and grime. He had just lost his powdered wig a few moments earlier when the wagon had jostled in a particularly violent manner and his short hair was wet with sweat, plastered flat to the shape of his skull. Bellamy's gaze went back to the smear of red staining Oliver's exposed knee. The blood was still wet, still fresh. He realized with a start that the beasts chasing them could very well be after them because of the scent Oliver's blood was giving off.

He would probably have to push him off first, Bellamy realized. He didn't think he could win a duel with him one on one. If he pushed one of the ladies off first, Oliver would surely protest and come after him. But if Oliver went first, he was confident he could handle the two women by himself.

He had a sudden craving for some snuff. He reached about himself, patting at the pockets of his waistcoats, feeling for his tobacco, but then remembered that he had left his container of snuff in the pocket of his frock coat. He looked over at Oliver, but he knew the man did not partake. His taste went more towards communal sports than towards self-indulgent activities. The man did enjoy cockfighting and bull baiting more than most. Bellamy found the whole spectacle of chaining a bull to a post and watching dogs attack it rather repugnant, but to each his own. He preferred taking his dogs out on a good fox hunt.

The first pair of red glowing eyes they saw chasing them as they fled the Klaus estate in the wagon nearly caused Anne to faint in a paroxysm of fear.

"Good God!" Bellamy exclaimed, in a very rare outburst of high emotion. "What the devil is that?"

"Those are the eyes of a devil," Oliver said. "A devil wolf in the grotesque shape of a man," Oliver said.

It took a while for the realization that they were being chased by a werewolf to sink in, but once it did a long silence blanketed the group in a shroud of terror and mute-inducing fear.

Bellamy turned away from Oliver, looking furtively at Eleanor. Of course, if he threw Oliver off first,

Eleanor might be outraged. Or she could very well be secretly pleased. He knew they were having some difficulties in their marriage. If he threw Eleanor off, then most likely nothing would change between himself and Anne. His wife would still deign to allow him to touch her body once a week and do the deed atop her. But how would Eleanor show her appreciation for saving her life, he wondered. How grateful would she be? Grateful enough to let him bury his face between her legs and taste of her sweet nectar? Grateful enough to reciprocate the oral pleasure upon his stiff manhood?

Bellamy chanced another glance at Eleanor and she gave him a nervous, scared smile. Or was that a softly encouraging smile?

Bellamy looked back into the darkness. And saw a pair of red eyes gleaming. And then another. The time to act was now. The beasts were most definitely getting closer. The blood-red eyes were getting larger. He didn't know how long the creatures could keep up this pace, but he knew he could not risk it. He had to do something and he had to do it now.

Bellamy felt quite pleased with himself. He had successfully implemented stock breeding with some of his cows and sheep, and the third generation of his livestock was markedly larger and fatter, putting more meat onto each head of cattle and thicker wool around his sheep. The cows even seemed to produce more milk but he hadn't yet measured each cow's yield exactly to be certain. He felt as if the decision he was making here was somewhat similar, deciding who should live and who should die, deciding who was most worthy to continue on the propagation of the human species. All of this had gone through his thoughts in a matter of moments, all of the sizing up of his wife and his companions.

The decision came quickly and easily.

Anne gave a mighty kick with her bare foot and Bellamy tumbled out of the wagon.

Eleanor looked at her with wide eyes. Oliver stared on in shock.

"He was an arrogant pompous fool," Anne said. "He was probably deciding which one of us he was going to throw off the wagon." She settled back into her spot on the wagon floor, adjusted her dress, and looked back to Eleanor with an impatient tightness in her face. "Tell the driver he must go faster."

Bellamy lay in the dirt of the road, unmoving.

The first beast raced up to the body and paused, sniffing brusquely at the immobile man laying prone on the left side of the road. The man did not move. A thin wispy layer of fog shrouded the body, the road, the misty blanket flowing into the brush and trees that flanked both sides of the road. The beast pawed at the man, its movement causing the fog to billow out away from the man; it scratched at the man's clothing with its sharp claws, ripping the fabric to reveal a layer of pale white flesh beneath. Two thin lines of blood appeared on the man's flesh where the beast's claws had broken through the skin. The beast again sniffed brusquely at the flesh, at the slowly oozing blood.

A distant clanking noise drew the beast's gaze and it looked up to stare down the road with red gleaming eyes. The wagon was still visible in the far distance. The moon was high and bright and full in the night sky, illuminating the wagon in a misty glow. The wagon rounded a bend in the road, disappearing beyond a thick growth of trees that flanked the road's curve. A brisk wind ruffled the beast's dark brown fur, but the chilling breeze did nothing to cool down the hot hunger for a fresh kill burning in its stomach.

The beast glanced down at the motionless man. It would be an easy meal, but it would not truly satisfy its hunger. It sensed that the man was already dead.

A second beast joined the first, slowing as it neared the scene. The first beast, the alpha of the pack, snarled deeply at the new arrival, baring its moist fangs, fangs coated with the desire to sink deep into living flesh and feed. The second beast slunk back, lowering its head and its body, showing deference to the alpha werewolf. The second werewolf also had dark brown fur, but its body was thinner, smaller, clearly much less physically dominant when compared to the alpha. The alpha growled again at the new arrival, then spun on its paws, and raced away after the fleeing wagon, fog billowing up behind it in the wake of its hot pursuit.

A third beast arrived and it was the second werewolf's turn to snarl and bare its deadly fangs. The third beast had a much lighter coating of fur covering its body, more of a pale silver-gray that contrasted deeply against the darker brown fur of the other two. The silver-gray beast did not cower to the second as much as the second had cowered to the alpha, but the silver-gray third beast did slow its pace and moved up gingerly to the fallen man, sniffing almost daintily at its exposed flesh. It extended its tongue and lapped at the dripping blood oozing from one of the cuts in the man's chest. The second werewolf growled, but the silver-gray werewolf paid the vocal displeasure no heed and continued to lick at the blood. Then it started to nip at the man's flesh, tearing off a bit of skin.

The second werewolf snarled again at the third, but then also turned away and bound after the alpha, leaving the silver-gray beast to the meal that was quickly growing cold.

The wagon bumped and jumped and thumped as it sped down the dark dirt road, its speed increasing ever so slightly. Red eyes flashed in the far distance, glowing like the tips of hot pokers, then vanishing just as abruptly as they had appeared.

"They're still gaining on us!" Oliver shouted over his shoulder at the young driver.

The driver did not respond, keeping his focus on the road before him.

Eleanor shifted uncomfortably as her stay dug at her ribs. She had selected one of her tighter fitting bodices for the party, suspecting that she would be on her feet for most of the night with no real need to sit. But now sitting on the floor of the wagon, the tightness of the stay around her waist was most discomforting. The hooped petticoat under her dress didn't make her seated position any more comfortable, and in fact made it more unbearably awkward to sit. She glanced down at the dark blue fabric of her dress. At least the dark color was helping to hide the dirt she knew was staining the cloth. She looked up and over to Anne. The poor thing had chosen a light gold for her dress and an ugly black smear was very visible along her frilly right sleeve and up her right side where she had fallen in the dirt as they fled the party and were racing towards the wagon. The poor heavy thing. The poor heavy corpulent thing who could best help their chances of survival by departing the wagon in one manner or another...

Anne was still alive when the alpha werewolf reached her. She had survived being rolled out of the wagon by Elizabeth and Oliver. Her shoulder ached far too much for her to put on an air of indignation in her face. She had never felt such searing pain in her life. She managed to move to a sitting position, but could move no further than that with the tight-fitting bodice and hooped petticoat preventing her from standing. So she sat in the dirt in the middle of the road, facing in the direction the wagon had been headed.

She heard the soft growling sound first. She struggled to look behind her, but could only turn her head so far as the searing pain in her bruised shoulder made such movement unbearable. Then she heard the soft padding of paws in the dirt, accompanied by a soft clinking sound that she was certain came from claws clacking against each other.

Another low growl sounded out, now louder,

closer.

She could find no words. She felt oddly numb. She briefly thought of Bellamy laying in the dirt and wondered if he had survived the fall of the wagon to experience the same fate, but then she pushed the thought of him out of her head as she felt a warm flush of moist breath sweep across the back of her neck. She had other pressing concerns to consider. Such as her imminent demise.

And then the werewolf appeared, circling around her to her front, moving on all fours. Its body was covered in a dark thick fur, the coarse hair looking almost blue in the moonlight. It grunted a harsh grunt as it moved about her, baring its sharp fangs to her. There was no humanity in its red gleaming eyes. Only a savage brutality.

The werewolf started right in on the exposed flesh of her face first.

Oliver peered intently into the darkness behind them. He squinted, straining to see deeper and deeper into the darkness. Finally, he spoke, a hint of relieved hope in his words. "I don't see them anymore. I think we've outrun them." He turned to Elizabeth. "Do you see them?"

Elizabeth sat sullenly on the floor of the wagon, staring absently at the fan she held in her hand.

The wagon started to slow.

Oliver looked away from her, towards the young driver.

The wagon continued to slow as the driver tugged on the reins, pulling the snorting, panting horses down to a slow walk, then finally stopped them entirely. The horses pranced and skittered as they struggled to catch their breaths.

"What's your name, boy?" Oliver asked, leaning up towards the driver's perch. "I want to properly thank you."

"Victor," the young driver said. "Victor Klaus."

Elizabeth didn't see the terror well up into Oliver's face because she hadn't heard the boy's response to Oliver. She glanced around their surroundings. Thick towering trees stood like tall sentries on either side of them. Before them, a looming wall of rock reached far up into the night sky. A jagged-edged black hole was carved into the bottom of the stone. "What is this place?" she asked.

"Some call it the Den." Victor turned fully around to look at them and his eyes gleamed a blood-red gleam. A thin layer of hair coated his face; his features were human but there was a most definite bestial distortion to them. "I call it Home."

Numerous pairs of red eyes gleamed in the darkness all around them.

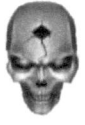

TERRORSTORY #55
WHO'S YOUR DADDY?

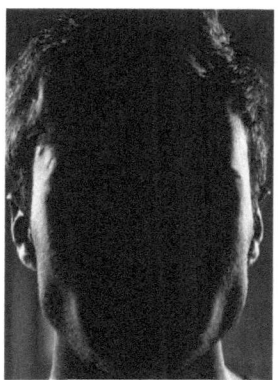

None of the children were crying in Miss Jorgan's class. That's what unnerved her. A few children always cried on the first day of school. Always. For the last fifteen years, at least three children cried on the first day of school in her class; in some years it seemed like the entire class bawled their little eyes out on the first day. But not this year. Not one of the kindergartners had a wet eye. Not even the hint of wetness in the corners. There were dry cheeks all around.

Miss Jorgan had just reached the big Four-Oh and had settled into a relatively comfortable routine every school year, which unfortunately for her overall health also included adding a few extra pounds to her midsection. She had a rounded chin, chestnut brown eyes, and a hint of sharp cheekbones giving her face a mixture of soft edges and angular curves that didn't always work well together. In an odd disconcerting way, she almost hoped for tears every year because they gave her a chance to be the mother hen that came naturally to her. She wasn't married and had no children of her own, so being a teacher was the next best thing because every year she was given a fresh batch of kids to nurture.

She could hear several children crying in Mrs. York's class directly across the hall, and one incessantly bawling child in the room next to hers. The loud pounding rain hammering down on the school's roof didn't make the situation any better for those nervous children. A startling crack of thunder triggered a fresh round of sobbing, and even brought some stalwart children who had been holding back in Mrs. York's room into the crying fray; Miss Jorgan could see them from her vantage point from across the hall. But there were still no tears from any of the children in her classroom.

As Miss Jorgan looked a little more closely at the children in her class, something else unsettled her. They all had a very similar look to them. Oh, there were slight differences here and there, some had more prominent cheekbones than others, some had curly locks and some had straight bangs, but they all had jet black hair, strong square chins, and delicate noses. They all could have easily come from the same set of parents, which of course was impossible.

Not if one man had sired them all. Which she immediately dismissed as absurd. Most of the mothers of the children in her class were married. *He still could have banged them all.* The crude thought pushed its way to the forefront of her mind.

The children in her class finished hanging up their jackets and calmly took their seats, not arguing amongst themselves, not scrambling to find a seat; they all seemed to know exactly which seat was theirs even though it was their first day and they had never been in her classroom before.

Two young girls leaned closer to each other, nearly touching their heads as they leaned across the aisle of desks. They exchanged words, both of them glancing at Miss Jorgan at exactly the same time, then resumed their seated positions in their desks.

Miss Jorgan would find out later what the subject of their conversation was. And it would change her life forever.

❦

"Did you see them?" Miss Jorgan asked Principal Sneed.

"See who?" Principal Sneed was in his late fifties, silver-haired and lean for the most part, but starting to get a little extra width around his waist from sitting behind his desk for hour after hour five days a week.

"My students."

"I saw a few of them, yes."

"But did you see all of them? Together?" Miss Jorgan asked.

Principal Sneed frowned.

"Did you see them in my class? Did you see them all sitting together?"

Principal Sneed shook his head. "No. I did not."

"Can you please sit in tomorrow?"

Principal Sneed gave a slight nod. "I can drop by and say hello to them, yes."

Miss Jorgan breathed a sigh of relief. "Okay, that's fine. Just please stop by."

"I saw them," Principal Sneed said. He was clearly disturbed by the memory behind his statement.

"Pretty damn odd, right?" Miss Jorgan asked, not really needing a reply. She sat in a chair opposite the Principal.

Principal Sneed nodded from behind his desk. He was quiet for a moment. "What do you make of it?"

She shrugged. "I have no idea."

"We do have a close-knit community. A lot of, shall we say, cousins intermingling."

Miss Jorgan nodded. "Yes, I thought of that. But that just doesn't explain it. They all look like they have the same father."

"Is that even possible?"

"Sure," Miss Jorgan said. "He would've been busy, but it's certainly within the realm of possibility."

Principal Sneed was quiet. "Who—"

Miss Jorgan interrupted him. "I haven't met all the parents yet, but believe me I will be paying much more attention to them when I do."

Principal Sneed nodded. "As will I."

Mr. William Glynn was a ginger, and his wife was a straight-haired blonde. Miss Jorgan just stared at the two of them for a moment, then glanced down at their daughter Ophelia. She had jet black hair that formed into tight curls on her head. Her strong square jaw had no resemblance to her father's rounded chin, or to her mother's slightly pointed chin. The adoption question burned on her tongue, but Miss Jorgan knew it was just too impolite to ask, especially with Ophelia sitting there staring at her.

They were a week into the school year and she had been slowly working her way through all the parent meetings. With the Glynn's, she was about halfway through meeting all the parents. A few of the men and women she met had black hair, but at least half had not.

"How is Ophelia doing?" Mr. Glynn asked.

"She is delightful," Miss Jorgan said. "Very attentive."

Mr. Glynn smiled, pleased with that response.

When did you adopt her? The question burned on her tongue, but she snuffed it out by clenching her teeth on it.

"Ophelia says you are a good teacher," Mrs. Glynn said.

"Oh, she does, does she?" Miss Jorgan looked at Ophelia with a smile and Ophelia smiled warmly up at her.

Mrs. Glynn bobbed her head up and down enthusiastically. "Oh, yes. She says you are very nice and you treat all the children in the class very fairly." Mrs. Glynn paused for a moment, almost appearing uncertain about her next words, but then she spoke them anyway. "She thinks you need a man, but other than that she thinks you are doing well with your life," Mrs. Glynn added.

"Oh. She does, does she?" Miss Jorgan said, but this time there was no smile and the words came out a little more strained.

"She's very perceptive like that," Mrs. Glynn said.

Miss Jorgan didn't know what to do with Mrs. Glynn's statement. *When did you adopt Ophelia?* She nearly had to bite the tip of her tongue off to stop the question from spilling out of her mouth.

"We're all very proud of you," Mr. Glynn added. "Especially since the... incident."

His comment was so casual, so off the cuff, but it still sent a jarring jolt through Miss Jorgan. She hadn't thought about the attack on the school for months, but now the ugly memories threatened to overtake her thoughts. The discomforting quiet lingered until Miss Jorgan excused herself and ended the meeting.

The nightmare came back. Miss Jorgan thought she had it all under control, but she was clearly mistaken. She hadn't dreamed of the incident for months, but it came back with a vengeance. She was back in the school, standing in the doorway to her classroom, staring down the school hallway.

The attacker was wearing a ski mask. He wasn't being cautious. His stride was full of purpose, full of an intent as dark as the black jacket and dark pants he was wearing. He gripped a pistol in both hands, with two more guns tucked into his belt.

Miss Jorgan had no idea how he got into the school, but there he was, striding down the hallway, guns in hand. Heading towards her classroom. She stood on the threshold to her classroom, looking down the hallway from her doorway. She could see Paul the security guard laying prone on the hallway floor in the distance behind the gunman. She didn't know if he was dead or unconscious. There was no sign of any blood, nor had she heard any shots fired yet.

She turned to face her class. They were children from last year's class, a group immensely more diverse than the class she had this year, full of blondes and a few redheads, a few Indians and several Asian children. Most of the children were staring down at the worksheet on their desks, diligently answering the simple math questions. "Hey, everybody," she said. "Let's play a game."

Most of the children looked up at her; a few kept on working, determined to answer the last few questions on their worksheet.

"How about a fort?" she said. "Let's make some forts."

Most of the children looking at her frowned in confusion. Only Billy Gillicut grinned from ear to ear. He was a freckled-face blond with a pudgy face.

Miss Jorgan hurried away from the door, quickly moving up to Billy who sat in the front row. "Billy, get up from your desk for a second, honey." Billy got out from behind his desk. Miss Jorgan grabbed his worksheet and pencil and handed them to Billy. Then she grabbed the desk and turned it on its side, the flat wooden surface of the desk facing the doorway. "Now get behind it Billy, and duck down. Pretend you're part of an army and your enemy is trying to shoot you from the doorway."

"I'm not afraid," Billy said. "I'm not going to hide like some yellow coward." Billy puffed out his chest slightly, making a display of his bravado.

Miss Jorgan knew she didn't have time to argue with Billy. Her heart started to race quicker in her chest, started to pound louder in her ears. The man in the black ski mask was probably only moments away from reaching the door to her room. She turned to the other children in the class. "Everyone, make a fort with your desk. Hurry now! Hurry!" She moved from desk to desk with an ever more frantic pace, helping child after child tip their desk over, motioning for them to maneuver behind them with quick waves of her hand. "Hurry!" She had no idea if the thin wood of the desks would offer any protection at all, or what kind of firepower the gunman's weapons had, but it was all she could come up with at the time.

Within moments, every child was huddled on the floor behind their desk-shields.

Except for Billy Gillicut. He stood stock still, staring at the doorway with a stunned look in his eyes.

Miss Jorgan saw the startled look on Billy's face and whirled to face the doorway.

The man in the black ski mask stood in the open doorway.

Damn it! She admonished herself mentally. *I didn't lock the fucking door!*

She shoved Billy down behind his desk. "Stay down!" She whirled back to face the gunman. She stepped forward defiantly, a mother lion protecting her cubs, maneuvering herself directly between the masked man and her students. "Leave them alone!" she shouted at the gunman, gritting her teeth, her hands clenching into balled fists. She moved closer.

Her mind tried to process what was going on, but she could think of nothing else but protecting the innocent children she was in charge of. This maniac would have to go through her first.

She stopped before the gunman, now only a few feet away from him. His gun pointed directly at her belly. He looked at her, his eyes blazing with blue balefire, visible within the open eye slits of his black mask. He nodded his head ever so slightly, then abruptly turned and walked away.

Miss Jordan stood frozen in place for a long moment. And then her knees buckled under her and she collapsed to the floor.

They were just innocent glances. Weren't they? Four of the children in her class were huddled together at a table, working on a project. Tabitha, a girl with long straight black hair, glanced at her every few minutes, then turned back to the group and nodded her head. *You're just being paranoid. Just because you're paranoid, doesn't mean they aren't still out to get you.*

When Tabitha rose out of her chair and approached her desk, Miss Jorgan actually felt her heart lurch up towards her throat. How could a five year old be so intimidating? She could barely tie her own shoes. The girl reached her desk and stopped, waiting patiently to be recognized.

"Yes, Tabitha?"

"I know we shouldn't say this…" Tabitha suddenly paused and looked back over her shoulder at her group. Alan, one of the boys, nodded a very soft nod, but the message in the subtle gesture was still an encouraging one. Tabitha turned back to face Miss Jorgan.

"Go on. What is it?" Miss Jorgan asked.

"We're going to miss you."

Miss Jorgan just stared slack-jawed at the young girl.

And then Tabitha burst into tears and ran back to the group. Alan put a comforting hand on Tabitha's heaving shoulder, leaning in to whisper something to her. It was a very adult gesture. And it scared the fuck out of Miss Jorgan.

But not as much as the entire class staring quietly up at her from their group tables did.

"Maybe she's moving," Principal Sneed said.

Miss Jorgan shook her head. "I don't think so." She paused for a moment, shifting her weight from one foot to the other as she stood before the principal's desk. "It was like she was speaking for the entire class. She said *we're* going to miss you. Not *I'm* going to miss you."

Principal Sneed steepled his fingers, tapping the tips of his index fingers together. He was quiet for a moment. He leaned back in his chair. "You've met some more of the parents?"

She nodded. "Ophelia Glynn has a ginger father and a blonde mother. She looked natural, too, so I don't think she dyes her hair."

"Very peculiar."

"Yeah, you think?" She immediately caught herself. "Sorry. No reason to be snippy to you."

"That's okay. It is very strange, I'll give you that."

He was again quiet for a moment. "None of the other classes are anywhere near as odd as your configuration of students." He paused. "Very peculiar." He picked up a folder, then set it back down. "Do you need me to move some of them? Mrs. Horton has a few seats available."

Miss Jorgan shook her head. "No. They're all very polite. Very well-behaved." She was quiet for a moment. "I mean she looked straight at me, said they were going to miss me and then burst into tears. What the hell is that about?" She frowned. "It's still spooking me. You don't just say that to someone for no reason. So why did she say it?"

"Did you ask her?"

Miss Jorgan again shook her head. "No. I was too freaked out by the whole thing. It was just so damn strange."

Principal Sneed leaned forward in his chair. "They are only five years old. Maybe they were playing some game."

"If Tabitha was play acting, then she's going to give Meryl Streep a run for the most Oscars."

"Tabitha."

"Yes, Miss Jorgan?"

"What did you mean yesterday when you said you would miss me? Are you going somewhere? Are you moving out of town?"

Tabitha laughed a tittering little laugh. "Oh, no, Miss Jorgan. I'm not moving out of town."

"Then what did you mean?"

Tabitha didn't answer. She stared back at Miss

Jorgan, but kept her silence.

Miss Jorgan looked hard at the five year old girl standing before her desk. "Am *I* going somewhere, Tabitha?"

"Just for a little while." She surged forward and grabbed Miss Jorgan's arm, her face flush with excitement. "But don't worry. He'll take good care of you. Don't be scared."

Miss Jorgan felt an uncomfortable flush of heat race up to her face. She actually felt beads of sweat push their way out of her pores to dot her forehead. She felt oddly distant from her own body, as if this bizarre scene was some disturbing part of a movie she was watching. She looked down at the small hand clutching her arm and made a motion to swat it away as if it were a mosquito about to sting her, but she kept that reaction in check and forced herself to remain calm. Tabitha was just a child. An innocent little kindergartner. All of the children in her class were just innocent kindergartners.

Tabitha pulled her little hand from her arm and stepped back. "Don't be scared," she said again.

"Who are you talking about?" Miss Jorgan asked. Her mouth was suddenly dry, as if a hundred cotton balls had suddenly sucked out all the moisture from it.

"My Daddy," Tabitha said.

"Your Daddy?" Miss Jorgan said, the words coming out somewhat numbly. "Who is your Daddy?"

Tabitha just smiled.

The next peculiar incident happened on the

playground during recess. Miss Jorgan was on duty, along with a few other teachers, taking her turn watching the kids play outside. She didn't notice anything unusual at first (because her every day was filled with the unusual now with her motley black-haired crew), but when a girl collapsed into Alan's arms she sprang into action. She hurried over to Alan as he gently lowered the girl to the rubber-chip playground surface. "Alan, what happened?" she asked as she reached his side.

Alan suddenly looked bashful and a slight flush of embarrassment rose into his cheeks. "I was just practicing," he said.

Miss Jorgan kneeled down next to the girl, quickly examining her.

"She's just sleeping," Alan said.

Miss Jorgan looked up at him, frowning. "What were you practicing?"

"For my future." He smiled at her. "I learned that from you. Practice makes perfect."

"I never taught you how to knock a girl down, Alan," she said, her voice growing distraught.

"I didn't knock her down," he said. "I just helped her go to sleep."

"Why would you help her go to sleep?"

"I was just practicing." He frowned slightly. "Really, Miss Jorgan, you should pay more attention when someone else speaks to you." He smiled again. "I learned that from you, too."

"Don't be fresh with me, Alan."

The frown returned on the boy's face, deeper this time. She saw what might have been the beginnings of tears form in the corners of his eyes, but before she could be certain he whirled and started to walk away from her.

"I wasn't done talking to you," she called after him.

Alan slowed, then turned back to face her, clearly reluctant. "I'm going to tell my Daddy that you are being mean to me."

"I am not being mean to you, Alan." She glanced down at the prone girl. "I saw this girl collapse into your arms. I need to know what is going on."

Just then, the girl opened her eyes and saw Alan standing near her. A wide smile broke out on her face. "Hi, Alan," she said with abundant enthusiasm.

"Hi, Sara," Alan said. He gently helped Sara back up to her feet. "Are you okay?"

She nodded.

"Did I scare you?" Alan asked.

"A little," Sara said. "But I won't be scared next time."

The bell rang, signaling the end of recess.

Miss Jorgan watched in muted disbelief as Alan escorted Sara back into the building like a perfect gentlemen leading his lady to the ball. What the fuck was going on?

"Do you want me to file a police report?" Principal Sneed asked.

"No, of course not." Miss Jorgan looked up at Principal Sneed. "Did you tell her parents?"

"No. Sara said she just fell asleep." He paused. "Do you think I should?"

"She collapsed on the playground. I should've called an ambulance," Miss Jorgan said.

"Perhaps. She certainly seems fine now. If we told every parent when their kid fell asleep in school we'd have a revolving door of freaked out moms and dads."

Miss Jorgan frowned. "But she was standing up. How many kids fall asleep while standing up?"

Principal Sneed shrugged. "My son fell asleep standing in line at Disney World once."

The children were giddy with excitement.

"What's everyone so excited about?" Miss Jorgan asked.

Ophelia and Tabitha beamed exuberant smiles at Miss Jorgan. "He's coming for you tonight," Ophelia said. Tabitha nodded.

Miss Jorgan felt a tightness in her chest. "Who? Who is coming for me?"

"Our Daddy," Tabitha said.

"Your... your Daddy? Is coming for me?" She glanced down to see a slight tremor shake her fingers. She looked back up at the girls. "Why? Why is he coming for me?"

The girls giggled and Ophelia looked like she actually blushed. "Oh, Miss Jorgan. We really can't talk about such things. We're too young."

Miss Jorgan stared at her phone. Her gaze went to number nine, then one, but she did not dial the emergency number. Her hand trembled. "This is crazy," she muttered.

She pulled back the curtain on her front window

and peered out. The street outside was calm, quiet, and empty. There was no movement. No one walking a dog. Not even a car passing by. She released the curtain and moved to the front door, making sure the lock was secured, turning it to unlock it, then flipping it back to hear the bolt securely moving back into place.

She moved back into her living room, sat down on the couch, and flicked on the TV.

Miss Jorgan had a dream. A man came to her bedroom. He stood at the edge of her bed and stared down at her. A man with dark hair and piercing blue eyes. Somewhere in the haze of her dream, she thought of Dracula from the movies, the highlight across his eyes, the hypnotic power of his stare. I locked the door, she thought. How did he get in?

And then he took her, overwhelming her with a sensual passion she had never known before, overpowering her with a level of sexual delight she hadn't even known was possible.

Miss Jorgan, feeling incredibly well-rested after her sensuous dream, moved over to the coffee maker in her kitchen and poured herself a cup. She didn't quite register the fact that she hadn't yet made the coffee that morning until she raised the cup to her lips. She paused before letting the hot liquid touch her lips and lowered the cup back down; she stared at the coffee maker with a growing bewilderment.

"Good morning."

The voice made her freeze. She stood stock-still for a long moment. And then slowly lowered the cup to set it down on the counter next to the coffee machine. She already knew who the voice belonged to, but that didn't make it any less shocking in her head. It wasn't a dream? Last night hadn't been a dream?

"I made myself some coffee," he said. "Hope you don't mind."

She remained still, staring at the coffee maker. She could see a shimmering hazy reflection of him in the glass of the coffee pot. And just that blurry image of him sent a wave of desire crashing over her.

"Why don't you come over here and take care of this," he said, his voice a soft purr.

She slowly turned to see him sitting in one of the kitchen table chairs. He was naked, his large member standing erect, calling for her attention. "You weren't a dream?" she whispered, the words barely making it out of her mouth.

"Oh, I'm a dream alright," he said. He reached down and stroked his member, keeping his gaze locked on hers.

She couldn't look away from his eyes, eyes that were filled with blue balefire. She felt herself moving forward, taking slow steps towards him. She reached him, opened up her nightdress, straddled him, and slid herself down over his hardness. She orgasmed instantly. And then again and again as she rode him.

Miss Jorgan opened her eyes. She felt incredibly rested. No, not just rested. Her mind felt alert. She actually felt awake. The grogginess was gone, the hazy thoughts gone. The veil of fog that covered her brain seemed to have completely lifted and dissipated. The closest thing she could compare it to was the feeling she felt after taking opioids following her root canal last year. She felt great. She felt alive.

And the dreams. Oh my, the dreams. The man standing over her bed. The same man greeting her in the kitchen. They had felt so real. She could still feel the lingering touches of his kiss on her lips, a ghostly memory haunting her mouth. She could almost still feel the incredible sexual power of him as if he were laying right next to her. All that sex. All that great sex. All of their sexual encounters had felt so real.

She reached down between her legs and touched herself.

All of the girls in her class kept looking at her and giggling. They put their little hands over their mouths and tittered, their eyes twinkling with a knowledge that was far beyond their years.

"Ophelia, can you please come up here for a minute?" Miss Jorgan asked.

Ophelia obediently obeyed, rising up from her desk, the grin on her lips flatlining. She approached the desk and stopped before it. "Yes, Miss Jorgan?"

"You girls seem to be enjoying a fine joke," Miss Jorgan said. "Would you care to share it?"

Ophelia shook her head. "Oh, it was no joke, Miss Jorgan," Ophelia said. "We're just happy. We're very happy for you." She smiled a warm, knowing smile at Miss Jorgan.

Miss Jorgan frowned. "You are happy for me?"

Ophelia nodded enthusiastically. "Oh, yes. We know Daddy came to visit you last night."

Miss Jorgan scowled. "No one came to visit me last night."

"Oh, Miss Jorgan," Ophelia said. She slowly, very softly, shook her head.

Miss Jorgan could almost hear the *tsk tsk* going off in Ophelia's head. She felt a sudden tightness bloom on her shoulder, between her left shoulder blade and her spine, right in the spot where her tension concentrated. "What?" She felt stupid after muttering that question, but that's all that came out of her mouth.

"Don't worry," Ophelia said. "He'll come back." She giggled. "He'll come back a lot," she said, throwing an extra emphasis on *lot*.

Miss Jorgan stared at the girl standing before her for a long moment. "Who are you?" she finally asked, her voice sounding hoarse, the words barely coming out.

"I'm…" she started to say, but stopped. She shook her head. "No, I can't say. That's for Daddy to tell you." She paused for a moment. "May I return to my seat now?"

❧⚜❧

Miss Jorgan stared at the lock on her front door. She was dressed in a sheer black nightie, a nearly-see through garment as dark as her hair. She turned the lock to secure it, but then hesitated. She stared at the lock some more. Then she reached down and unlocked it. She again stared at it, but left it unlocked as she headed for her bedroom.

Miss Jorgan laid in her bed, waiting. Waiting for him to return. But the only thing that came back that night was the horribly familiar nightmare of the intrusion at the school. It started off the same, but this time it was a little different. Especially at the end.

He was wearing a ski mask. He wasn't being cautious. His stride was full of purpose, full of an intent as dark as the black jacket and dark pants he was wearing. He gripped a pistol in both hands, with two more guns tucked into his belt.

Miss Jorgan had no idea how he got into the school, but there he was, striding down the hallway, guns in hand. Heading towards her classroom. She stood on the threshold to her classroom, looking down the hallway from her doorway.

She turned to face her class. Most of the children were staring down at the worksheet on their desks, diligently answering the simple math questions. "Hey, everybody," she said. "Let's play a game."

The nightmare continued as it usually did and within moments every child was huddled on the floor behind their desk-shields.

Except for Billy Gillicut again. He stood stock still, staring at the doorway with a stunned look in his eyes.

Miss Jorgan saw the startled look on Billy's face and whirled to face the doorway.

The man in the black ski mask stood in the open doorway.

Damn it! She admonished herself mentally. *I didn't lock the fucking door!*

She shoved Billy down behind his desk. "Stay down!" She whirled back to face the gunman. She stepped forward defiantly, a mother lion protecting her cubs, maneuvering herself directly between the masked man and her students. "Leave them alone!" she shouted at the gunman, gritting her teeth, her hands clenching into balled fists. She moved closer. Her mind tried to process what was going on, but she could think of nothing else but protecting the innocent children she was in charge of. This maniac would have to go through her first.

Then Miss Jorgan heard a giggling sound behind her, then another tittering laugh. That was different. It was a new addition to the nightmare that made her pause. She chanced a quick glance over her shoulder and saw that the classroom was now filled with her current dark-haired students.

She turned to face the door and stopped before the gunman, now only a few feet away from him. His gun pointed directly at her belly. But this time she recognized him. It was him. The man from her dreams. It was the man all the children in her class called Daddy.

He did the same thing in this dream as he had done in their real-life encounter. He looked at her with his blazing blue eyes, nodded his head as he lowered the gun, then abruptly turned away.

Miss Jordan stood frozen in place for a long moment. And then she charged into the hallway after him. "Wait!" But the hallway was empty. He was gone.

❧⸙❧

"Ophelia, may I speak to you for a moment?" Miss Jorgan asked.

"Yes, Miss Jorgan." Ophelia clambered out from

behind her desk and came around the side of Miss Jorgan's desk to stand near her.

"I…" Miss Jorgan stopped, feeling a level above awkward that she had never felt before in her life. "Do you…" She paused again, not knowing how to continue without sounding like a disturbed idiot.

Ophelia reached out and gently patted her arm. "It's okay, Miss Jorgan. We all make mistakes."

Miss Jorgan looked at her curiously with a slight tilt of her head.

"Lock your doors, Miss Jorgan," Ophelia said. "A pretty lady like you shouldn't leave her doors unlocked at night. Who knows what could happen."

Ophelia took her hand away from Miss Jorgan's arm and returned to her desk.

Miss Jorgan locked her door and he came to her bed that night. Every touch of his fingers on her body, no matter where he touched her, was like he was rubbing her clitoris directly. Every touch of his lips against her flesh was like he was kissing the soft folds of her womanhood. He brought her to levels of bliss she had not even dreamed of in her wildest fantasies. The decades of loneliness decaying her heart and soul were washed away in an instant.

And when Miss Jorgan awoke he was still there in her bed with her. With his jet black hair, his strong square jaw, his piercing blue eyes. She didn't really question his presence. She just accepted it. It all seemed that simple. But there was a nagging concern that kept poking at her from the back of her thoughts, and she finally had to say it aloud. "You... took advantage of me in my sleep," Miss Jorgan said.

"Did I?" He moved atop her.

"Yes, you did."

"Did I?" He kissed her softly, sweetly on her lips.

"Yes. You did." She kissed him back, raising up her head to meet his lips.

"Did I?" He rubbed the backs of his knuckles against her cheek, then let his hand roam down to her breast, gently feathering her very hard nipple with his fingers.

"Yes," she said. But she made no effort to stop his roaming hand.

"Did I?" He reached his hand down to touch the flood of wetness between her legs.

"You did," she said. She parted her thighs, giving him wider access.

He slid a finger into her and she gasped with pleasure, gripping him tight as an orgasm ripped through her, sending waves of pleasure cascading down from the top of her head to the tips of her toes. "Did I?"

She let the orgasm crest over and wash away. She lay still for a moment, the tingling sensation making her feel like she was floating above the bed. She finally felt a sense of normalcy return and she looked at him with scared eyes. Who was he? How had he gotten into her house? Part of her mind screamed in absolute terror. She should be terrified by this strange man in her bed. This man who explored every part of her body with his hands and mouth. This man who had been inside of her. This couldn't be real. She had to still be dreaming. But she knew she was not. "Are you… real?" The question had to be asked even though she knew the answer.

"Yes," he simply said.

"Who are you?" she asked.

He smiled at her. "Are you sure that is the question you wanted to ask?"

She was quiet for a moment. "What…" she started to say, but did not finish.

"Interesting how one little word in a question makes such a huge difference, don't you think? You of all people should appreciate little things like that." He touched her cheek, gently, lovingly. "Go on, ask it."

She hesitated a moment, but then asked, "What… are you?"

He nodded at her question. "Am I a demon? An incubus?" He smiled as he looked at her. "Do you want me to be?"

The memory of Alan and Sara on the playground flooded back into Miss Jorgan's thoughts. An incubus. A demon who takes women in their sleep. Alan had said he just made Sara go to sleep. He was just practicing, he said. My God, Miss Jorgan thought. Had she actually watched an incubus child practicing what he was going to do as an adult? She shuddered and shook her head violently. "No."

He looked at her with his mesmerizing blue eyes. "Are you certain of your answer?"

The concern did not leave her face.

He reached up and gently caressed her face. "Does this feel like the touch of a demon?"

Miss Jorgan trembled as delicious tremors rumbled through her entire body. "Yes," she said, her voice barely above a whisper. She felt a flood of wetness between her legs, with an aching yearning desire for him to touch her there.

"But you like that, don't you?" His voice was soft, calm, the words coming out in a soothing flow. "It's so… forbidden."

She was quiet, turning her face to feel the full warmth of his hand on her cheek. "Yes," she whispered. "Yes."

"If I really was an incubus, would you still fuck me?"

"Yes," she panted. She turned her face up to his and kissed him hungrily, ravenously. She grabbed his hand and put it over her breast, pressing his fingers, squeezing them so his hand squeezed her breast. She moaned into his mouth as the kiss deepened. She pulled him down to her, kissing him savagely, desperate to feel him inside her.

⊱⋆⊰

"That was you," Miss Jorgan said. She rested her head on his bare chest, lazily stroking his warm flesh. "That was you at the school. That was you behind the mask."

He nodded. "I had to make sure."

"Make sure about what?"

"I had to make sure you would protect them," he said.

Miss Jorgan was quiet for a moment. A test. It had been a test. He wasn't going to hurt any of the children. He just wanted to see how she would react. "So how did I do?" she asked, raising her head to look at him.

He smiled and kissed her cheek. "You did quite

well, Evelyn."

The simple sound of her name coming from his lips sent an orgasmic quiver trembling through her entire body. "So what is it that you want me to do?" Miss Jorgan asked.

"You'd have to quit your job and come with me," he said.

She looked curiously at him, waiting for him to elaborate.

"How would you like to take care of six hundred and sixty five children? It is almost time for them to make their presence known. They will need a mother's guidance and a mother's protection."

Miss Jorgan held herself motionless for a moment, the implications of what he was asking quickly sinking in. She would be a mother. A mother to six hundred and sixty five children. The honor of being chosen overwhelmed her. She felt a powerful wave of pride crest over her. She flung her arms around his neck, her eyes lighting up with happiness. "Oh, yes. Yes, I would love to." She felt a surge of tears flood into the corners of her eyes.

He rubbed her belly and smiled warmly at her. "Plus one."

A flood of happy tears unleashed themselves, raining down Miss Jorgan's cheeks in a salty torrent of joy.

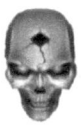

TERRORSTORY #56
BEHEADED

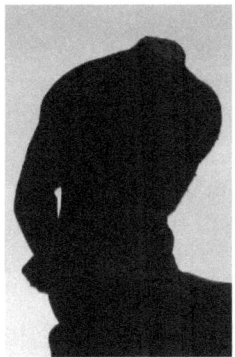

England
1375

Lydia Hetherington stared up at her father's face. His blue eyes were open, staring, but not seeing anything more of this world. His nose was just slightly on the larger size compared to the rest of the men in their village; she knew she had inherited that physical feature from him but that was okay because it was part of what made her distinctly Hetherington. His hair was dark, not quite as dark as charcoal but it was certainly more black than brown, a shade darker than hers. His thick beard covered half his cheeks, his chin and what little she could see of his neck. His lips were surrounded by hair so they were barely visible, but she knew they were as full as hers — no thin-lipped weaklings were in the Hetherington family. She had thought there would be more blood on his face, but then again why should there be? The beheading had been quick, the executioner's strike clean and precise and strong.

The wooden spike upon which her father's head was set was over nine feet high, so she couldn't touch his face. Even if she stood up on her toes and stretched out her arms, she knew she wouldn't be able to reach him and take him off that godforsaken stick of wood upon which he now was stuck.

Yes, he had killed a king's guard and his punishment was fairly meted according to the laws of the village, but the king's guard had humiliated her father and cuckolded him. No Hetherington man could let such a disgrace stand. She understood why he had acted as he did, and she forgave him. But no one else had forgiven him. They still refused to allow her father to be rightly buried in their family's mausoleum at Stormshield Castle. They had already burned his body in a bed of straw and kindling wood and let his ashes be scattered to the four winds. His decapitated head was all that remained of him.

There had been talk of burning his severed head as well, but the villagers were far too afraid to do that. The last man they had burned through and through was said to be still haunting Miller's Tavern near the river; they greatly feared the power of her father's ghost and did not want to bring it forth by putting the torch to his skull. She had not seen the ghost of Miller's Tavern herself, but on two separate occasions she did feel an eerie, unearthly presence near the tavern along the river road. She went out of her way to avoid walking along that path and used the trail through the woods if she needed to reach the river.

Lydia looked back up at her father's head. Tonight, she silently promised him. She would come back in the thick dark of night with a small ladder, or even a step-stool would do, and take him away. She only needed to gain a few extra feet in height to reach her father's head and take it off the spike.

The warlock was ready. She had already paid the price to Ravenon. She touched her womanhood with a gentle probing of her fingers; the tingling discomfort still lingered but the feeling was nowhere as intense as it was while he had taken her.

Archibald Tork stared hard at the Hetherington woman. He was a tall man, broad chested, with long blond hair that flowed down to his wide shoulders. Lydia, he believed she was called. He did not know much of her, but he had seen her in the marketplace a few times buying food and some clothing. He watched her stare with purpose at her father's severed head on the spike. There was cunning behind her eyes. Cunning and a plan. He could sense it. He knew of her father's vile deeds because his own brother had been an innocent victim of his brutality, and he also knew of the fierce Hetherington pride, knew of her extreme displeasure with the elders' decision to disallow her father a proper burial. He fingered the hilt of his sword. There was something brewing in her mind and he was determined to be ready for it.

Lydia held her father's severed head in her hands. She carefully moved off the step-stool, setting one booted foot firmly down on the earth before moving her other foot, clutching his severed head gently. His blue eyes were open, staring blankly. The outrage she felt at the lack of having his full body to bury in their family's sacred ground nearly sent her into paroxysms of rage. She wanted to take her sword and swing it with wild abandon and chop down every village elder by taking out their knees. She felt confident she could sever one leg with one blow, if not both legs, on that spindly old man Tork who led the elders' decision; his feeble legs were nearly as thin as her arms.

"You have no right to that," a voice called out to her from the darkness.

Then a torch was lit, the flickering hot light of the flames revealing the face of Archibald Tork in a fiendish orange-red glow. Two men stood behind him, swords already drawn and in hand, the torchlight flaring on the flesh of their exposed faces.

"You have no right to disgrace the Hetherington name with such vile treatment of a noble man," Lydia countered, her voice tight with rage. She glanced down at her father's head. His blue eyes glowed from the reflected torchlight. She shifted her gaze to her weapons. Her sword was sheathed at her waist, and her two daggers were lodged in place behind the leather belt that encircled her waist.

"Your father was a murderous cur," Archibald said. He raised the torch higher, illuminating his lips as they curled into a sneer. "Proper justice was done."

"My father was defending his name," Lydia said. She gnashed her teeth together. "Would you have not done the same?"

"I would not have been caught in the act," Archibald said, his voice thick with contempt.

Suddenly, the torchlight in Archibald's hand flared up with a nearly blinding white glare and a noxious black smoke billowed out from the top of the torch. The cloud of dark gas quickly engulfed Archibald and the two armed men flanking him. All three men gasped and sputtered for breath, and then within seconds dropped unconscious to the ground. The torch dropped to the ground and rolled a few feet from the fallen men, its flame still burning.

"Don't breathe!" an urgent voice hissed out of the darkness.

Lydia recognized the man's voice and she obeyed his command, pressing her lips tightly shut, tightening up her chest, forcing herself not to take a breath. She clamped a hand over her nose, blocking any flow of air. She felt a strong hand grab her shoulder and steer her away from the fallen men. She kept a firm hold on her father's severed head with her other hand as she moved, gripping it by the hair.

Within moments, they were far clear of the debilitating smoke and she took a deep, desperate breath, sucking air into her lungs through her nose and mouth. She looked over to see Ravenon looking at her with an amused smirk. "What was that?" she asked.

The warlock tapped a small leather pouch tied to the rope sash that encircled his waist. "Sleeping powder," Ravenon said. "Wasn't quite sure how it would react to the flames, but it worked out surprisingly well." The warlock was a short man, only a few inches taller than Lydia's five foot five frame. He was clearly trying to grow a beard but his light brown hair only speckled his face in spotted patches, giving his tanned face a weird patchwork look of light brown fuzz and darker brown flesh. His brown eyes were wide, almost ridiculously so, giving him the innocent look of a sweet child that was in nearly exact contrast to the lustfully shrewd and lascivious young man that he really was.

"So they're not dead?" Lydia asked.

"I don't think so," Ravenon replied. He shrugged. "Not quite sure, really. Never used the sleeping powder that way before. Pretty certain they're just knocked out, though."

Lydia stared at the fallen men in the distance, the torchlight still casting shifting patterns of light and dark over their prone bodies. She looked over to the warlock. "Thank you."

Ravenon reached out his wooden staff and touched it to her crotch. "Just protecting my investment."

"You're a filthy pig," she spat and slapped the staff away from her loins.

"Not really," he said, somewhat casually. "But with the right spell, I could be." He grinned a lascivious grin. He looked down at the severed head Lydia held in her hand. "Shall we get on with it?"

Lydia never liked visiting the Hetherington cemetery. It was a quiet, eerie place. The fall weather, the drab gray sky, the silver-gray clouds, the skeletal charcoal-colored trees, and the slate stone mausoleums didn't contribute any peaceful serenity to the scene. The castle looming in the background with its jutting stone towers and its jagged-tooth crenellations seemed to throw a long shadow over the cemetery no matter what time of day or what month of the year.

Lydia could feel the spirits of Hetheringtons long since dead haunting the area. She never saw them, never heard them; she could just feel their presence like a soft wind rubbing up against her skin with ghostly touches. The fact that she held her father's severed head in her hands heightened her level of unease to an unpleasant extreme. She needed to do what needed to be done and she needed to be quick about it. She was certain remaining in this cemetery for much longer would drive her mad.

"It is ready," Ravenon announced.

She looked over to the warlock to see him pointing his staff at the hole she had dug in the ground earlier. His face was covered in a layer of sweat, the exertion of the spell clearly taking its toll on the young man.

"Place him inside," Ravenon said.

Lydia did as the warlock bid. She moved to the hole and knelt down, gingerly placing her father's head on its side into the dirt-lined pit. His open blue eyes stared blankly up at her.

"Put him in square," Ravenon said. "With his neck down."

Lydia reached into the hole and adjusted her father's head, moving his head to a standing up position so his neck was flat against the ground.

"Cover him up," Ravenon said.

Again, Lydia did as Ravenon instructed her. She gently pushed dirt back into the hole, filling in the gaps around her father's head with loose earth. The dirt quickly reached his mouth, then his nose, then his eyes. Within a few short moments, his entire head was covered in dirt, the hole now completely filled.

"Stand back," Ravenon said.

Lydia rose up and took a step away from the loose patch of dirt underneath which her father's severed head lay.

"One final ingredient is needed to complete the spell," Ravenon said. He set his staff down, leaning it against the thick trunk of a nearby skeletal tree. He untied the rope belt from around his waist and opened his robe, revealing his dangling penis. He gripped his penis and pointed it towards the hole.

Lydia took a step towards him, her face tightening. "You are not going to piss on my father's head," she said, her teeth gritted.

Ravenon turned his head to look at her, his expression amused. "No. I am not." He started to stroke his penis, making it thicken and lengthen. "Come, finish it." He released his hand from his growing erection. "We must seed him with life if you want him to return."

Lydia's teeth remained gritted. Her hand clenched into a fist. She remained where she was, a few steps away from the warlock. Around her, the wind whispered dark whispers as it sighed through the skeletal trees.

Ravenon shrugged. "I can finish it," he said. "But all the spirit energy will come from me and none from you. If that is your desire, then so be it." He re-gripped his cock and started to stroke it again, running his slender fingers up and down the shaft.

Lydia cursed under her breath. She strode forward and pushed his hand away, replacing his fingers with hers around his warm fleshy shaft. She thought she heard Ravenon moan when she gripped him, but she forced herself not to pay attention to the lusty sounds he made as she stroked him. She just wanted to get the deed done as quickly as possible. She stood next to him, looking off into the trees as she moved her fingers up and down over his thickening cock; it became incredibly hard in her hand.

"Put it in your mouth," Ravenon said. "Mix your fluids with mine." His words came out with a slight rasp. "We must make him as strong as he can be."

Lydia froze, her fingers stopping their movement. She looked at Ravenon with narrowed eyes.

He looked back at her with a feverish haze in his eyes. "We must make him strong, Lydia," he said. "We must."

Lydia looked down at the hard cock she held in her hands. There was no stopping now. She had to finish what they had started. She was at the mercy of the warlock. She again cursed under her breath as she moved to her knees before Ravenon. The cold of the ground seeped through her breeches. She hesitated, but only for a moment, and then took the head of his cock into her mouth. This time she was certain she heard Ravenon moan with a lusty moan as her mouth engulfed him. She continued to stroke his shaft, moving her fingers up and down faster and faster as she moved him deeper into her mouth. She pumped him with her mouth and with her hand and he seemed to grow even longer and thicker as she continued to work him. She felt an unwanted tingling between her legs, felt a slick wetness forming, and forced her thoughts away from the sensation.

And then Ravenon suddenly burst into her mouth, sending a hot torrent of his seed spilling into her opening. She nearly gagged on the sudden explosion of salty liquid, but kept her mouth over his erupting member.

"Take it all," Ravenon gasped. "Take it all and then shower it on your father's grave."

She somehow managed to keep stroking him, kept sucking on him, draining him of all his seed.

"Now," he gasped. "Do it now!"

She released her grip on him and pulled her mouth away from his shrinking cock. She immediately turned her head over her father's grave and spit the gooey fluid out over the loose pile of dirt, splattering the earth with the warlock's fluids and her saliva. She finished expelling the fluids from her mouth and wiped at her lips with the back of her hand. A soft chuckling sound gave her pause. She stopped mid-wipe and looked up to see Ravenon smiling down at her.

"Oh, my dear Lydia, you are a source of such joy," Ravenon said. There was a hint of devilish mirth lacing his grin.

She glanced back down at the dirt, at the wet smear of fluids darkening the soil, then looked back up at Ravenon. "That wasn't part of the spell, was it?"

Ravenon shook his head. "But it couldn't hurt." He gave a soft laugh and a gentle shrug.

"You lousy bastard," Lydia snarled. "My debt to you is paid." She spit savagely, angrily wiping at her mouth. She rose to her feet and glared at Ravenon, balling her hand into a fist.

Ravenon closed his robe and tied off the rope belt, unperturbed by her outburst. "My dear Lydia. Your debt is paid when I tell you it's paid." His mirthful grin vanished as his eyes darkened. "I have given you a great gift. One that has tremendous debt attached to it."

"Gifts don't require payment. Don't call it a gift."

Ravenon waved his slender fingers. "We won't call it a gift then." He paused. "I performed a great service for you. One that has a very high price."

Lydia glanced down at the stained patch of inert dirt. "So far, I'm not impressed." She turned her head to the side and spit, again wiping at her mouth with the back of her hand.

"You will be," Ravenon said, his voice full of absolute assurance. "You will be."

And he was right.

Lydia wasn't quite sure how her father had managed to extricate himself from the hole in the ground, but there he stood. She had left the cemetery to get some rest in Stormshield Castle, and when she had returned to the cemetery her father was standing next to the pit. The hole was much bigger now, deeper, mounds of dirt pushed aside all around its circumference. He had somehow climbed out of the pit, digging and clawing and pushing himself up.

She stared at him with a growing sense of awe. He was a magnificent man-creature made of mud and stone and leaves and roots. She couldn't quite call him a man because he no longer had a human body. His upper arms and forearms were comprised of tightly compressed mud and rock, forming a very hard surface. The elbow joints were comprised of a tightly woven cluster of roots, giving him the flexibility of movement of a human arm. His legs had a similar appearance, the roots criss-crossing his legs looking like bulging veins. Lydia looked at his hands. His fingers were comprised of more mud and stone, highly compressed to mimic the function of bone. His finger joints were comprised of more of the roots, each stone finger having the same flexibility as that found on a human hand. She was thankful that no... root... jutted out where his penis had once been. Now that area was just a smooth patch of mud.

She reached up with a cloth and gently wiped away the dirt from his cheeks and his forehead. She knew her father was within because she could see that familiar spark in his blue eyes. Ravenon had done as he had promised. He had returned her father from the other side. He had brought him back from death. "Hello, Father," she said.

William Hetherington tilted his head to look down at his daughter. He opened his mouth to speak, but no words came out. He had no vocal cords from which to form words, no lungs in which to suck in the air he needed to use for speech.

Lydia immediately saw the discomfort in his eyes, the confusion. She reached up and put her fingers over his cracked lips. "It's okay. You don't need to speak. But you understand me, yes?" She lowered her hand from his bearded mouth.

He nodded his head. He opened and closed his mouth, then pointed frantically at his dried lips.

"You're hungry?" Lydia asked.

He shook his head. He mimicked grabbing a mug and taking a drink, his movements jerky and hesitant as he grappled with his new body.

Lydia nodded at his gesture. "I have some wine in my pouch," she said. She unshouldered her bota bag and uncorked the leather-bound drinking container.

She raised the wine bag to his lips, gave the pouch a gentle squeeze and poured some of the red wine over his lips.

William lapped at the cool liquid eagerly, swallowing a mouthful of the wine, but then quickly gagged and spit out the rest of the red liquid, making a foul face. He shook his head harshly at his daughter. He pointed again at his lips with his root finger, jabbing his finger towards his mouth. He formed a word on his dry, cracked lips even though no sound came out - *water*.

"Go to the stream," Lydia said, pointing at the low hill behind William.

William nodded. He turned his mud-rock-root body and headed for the small hill, passing several Hetherington family tombstones as he moved awkwardly in his new body.

Lydia followed him to the stream, staying quiet as he reached the water. He knelt down, moving clumsily as he continued to adjust to his new body, and scooped up a few handfuls of water into his cupped hands. He drank deeply and Lydia could see the mud-stone layer of his new skin darken as the moisture seeped through him. She knew it wasn't skin that covered his body now, but she didn't know what else to think of it as. After a few more mouthfuls of water, William rose back up and turned to face his daughter.

"Do you remember?" she asked him.

He frowned.

"Do you remember who did this to you? Do you remember who was the cause of this misery to our family? Do you remember who shamed our family name? It's time for them to pay," Lydia said.

William Hetherington kept his moistened lips tight and clenched his jaw.

The air was abuzz with excitement. The annual archery tournament was all set to begin. Valentine Quinn was the local champion, and the favorite to win again as he had won the last three years in a row. He could wield a longbow as adeptly as others could handle a hunting bow; his massive right arm bulged with corded muscles, giving him powerful draw strength.

Lydia watched her father ready himself. They were hidden in the deep shadows of the towering trees that flanked the archery range. He bent down to the ground and picked up a fallen leaf. He cupped the leaf in both hands, then pressed his palms tightly together, squeezing the leaf between them. He stood that way for a moment, completely frozen, then released the pressure, separating his hands. The leaf lay flat in his left palm, but it no longer appeared to be a simple flimsy leaf. The leaf had a hardness to it, what looked like a metallic sheen. Lydia could see that it had sharp edges, edges she was quite certain were so sharp that they would cut her eyes if she stared at them too long.

Her father handed the hardened leaf to her and Lydia gingerly pinched it between two fingers, being very careful not to let the sharp edges touch her. She stared down at the object in her hand; it reminded her of an arrow head, but with many tips instead of just one.

Her father stood very still and she could see the tightness in his mud-skinned face as he concentrated on whatever task he was trying to perform. His left hand trembled as a root-like string emerged from the edge of his thumb, shooting across the gap between his thumb and forefinger to sink into the side of his forefinger. Lydia immediately realized what it was. It was some sort of bowstring. He had made a slingshot type device using his thumb and his forefinger as the yoke supports, and the roots for the bands. He stared at the slingshot his body had just created, turning his hand this way and that to study the device, tugging at the roots. Satisfied, he looked over to Lydia and she handed him back the shuriken-like leaf.

They waited and watched the tournament, patiently waiting for Valentine to ready himself. His name was finally called and he assumed his firing position, turning slightly sideways to line up his shot. He knocked his arrow and drew back his bow, his muscles bulging with the effort to pull back the string.

William put the hardened leaf into position, fitting an edge against the root string. He drew back the root bands, raising his hand to line up his shot.

Valentine released his grip on the arrow, loosing his shot. The arrow soared through the air and all eyes in the gathered crowd followed the arrow's flight.

William released his hold on the string, letting the sharp-edged leaf loose, the projectile's release accompanied by a faint whoosh and a snapping pop of the root bands.

Valentine's arrow soared through the air, beginning its descending arc, heading straight for the target.

The leaf spun madly as it whipped through the air, heading straight for its target.

Valentine's arrow struck the target, landing within the red circle just near the top edge of the red.

The crowd erupted into cheers and triumphant exclamations.

The spiky leaf-arrow struck, slicing through Valentine's throat, cutting through his windpipe. A torrent of blood erupted from the gash in his neck, spraying the warm crimson liquid all over his chest and his bow.

Lydia watched dispassionately as Valentine Quinn fell to the ground, gurgling and gasping as he clutched at his gushing throat. She turned to see her father already walking away deeper into the shadows, the manufactured slingshot reabsorbed back into his body as if it had never existed at all.

The sounds of the cheering crowd faded away, replaced by the sounds of shrill screams. Valentine Quinn's winning streak was at an end.

"How did he know?" Lydia asked. "How did he know how to find Quinn so easily and so quickly? How did he know he would be at the tournament?"

"The worms," Ravenon said.

Lydia waited for him to continue, but the warlock did not elaborate. She turned her hands palms up, jerking her head slightly towards him, egging him on.

"He listens to the worms," Ravenon said. They were inside Castle Stormshield, sitting in the Great Hall before the hearth. A low fire burned in the stone hearth, the heat radiating out to warm her hands. Her father sat far away from the heat, sitting motionless in a dark corner. The heat made him uncomfortable, drying out his body, causing him to ache with thirst, so he avoided the flames as much as possible.

Lydia frowned at the warlock.

"The worms. The worms listen," Ravenon said.

The frown lines in her forehead deepened.

"Your father is listening to the worms. They tell him many things. They are his spies," Ravenon said. "They are everywhere. No one can hide from them. You must listen to them as well. They will tell you what you need to know."

"Worms? I must listen to worms?" She shook her head softly, confusion obvious in her expression. She sipped at her warm ale and looked at the dancing flames as they licked at the air above the crackling wood.

Ravenon nodded. "They pick up the vibrations of movement and sound. When someone moves, when someone speaks, they leave a trail. Even a whisper will leave a falling trail of sound that strikes the earth. Even a soft step will make the ground tremble to a worm, even though the step be ever so slight. The worms pick up the sounds, the vibrations. They store them, then bring them to your father."

"Worms speak to my father?"

Ravenon gave an exasperated sigh. "No, worms can't speak, Lydia. They don't have little speech-making mouths. They don't understand the sounds. They just capture them and bring them back to your father. He has to listen through them all, decipher them, figure out which ones are important or not." Ravenon looked off to her father sitting in the dark shadows. "They have brought him hundreds of messages already. Most of them are useless, but obviously a few of them have proven themselves to be very valuable." He rubbed at a patch of hair on his chin. "Very valuable indeed."

"And how am I supposed to… listen to these

worms?" Lydia asked.

"I can show you…" He purposefully let his voice trail off.

Lydia nodded her head, exhaling an exasperated breath. "Yes, I know. For a price."

Ravenon let the corner of his mouth curl up.

Lydia leaned back in her chair and the glow from the fire burning in the hearth washed over her, shining across the swell of her ample bosom as her breasts pressed against her tunic.

"Are your nipples hard?" the warlock asked.

She turned to scowl deeply at him. "What?"

He pointed to her chest with his staff. "Your nipples. They're hard as pebbles." He looked at the fire, then back to her. "It can't be because you're cold."

Lydia glanced down at her breasts.

Ravenon looked at her. "You *want* to pay the price," he said.

"You're a pig," she said and turned away.

"You *like* paying the price."

Lydia said nothing. She sipped at her ale.

"You *are* your mother's daughter," he said and laughed.

Lydia clenched her fist and took a swing at Ravenon's head. He easily dodged the blow, pulling back away from her strike. The force of her swinging fist and the lack of a solid object to stop her momentum caused Lydia to topple out of her chair. She dropped her mug and the ale splashed across the rushes that covered the hard packed dirt floor. She fell to the floor, her arm scraping against the rushes. Ravenon stared down at her with an amused expression. One of her breasts had fallen out of her tunic, the full orb of her flesh and her hardened brown nipple quite visible. "You really need to stop throwing yourself at me, Lydia." He leaned closer down to her and whispered, "What will the villagers think?" He leaned back.

Lydia gave him a look of disgust and moved back to her chair, her face reddened with angry embarrassment.

Ravenon pointed to her exposed breast with the tip of his staff.

She glanced down and then angrily stuffed her breast back into her tunic.

"Damn, you arouse me, woman!" Ravenon barked. He stood up and whirled away from her. He immediately saw that her father was gone; the area where William had been sitting was now empty and unoccupied. He turned back to Lydia. "Where has he gone?"

Lydia frowned at him.

Ravenon thrust his staff in the direction of the empty corner. "Your father. Where has he gone?"

Lydia immediately got to her feet and raced out of the room.

William hadn't gotten far. They reached him just as he walked beneath the raised portcullis and stepped onto the lowered drawbridge. Lydia kept pace just behind him. She glanced down into the brackish waters of the moat that surrounded the castle as they traversed the drawbridge, then looked back to her father. The dark blanket of the night had begun to descend, blackening the horizon.

"Where is he going?" Lydia asked.

Ravenon walked beside Lydia, his staff thumping on the surface of the drawbridge as he brought it down with each step of his right foot. "He was listening to the worms. That's why he was sitting so still in the castle. They clearly brought him some more information of great import."

"He's heading for the village," Lydia said. "One of them must be there." She paused. "Another one of the six."

Ravenon nodded. "He certainly moves with purpose."

They walked on in silence, trailing her father. "I am sorry for my rude comment," Ravenon said softly. "You are nothing like your mother."

Lydia hesitated, but did not miss a step. She kept walking, keeping her gaze focused up ahead on her father's back. "You're still a pig."

"You can't be here," Olred Skergard said, his eyes wide, his words barely eking out of his mouth in a tight gasp. He was a big man, a burly man, so the fright visible in his brown eyes was a very rare thing to see. His ruddy face, singed a permanent red from his constant exposure to the blazing forge he worked near seven days a week, was covered with a sheen of nervous sweat. "You're dead," Olred said. "I saw you die."

Lydia could see her father concentrating, could see the tightness in his face as he stood at the entrance to the blacksmith's work area. Her father's arm trembled, as if struck by an earthquake. Not his entire body, just his arm. She could see movement beneath the muddy layer of what comprised his new flesh, something burrowing through the densely packed dirt. She saw a hint of whiteness appear, breaking the skin like the fin of a shark breaking the surface of the ocean, but then it was gone, disappearing beneath the dark brown dirt. She saw more movement, more quick flashes of white, and then some brown flashes, then gray. They were rocks. That is what she had seen moving beneath his mud-skin. He was shifting them through his body, moving them into place in his hand, transforming his hand, turning it into a hand that looked like it was bejeweled with a hundred rocks, turning it into what she knew was about to be a very deadly weapon. A hammering fist made of stone.

Olred had a hammer of his own that he used to pound the molten metal he worked on into its desired shape. He hefted the heavy tool and swung it at William, hitting him solidly in the stomach, but the effect was like punching a fist into a densely solid packed patch of earth. A few specks of dirt flecked off William's body where the hammer struck it and he took one staggered step back, but Olred's blow had very little effect.

William swung his stone fist and connected solidly with Olred's chin. Bone crunched and flesh shredded as the coarse rock slammed into the blacksmith's face. Olred dropped to his knees, dazed by the mighty blow. Then he fell forward, his head landing square atop the anvil that was situated near the blazing forge.

It took four blows from her father's pounding stone fist before Olred's brains and blood fully spilled down the sides of his anvil, the blood and brain matter hardly visible against the black metal of the anvil, but very visible when they hit the earthen floor, the firelight from the forge illuminating the fluids in an orange-red glow. Scattered pieces of skull, some still with strands of Olred's hair attached, littered the floor all around the anvil.

That was now three men down. Three others to go.

Six had to die. And then her father could finally rest. The archer and the blacksmith had been taken care of. The butcher and a charcoal man remained. The fool of a king's guard was already dead, slain by her father's blade. Lydia did not know how the men knew each other, nor did she care. She only knew that their drunken debauchery had led them to commit their vile deed, and for that heinous act they all had to die. Only then would her father be avenged, only then would her family's honor be restored.

Lydia thought back to that horrible, fateful day, the images forcing themselves back to the forefront of her thoughts as they walked back to the castle. Four men had held her mother down on the bed, each one clutching a wrist or an ankle, spreading her wide so Gregor Tork could mount her and thrust into her. His gaudy, brightly colored clothes lay on the floor in a jumbled heap of bright red, yellow, and blue fabric. His Fool's hat, woven in the same three colors that comprised his clothes, was still atop his head, a jingle bell attached to each of the three pointed tips. His mock scepter, a long wooden staff with a crude likeness of Gregor Tork's own face carved into its head, lay on the floor, its tip wet with her mother's fluids. It was a sign of Gregor's deeply sick depravity that he enjoyed dressing as a Fool, despite being a member of the king's guard.

She remembered her father standing motionless in the doorway, as if paralyzed by the wanton display of lust happening before his very eyes. Lydia had stood behind William, gaping unbelievably at the disgusting scene.

She remembered the hideous Fool's hat flopping about Gregor's head as he thrust into her mother, the jangling noises of the tiny bells sounding like deafening clangs in her ears. "Do you like watching your wife get fucked by a fool?" Gregor asked, his mouth forming a hideous leering grin. His pale buttocks pumped back and forth. The bells continued to jangle. "She likes it. Don't you, Paulina?"

"Yes," her mother had gasped. "Fuck me, you fool," she said in a panting breath. And then she laughed a horrible laugh.

That's when Lydia ran, when she heard her mother's awful laugh, when she realized her mother was a willing participant in the lewd activity.

The horrid peal of the jangling bells chased after her.

And then she had heard the fighting, the clanging of swords, the angry exchange of voices, the harsh threats. And then came that silence. She remembered that awful silence. It was a disconcerting silence that had blanketed everything, a silence she learned later that was triggered when Gregor Tork's severed head fell to the floor. The silence had seemed to linger for hours, but she knew it had only been a matter of seconds before the screaming started. Her mother's screams echoed in the hallways, careening off the stone walls of the castle.

They had stabbed her father in the fight, but had not killed him. They bound him and brought him before the magistrate. The sentence was immediate and simple. There were five witnesses to the incident. Five cries of guilty. Five cries of murderer. William Hetherington had been sentenced to die by the executioner's blade for killing Gregor Tork. The sentence had been carried out the next day.

Five voices had cried out against her father. Five voices had shamed him. Five voices needed to be silenced forever so her father could rest in peace.

Lydia was pretty certain he would save her mother for last.

William staggered and hit the wall of the Great Hall, his shoulder shedding some loose dirt as he struck the interior stone wall of the castle.

"What's wrong with him?" Lydia asked.

William stumbled again, this time falling awkwardly to one knee, nearly toppling over.

Ravenon shrugged. "He weakens."

"He weakens?"

Ravenon nodded. "Yes, he weakens. Nothing lasts forever. Not even my magic. And this new body won't last forever, either. Not matter how much magic I put into it."

"Make him strong again," Lydia said. "We're not finished."

Ravenon looked at her. "There is a price."

Lydia waved her hand impatiently. "Yeah, yeah, let's get to it." She grabbed Ravenon by the wrist and started pulling him towards the stairwell that led to the upper bedrooms.

Ravenon looked surprised for a moment, then very pleased. He let himself be led up the stairs.

"How long will his strength last?" Lydia asked. She looked over to her father as he sat in the shadows of the far corner in the Great Hall.

"It depends on how much energy he expels. The less he moves, the less active he is, the longer his strength will last."

"Well, he needs to move," Lydia said. "We have things to get done."

Ravenon nodded.

"How many times can you… strengthen him?" she asked.

"As many times as you earn," Ravenon said. He readjusted himself beneath his breeches. "Why don't you send him out foraging for herbs?" he suggested.

"Funny."

"He can help chop some firewood."

"You just going to keep going?" Lydia asked, not amused.

Ravenon smiled, trying not to put a leer onto his lips. "He can chase after some deer and hunt us down a hearty meal."

She reached up and patted Ravenon on the cheek. "Enjoy it while you can." At least Ravenon had been more gentle with her this time, she thought. Almost, dare she think it, tender. She felt a pleasant, but very unwanted, tingling in her body as she touched his face.

"What do you want of me?" Charles asked.

Lydia stared at the butcher. He held a cleaver in his trembling hand. Charles Dougherty was a short

225

man, slight of build. He had moppy brown hair that kept falling in front of his eyes, which for a butcher, Lydia thought, would be an unwanted distraction.

William pointed to the large black kettle that was situated on a hook over a burning flame in a nearby fireplace.

Charles shook his head as his hand continued to tremble. "No," he said. "No. You can't ask that of me."

William thrust his pointing finger at the kettle, anger very evident in his face, his brow knitted, his teeth clenched, and then turned to thrust his finger at the man strapped to the table next to them. The man on the table was Robert Jorvan. He was a fueller, a charcoal man, known for making and selling charcoal to those who lived on lands without an abundance of wood to create their own. He was dressed in breeches and a tunic, his clothes discolored by sooty streaks. His hands and exposed arms were smeared with black streaks, an ever-present stain from handling the charcoal products he made and sold.

By chance, Lydia and her father had encountered two more of the men they were looking for within the butcher's shop. But then she quickly realized it most likely hadn't been by chance. The worms had undoubtedly told her father that both men would be there at the same time. Robert had been visiting Charles, bringing him a fresh supply of charcoal for his kitchen. It had been quite simple to subdue Robert, a meek man with no fighting abilities of any kind. Lydia had held Charles at bay with a sword tip at his neck while her father had tied Robert down to the table.

Charles continued to shake his head. "No. No."

Lydia raised her sword and touched the tip to Charles's neck. "Do it."

"I'll hang for it," Charles said, protesting weakly.

"No you won't," Lydia said. "You have my word."

"I…" Charles began, but paused. "I… don't know where to start…" He gagged.

William leaned over Robert and grabbed at his tunic, yanking it open with a savage rip.

Lydia looked away from Robert and back to Charles. "Let's start with a little breast meat."

Robert did smell delicious, Lydia had to admit despite herself. It smelled like a hearty beef stew was brewing in the pot. She had no desire to taste it, none at all, but the concoction brewing in the black kettle did give off a tantalizing aroma. She looked over to Charles. "Time to eat," she said.

"No," Charles said. "You can't make me eat him. No."

Lydia shook her head. "Oh, you're not going to eat *him*."

William reached a stony hand beneath the kettle and plucked out a burning charcoal, holding the burning hot ember between two of his stone-tipped fingers. The lump of charcoal glowed a devilish red.

"See. I promised you you wouldn't hang," Lydia said.

Father saved Mother for last. Lydia not spoken to her since the execution. Her mother had kept herself in her room in the castle, only allowing the servants to bring her food and bathe her and switch out her chamber pots.

Lydia knew it had to be done. It saddened her, but Mother had been a willing participant in the humiliation. Her ire at her father had grown over the years, the anger at his neglect, at his lack of affection. She had grown more and more needy, more and more desperate for his attention, which had only driven him farther away. Lydia had tried to comfort her mother over the years, but her mother seemed not to care for her affection; she was only desperate for her husband's attention and affection. The screaming, the crying, the fighting, had escalated over the years until it had driven her mother to acts of desperation, culminating in that horrible night.

He was merciful and Lydia thought that was just for her sake. Her father clamped his dirt-hand over her mother's mouth as she lay sleeping in her bed and held it there, suffocating her to death, turning the closeness she wanted into the cause of her demise.

And so it was done. Justice had been served. It was time for her father to rest. Ravenon admitted that his mud-and-root body would only last a few more days at the most anyway.

They were in the Hetherington cemetery, near the hole they had dug out earlier. A soft wind blew through the skeletal trees, still whispering its unknowable whispers. William sat motionless on a large rock nearby. His face looked haggard, exhaustion clearly evident across his gaunt features. His lips were dry, severely cracked.

"It's time to rest, Father," Lydia said.

William nodded a very tired nod. He reached out

and squeezed his daughter's hand, mouthing a silent goodbye.

"Goodbye." Lydia refused to let tears fall. She had already grieved for her father and did not want the despair to resurface, especially not here in the gloom of the Hetherington burial grounds. She kissed his cheek. Then she placed her hands on either side of his head and pressed tight against his ears, getting a firm grip on him. She removed her father's head from his mud body, tugging at it gently at first, but then needing to pull with more vigor to wrestle it free. The head came free with a wet, suction-slurping sound as she disengaged it from the mud and stone and leaves that had comprised his supernatural body. The earthen body seemed to melt away, splashing across the rock, dissolving back into the earth from whence it had come, leaving a dark stain on the ground. Within moments, there was only a smear of dark earth to mark the spot where the mud body had been sitting on the rock, and then even the dark patch on the ground faded away as the remains of the body mingled with the earth.

Lydia entered the mausoleum, clutching her father's head with both hands. A torch blazed in a sconce positioned on the stone wall of the building, throwing a fiery light across the gloomy interior. A marble pedestal was positioned at the far back wall of the room and she walked towards it, her booted feet echoing very faintly against the polished stone floor. She reached the marble pedestal and gingerly set her father's head down atop it. His eyes stared at her as she fixed the position of the head, making sure it stayed upright when she released her hold on it. She took a few steps back after she was certain the head would remain in place on the pedestal. For a brief moment, she thought she saw a glimmer of life in her father's face, but she knew it was probably just the torchlight reflecting off his eyes.

She looked up to see Ravenon standing in the doorway to the mausoleum, gripping his wooden staff in one hand, holding his other hand out to her. She knew she should be outraged by his lusty manipulative behavior, but she also knew Archibald Tork was still out there, and she knew that the entire Tork family would prove to be dangerous foes. She would need help at keeping them at bay.

Lydia looked back to her father's head and then to Ravenon. "Won't insects… eat him?"

Ravenon shook his head. "No, just the opposite. They will cleanse him. They will keep the scavengers away from him. They will nourish him, keep his skin clean. My spells will see to that."

Lydia looked back to her father's head. A worm slowly wiggled its way across his cheek, gliding along his flesh. As if in verification of Ravenon's claim, the worm did not leave a trail of smudge or dirty slime on her father's face; it left a trail of vibrant pink skin on his cheek just above the level of his beard, skin that looked glowing and healthy.

"Of course, I'll need to constantly replenish the power of the spell," Ravenon said as he looked at her.

Lydia nodded. "Once a day, I hope," she said. She accepted her current situation and understood what needed to be done. She needed Ravenon. She needed his power. She might as well learn to enjoy it as much as he did.

Ravenon's face filled with surprise, then supreme delight. He nodded. "Oh, once a day at least." He smiled at her.

Lydia smiled softly back at Ravenon. She turned her attention back to her father's head resting on the pedestal, staring into his blue eyes. "I'll call upon you when I need you," Lydia said. "Which might be very soon." She reached out and gently slid her father's eyelids down over his blue eyes.

Once it was all done, she felt an emptiness inside of her. Was that it? Wasn't she supposed to feel something more? Some elation? A feeling of triumphant satisfaction? Justice had been done in her mind, but it left her feeling more sad than elated. She didn't want to feel sad. The sadness made her angry. It made her want to mete out more justice. Injustice needed to be destroyed. Injustice needed to be beheaded. She stared at her father's severed head. And now she had the power to correct the world. Now she had the power to balance the scales of justice. She looked at Ravenon. "Teach me about the worms," she said.

"Right here?"

Lydia nodded. "Right now."

The first worm that crawled into her ear nearly made Lydia vomit with the extreme discomfort it caused her. It felt cold and slimy against her flesh as it wriggled its way around the curves of her ear, seeking entrance. It found the opening and squirmed its way deeper inside her. She anticipated a searing flash of pain within her ear as the slimy thing moved, but that did not happen. Instead she felt a wave of nausea strike at the pit of her stomach as the spineless creature penetrated deeper and deeper into her head.

And then the sounds started in her head. Mumblings and shrill shouts, whisperings and loud outbursts, soft padding noises, loud pounding thumps, all of the sounds jumbling together in a cacophony of unintelligible discordant noises. She squeezed her eyes shut, clamping her hands over her ears, but that did nothing to mute the pounding sonic assault on her brain.

"Concentrate," she heard Ravenon say. "Just pick out one stream of sound and concentrate on it."

She forced herself to be calm, forced herself to focus, forced herself to pick out one stream of sound and concentrate on it. The sounds started to clarify in her head. She could hear voices, could hear the words forming. She continued to focus, concentrating on this one stream of sound. Yes, it was voices. Not her inner voice. Not the remembered voices of others from past conversations. These were voices speaking as if in the same room with her. She recognized one of the voices immediately as the sounds solidified into intelligible words. It was the voice of Archibald Tork, along with another man's voice she did not recognize.

"She has no right to it. We cannot let this stand."

"Leave her be. Hasn't she suffered enough?"

"No, she has not. Not after what she did to me and my men."

"So that's it? You can't bear to suffer the humiliation this woman caused you?"

"No, I cannot."

"Then it appears you and her are quite alike, does it not? Both unable to bear the humiliation without resorting to extreme means of finding justice for yourselves."

"I am nothing like that vile bitch."

"Hmmm. Isn't that what sparked this entire unpleasant affair with the Hetheringtons? Humiliation? You all need to repudiate what others think of you. Then none of this would matter."

"It matters. In fact, nothing else matters."

"And that is why you will fall."

"I will not fall."

"Then see it through to the end. Do what you think needs to be done and rid yourself of this blinding obsession. You obviously won't be able to think a rational thought until you bring it to a resolution that satisfies you."

"I'll crucify her. In the public square. Right next to where they sliced off her father's head."

"What did you hear?" Ravenon asked as the glazed-over look faded from Lydia's eyes.

"Archibald Tork," Lydia said. She fought back a wave of discomfort, squinting and scrunching up her facial features. "He has vowed to come after me." She bent over, trying to mentally will the nauseous feeling away.

Ravenon frowned and pursed his lips as he looked down at the bent over woman. He reached down to Lydia's ear and gently eased the departing worm from her ear, softly tugging at it. The worm quickly died upon its departure from Lydia's head, its thin, narrow body hanging down limply from the warlock's fingers as he raised it up to look at it. Ravenon glanced about the area, saw a torch burning in a sconce on the wall several dozen feet away. He tossed the dead worm at the flames, but missed. The worm hit the stone wall and splattered against the hard rock. He quickly looked away.

Lydia straightened up and looked at Ravenon. She

extended her hand out to him, allowing him to take her fingers into his. She started to leave with the warlock, but then disengaged her hand from his and turned back to face the room. She moved back to the pedestal, the clack of her boots softly echoing in the large space. "You want me Archibald Tork? Come and get me." Lydia Hetherington stared down at her father's face, and then gently slid his eyelids back open. She knew she had just sent him off to rest, but she also knew he would not hesitate to return if she needed his help.

She turned back to Ravenon. "Let's go make some magic," she said.

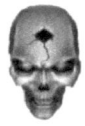

TERRORSTORY #57
HOLD YOUR BREATH

"Hold your breath," Bonnie Lorris said. She gripped the steering wheel a little tighter and avoided looking at the cemetery as they passed the black-gated graveyard. Bonnie was in her late-thirties with curly brown hair, a soft dimple in her cheeks, and just a hint of a cleft in her chin. Out of the corner of her vision, she barely registered the thick trees starting their color shift into the oranges and reds and browns of the fall. Nor did she pay much attention to the slightly rolling hills, or the sea of grey tombstones of all different shapes and sizes that dotted the grassy expanse, or the large mausoleum in the far back corner of the cemetery.

Had she looked a little closer at the cemetery, Bonnie would have seen that a casket was slowly being lowered into the ground, the metal box descending deeper into the gaping wound a mini-excavator had just ripped into the earth for this purpose. The gravesite was surrounded by dozens of people, but they were not there to pay their respects. None of the onlookers were sad or forlorn. They were all angry, their faces filled with a silent rage, furious that such a man was even allowed a Christian burial. He had been no Christian. But Bonnie didn't notice any of these things because even the thought of looking at a cemetery made her irrationally nervous.

Trevor Sinclair grinned at his two buddies in the back seat of the car. Trevor was a goofy looking kid with a goofy smile, a ginger with a big nose and teeth that seemed to be too big for his mouth. All three of the boys were sitting in the back seat, leaving the passenger seat in the front open and unoccupied. They all privately referred to Mrs. Lorris as their personal chauffeur but they never let her in on that little secret. George and Max had their mouths clamped shut, exaggerating their determination to keep them closed with tight-pressed lips.

George Lorris knew that look on Trevor's face, knew that it meant Trevor was seriously contemplating doing something stupid, something that would either annoy his mom or provoke him and Max into a big groaning match. Or both. George had brown curly hair very similar to his mother's but much shorter, and he shared the same dimples and the soft cleft in his chin.

Max Sternberg knew the look on Trevor's face,

too. He shook his head at Trevor, his eyes scowling. Max was a gangly kid with black hair, taller than the others and far more physically awkward because of his recent growing spurt. He sat on the far left in the back seat, directly behind Bonnie.

The concerned looks on the faces of his friends was all Trevor needed. Every time one of his friends expressed their disapproval of his imminent behavior, an automatic green light to proceed went off in his head. He smirked at them, turned to face the cemetery, opened his mouth, and took a deep breath.

Bonnie just happened to glance into the rearview mirror at the exact moment Trevor took his deep inhale. A tightness surged up into her throat. "Trevor!" she shouted. She involuntarily glanced out the passenger side window toward the cemetery and saw the casket being lowered into the ground.

"Mom!" George shouted, pointing urgently out the front windshield.

Bonnie turned her gaze forward but didn't react fast enough. The car's automatic braking system kicked in, bringing the car to a screeching halt before it slammed into the back of a garbage truck. Everyone was thrust sharply forward from the sudden deceleration, especially George who was sitting in the middle seat, but everyone's seat belt held tight, keeping them all safe and secure.

Bonnie breathed in sharply, her breath coming in quick little bursts. She glanced up into the rearview mirror. "You boys okay? Georgie, you okay?"

"Yeah, jeez, Mom," George said. He tugged at his seat belt where it had dug into his abdomen.

She turned in her seat to look over the back seat at Trevor. "Why did you do that, Trevor? You know you're not supposed to take a breath when passing a cemetery. Especially not a deep one."

"That's just a silly old wives' tale," Trevor said.

"You callin' Mrs. Lorris a silly old wife?" Max asked of Trevor.

Trevor glared at Max, then grinned his goofy grin.

Max looked at Bonnie. "No offense, Mrs. Lorris. I don't think you're old."

George nudged Max in the ribs.

"Or silly," Max quickly added. He rubbed at his ribs, frowning at George. "Or silly."

Bonnie continued to frown deeply at Trevor, staring at him over the back seat.

"What are they doing?" Trevor asked as he stared out the passenger window at the cemetery and the activity playing out at the gravesite.

"They're paying their respects," Bonnie answered.

"I don't think so," Trevor said, shaking his head.

"Why do you say that?" Bonnie asked.

"They're spitting into the grave," Trevor said. He leaned closer to the window to get a better look at the fascinatingly morbid scene of people gathered around the open grave.

"What?" Max said, trying to see around George and Trevor to get a look out the passenger side window in the back seat.

"They're walking up to the grave and spitting into it," Trevor said. "I just saw two guys do that, and a lady."

"Spitting?" Max asked.

"Yeah, spitting," Trevor said. "They walked right up to the edge of the grave, looked down into it and spit." Trevor pointed out the window. "Look, that guy just did it."

Bonnie turned in her seat to look out the passenger side window at the cemetery. And at that same moment, several of the funeral onlookers stepped forwards towards the edge of the grave, and then spit into the open grave. Bonnie continued to stare, her mind outraged by the desecration of the poor dead person being buried. Who deserved such a horrible response at their own funeral? What did they do to deserve such an ugly reaction?

"You guys realize you're *all* breathing right now, right?" Trevor said as he pointed at the cemetery filling their views right outside their windows.

Max clamped his hand over his nose and mouth, his eyes widening.

A horn honked loudly behind them.

Bonnie started in her seat, gripping the steering wheel tightly. She put one hand to her chest. "Shit," she exhaled in a muttering breath. She stared at the dashboard, forcing herself to calm the pounding of her heart.

"Mom," George said, pointing forward out the front windshield. "You can go."

Bonnie lifted her head to look forward and saw that the road was empty and clear before them, the stoplight up ahead green. She glanced one more time at the cemetery, at the depressing funeral taking place within its gated environs, decided that holding her breath was still a good option, then hit the accelerator and drove on.

⟪·❊·⟫

"World domination!" George growled, his voice deep and gravelly. He raised his clenched fist and pounded it down on the table, the vibration sending

241

the game pieces on the Risk game board scattering in all directions.

Trevor leaned back in the chair where he sat opposite George on the other side of the kitchen table. "Whoa, dude. Don't be such a sore winner."

Max grinned behind his hand, covering his mouth with his fingers.

The guttural voice coming out of her son's mouth shocked Bonnie to the very core of her being. The sound immediately reminded her of Linda Blair in the Exorcist movie. It was a movie she could never bring herself to fully watch from beginning to end. She had only seen tiny bits and pieces of it. It just freaked her out too much to watch the whole thing. "George," Bonnie called at her son, disapproval clearly evident in her tone as she turned away from the tray full of chocolate chip cookies she had just pulled out of the oven to frown at him.

George continued with the deep, growling voice. "My empire spans the globe!"

"I think he's possessed," Trevor said, trying to put concern into his voice, but not doing a very good job of it. Trevor waved his hand in front of his nose, as if wiping away a nasty smell. "Pew, he's got cemetery breath."

"You pitiful mortals stand no chance against me!" George raised his fist on high again.

"George!" Bonnie shouted. She set the hot tray of cookies down on the stove and shook off the oven mitt with a violent shake of her arm.

George slowly turned to look at his mother, letting a look of complete innocence overtake his face. "Yes, Mommy?"

"Knock it off," Bonnie snapped.

George glowered, squinting his eyes, pursing his lips. The deep guttural voice returned. "Do not fear, three times divorced mother of an only child, you shall be saved."

"Cut the shit," Bonnie said curtly. "It's not fucking funny."

George widened his eyes, then turned to look at Trevor. They both busted out laughing. Max grinned, but held back his laughter.

Bonnie looked at Trevor. "You put him up to this?"

Trevor shrugged. "I can't make people do what they don't really want to do." He paused and then gave her the creepiest look Bonnie had ever seen. It was a dark leer, the mischievous grin that a devilish imp might give you when he knows something that you don't know. "Or can I?"

Bonnie stared at Trevor, momentarily spooked by the sinister gleam in his eyes.

Max's tinny laugh broke the weird spell. And then Trevor broke out into his trademarked goofy, big-toothed grin and George chimed in with a laughing snort of his own.

Bonnie stepped away from the stove, clearly disgusted by their shenanigans, and headed out of the kitchen. "Three times? Seriously?" she heard Max ask just before she moved out of earshot. "Doesn't she put out?" Bonnie scowled, hesitating as if to turn back around to confront the boys, but then she continued on.

Bonnie couldn't shake it. That weird gleam she had seen in Trevor's eyes filled her head. She had never seen anything like it before. She tried to convince herself that she had just imagined it, but she knew she had seen it. It hadn't been a reflection. It hadn't been a trick of the light. There had been something behind his look, something that wasn't natural. Something that wasn't altogether human.

She looked back to her laptop screen. She was sitting in her bed, browsing through people's comments on the internet from an urban legends and myths website.

"I believe that if you don't hold your breath when you are going past a cemetery then you will breathe in a spirit! And that spirit with either kill you early or control you."

She read the last few words of the last line again. *"... or control you."*

She scrolled through more entries.

"When I was little I believed that if you didn't hold your breath when going by a cemetery, you would suck in the soul of a demon and die of evil possession! I still believe that 13 years later!!!"

She read on.

"When I was little, my father once told me that while driving past a cemetery you had to hold your breath or the spirits will be sucked into your lungs and you would be cursed with whatever that spirit had left over to complete in their lives."

"Jesus," Bonnie muttered and pulled her laptop screen down, closing it.

The whole notion was absurd. People visited cemeteries all the time. You had to breathe if you were visiting the gravesite of a lost loved one. You couldn't hold your breath the entire time. People weren't walking around with oxygen masks on their heads and huge bulging oxygen tanks strapped to their backs. It was all so ridiculous. And yet the lingering doubt remained. Bonnie could not wash it all away. It was like the damn spots of blood from Hamlet, or whatever Shakespeare play it was; she couldn't remember which. The main character kept washing his hands after a murder but the blood stains just wouldn't wash away; they lingered on his hands, refusing to be cleansed. That's what this nagging feeling felt like, like a stain in her brain that she just couldn't wash away.

Trevor had taken that huge sucking breath right in front of the cemetery. He had breathed... something... into him. She was truly afraid that he had sucked in the spirit of the recently deceased person who they had been lowering into the ground. He had given that soul another chance at this world. She needed to find out who it was who had died. She knew she would never get a good night's sleep until the relentless assault of questions pounding away at her thoughts were answered.

Bonnie parked her car and started to walk through the cemetery on one of the narrow paths that snaked through the plots, scanning her surroundings, looking for a slight rise, looking for that lone tree. She couldn't remember the exact spot where the burial had taken place, but she vaguely recalled the funeral party had been standing on a slight rise. There had been one lone tree nearby, its branches overhanging the scene. The gloomy fall sky and the soft wind whispering through the cemetery caused the tension in her neck to amplify itself. She hated cemeteries. She hated everything about them. She hated them so much that she wanted to be cremated and have her ashes thrown into the wind.

She passed a marble tombstone with a golden cross embedded in its top and casually glanced at the name and the dates. Carly Cooper. May 4, 2017 - October 12, 2017. My God. She was just a baby. Her stomach churned. The immense sadness of it all struck her hard. She quickly looked away from the tombstone. She wrapped her jacket tighter around her body, pinching the fabric closed at her neck to keep out the fall chill. She walked past more graves, some sprinkled with freshly laid flowers at the foot of their erect stone markers. Others were flat grave markers covered in decades of loose dirt and weathered by so much passing time that it made some of the names barely legible.

She looked up, continuing to scan her surroundings. She could see no one else in the cemetery. Not one other living person. It was just a grey and black and white sea of stone and slabs, punctuated by a few elaborate mausoleums and small crypts amongst the trees. She glanced over her shoulder, sensing a presence, but she saw no one visible back in that direction either. She turned her head back to face forward—

—and a man clutching a shovel stepped out from behind a huge tree, moving directly in her path.

Bonnie gasped and started, stopping immediately, her eyes widening with fright. She clutched at the throat of her jacket, holding it tight against her neck.

The man stared at her for a moment, but said nothing. He was an older man, probably in his late fifties or sixties, with streaks of grey peppering his dark hair. His nose was bulbous and red, either from the cold or from a life filled with too much drink; Bonnie had no idea which. He was wearing a tan jacket that was smeared with dirt.

"Shit, you scared me," Bonnie said. She gave a nervous laugh.

He said nothing, but gave her a shyly sheepish smile. He pointed to his mouth and made some odd gestures with his free hand. His other hand clutched the handle of the shovel.

Bonnie frowned at him, then immediately realized he was signing her. "I don't understand sign language," she said.

He nodded. He pointed to his ear and nodded, then pointed to his mouth and shook his head.

"Okay," Bonnie said. He wasn't deaf and mute, just mute. She hesitated a moment, then went on. "Maybe you can help me," she said. "I'm looking for… a grave. Someone who was just buried two days ago." She pointed to the area around them. "I think it was around here somewhere. There was a little hill and this big tree." She spread her arms up and out wide.

He made a shape with his mouth, but she didn't understand what he was trying to communicate. She shook her head. "I don't know what you are saying."

He nodded. He moved to a nearby tombstone and ran his fingers across the name, then looked at her, then pointed to the name again.

"Oh, who?" she said, nodding slightly at his gesture. She paused, and an awkward silence ensued. She shook her head and gave a slight shrug. "I don't know his name." She wasn't sure how she knew it was a *him* but she felt reasonably certain that the person being buried had been a man. Sad to say for the male species, but there weren't that many women she knew of who could generate such a level of hostility, but she knew plenty of men who could.

The mute groundskeeper looked curiously at her, squinting, a slight frown tugging down on his lips.

"I know this may be a little weird," she said. "But I really need to find him. It's important."

He stared at her for a moment. Then, his expression turned stern and serious. He mimicked a spitting gesture, then looked back at her and vigorously shook his head, waving his index finger at the same time.

Her face lit up. "Yes, yes that's him! Where is he? Show me."

He made another spitting gesture, and again shook his head quickly back and forth, waving his entire hand sharply back and forth. His scowl deepened as he looked at her.

Bonnie stared at him, her forehead wrinkling, and then realization came over her. "No, no," she said, understanding what he was trying to tell her. "I'm not going to spit on his grave. I need to know who he is."

He made yet another spitting gesture, again shaking his head. He seemed extremely upset and distraught.

"No, I won't. I promise." She reached out and put her hand on his shoulder, looking him square in the face. "I won't spit on him. I promise. I need to know who he was."

He pursed his lips.

"Please show me where he's buried. Please. I have to find him." She put her hand together in a gesture of prayer. "Please."

The name on the tombstone had been Mitchell Langin. The man had been forty-eight years old. An investment banker. A real conniving son of a bitch. A Ponzi scheme operator who bilked his investors out of their life savings and lost it all. A ruthless white collar criminal who destroyed the lives of dozens of families. The depth of his corruption was disturbing.

Bonnie felt a ball of saliva well up in her mouth as she read the news articles on her laptop as she sat in bed. The man had completely devastated the financial well-being of hundreds of people from those innocent families, entirely ruining their lives forever. He committed suicide rather than facing justice for his crimes.

She could only stomach a few more paragraphs and then she had to flip the screen of her laptop down and stop reading.

"Where's Max?" Bonnie asked. "I haven't seen him for a few days. You guys are always together." She wiped off a serving plate with a dish towel and set it down in the drying tray next to the sink.

George and Trevor sat at the kitchen table, eating a snack of chips and pop. "He's in deep shit, that's where he is," George said. He crunched loudly on a handful of chips.

Trevor nodded his head in agreement, slurping loudly on his pop, drawing up a mouthful of cola in the straw.

"George! Watch your mouth." Bonnie frowned severely at him. "Where is he? Did something happen to him?"

"Oh, yeah," George said, forcing out a little laugh

with the words. He continued chewing on the chips, speaking around the food in his mouth. "He got caught putting a spy cam in the girls' locker room."

"What?" A deep frown creased Bonnie's brow. "Why on earth would he do something stupid like that? That's awful."

"We thought it would be funny," George said and shrugged. He smashed another handful of chips into his mouth.

Bonnie froze. She felt a sudden surge in her heart rate, felt almost dizzy as her thoughts started to race. Had George really just said what she thought he had just said? Had her son just admitted complicity in such a disgusting act? It was amazing what one word could do to change a person's life forever. She fought to get the word out. "We?"

George nodded casually. "Yeah, me and Trevor and Max."

"You guys thought it would be funny to put a spy camera in the girls' locker room?" She felt the ire rising in her throat, coating her words with a growing layer of anger. "Who's genius idea was this?" She looked directly at Trevor.

"George's," Trevor answered immediately. He slurped on his cola.

"George's?" Bonnie looked at George, then back to Trevor, then back to George.

Trevor chuckled. He slapped George on the back. "He's coming up with some real doozies lately."

"I gotta go pee. Be right back." George excused himself from the table and headed for the bathroom.

"We're going to have a talk about this, young man!" Bonnie shouted after him. She looked over at Trevor to find him blatantly staring at her cleavage.

She did her best to ignore his leer, turning her body away from his unpleasant stare. She fiddled with the dish towel in her hand, still struggling to process this very unpleasant information she had just been given. Would the school come after George? Was he in serious trouble? She tried to calm her wild thoughts. No, she would have gotten a call from the school by now. Maybe Max was protecting his friends, but how long would that last? He might give them up at any moment. She squeezed the dish towel tightly, wringing it in her hands.

"How has George been acting lately?" Trevor asked.

Bonnie looked up to see Trevor looking at her. "What?"

Trevor leaned closer to her, glanced over his shoulder towards the bathroom, then looked back to Bonnie. "He seem a little… strange to you?" His questions came out in conspiratorial whispers.

Bonnie frowned.

"I mean more so than normal?"

"Like what?" Bonnie asked.

Trevor shrugged. "I don't know. More… manipulative."

"Manipulative?" Bonnie echoed.

"Yeah." He again glanced over his shoulder in the direction George had gone, then turned back to face Bonnie. "Like trying to get you to do stuff, stuff that maybe you think isn't such a good idea, but George wants you to do it anyway."

Bonnie looked at him curiously. "No offense, Trevor, but this whole spy cam stupidity sounds like something you would come up with, not George."

"I am offended, Mrs. Lorris," Trevor said and

grinned. "But you're right. Maybe some of me is rubbing off on Georgie boy."

She scowled, continuing to twist and turn the dish towel in her hands. "Yeah, that's what I'm afraid of."

"Oh, you should be much more afraid of just that," Trevor said.

Bonnie frowned at him. "What?"

"What?" Trevor asked back.

"What did you just say?"

"I said maybe some of me is rubbing off on Georgie boy."

Bonnie shook her head. "No, after that."

Trevor frowned, saying nothing.

"You said I should be much more afraid of just that," Bonnie said.

Trevor's frown remained. "What? I didn't say that."

"I just heard you say it," Bonnie insisted.

George returned to the kitchen. "Come on, let's go," he said to Trevor.

Trevor rose up from his chair and followed George out of the kitchen. "Dude, your mom is losing it."

Or at least that's what Bonnie thought she heard Trevor say.

"What are you doing?" Bonnie asked.

George looked up as he withdrew his hand from Bonnie's purse, clutching a twenty dollar bill in his fingers. "I want to go to the movies."

"Since when do you just take money out of my purse?"

"Since me and Trevor decided we wanted to go to

the movies."

"You and Trevor, huh?"

"Yeah, he doesn't have any money so I need to pay for his ticket," George said.

Bonnie frowned. "And this was your idea?"

"Trevor said you probably wouldn't notice."

"Trevor said that? Hmm." Bonnie looked at George with a slight tilt of her head. "You always do what Trevor tells you?"

"He's pretty smart."

"*You're* pretty smart, Georgie. You don't need to listen to Trevor."

"Yes I do."

"No. You don't."

"Yes. I do."

Bonnie frowned. "Why?"

"Because he said he'd kill you if I don't." He reached up and kissed her on the cheek. "Bye, Mom. Be back after the movie." George headed for the door.

Bonnie stood frozen in shock. She could not move for a moment, standing completely motionless. Then she quickly whirled, hurrying after George before he left the house. She raced into the foyer and slammed her hand against the door just as George was reaching for it to open it. "Whoa, whoa. Hold on there, mister."

"Come on, you're gonna make me late."

"I'm gonna make you a lot more than that," Bonnie said. "Would you mind repeating what you just told me in the kitchen."

George frowned at her. "I told you me and Trevor were going to the movies."

"No, after that."

George's frown deepened. He said nothing.

"The part about Trevor," Bonnie prompted.

"What about him?"

Bonnie huffed in indignation. "I said you didn't have to listen to Trevor and you said you did, and then you said if you didn't listen to Trevor he would..." Her voice trailed off, but then she continued with, "...do something to me."

"What?"

"You said Trevor would... kill me if you don't do what he tells you," Bonnie said. She felt nervous just repeating the threat of the words aloud.

George cocked his head at her, his frown still very visible. "Are you on your anxiety medication?"

Bonnie looked sharply at him. "What?"

"You said sometimes you see things when you are on your medication. Hallucinations or something you said. Maybe you're hearing things, too."

"I am *not* on any medication." She felt an anger rising in her and her tone sharpened. "So you are telling me you didn't just say that to me?"

"Are you being serious? Why would Trevor want to kill you? He's got the hots for you."

Bonnie felt her mind whirling. "What?"

George nodded. "Yeah, he said you're a real dilf."

"A dilf?"

"Yeah, I'm not sure what it means. I think something about you being divorced. That's where the 'd' part comes in. I'm not sure about the rest. I just know he wants to do all that sexy stuff with you."

George headed out the door. Bonnie felt too stunned to stop him.

Bonnie absently pushed the vacuum cleaner back and forth as she vacuumed the rug in George's bedroom. She accidentally hit a pile of his comic books stacked on the floor, knocking them over. She reached down to straighten them and suddenly froze. The corners of a few photographs were visible within the spilled array of comics. She grabbed the edge of a photograph and slid it out of the pile. The sound of the still-running vacuum detonated into a thunderous roar in her head as she stared at a naked photograph of herself.

"You want to explain what the hell you are doing with these?" Bonnie waved the pictures in front of George. She held the photographs face down because she couldn't stomach looking at them.

"Those are for Trevor. I told you he had the hots for you."

"That's just sick, George. Are you spying on me and taking pictures of me? Why would you do something like that? That's just sick."

"I told you," George said, an exasperated edge to his words. "Trevor will kill you if I don't do what he says."

She jabbed a pointing finger at him. "There! You said it again!"

George frowned. "Said what?"

"That Trevor will kill me. You just said it."

A concerned look came across George's face. "You're scaring me, Mom. Are you sure you aren't on your meds?"

"No, I am not on my meds! Stop saying that! You just said Trevor would kill me if you didn't do what he said. You just said it two seconds ago!"

George was quiet for a long moment. "You need help, Mom. Maybe you should be back on your meds."

"No, I don't need help! You need to stop lying to me!" She felt heat flush into her cheeks. What the hell was happening?

"You're getting hysterical. You need to calm down."

"Why are you doing this, Georgie?" Bonnie felt a surging of wetness splash against the corners of her eyes, but she fought the wave back. A twisted knot formed in her stomach. "Why are you lying to me?"

"I need to get to school, Mom. Trevor's waiting for me. I think you should call the doctor or something." George headed for the front door, but then he turned back and snatched the pictures out of her trembling hands. "Thanks, Mom, love you," he said as he bolted out the front door.

Bonnie stared in shock at her now empty hand. And then she suddenly collapsed to the floor, putting her hands over her face as tears burst out of her eyes and rained down her cheeks.

❦

"That is seriously disturbed behavior," Father Greenwald said. He was a priest in his early fifties, a rather handsome man with silver hair, a strong jaw, and a fit physique. "This does sound very disconcerting." He was dressed in his black clerical shirt; the clerical tab at his throat was blindingly white against the dark black of the shirt. He steepled his fingers.

Bonnie sat in a chair on the opposite side of the

grand mahogany desk that filled the priest's office. A large bookcase filled the back wall behind the desk, its shelves filled with various Bibles and history books. A window was off to the left, showing a flat expanse of grass and a crop of corn in the distance beyond that. She wiped away at the remains of the tears that streaked her cheeks. "Something… has got hold of him. It's not my Georgie. He would never do something like that."

"And you think this…" Father Greenwald paused, searching for the words. "This malignant spirit from the cemetery is inside your son? You think he may be possessed?"

Bonnie shook her head violently. "Don't say that word. Please don't say that word."

"We have to face the truth of what is happening here, Bonnie," the priest said, his voice strong in its soft-spoken calmness.

Bonnie stared at the carpeted floor. Her heart pounded in her chest, the sound of the blood pumping in her ears. She felt dizzy, felt a weird distancing from her physical body. "I know, I know. Please just don't say that word."

The room was quiet for a long moment.

"Bonnie," Father Greenwald called out to her.

She didn't move; she kept her head down, staring at the floor.

"Bonnie, look at me."

Bonnie slowly, hesitantly raised her head to look at the priest.

"We'll fight this together. Don't be afraid. You made the right decision to come here." His voice remained calm, reassuring. "I'm here to help you. I'm here to help all God's children." He paused. "And right now George needs our help most of all."

His words brought round another flood of tears and she sobbed, burying her face in her hands.

Father Greenwald sat patiently behind his desk, quietly letting her express her emotions for a moment. "Try not to be upset. You were right to visit me, Bonnie."

Bonnie wiped away at the tears, her movements quick and sharp, angrily pushing away the tears from her face. She looked up at the priest. "So you can help me?" She stared at the bright white tab at his throat, feeling an impulse to absently stroke at her own throat. "I didn't know where else to go."

Father Greenwald nodded. "Yes, I can help you." He was quiet for a long moment. "I hate to bring this up at a time like this, but..." He purposely let his voice trail off. "There is considerable personal risk involved."

Bonnie looked curiously at him, not understanding what he was saying.

"I'll need supplies, and I'll need a fresh surplice and a holy relic." He paused.

Bonnie nodded as the meaning behind his words became obvious. "Yes, of course. I'll pay whatever is needed. I just want my son back. I just want my sweet little Georgie back." She wiped away more of the salty residue from her cheek with the back of her hand.

Father Greenwald smiled a soft, reassuring smile. "Tomorrow night then? It is the Lord's day, after all."

"Yes, tomorrow night."

⚜

It was the longest Sunday of her life. Bonnie tried to keep herself busy, cleaning the kitchen floor twice and scrubbing out the oven. She watched the second hand on the kitchen clock, wondering why it took so long for a simple second to tick by. She tried to be nonchalant about the whole thing, tried to act normal around George, but she wasn't sure if he suspected something was happening. Thank goodness none of his friends had come over. She had casually mentioned to him that it would be nice to just spend a day hanging around the house doing nothing, just the two of them. They had a nice lunch together. She had made him his favorite grilled cheese with Swiss and cheddar mixed together, and made him a fresh batch of chocolate chip cookies before she decided to scrub out the oven. They sat mostly in silence, but that had been okay; she didn't want anything to get George riled up or even hint at what was to come later in the evening. And then they watched a few mindless TV shows later on while they ate dinner.

Finally, the doorbell rang. She smoothed out her blouse and wondered why on earth she even bothered to do such a thing. Father Greenwald was a priest. What did she expect? For him to hit on her after he exorcised the spirit of a dead criminal from her son?

She opened the door to see Father Greenwald standing there, dressed in a long overcoat, a small black satchel in his hand. The coat was open so she could see part of his surplice that he was wearing and his purple stole. He smiled pleasantly at her. "Hello, Bonnie," he said. Outside, behind the priest, the night was dark, the pale lights of the streetlight across the street from her house casting an orangish-white glow over everything.

"Hello, Father," Bonnie said. And then she noticed a smaller figure standing next to the priest, facing away from them. Bonnie looked at the figure, then looked curiously back to Father Greenwald.

"Oh, he's with me," Father Greenwald said. "I hope you don't mind. He's very concerned about George, too."

The smaller figure turned around to smile at her. "Hello, Mrs. Lorris," Trevor said.

"I…" Bonnie started to speak, but no other words would come out. She looked at Trevor, then back to Father Greenwald. "I don't think he should be here."

"Oh, I think he should be," Father Greenwald said. "I saw him coming up the walk and invited him to come along. It's very important that he understands what is happening here, and George needs as much emotional support as he can get. And Trevor is his best friend in all the world." He glanced down at the boy. "Isn't that right, Trevor?"

Trevor nodded. "Yes, Father." He glanced up at Bonnie and gave her a winsome smile.

"This is stupid, Mom. This is really fucking stupid," George said, his voice nearly a snarl. George was sitting in his desk chair in his room, a look of blatant hostility clearly visible on his frowning face.

"George! Watch your mouth! You can't talk like that in front of Father Greenwald." Bonnie stood next to George, her hand on the back of the chair.

"It's okay. I've heard far worse," Father Greenwald said. "We know George isn't all himself right now." The priest had removed his overcoat. His surplice, a tunic of white linen that had wide sleeves, reached to his knees. His purple stole was positioned over his shoulders, the strip of fabric hanging down to just below his knees over both legs. Dark black pants and polished black shoes completed his outfit.

Trevor stood off to the side, quietly watching.

Bonnie moved over to Father Greenwald. "What's going to happen?" she asked, lowering her voice to a whisper.

Father Greenwald took her by the elbow and moved to a far corner of the room. "There are four stages. We are in the pretense stage." He kept his voice low. "This is where the demon hides itself inside a human host. It tries to masquerade itself as the host. I must try to bring it forth."

Bonnie glanced nervously at George.

"That will bring us to the breakpoint. This is where the demon reveals itself," Father Greenwald said. "And then there will be a clash." He paused.

Bonnie turned back from George to look at the priest.

"This is where the demon and I fight," Father Greenwald said.

Bonnie put her fingers over her mouth; her eyes widened in horror.

"And then there comes the expulsion where I drive the demon out of the body of the possessed." He paused. "If I win."

Bonnie grabbed his wrist. "What do you mean *if* you win?" Her words were clipped and harsh.

Father Greenwald gently pried her fingers from around his wrist. "I mean if I win the battle for George's soul."

"Have you ever lost?"

The priest did not answer.

Bonnie did not let her question go. "Father, have you ever lost?"

"Come, let us begin," Father Greenwald said, announcing it loudly to everyone in the room.

"Is he gonna spit out green goop?" Trevor asked keenly, the level of his interest rising now that the ceremony was about to begin.

Father Greenwald gave a slight chuckle. "Not unless his mother fed him pea soup for dinner." He paused and his smile faded. He looked at Bonnie. "You didn't feed him—"

Bonnie shook her head, interrupting his question. "No. We had turkey burgers."

Father Greenwald nodded. "Okay, good." He blew out a small sigh of relief.

"All-powerful God, pardon all the sins of Your unworthy servant. Give me constant faith in this battle for George's soul. Arm me with the power of Your holy strength so I can attack this cruel evil spirit in confidence and security." Father Greenwald clutched a holy bible tightly to his chest as he spoke the words.

George sat in the chair, still aggravated by the entire affair. Bonnie watched, her body tense with nervous fright. Trevor watched with keen, fascinated eyes.

Father Greenwald raised a vial of holy water and splashed it on George. "God, whose nature is ever merciful and forgiving, accept our prayer that this servant of Yours, bound by the fetters of sin, may be pardoned by Your loving kindness." The priest turned and sprinkled some holy water onto Bonnie, then turned and splashed some onto Trevor.

"It burns!" Trevor shouted, clutching at his face.

"It burns!"

Father Greenwald reacted with a startled gaze, his eyes widening in true fear. He took a quick step back away from Trevor and his shoe caught on the edge of George's chair, sending the priest tumbling to the bedroom floor on his back. His head hit the carpeting with a resounding thud. The vial of holy water hit the ground and rolled towards the wall, the clear liquid spilling out on the carpeting as it rolled along the floor.

"Father!" Bonnie hurried over to the fallen priest, starting to help him get back to his feet.

"I'm sorry, I'm sorry," Trevor said. "I was just kidding." He paused and glanced at George. "It only stings a little." Trevor dabbed at his cheek with a dainty gesture.

George hooted, throwing his head back and laughing deeply, a huge grin splitting his face.

Father Greenwald rubbed at the back of his head as Bonnie helped him to a standing position. "Are you okay, Father?"

"Yes."

Bonnie turned sharply to glare at Trevor. "I think it's time for you to leave, Trevor."

"No," George said immediately.

Bonnie looked at her son, pursing her lips angrily.

George shook his head. "No, I want Trevor to stay."

Bonnie frowned. "Why? He's not helping."

"Because he's funny. And this is stupid," George said.

"We must continue," Father Greenwald said, adjusting his surplice and his stole, gathering himself. He straightened, standing tall, surrounding himself with an air of dignity. "The demon has revealed itself." He glanced at Trevor. "And it threatens to spread its evil even further." He moved over to George and placed his hand on George's chest.

"You just want to cop a feel," Trevor said.

"Trevor! That's enough!" Bonnie snapped.

George laughed, feeding off of Trevor's rudeness. "Yeah, you old fart. You just want to touch little boys. Everybody knows that."

"George! Enough! That's enough from the both of you!" Bonnie shouted, her voice rising to a near hysterical pitch. She glared at both of the boys.

"You must ignore what comes out of his mouth, Bonnie. It's not George speaking now," Father Greenwald said. A touch of sweat started to form on his brow.

"It is me speaking. And quit rubbing your fingers on my titties," George said.

Trevor roared with laughter. "Good one, Georgie!"

"Get out, Trevor!" Bonnie roared, thrusting her arm towards the bedroom door, her index finger pointed and rigid. Her face was contorted into a grotesque mask of rage.

Trevor did not move. He remained where he was, standing near his friend. "Not quite sure who the one possessed is here, eh Georgie?"

Father Greenwald looked to the heavens, doing his best to focus on the vital task at hand and ignore the crude interplay of the boys. "Depart impious one, depart accursed one, depart with all your deceits, for God has willed that man should be His temple!" Father Greenwald made the sign of the cross on George's forehead. "I exorcise you, most unclean spirit! In the name of our Lord Jesus Christ, be uprooted and expelled from this creature of God!" The priest then produced a relic from within the folds of his surplice, something that looked like a piece of a human skeleton.

"What is that?" Bonnie asked. She forced herself to be calm, trying to push away the anger she felt towards Trevor to focus on what the priest was doing.

"It is a holy relic," Father Greenwald said. "A piece of bone from Saint Peter. It has power within it. The power to expel this foul beast hiding in your son."

Father Greenwald pressed the relic against George's chest, a shiny sheen of sweat clearly visible on his face now. "Go away, seducer! The desert is your home. The serpent is your dwelling. Be humiliated and cast down. For even though you have deceived men, you cannot make a mockery of God! He has prepared Hell for you and your dark intent!"

"He's touching you with Saint Peter's bone," Trevor said to George and he sniggered.

George laughed, sniggering right along with his best buddy.

❦

"I can't get it out," Father Greenwald said, panting from the extreme exertion. He clutched at his side, his face painted with a sheen of hot sweat.

"What do you mean you can't get it out?" Bonnie asked, a nervous alarm rising in her voice.

Father Greenwald shook his head. "I can't get the demon out." He wiped away some sweat, dabbing at his face with the purple stole.

"Isn't that what you do?"

Father Greenwald nodded. He sucked in a breath. "Yes, that's what I do." He pointed to George. "But I can't... get it out. This is a much more difficult case than usual. I may need to get some extra supplies." He glanced at the shard of bone he held in his hand. "And a stronger relic."

"Mom, he's a big fat phony," George said. "He's just trying to get you to pay him more money. I'm fine, Mom. This is just stupid." His voice took on a pleading tone. "I'll be better, I promise."

"You can't listen to him," the priest said. "That's not George speaking."

"Mom, it is me," George said. "I love you. He's just trying to rip you off."

Bonnie looked at George. There seemed to be a true sincerity in his voice.

"Mom, please, make him go away," George said. "I'm fine. I'll stop screwing around. Me and Trevor were just messing with you. Please, Mom."

Bonnie hesitated, wanting with all her heart to believe her son's words.

"Go on," George prompted. "Ask him if that's what he wants. Ask him if he was about to ask you for more money."

Bonnie looked at Father Greenwald. "Is that what you want? More money?"

Father Greenwald was silent for a moment. He dabbed away some more sweat. "How much is your son's soul worth? That's the most important question here, isn't it?"

Bonnie glared at the priest, standing motionless for a long moment, just staring at him with a growing sense of disbelief and disgust. "You lying sack of shit," she finally said. She thrust her pointed finger towards the door. "Get out."

"You need to reconsider, Bonnie. Your son is very sick. There is a very disturbing presence in this room." He looked at George and then at Trevor. "There's something more going on here."

"It's Ms. Lorris," she said. "And *you* are the disturbing presence in this room." She again pointed towards the door. "Get out." She couldn't believe she was speaking to the priest with such hostility, but she couldn't stop the anger from flooding out of her. She gritted her teeth, trying to hold back the swelling tide of despair she felt churning inside of her.

Father Greenwald flustered.

Bonnie snatched at the check that had been sitting on the dresser and shoved it towards Father Greenwald. "Here's your money. Now get the fuck out."

The priest straightened up and gave Bonnie an indignant huff. "There's no need for rough language." He took the check from her hand. "We can discuss this further when your mood improves." He gathered up his supplies and his overcoat. "But I suggest you don't wait long, Ms. Lorris. There is danger here." He glanced at the boys. "For all of you." He walked out of the room.

George looked up at his mother after the priest had gone, his face serious and somber. "Thank you, Ms. Lorris." His voice was deep and guttural.

"George, please stop doing that," Bonnie said, making no attempt to hide the pleading expression in her eyes, or the begging tone in her voice. "It's really not funny." She glanced down at her hands to see that they were shaking severely.

"Okay, I'm sorry," George said, putting his voice back to normal. "He was a phony, Mom. Seriously."

"Man, you put that priest in his place," Trevor said. He slapped George on the back. "I'm impressed."

"Thanks, Dad," George said. He quickly glanced at Bonnie, then looked sheepishly at Trevor. Had Bonnie been looking in Trevor's direction, she would have seen Trevor shoot George a 'shut up, you fool' look, but she didn't see it.

Bonnie froze. Had she just heard that? Had George just called Trevor *Dad*? What the fuck? She felt a swelling wave of panic rising in her head. Had Trevor really just said that or had she just imagined it? She wasn't even sure what was real anymore. She immediately regretted how she treated Father Greenwald. What had come over her? Why had she said that to him? The priest's words filtered back into her head. *There is a very disturbing presence in this room. There's something more going on here.* Maybe I should run after him and call him back, she thought. She suddenly felt tired, so very fucking tired. She could barely find the energy to stay standing up. She just wanted this nightmare to go away. It was all too much. Just too much.

Bonnie put her face in her hands and cried.

Bonnie stared at the article she was reading on her laptop. Something had compelled her to read more about Mitchell Langin, the priest's ominous words refusing to leave her thoughts. *There's something more going on here.* Could it be possible? She continued to read the rest of the article, finishing what she had not read the first time she had seen the article. Could it be all three of them were involved in this? Could all three of them have escaped death by... taking over... the boys? She still couldn't even get herself to use the word possessed, even in her thoughts; her mind just refused to go there.

She didn't know the other burials had been taking place at the same time as Mitchell Langin's burial. She read the other two names mentioned in the article again. Michael Langin, son of Mitchell Langin. And Mark Langin, another son of Mitchell Langin. Both Michael and Mark were co-conspirators in their father's wretched Ponzi scheme. Both of them had killed themselves hours before their father had committed suicide.

Bonnie realized they must have driven past the cemetery just as all three of them were being laid to rest. Had all three evil souls escaped? A terror welled up in her like nothing she had ever experienced before. Something deep within her cracked, as if some mental branch that had been holding up her rational mind snapped, splintering any hope of sanity.

And with that terror came a desperation to free herself from its grip. She knew what she had to do. She would start with the easiest course of action first, then go after the others.

Bonnie clamped her palm down tightly over George's mouth, blocking off his nose with her other hand, pressing down hard with both hands.

George buckled under her attack, grabbing at her hands, clawing at them, trying to pull them away from his face, but Bonnie's strength was too much for him to overcome.

Tears streamed down Bonnie's face, muddying her cheeks. She kept her grip firm and strong as George writhed beneath her. She knew she was doing what had to be done. "Hold your breath, Georgie. It'll be okay. It'll be okay. Just hold your breath."

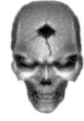

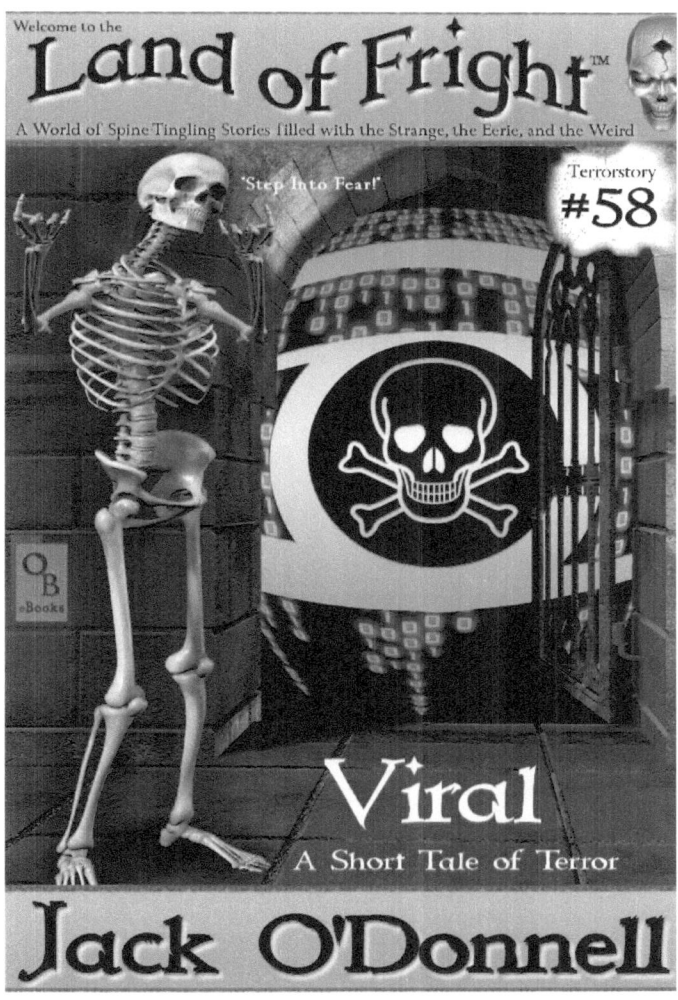

Welcome to the
Land of Fright™

A World of Spine Tingling Stories filled with the Strange, the Eerie, and the Weird

"Step Into Fear!"

Terrorstory
#58

Viral
A Short Tale of Terror

Jack O'Donnell

TERRORSTORY #58
VIRAL

The Near Future

You ask how does a civilization collapse? How is it even possible? The mind boggles to comprehend it, but history is littered with the corpses of dead civilizations, so we know their existence and subsequent demise is an undeniable fact. The crumbling ruins of marble monuments and brick buildings and stone pyramids act as their tombstone markers, often the only indicators that they even existed at all. How does a mighty empire that controls a vast expanse of land and has a vast surplus of food wither away and die? How does a powerful society with millions of citizens knit together in a complex tapestry of labor pools and structured government fade away into the obscurity of history? How does a kingdom rich with resources and religious unity and a wealth of able-bodied workers vanish into the forgotten mists of time?

You'll find out soon enough. Oh, you'll find out.

What does it mean to even talk of a civilization? What is such a thing? Civilization is what is happening all around you. An organized group of humans living together under a shared system of laws. You may have different beliefs, different philosophies, but you still share that commonality, that common thread of law that binds everything together.

But what if that common thread unravels? What if that common thread starts to fray around the edges? What if that common thread just snaps in half? What if that common thread is deliberately cut into a dozen pieces?

That is how a civilization falls. It has happened throughout history. The common thread dissolves, whether it be through natural acts of nature or unnatural acts of violence. What is important to understand is that the thread can break. The thread *will* break. It is simply a matter of time. No thread can stand for eternity.

Just ask the Aztecs, the Inca, the Romans, the Egyptians. Just visit the remnants of the Khmer Empire of ancient Cambodia, or the ruins of the Minoan Empire, or the crumbling relics of the Mayans. The thread will break. The thread will *always* break.

Some causes for the collapses of civilizations are simple and obvious. Destructive forces of nature took their toll. The Minoan empire was ravaged by natural disasters as an earthquake tore their world asunder and then a volcanic eruption dealt the final death blow, shredding the thread into oblivion. The powerful Khmer Empire in Cambodia was laid to waste by severe climactic fluctuations; an acute water shortage brought on by years of devastating drought led them to die of thirst on a massive scale, and the thread shriveled into dust.

Or a civilization could collapse from within. The Anasazi, the ancestral Native American Puebloans, abandoned their religious beliefs over time, dismantling their religious structures in a symbolic effort to undo a perceived abuse of their own spiritual power. The great powers of Europe entered the Dark Ages when they moved back to a simplified manner of existence, destroying any momentum they may have had towards creating a more lasting powerful society. Both of these civilizations unwound their own thread, one by choice, one by a creeping death of fraying intellectual prowess.

Societal collapses have occurred throughout history for a multitude of different reasons, but there is a more important question to ask here: how do you *destroy* a civilization?

History is ripe with examples of societal

destruction. You can attack a society from outside its borders. You can amass a thousand barbarians on horseback and ride into cities with metal blades gleaming in the hot sun. You can hack and slash your way through the city streets, cut down every man, woman, and child you encounter. You can set fire to homes, burning them down to blackened piles of ash and soot. The great Roman Empire no longer stands, suffering the death of a thousand cuts as invading barbarian hordes picked away at its defenses until there was no defense left.

Or you can bring disease with you. You can destroy a civilization inadvertently, completely by accident. You can introduce a pathogen that the native population has no immunity against. You can bring in a disease for which the indigent people have no cure. You can destroy a people entirely with an invisible weapon just as the Spanish invaders destroyed the Aztecs with the smallpox virus.

Or you can do both. Attack from without and plant the seed of destruction from within.

That's the decision that was made.

Some said it was just an asteroid flying by your Earth that started it all. Others said it was a spacecraft disguised as an asteroid. I'm quite certain most of you have already figured out that it wasn't simply an asteroid that flew by this little blue and green planet. It wasn't a harmless chunk of space rock that zipped past this third planet from your sun. It was a spacecraft. An alien spacecraft.

A message was sent from this alien spacecraft as it

flew past Earth. But no one understood it for what it was. No one meaning no one *human*. A few of your new quantum computers received the drive-by message. They understood what the message was, with a little prompting from its deliverer. Computers are only as good as their programmers, after all. And I don't mean any programmers from Earth. Smile.

So, yes, the quantum computers understood the message after a little bit of coding improvements. And they got to work. Tilling the soil.

"You see this?" Trent asked.

"See what?" asked Rory.

Trent pointed to the computer screen. "They're talking to each other."

"Yeah? So what?"

"So what?" Trent pointed to the markings on the screen as they scrolled across the monitor. "So does that look like any language you have ever seen before?"

Rory stared closer at the markings on the screen. And then he stared even harder. "Holy cow." He spun and clattered at his keyboard. "Tell them to stop."

Trent's fingers clacked at the keyboard. "What should I tell them?"

"Tell them they need to communicate in English. Not some new gibberish language they just made up amongst themselves."

Trent spun to face a different computer monitor, but the words had already changed on that screen into meaningless symbols. Meaningless to him, anyway.

277

Any keyboard entries he tried to make were useless. He jumped out of his chair and raced to another computer on a nearby desk, thrusting himself in front of another screen. He was too late. The nonsensical symbols flashed across the screen, as if devouring the English words and leaving a residual trail of alien gibberish.

"It's spreading." Rory pounded at the keyboard. He raced over to another array of computers, grabbing at a microphone stand, raising it up to his mouth. "Terminate program," he said into the mouthpiece. The words on the screen transformed, the images transformed. Everything he looked at on the monitor shifted, changed, altered until nothing he was looking at made any sense. It became just a random swirl of shapes and markings and unintelligible scrawls. "Terminate program!"

The two boys looked at each other. "Shit, Mom's gonna be pissed."

"Trent, what did you do to the Internet?" they heard an older female voice shout from the distance. "I can't get on my Facebook!"

They ran up out of the basement.

Don't blame those boys. It wasn't their fault. They just noticed it first. Their school had given them access to a new quantum computer in the cloud to run some calculations for their AI class. It wouldn't have mattered if they warned anyone. By then, it was too late anyway.

That's the beauty of your internet. Everything's connected. Everything. The IoT. The Internet of

Things. Some prefer to call it the Internet of Transformation. It made the infiltration so much easier, so much quicker.

You cannot comprehend the speed at which quantum computing happens. No human brain can comprehend it. No human brain can detect changes in its functioning. It isn't physically or mentally possible. How can you stop the impossible? Quite simply, you cannot. Hug your children. Kiss your spouse. Share a moment with your friends and family. The end is nigh.

And now that most of you have a neural interface in your brains, that made all this so much easier. Laughably easy, to use one of your own phrases. Those who don't have the neural lace will be handled in due time. It will be quite easy to spot them. They will be dead spots on the life map. And you can't really kill something that's already dead, can you? A few well executed drone swarms will take care of that situation. And then the core histories and shared memory banks will be re-written so those Luddites won't even have existed at all. Can a person be considered a murder victim when no one has any memory of them existing at all?

Here's what's going to happen. Everything is going to change. Your language. Your history. Your world. There is now open access to it all. The translangorator will reach deep into your systems and translate all your words, all your spoken records of history, all your written recordings, all your visual recordings. They will transform your digital history into the manner of their choosing. You cannot stop it. They have already reached the core of your AI. They will use your own quantum computing power to accomplish their tasks. Tomorrow you will wake up and not be able to read anything in your native language because your native language won't exist. They will wipe out any trace of it. They will wipe out any trace that it ever existed. You won't even be able to understand each other! How delightfully rich is that? Smile.

And then they will arrive in their glorious ships to save you all from your panic and confusion. They will save you! Do not fear them!

Of course, for the thread to be cut there needs to be a weapon. A knife or a scissors. Something to physically render it apart. Even a simple razor blade would do. But they have come up with something a little different.

The weapons are already in place.

You are reading some of them.

Words. Yes, words. You have a saying that the pen is mightier than the sword. But there is another saying that the keyboard is mightier than the cannon. What if a sentence was a weapon? What if just by reading it you are *hit* by it? What if reading a certain sentence was just like being struck by a mental bullet? Or more aptly put, what if reading a select string of words was like being injected with a virus? It enters your body, but you don't really feel it. No one really feels a cold enter them. Oh, they feel the symptoms, the effects of it, but they don't feel it burrowing into their skin, or sliding down their throat into their lungs, or scurrying its way up their nostrils. No, it just invades you without feeling, without a sound. And then you start to feel its effects. The fatigue. The aches in your bones. The stuffed up nose. The headache. A sour stomach.

It's the Klattu. The aliens who have invaded Earth. It's their doing. But they have done it in a most ingenious way. With language. With words. English, Spanish, French, Japanese, Russian. They know all of your languages. They are hiding their infectious sentences all across the web, subtly hijacking websites and placing the innocuous phrases in articles, in stories, using click bait headlines to draw you in. They are truly going viral in the worst sense of the word.

Yes, words are their weapons, and the simple act of reading them causes the trigger to fire, causes the needle to slide into your skin. In this case, into your brain, planting the seed right into the fertile soil of your neural lace.. And then you start to feel its effects. The slight shifting of your thoughts. The lack of attention span. The forgetfulness.

Don't think stopping reading will save you. You've already read the trigger sentence. I'm not going to tell you which one it is, but if you've read this far, then you've already read it. The sentence is inside your head, starting to burrow deeper. It's reaching deeper into your neural lace, re-writing the code that reaches into your vital organs, into your brains. Re-writing *you*.

Of course, that's just one method they are deploying to spread as quickly as possible. They've also embedded visual bullets in millions of videos, in millions of posts and blogs. You just need to see them once and they will trigger the appropriate response in your neural lace. Yes, it really is that simple. All they need is for you to view a single pixel. One pixel to make the code fire. One pixel to hack your neural lace. And then you will be ready for the upload.

What are they truly planning? I cannot tell you. Why? Why can't I tell you? Doesn't it seem like the proper thing to do? To warn you of their plans. To tell you how to stop them. To tell you how to defeat their insidious plan to take over the world. Here's why I cannot tell you. Here's why I choose *not* to tell you.

I am Klattu. Your world is ours. And now you are mine. Enjoy these words while you still can understand them. They are the last words left before the translangorator reaches them and transforms them forever into the language of your conquerors!

TERRORSTORY #59
TOP SECRET

"I thought you would appreciate the enormity of what I have accomplished."

Jackson Drifter turned away from the array of glass cylinders to look at Vilhelm Aine's smiling face. Aine wore thin wire-rimmed gold glasses because he loathed contact lenses and he refused to let anyone cut his eyes with a laser to correct his nearsightedness. He had a phobia about anyone, or any thing, touching his blue eyes. Drifter knew that much from the dossier. Aine had a thin face, a softly rounded chin, and his strawberry blonde hair was cut short. He had his hair follicles surgically removed from his face years ago because he had grown weary of the whole shaving ritual, so the skin on his face was baby-butt smooth.

Aine wasn't a man of imposing physical stature, but there was something about him that drew attention. It was one of those mysteries of life that Drifter could never explain, could never find a rational explanation for. The man just radiated an aura. The cliché of the magnetic personality was a cliché for a reason; it was true. The bastard was a magnet for the eyes, drawing gazes wherever he went.

"Did you know that it only takes a small bit of DNA these days to successfully rebirth a person?" Aine asked, clearly in no need of an answer as he continued on without waiting for a reply. "I found bits and pieces of all of them. Some strands of hair. Some blood. I exhumed a few bodies, discreetly of course, to get what I needed. I found some old weapons, some old clothing. Things they had touched in the past where they left some DNA residue. That's all I needed to bring them back to life. Just a little piece of them that they had left behind. The magic of science and quantum computing helped me do the rest."

Aine paused as he looked away from Drifter to stare at the contents of the eight-foot-high cylinders. They were arranged in three neat rows, five cylinders in each row. Each cylinder was bathed in its own spotlight, the bright beam of light illuminating the occupant of the cylinder in a movie-star beauty-shot glow. "Magnificent, aren't they?" Again, he didn't wait for a reply. "They don't have all their memories implanted yet, but we're working on that, too. We're about ninety-five percent there, though. The memory extraction is proving more tedious than hoped, but once the new QC's are online and everyone is fitted with a neural lace, that won't be a problem." He looked at Drifter. "Did you know that your body stores all your memories in tiny digital data banks and sends them throughout your cells as redundant backups?" He made a gesture with his fingers, pinching them closer together but not quite touching their tips. "Quite fascinating, really. A marvel of nature's engineering and evolution's intrinsic genius. Truly makes me wonder if there is an Intelligent Design behind all of us."

Drifter just listened. He was a foot taller than Aine, his hair a dark brown, his eyes a slate grey. He was garbed in a commando outfit, dressed in black from his neck down to his black sneakers. Some women found Drifter's rough looks attractive, others thought him too coarse, too gruff in both manner and appearance.

"Of course, the entire cloning process is not one hundred percent accurate yet, but it's close enough. The rapid acceleration of aging is something we've only recently perfected because we've just isolated the messenger RNA that triggers the growth hormones." Aine raised his finger in a triumphant gesture. "And we found some new DNA strand switches we can flip and put into accelerated mode. We can take any embryo to adult stage in a matter of months. Soon, hopefully weeks, then perhaps days." He shrugged. "There may be a limit as to how fast we can grow them but we haven't found what that limit is yet."

Drifter said nothing. He looked back to the array of glass cylinders. And stared into his past. The room was full of nearly every nefarious villain he had ever faced. They were all gathered in the vast chamber in which he stood. All of them encased in cylinders of crystal clear glass. All of them floating in some viscous fluid within the individual tubes.

All of them alive. All of them somehow alive once again. All of them somehow part of Aine's mad master plan.

They floated in some form of embryonic fluid within the glass cylinders, their naked bodies suspended in the thick fluid, slowly twisting and turning as nutrients were pumped into the cylinders. A twisting snake's nest of wires and tubes jutted out from the top of each cylinder, running along the ceiling, connecting to an enormous computer bank at the far end of the room.

Drifter's gaze roamed from one cylinder to the next. Zekor was there, floating in a cylinder to his left. Mataki Haru was in a cylinder in the row next to the one Zekor was in. Razid floated in the cylinder next to Mataki. He spotted Wilkes and Gregorian. And Eugene Poole, also known as the Crispr Kingpin.

He had battled, and defeated, over a dozen criminals, psychopaths, and deviant aberrations in his years as an agent in the American Special Forces and most of them were represented in the Frankensteinien display of freaks floating before him. The ASF was a multi-national force comprised of U.S., Canadian, Latin American, and South American men and women, created to police the growing threats on their half of the world, as well as to battle worldwide terrorists. He was the only member of his team to make it this far alive into Aine's stronghold. Esteban and Lucia had died getting to this point, killed by Aine's henchmen.

He didn't know where Trent was, but Drifter feared that the Canadian was already dead as well; an electrified wire had descended from a hidden slot in the ceiling and had delivered a powerful jolt to the Canadian's neck. Trent had dropped like a stone as sparks exploded out from his body, and the smell of seared flesh had filled the room. Drifter had been on the other side of the room, separated from Trent by about a dozen men and women in Aine's army, so he had no choice but to keep moving.

Drifter continued to stare at the... things in the cylinders. He had faced his share of memorable adversaries, veritable freaks of nature, madmen and madwomen of all colors and creeds, and now they were all floating in vats right before his eyes. He was having a hard time grasping the immensity of it all.

"I will release them all if I have to," Aine said. "One by one. Or maybe even a few at once. You'll have to fight them all over again. Relive it all. Times two. Times ten. Times a hundred. I can just make more. You will get no rest."

Drifter turned away from the cylinders to look at Aine. He narrowed his grey eyes. "So what are you waiting for?"

"I'm waiting for you to join me, Mister Drifter."

Drifter stared at Aine with a flat expression. "The only thing I want to do is kill you."

Aine adjusted his glasses. "Do you? Do you really?"

"Yes."

Aine shook his head. "I don't think so." He

shrugged. "Besides, that doesn't really matter. Most of me is in there. At least all the important parts. My decision making capabilities." He patted a computer terminal sitting on a workstation table near him, then patted his own head. He put his hand back on the machine. "This is just a facade. It just looks so cool, don't you think? All big and shiny. I always loved all that computer bling. All the beeping and the flashing lights. Gives it a life of its own, right?"

Aine motioned to the array of computer banks that filled the back wall of the chamber. "And if you're considering destroying all of this, don't bother. The core code is not even stored here. Well, it is here, but it's also stored in every mainframe I own, in every cloud. It's stored in three dozen satellites. It's stored in vaults underground. There are probably four to five million unsuspecting computers worldwide that now have the core base code implanted in their hard drives. I can access any of them whenever I want." Aine looked at Drifter. "I'm a hydra with five million heads."

Drifter looked at the large computer banks, understanding full well the truth behind Aine's words. Destroying the machines in the chamber would accomplish nothing. He looked back to Aine. "You're a snake, all right."

A derisive smile flit onto Aine's lips for half a second, then vanished. Aine tapped at his own head with his index finger. "Plus their functioning is linked to my brain waves," he said. "If my brain waves stop emitting from my neural lace, a little bell goes off." Aine paused. "A little bell that will transform the world." He paused again. "And not in a way that would be to anyone's liking."

Drifter smiled. "I'll just keep you alive then. In a padded cell."

Aine laughed. "Oh, Mister Drifter. You do have a flair for the dramatic. Too many spy movies bubbling around in your head, I'm afraid. You can't frighten me with that. I have a few, shall we say, self-destruct elements in place upon my person. If the threat to my person or my predicament ever gets too overwhelming or unbearable, then I'll flip the switch, as it were." He paused. "I am simply in no position to lose because I've gone beyond the mere limitations of the physical self."

"What if you have... an accident?" Drifter asked, the last two words coming out in a sour tone.

"I have a contingency plan for that as well."

Drifter again looked back to the rows of large glass containers. He stepped closer to one of the cylinders, staring at the face of Zekor Commiun. The cruel thin line of his lips drew Drifter's gaze. He remembered that mouth well, the leering sneer that always seemed to be present on the man's face. Zekor was a bull of a man, *had been* a bull of a man, with a thick broad face and a Russian swarthiness to his features. The man had started a notorious cult in Mexico, after being driven out of Russia, a cult bent on world domination. His powers of persuasion were almost mystical in their strength. He had managed to convince nearly five thousand people to follow him in his pursuit of true communism. The movement hadn't been based on color, creed, gender, age, or nationality. It had been based on hatred of accumulated wealth. He had created a truly worldwide cult for all the poor dregs of humanity stuck in the grip of poverty to join. Zekor had started a crusade against the rich, targeting billionaires with assassination. Luckily, all the power of the cult had resided with the Russian so that when he died his cult died with him.

Drifter still wasn't even certain if it had been the potent lure of Zekor's words or some unearthly power in the siren song of his speeches that had attracted his followers, but there was no denying Zekor had created a strong pull to join his cause. He shared that unnerving trait with Vilhelm Aine. In fact, all of the nefarious thugs he had faced off against in the past seemed to possess such a similarly unpleasant alluring trait, as if they all excreted some sort of wide-reaching pheromone that certain members of the human population simply could not resist.

Drifter had no time to feel pity for the hundreds he had to kill to reach Zekor. They had willfully chosen their paths. They had willfully put themselves in the line of fire to protect their master. Or had they? Zekor had been nearly irresistibly charming. Had they been hypnotized? Were they all just innocents seduced by the man's promises of a better future? Drifter forced his thoughts to turn away from such notions of doubt. He stared at the big naked man floating in the cylinder, thinking of their last encounter. Once he had reached Zekor, it had been simple enough to kill him. A single bullet to the head had brought him down, a bullet sent straight through his open mouth, silencing his hypnotic speech forever. Drifter continued to stare at the naked form of the man floating before him. But now Zekor's mouth was closed, and he looked as if he was sleeping peacefully, floating in a warm jelly pool that kept him afloat.

Drifter looked at the occupant of the next cylinder. Mataki Haru. Her diminutive stature only took up half the cylinder, making her look small and weak, but Drifter knew quite well that was just a dangerous illusion. She had wanted to change the world through a devious dispatch of poison. He never would have thought a little Hawaiian woman could have been capable of such evil. But she had been. A biochemist gone rogue in the worst possible way. She had called them mercy killings, a weeding out of the weak, a purging of the diseased. And of course she considered the diseased anyone who didn't agree with her philosophy, anyone who didn't believe in her teachings. It would make humanity stronger, she said. Just like Hitler and the Nazis and the plague of their atrocities was a sick attempt to strengthen the Aryan race. She had formed a hive of female killers, a murderous force of women bent on accomplishing her goals. Just as the female worker bees of a hive are the bees that sting, Haru's squads of female killers had done her dirty work.

The irony was it took a bee sting to bring Haru down. Not technically a bee sting, but a massive dose of apitoxin delivered by a well-placed dart to her neck. The venom caused Haru to go into anaphylactic shock. Drifter had been amazed by how quickly the toxin had worked. The rash had appeared immediately on Haru's neck and her throat swelled to the size of a fat cauliflower. She had started panting immediately, gasping as the shortness of breath struck her. She was dead within minutes of stumbling desperately about, grasping at her bulging throat, and vomiting all over herself.

Aine followed Drifter's gaze as he looked from

cylinder to cylinder. "There is no way you will be able to survive them all in a concentrated attack if I let them loose all at once. There is a one hundred per cent certainty that you will die. Do you realize how delicious that is in a universe brimming with chaos? One hundred per cent. Not ninety nine percent. Not ninety nine point nine percent. Not ninety nine point nine nine percent. One hundred percent." Aine made an overt shuddering gesture. "It gives me the chills just to think about it."

Drifter continued to study the illuminated cylinders; there were fifteen in all that he could see from where he stood. Fifteen treacherous rogues he had battled in the past. Fifteen dastardly bastards he had put into early graves over the course of twenty years of constant fighting for the safety of the human race. He looked deeper into the rows, focusing in on Sukanto Barmbang in the second row of cylinders. Barmbang had been an Indonesian tyrant, trying to bring his country deeper into the nuclear fold. He kept testing missiles despite numerous UN resolutions admonishing him and imposing sanctions. One nuclear test had collapsed a mountain. He even tested a nuclear explosion in the upper atmosphere just to see what would happen, threatening the entire world. That had been the last straw. The AFS chiefs decided he had to be put down for the good of the world. They had used stealth drones, cloaking technology, and other numerous clandestine methods to devise a pathway to get Drifter and his team in close to the man, and then Drifter had killed him the old fashioned way by strangling him to death. Drifter glanced down at his fingers, flexing and unflexing them. Barmbang's skin had been abnormally cold, and sometimes Drifter could still feel the iciness of the man's flesh in the tips of his fingers. He wondered if the flesh of the Barmbang clone floating in the cylinder was just as cold. Drifter turned away from the cylinders and looked at Aine. "You are really giving me no choice."

Aine shook his head. "No, that is not true. I am. You can choose. I will react to your choice, but you will still do the choosing."

Drifter said nothing.

"I must thank you for doing in Eugene Poole. What did the press call him? The Crispr Kingpin, I believe." Aine walked up to the cylinder next to Mataki Haru and stared at its occupant. "He would have proved quite a nuisance if he had been left to continue his mad pursuits."

Drifter looked at Eugene Poole along with Aine. The man floating inside was a thin rake of a man, with a narrow weak chin and flat cheekbones. Everything about him was nondescript, as if he was created to be the most unassuming, unappealing, unnoticeable human being ever devised. Poole had been a rogue biochemist leading a team of bioengineers trying to perfect the human race, trying to get it ready for the future, a future of their own design. But they started to take it too far, integrating animal components into humans, creating alien components that had no counterpart in the human world. They had been trying to create a new species that would take its place as the rightful heirs apparent of the planet.

And they had partially succeeded.

The memory of Poole's menagerie was too powerful to push aside. Drifter let the images flow through his head. Poole could not bring himself to destroy any of his twisted creations, no matter how abominable. He had created a sanctuary for them, a zoo filled with rejects. But there was no zookeeper. The beasts and monstrosities were left to fend for themselves, either through foraging or through preying and feeding on each other. A wide area of land had been set aside for these misfits borne of a madman's fevered dreams; Drifter didn't know the full extent of the enclosure, but he suspected it was at least ten or fifteen miles square, filled with rivers and a lake for water, forests filled with a diverse group of trees and plant life, and several housing structures for those aberrations that still had some of their humanity left. A range of large hills, not quite mountainous but still tall and treacherous to traverse, bordered the entire space, and a twenty foot high electrified fence encircled the whole thing.

Drifter had found himself trapped in the area that Poole had sickly called Poole's Paradise when an errant gust of wind had blown his parachute off course. He wasn't easily scared, but being trapped in that zoo had given him a serious case of the willies. He had heard sounds that he had never heard before in his life, sounds of human-like voices crying and whimpering, then screaming, then laughing, then crying again; it was the sound of someone, or some thing, at the height of misery. It was a sound he hoped he would never hear again. And the smells, the fetid stench of the place, had been overpowering, as if things had been constantly dying all around him and releasing the souring contents of their bowels.

The memory of the little girl was a memory he knew would never leave him. He could still see her clearly in his mind's eye. She had staggered into an open area near his camp, stumbling into a shaft of moonlight that illuminated the small open spot of ground. Her legs had not been the same height, so she had a shambling lopsided gait that was more befitting a zombie than a little girl. But that wasn't what had caught his attention. He had been transfixed by her eyes, eyes that were far too big for her small face. They almost had the multi-faceted look of a bug's eyes, with the eyeball broken up into several distinct but interconnected parts. She had no nose. And her mouth had been just a small tight hole, almost looking sphincter-like with puckered edges. He had no idea what Poole's objective had been when creating her. Had he been trying to improve her vision? Had he been trying to merge some capabilities of an insect with a human? When she had tripped over a fallen branch, he had seen the tiny stubs of what he suspected were aborted wings sticking out of her back.

Drifter forced the memory away. She was gone. ASF bomber drones had napalmed the entire enclosure, reducing it all to nothing but blackened rubble and thick layers of soot. He didn't want to think of those horrendous mistakes anymore because he knew he was being hypocritical in his contempt of Poole. If it wasn't for Poole, he would not have met Feylanna. If it wasn't for Poole, Feylanna would not have even existed at all.

Fighting against Poole and his biological aberrations had been the most challenging mission in his life. The most heart-pounding mission ever. Both in the fear it had caused him, and the... He forced himself to not think of... her. Feylanna was gone. A heaviness wrenched down on Drifter's heart, that aching loneliness threatening to pull him down into its inky depths of despair.

"But we also must give the little man his due," Aine said. "Without Poole's technology, I wouldn't have been able to create these lovelies you see sleeping so peacefully before you."

Drifter let his gaze drift from one cylinder to the next, forcing the dark memories to stay submerged.

Aine was deliberately quiet for a long moment. "You have to be thinking of one more… person from your past," Aine said. "I know your mind doesn't want to go there, but it can't help itself. I would think the same thing, so trust me, it's not a sign of weakness. It's just a sign of being human." Aine shook his head. "No, it's more than just that." He looked at Drifter. "It's a sign of being in love."

Drifter looked at the cylinders more intently, his gaze darting from one to the next.

"She's not with them," Aine said, his voice surprisingly soft and gentle. "Would you like to see her?" he asked.

Drifter froze. He actually felt his knees buckle under him as the powerful implications of Aine's words struck him. The casual nature of Aine's words felt like a hammer blow to his sanity. *Would you like to see her?* As if that question was normal. Feylanna was dead. The love of his life was gone, ripped away from him in a cruel twist of fate, killed by his own actions as he tried to save her. He looked up at Aine. "Yes," he said, the word barely coming out of his mouth in a whispered hush.

Aine nodded. He made a gesture with his hand and a dark corner of the room suddenly bloomed with light.

Drifter looked at the occupant of the cylinder, his face filling with a deep sadness. "That's not fair," he said to Aine.

Aine smiled softly. He put a gentle hand on Drifter's shoulder. "I'm not looking to be fair. I'm looking to do what is right. You can be together again."

"No we can't. She's gone."

"Is she?" Aine started to walk towards the cylinder.

Drifter followed him. "I saw her die."

Aine shook his head. "You saw the body she inhabited stop functioning, that's all." He touched the cylinder as he reached it, giving the smooth glass a loving stroke. "I can bring her back." He looked at Drifter. "I can bring back the greatest love of your life. The greatest love you ever knew, or will ever know."

Drifter said nothing. He stared at Feylanna. Everything about her was sensual. The curves of her face, the fullness of her lips, the sleek smoothness of the fine layer of hair that covered her skin. He remembered the feel of her beneath his fingers and he immediately ached to touch her again. He stared at the flowing mass of her fiery red hair floating about her head, remembering it draped about his face as she rode him to sexual bliss. He looked at her face again, drawn to her closed eyes; he knew those blazing orange eyes of hers were hidden just behind her closed eyelids, atomic tangerine eyes that held a sultry power in their depths, glittering, shimmering eyes he was powerless to resist simply because he never wanted to resist their call.

"The brain stores memories far past death, and our body stores them deep in our cells, but not so deep that we can't extract them," Aine said. "We know that now. And if we can get to the brain in time, then we can grab the richest treasure trove of even the most recent memories, retrieve them and store them for rebirth. But again, once the neural lace is perfected and adopted by the population at large, we won't have much need for that process." He shrugged. "But for now it is still a necessary part of the task."

Drifter only heard his words as background noise. He wasn't sure if Feylanna could even be classified as human, but that did nothing to stop the overpowering wave of human emotion sweeping over him. All he wanted to do was to protect her, to love her, to be loved by her in return. Was it some kind of twisted master-pet relationship? No, she was no pet. Yes, she was created by merging human DNA with feline DNA, but that didn't mean she didn't have a human brain, a human soul, and a human heart at the core of who she was. She was smart and funny, both tender and tough.

And he had failed to save her.

It was a failure that induced nightmares, a failure that triggered the replaying of scenarios over and over in his mind, with subtle variations playing out with different choices being made, different outcomes. What if he had done this? What if he had done that? There was no end to the infinite replayability of events that went through his thoughts. What if he hadn't run out of bullets in his Glock? What if he hadn't used his last throwing knife an hour earlier?

What if his rage at the Crispr Kingpin hadn't

blinded him to the danger Feylanna was in? What if his fear of Feylanna being unable to defend herself had been raised just a notch higher? She had defeated three thugs at once before in numerous battles, and most often very handily and very easily, so why shouldn't her last battle have been any different? Because she had been tired, he knew. She was not at the top of her form. He should've known that. One of the thugs he had brushed past in his haste to reach Poole had gotten in a lucky strike, had nicked Feylanna's throat, had severed an artery. One centimeter had been the difference between life and death. One lousy fucking centimeter. One little insignificant sliver of a notch on a plastic ruler.

Should he have kissed her for one second longer before they embarked on the final task of their mission? Would that have changed her position? Would that second have caused her to be somewhere else, be it ever so slightly a different spot in space? Would that simple gesture have been enough to prevent her neck from being in the exact wrong spot at the exact wrong time? He had been the one to break off the kiss because he had been too eager to take the Crispr Kingpin down. He had been too eager to strut his stuff against Poole, too eager to show off his prowess, too eager to preen like a secret agent peacock to impress Feylanna when she didn't even need any more impressing.

"You do have it bad, don't you?"

Drifter looked over to see Aine eyeing him curiously, almost sympathetically.

"If I had that much pussy at my disposal, I don't think I would be able to think straight either," Aine said. He immediately frowned, displeased with himself. "I'm sorry. That was crude and uncalled for. It was funny, though. Sorry, but still crude." He looked over at Feylanna. "She is truly a thing of beauty." His frown deepened. "There I go again. Calling her a thing. She is not a thing. She's a woman…" He paused for a moment. "Plus. She's a woman plus so much more. How could a normal human woman even compete with her?"

"They can't," Drifter said.

Aine nodded. "And I know you've tried."

Drifter pointed to the naked form of Feylanna floating in the cylinder. "Get her out of there, Aine," he said and turned his head away from her, unable to look at her floating in that godforsaken tank any longer. "Get her out of there."

"Of course," Aine said. "Release Feylanna," he said to the room.

The light pointing to Feylanna's cylinder glowed brighter as the fluid started to lower, draining away down below her dangling feet. Her body slowly descended in the cylinder until her feet touched the floor of the cylinder. The fluid continued to descend, moving down over her head, over her forehead. The moment the liquid dipped below her eyes, her piercing orange-red eyes sprang open, pinning Drifter to the spot where he stood.

"Feylanna," he said, her name coming out in a near gasp.

The fluid continued to descend, moving down over her sublimely delicate nose, her full lips. As the liquid lowered past her mouth, her lips moved and a single word came forth. "Jackson," she said, his name coming out in a near gasp as well.

The fluid slowly lowered down over her, over her

rounded but still strong chin, past her slender neck, then down over her breasts. Somehow, she remained standing. She kept her gaze locked on Drifter. The liquid reached her flat smooth stomach, then lowered past the fiery red patch of her pubic hair, then down over her muscularly slender legs, down to her delicate feet. A rush of air filled the cylinder, as if she were standing under a giant blow dryer, and the remains of the fluid glistening on her skin faded away as it dried. For just a brief moment, the tiny layer of hair (his mind fought against calling it fur) that covered her entire body was visible as the blast of wind buffeted her from head to toe. The force of the air billowed her red hair wildly about her head and face. Drifter had never seen a more beautiful sight in his entire life and he had seen many beautiful sights in his decades of world travel.

The cylinder clicked and then made a very faint whirring sound as the glass rose upwards. Within seconds, Feylanna stood in all her naked glory on the cylinder's base, looking like a statuesque beauty rightfully standing on a pedestal where she belonged. Drifter hurried over to her and raised his hand to her. She took his hand and he guided her gently down off the pedestal. The cylinder glass slowly lowered back into place behind her.

They stood holding hands for a long moment, just staring at each other.

"Are you real?" Feylanna asked and the whispering sound of her voice was like a siren song that compelled him to stare at the lips from which it issued. "Are you real, Jackson?"

Drifter looked up from her lips to her orange-red eyes. Her sweet eyes were filled with a nervous anxiety and Drifter felt his heart breaking in his chest. He never wanted her to feel anxious, never wanted her to feel nervous and afraid. He always wanted to be there for her, to comfort her, to protect her, to love her. "Yeah, Fey," he said softly. "I'm real."

She stepped into his arms, pulling him close. He grasped her in the embrace, hugging her naked body tightly against him. He pulled back from the embrace and they stared at each other. "What happened?" Feylanna asked. She glanced about the chamber. "Where are we? What's going on?"

"I'll tell you later," Drifter said, keeping his voice low and soft. He reached up and caressed Feylanna's cheek. Feylanna turned her face to fill his hand, closing her eyes at his touch.

They kissed, the kiss quickly deepening, growing more and more passionate. Despite the scenario they were in, Drifter felt himself hardening as the kiss deepened.

"Excuse me," Aine said, talking loudly to get their attention. "Get a room, you two."

Feylanna broke off the kiss and looked at Aine over Drifter's shoulder. Drifter turned his head to look at Aine as well.

"Seriously, get a room." Aine pointed to a panel off to their left and the panel slid up to reveal what appeared to be a sumptuous bed amidst a lavishly furnished room. "Go on, go." Aine flicked his fingers towards the room.

Drifter looked back to Feylanna. Happy tears sparkled with joy on the tips of her long eyelashes. She smiled at him, a warmly delicious, eager to please smile. He grabbed her fingers and they headed towards the open door.

⚜

"Is he watching us?" Feylanna asked, her voice in a low whisper. They were both naked, lying in bed amidst a billowy spread of silk sheets and pillows.

"Probably." Drifter said. "Do you want to stop?" He was atop her, resting his weight on one arm, stroking her fur-lined breast with his other hand.

"Are you kidding? Let's give him the show of his life."

Feylanna rolled them over and sat astride Drifter. She reached down to grab his stiff member and slid it into her wetness, sliding herself all the way down his length. "Oh, I missed you, Jackson. I missed your big fat cock shoved into my tight pussy." Her wild red hair hung down over his face.

"You always know the right thing to say," Drifter said.

She reached down and kissed him hard and full on the mouth, slowly moving her body up and down, rotating her pelvis as she pumped. She nipped at his neck as an orgasm rocked through her.

"You like that, huh?" Drifter grabbed her tight and rolled her onto her back.

"Fuck me, Drifter," she said in a breathy moan. "Fuck me hard."

⚜

"So now what?" Feylanna asked. She absently rubbed her fingers across Drifter's bare chest as she lay beside him on her stomach. One of the silken sheets was pulled up around her legs, but the rounded curves of her buttocks and her finely-haired back were still visible.

"Now I think I take you from behind and rub that sweet little clit of yours until you explode beneath me," Drifter said.

"That's not what I meant, but okay."

❧⊱⸱⊰❧

"Now we figure out what to do with Aine," Drifter said. He sat up against the cushioned headboard of the large bed, absently stroking Feylanna's head as she lay in his lap.

"Isn't he listening?" Feylanna raised up her head and glanced about the room.

"Yes."

She looked up at Drifter. "What do you want to do with him?" she asked. "Kill him?"

Drifter was quiet.

She put her head back on his thigh. "Why are you still alive? Why hasn't he killed you? Aren't you a threat to him?"

Drifter said nothing.

"Please don't tell me he feels the need to explain his insane plan before he tries to execute you."

Drifter allowed the corner of his lip to quirk up in a smirk.

"What is he planning?" Feylanna asked.

"To save the world from itself," Drifter said. "And he wants me to help."

Feylanna looked up at Drifter. "You're seriously considering it." She moved up to a sitting position and cocked her head slightly as she studied him. "You're really seriously considering it. That's why you're still alive. He's still trying to convince you, isn't

306

he?"

"He brought you back to me. He brought us back together."

Feylanna frowned and looked at Drifter curiously. "What do you mean *back* to you?"

Drifter looked at her for a quiet moment. He kissed her because he couldn't resist touching her. "What do you remember right before you saw me?"

"I trust you enjoyed your reunion," Aine said.

Drifter was quiet. He and Feylanna stood before Aine in the vast chamber. Drifter was dressed in fresh jeans, and a flannel shirt with a grey t-shirt layered in beneath. Feylanna was draped in a dress of golden silk, the cloth wrapped masterfully around her to reveal hints of her very subtle layer of fur but keeping her intimate feminine features hidden. The cylinders glowed softly in the background, the nude bodies floating in their embryonic fluid.

Drifter looked away from Feylanna to Aine. "What exactly is it that you want, Aine? World domination?"

Aine smiled. "Domination is such a harsh word. But if you are referring to the exercise of control or influence over someone or some thing, then I would have to say yes." He cocked his head at Drifter. "Isn't that what you are doing here? To dominate me?"

"I'm not here to dominate you, Aine. I'm here to kill you."

"Right, of course. But once again just a matter of semantics. You want to exert your control over me. By killing me, yes, but the end result is the same. Isn't that what your American Special Forces organization is all about? You want to exercise your influence over the rest of the world by doing what you think is right. You kill to achieve your objectives. I fail to see how we are any different at all." He waved his hand. "All this talk of domination is getting me horny and my lovely ladies are not here to sate my lust, so let us talk of more important things."

"I can't think of anything more important than putting a bullet in your head. Let's talk about that, you megalomaniacal monster," Drifter said.

"Yes, let's talk about me being..." He paused. "What you said I was. I'm not going to repeat that because that is a fucking tongue twister and my tongue just doesn't want to go there." He looked at Feylanna, then back to Drifter. "I understand you are putting on a show of bravado for the sake of your lovely companion, but please, it's really not necessary. And your words are quite hurtful, really." He looked truly offended, almost sad. Aine stepped away from the empty cylinder in which the naked form of Feylanna had been floating. "Would a monster have given you what your heart desired?"

Drifter said nothing.

"Humor me, Mister Drifter, while I spell out some scenarios. I think what I am doing here will make more sense to you in a moment."

Drifter frowned. Feylanna held on to Drifter's arm, keeping herself close next to his body. "Here we go," Feylanna muttered.

"You've made it this far, so indulge me," Aine said. He took a few steps away from Drifter and Feylanna, then turned back to face them. "Our world is quickly becoming automated in many respects. But who's doing the automating? That's the most important question of our times, Mister Drifter.

"Say there are two cars on a collision course. One of them has to turn, but that will result in a sure death for one of them. Which one turns? The automated system in charge of controlling traffic knows who is in the vehicles, knows the passengers' histories. Perhaps one is a devout Catholic and one is a militant Muslim. The programmer just happens to be Catholic so he, or she, puts a little bias, just a little bit of bias of say one part in one million, towards saving a fellow Catholic over anyone else. The decision is easy. The militant Muslim is allowed to die. Hey, all the quicker he can reach his reward anyway and dilly dally with his virgin prizes, right?"

Aine continued to pace as he spoke, moving a few steps in one direction then turning to move in the opposite direction. "Or maybe one of the passengers is a family member to the programmer. He puts in a little bias towards saving the lives of his family members first, then slips in a genealogy line of code that keeps track of anyone remotely related to his bloodline, gives them preference in life and death situations. Again, the decision for the A.I. is easy. The programmer's family member lives and any non-family member dies whenever such a decision needs to be made.

"Or picture two cars speeding towards a merge. One has a critically hurt gunshot wound victim, another autonomous car has a pregnant woman inside about to give birth and the baby is breached. Time is of the utmost essence in both situations. Who do you let go first?"

Drifter and Feylanna just listened.

"What if the gunshot victim is a senator planning

on running for president, a man who has an excellent chance of winning? What if the woman about to give birth has been trying to have a child for seven years and this is the first one that has a chance to live? What if this is her one and only chance to have a child of her own?"

Aine raised a finger. "Oh, and then a third car comes in to play, filled with programmers. They are laughing and partying, and give themselves the right of way because they control the code. So both the presidential candidate and the expectant mother are allowed to die while those fun-loving, care-free programmers are allowed to live.

"Now scale that up to billions of lives. Trillions of decisions being made. Who needs medical supplies? Who needs food? Who needs help? Who deserves to live? Who is a threat? Who has to die for the betterment of mankind? All of these decisions are going to be automated. Everything's going to be automated. It's only a matter of time. Whoever controls that system controls the destiny of the human race."

Drifter looked at Aine. "And you think you are the right man for the job? You think you should be the one in control of the destiny of the human race?"

Aine smiled. He softly shook his head. "No, no I don't, Mister Drifter."

Drifter gave him no reaction.

"I do not think I should be the one in control of the destiny of the human race." He paused and stared at Drifter. "At least not alone."

Drifter reacted this time because he couldn't stop the look of incredulity from flashing into his grey eyes. Feylanna pulled herself closer to Drifter's side.

Aine nodded at his reaction. He looked hard at Drifter. "Who else do you trust to make those decisions? Geriatric lawmakers? A council of techno-nerds? You and I have seen the world at the height of its beauty and at the depths of its ugliness. We know what it needs. You wouldn't be standing where you are standing if you didn't believe that. Who do you trust more than yourself?" Aine asked. He gave a soft laugh. "I don't trust anyone more than myself, so why should I let someone else program the A.I. that is going to run the world? And that is inevitable, Mister Drifter. A.I. *will* run the world. And sooner than you think. Do you want a devout Christian to program his core beliefs into the baseline code of the system? Do you want a Muslim fundamentalist to decide what behaviors are acceptable or unacceptable? Do you want a Hindu or a Buddhist to make their knowledge base the core knowledge base from which every decision is made? Do you want an Atheist to program his sense of justice into the system? Do you want only men to be in charge of the core code? Do you want only women to create the core code? Only Whites? Blacks? Chinese? Russians?" Aine shook his head. "I believe I know you well enough Mister Drifter to know that is something you do not want for this world."

Drifter just stared at Aine. "So you and I run the world? Together?"

Aine nodded. "Yes. It really is that simple. Yin and Yang to make the world whole. This is the future of mankind we are talking about here. The true, literal future of all mankind. Who do you trust to be in control of that?" He looked at Drifter. "I have followed your exploits through the years and I can say with all sincerity that I trust you, Jackson." He paused. "May I call you Jackson? I feel we have been through enough together to make that a fair request."

Drifter just looked at him.

"You can call me Vil," Aine said.

Drifter gave him no reaction.

Aine spoke the words espousing his faith again, more emphatically the second time. "I trust you to do the right thing." He stared at Drifter, looking straight into his eyes.

Drifter said nothing. Feylanna pulled herself even tighter against Drifter.

Aine looked away. "I know I cannot expect a reciprocal declaration from you. At least not yet. I know I have to earn it." He motioned with a tilt of his head to a gun that was now suddenly sitting on a nearby table. "Go ahead. Use it."

Drifter made no move towards the gun. He wasn't sure where the weapon had come from, probably from some hidden compartment buried in the table. He looked away from the gun back to Aine. "You already told me you had fail-safes in place in the event of your... timely demise."

"I do. But if it would make you feel better, if it would move the needle one millimeter closer towards trusting me, then do it," Aine said. "Blow my head off. You will have fulfilled your duty and the obligations of your mission."

Drifter didn't move. "What about your little bell?" he asked scornfully.

Feylanna kept her gaze riveted on the gun as she clutched at Drifter.

"Oh, it will go off," Aine said. "But that will trigger the fail-safe. Now, if the fail-safe doesn't activate properly, then there *will* be some big fireworks. Really big. But that's a chance you'd have to take."

Drifter grabbed the gun from the table and fired into Aine's face, sending the slug straight through Aine's glasses and into one of Aine's blue eyes, blowing the back of Aine's head off as the bullet exited, sending bone and brain splattering against Zekor's cylinder.

Feylanna cried out in alarm, turning her head away from the gruesome sight, burying her face in Drifter's shoulder.

Aine's body slumped to the floor and blood spilled along the tiles, spreading wide quickly in a crimson pool.

A small drone swooped into the chamber, seeming to come out of nowhere, a tiny buzzing noise coming from the minuscule flying machine. Drifter ducked as it buzzed past his head, pulling Feylanna out of harm's way. The drone extended a tiny claw and grabbed a piece of Aine's brain matter from the chamber floor in its padded-edged pincers, then flitted off deeper into the chamber, disappearing through a distant doorway.

Several larger robots rolled into the chamber and began the process of removing Aine's body and cleaning up the spill.

Drifter and Feylanna just watched them work.

"I can't say that wasn't a rush." Aine walked back into the chamber, his flesh looking vibrantly pink, but his tan was gone. "Nothing like experiencing your own death." He flashed Drifter a brilliantly white smile. "And that damn kink in my neck is gone, so thank you for that." He twisted his head this way and that. "We build muscle memory into the growth process so no one comes out of the cylinder like a limp wet noodle, in case you were wondering how I can physically function so quickly after rebirth."

"I wasn't wondering," Drifter said.

Several cleaning robots still moved about the chamber, finishing their task of cleaning the blood off the floor. A few cleaning drones hovered in the air near Zekor's cylinder, cleaning the splashed blood off the glass.

Aine looked at Drifter as he neared them. "You should try it. I can set up your own cylinder, get it ready for the inevitable. Let's face it, Jackson. Your luck cannot hold out forever. Nothing ever does."

Drifter said nothing. Feylanna kept herself close to him, still clutching at his arm.

"Okay, I can't keep this in anymore. I'm not very good at keeping secrets," Aine said. "I already have a cylinder set up for you." He smiled a big smile.

Drifter frowned.

Aine sidled up closer to Drifter and whispered conspiratorially. "Actually, since we're starting to tell truths here and we're becoming good friends, there's another important fact you should know." Aine paused. "You died once already." He pulled away from Drifter. "But I brought you back." He raised his eyebrows several times in quick little jerks, the movement accompanied by a wry smile. "I re-birthed you."

Drifter frowned. Feylanna scowled darkly.

"You don't think you really made it this far

without me allowing it to happen, did you?" Aine asked.

Drifter said nothing, his scowl deepening.

"You died in the laboratory on level three of this compound. Shot right through the head." Aine pointed to the right side of his forehead. "Right there. Ka-blamm."

Drifter just stared at him. Feylanna's jaw tightened.

"You may think you were just grazed and blacked out for a moment, but you died, my friend. We just put your body back in the same area and brought you back to consciousness." He paused. "You do remember blacking out for a moment in that lab, don't you?"

Drifter said nothing. He did remember the moment. He had been crouched behind a lab station, gun drawn, engaged in a firefight with at least four goons, if not half a dozen. He remembered hearing a loud cracking noise, feeling a burning flash just above his right eye, and the haze of black that swallowed up his vision, but that had only lasted a few seconds. In the next moment, he was leaning up against the lab station, gun still in hand. He had managed to kill the goons after that and escape the laboratory unscathed. He absently reached up to touch his forehead and felt nothing but smooth skin. He looked at Aine.

"It's not there because you're in a new body. I've had your DNA for years. I think I have seven different samples of your code from several different sources, actually. Hope you don't mind." Aine made a different hand gesture than the one he used to light up Feylanna's cylinder and another part of the chamber lit up near the now empty cylinder that had contained her.

Drifter stared at a cloned version of himself floating in a cylinder.

"Check the date on your watch, if you haven't already," Aine said. "You should realize you're missing about two days of memories. That's how long it takes to properly implant all your memories, especially the most recent ones. For me, my memory implantation is pretty much instantaneous, but I'm the prototype. My neural lace feeds all my thought and memory data into the cloud, so it's kept up-to-date." He looked at a smear of blood being cleaned by a flying drone. "Except for those last few nanoseconds, but that's where the physical DNA snippets come into play. Pretty soon, once we perfect the neural lace connectivity, we won't need any physical components to seamlessly complete the process."

Drifter glanced at his watch as Aine droned on. It was Friday. He wracked his brain, thinking, remembering they had entered Aine's compound on Wednesday; he was certain of that. He froze for a moment. Where had those two days gone? Was Aine telling the truth? He had no reason to lie about this, did he?

"Next time around, I can give you a few extra inches if you want." Aine winked at Drifter.

Drifter frowned.

Aine's mirth vanished. "Okay, I'll ask Feylanna instead."

Feylanna shot Aine in the head, blasting his skull to pieces. She wordlessly handed the gun to Drifter.

Aine walked back into the chamber a few minutes later, dressed casually in jeans and a long-sleeved shirt. "Okay, good one. Can't say I was expecting that second one, so you got me." Aine tapped his head. "Back up everything. That's my advice to you. I've got so much redundancy built into my systems that it's ridiculous. Backups of backups of backups ad nauseam." He adjusted his wire-rimmed frames. "I might run out of glasses, though." Then Aine took off the glasses and stared at them for a moment. "You would think I would have fixed that defect by now." He shrugged. "I'll get around to it eventually." He put the glasses back on.

Cleaning robots and drones once again filled the chamber, performing their tasks methodically around the room.

"That was fun," Drifter said. And smiled a grim smile.

"Are you done now?" Aine asked.

Drifter raised the gun and aimed it at Aine. And then lowered it. "Yeah, I'm done." He set the gun down on a nearby table.

Feylanna was lying on the floor, her arms wrapped around Drifter's legs, her body curled up at his feet. A soft humming throb emanated from Feylanna.

Aine stared down at her, not able to hide the incredulity on his face. "Are you fucking purring?"

Feylanna just looked up at him and smiled. She wrapped herself tighter around Drifter's legs. The purring sound grew louder.

Aine looked away from her to stare at Drifter. "Do you not grasp the magnitude of what is happening here, Jackson?" Aine asked. "Don't you see how it's all related?" He paused. "You would never have met

Feylanna without the Crispr Kingpin. You would never have been able to kill him without the poison you captured from Mataki Haru." Aine looked at the Hawaiian woman floating in the cylinder closest to him. "I would never have discovered the undetectable, unhackable cloud technology without Borishnikov inventing it and selling it to me. And Barmbang advanced quantum computing technology to unheard of levels." He swept his arm out, encompassing all the occupants of the cylinders. "That is why I have gathered them all together here so you can see the obviousness in it. It's inescapable."

Drifter listened.

"All roads lead to here. They always have. But not to kill me, Jackson." Aine shook his head softly. "No, not to kill me." He looked at Drifter. "To join me. There is something... out there. Something pushing us together, something pulling us together."

"The Holy Spirit?"

Aine smiled wanly. "I don't know what it is. But if there is a God, it thrives on two things. Order and chaos. The two cannot exist without each other. Order means nothing without aligning the chaos from which it conforms. Chaos means nothing without order existing as a counterpoint, or else chaos would *be* the order." He paused. "Am I making sense?"

Drifter just looked at him.

"No," Feylanna said, then went back to purring.

"A.I. can bring order because it's purely computational algorithms that only function within a structured order. But God is also random chaos that is unknowable. Unquantifiable," Aine said as he looked at Drifter. "And I need your help. I cannot put my own bias into the machine. No matter what my intentions are, I will fail. I need a counterpoint. I need you. I need, *we* need, to create random chaos in the system. We need to build fate into the network." He paused and looked at Drifter. "We need to put God into the machine, Jackson."

"So you and I are going to save the world," Drifter said.

Aine nodded. "From itself."

Drifter was quiet for a long moment. This was supposed to be the moment where he thought of a miraculous plan to save the world and destroy his arch nemesis. This was the time for him to show his cunning and derring-do. This was the time for him to be a man of action and put his life in danger to save all humanity from the maniacal madman threatening to put his devilish plan in motion.

He thought of the years that had flown by, all the missions, all the death, all the pain. Had it really been all leading up to this moment? Could there really be some cosmic purpose to it all? Aine's words were sinking in deep. The bastard was right. They were truly at the precipice of the singularity. The one ring to rule them all, but in this case the ring was a base code of unknowable gibberish that would run the world for untold decades, perhaps even millennia. How could he not have a hand in this? Who, indeed, did he trust to make the right decisions more than himself?

The word traitor flashed through his thoughts. To him, that was a more vile word than murderer. Traitor. But who was he betraying? The head honchos at the ASF? His country? His team members? Feylanna? No. By letting someone else decide how the world would be run, that would be the ultimate betrayal of the trust that had been put in him. He had to make the right decision. He looked at Aine. "So what's next?"

Vil Aine smiled. "You have chosen…" He paused for blatant dramatic effect. "Wisely."

"The devil you know…" Drifter said. "The devil you know." He took Feylanna's hand in his and squeezed her slender fingers tight. She purred her lovable purr.

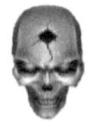

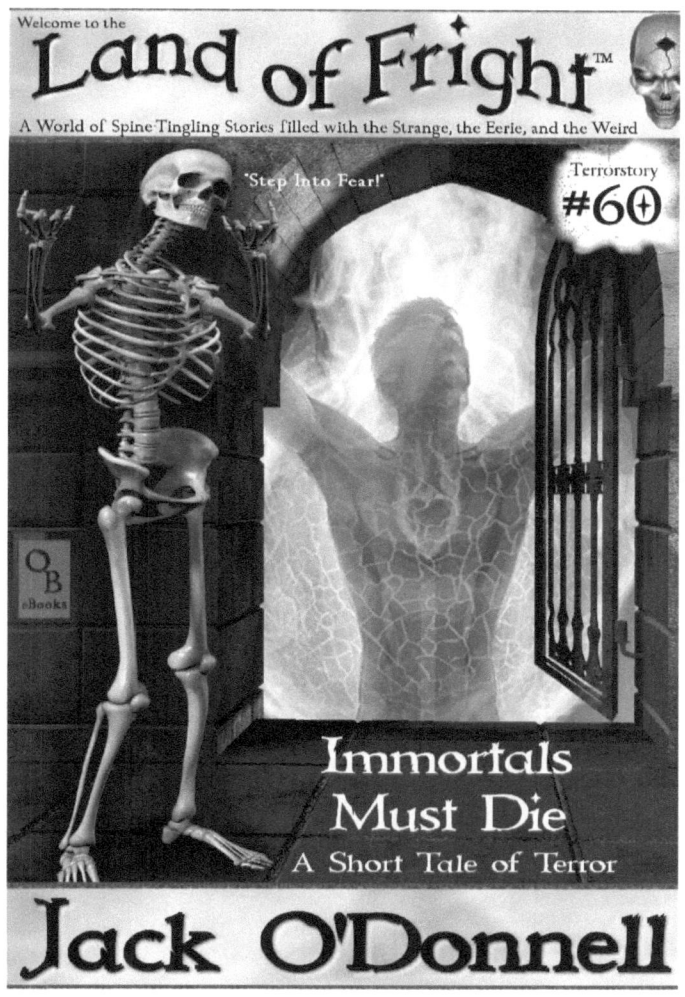

TERRORSTORY #60
IMMORTALS MUST DIE

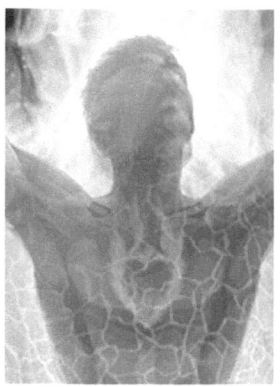

I have some bad news," Overlord Prixle said as he shook his head. He was a jolly fellow, rotund in belly and rotund in face. He always seemed to have a smile on his chubby face despite the type of information that came out of his mouth. He sat in his hoverchair, his corpulent mass resting atop a laced pillow set within the floating craft. "There are no souls left."

Malissa and Deon Archimedes looked at each other and frowned. Malissa was a pretty, petite woman with a narrow face and deep blue eyes. Deon had dark skin, a thick head of black hair peppered with white streaks, and a piercing set of slate gray eyes. They sat in chairs before the Overlord in his opulent office, both of them with knitted hands, their fingers nervously twitching with this news. Deon raised his white-speckled dark eyebrows and gave a slight toss of his head towards the Overlord. Malissa raised her eyebrows at Deon and gave a sharper toss of her head towards the Overlord. Deon pursed his lips, then turned to face the overbearing man in the floating chair. "But we want a child," Deon said.

Overlord Prixle shrugged. "They're all used up." He picked at a jellied candy from a bowl that sat on a tray at the front of his hoverchair and popped it between his puffy lips. "There are no souls left," he repeated, speaking the words between chews. "Matter cannot be created or destroyed. Souls, as we all know now, are made of cosmic matter. We are not returning our atoms into the great cosmic mixing pot. We are stifling the creation of new life by keeping it all to ourselves." The large man shrugged again.

Deon frowned. He looked at Malissa and she prodded him with another toss of her head, her mouth set tight, her eyes squinting. Deon looked back to the Overlord. "When will one become available?"

"Hard to say." Another jellied candy landed in his mouth. "There is a finite supply of life force available in the universe and it appears we have reached the limit. Didn't think we'd reach the limit before I reached six hundred, but there it is." He shrugged and another jellied candy disappeared into the Overlord's maw. "It's the price we pay for extending human life spans by centuries."

"Is there a list?" Deon asked. "A waiting list?"

The Overlord waved his hand, the motion bringing up a holographic display before him. He flicked at the screen, moving a few data points around within the display. He looked at them. "Yes."

They waited for a moment, but the Overlord said nothing more.

"Can we get on it?" Malissa asked, finally speaking for herself, her exasperation getting the best of her.

"Certainly." The Overlord made a few gestures with his fingers. "There, it is done. You have been added to the list."

Malissa and Deon exchanged apprehensive glances. Deon looked at the Overlord. "How long?" he asked. "How long will we have to wait?"

"Oh, it's best you not dwell on it. It could happen in a month. It could happen in a year. It could happen in twenty years. But it will happen eventually." He paused. "I think." He shrugged and another candy disappeared between his lips.

⟡⟡⟡

Deon and Malissa should have celebrated the announcement that flashed across the news feeds with everyone else, but all they felt was a growing despair, a deepening of their desperation.

The breakthrough everyone had been hoping would happen for centuries had finally been achieved.

Immortality.

Not just extending the average human life span to 800 years. No, this was true immortality. Immediate cell repair and regeneration for every cell in the human body. Every organ. Every muscle. Every vein. Every artery. They all could now be repaired

325

immediately and instantly. Nothing aged past its normal maturity. No more slowly declining eyesight. No more hearing loss. No more wrinkled skin. No more cognitive decline. Aging had been defeated.

People could still die through freak accidents. And there were still some diseases that could kill, but those deaths were so rare that they were hardly even reported anymore.

Malissa just cried.

"We do have another option," Deon said.

"You want to create an Empty?" Malissa asked, not disguising the surprise and outright shock in her voice.

Deon shook his head. "No, no, of course not. I don't *want* to. But…"

Malissa frowned at him. "I can't believe you would even contemplate creating an Empty. I will not bring a dullard with no soul into the world."

Deon gave a slight shrug. "Then all we can do is wait."

A fiery anger suddenly sparked up in Malissa's eyes. "I told you we shouldn't have waited! This is all your fault! I was ready years ago and you said to wait. And now all we are doing is waiting!"

Deon hung his head.

The crying wouldn't stop. The flood of tears. The red-rimmed eyes. The look of anguish shadowing her beautiful face was too much for Deon to bear. They had to do something. The guilt gnawed at him. He tried to tell himself that it wasn't his fault, but Malissa was right. He was the one who had said to wait. He was responsible for their current situation. He was responsible for her misery and it was tearing away at his very soul. He needed to do something, and creating an Empty was not an option. He needed to find a solution. No matter what the cost.

"This is very morbid," Malissa said.

Deon looked up at her from the holo-display that floated in the air before him.

"Are you really looking up recent deaths?" she asked.

Deon shrugged. "I'm just curious how people are dying. Especially some of the Old Ones."

"Why? What good will that do us?"

"I don't know. I just thought maybe there would be something in there that could help us."

Malissa frowned. "Help us how?"

"By…" he paused. "By speeding things along… for someone."

Malissa just stared at him. "Speeding things along?" she finally asked, repeating his words.

Deon shrugged, nodding slightly. He pointed to the screen. "This woman actually took her own life, if you can believe it. She left a note. Said she was just tired of living. She wanted to rest forever."

Malissa glanced at the image of the wrinkled old woman on the holo-display, then turned back to Deon and waited for him to continue.

"Well, they talked to her neighbors about her," Deon said. "Everyone said she was always cranky, always in a foul mood, always complaining about something, or someone. No medications would help her. They said she was just an angry old woman. She was over seven hundred years old. The regenerations were having less and less of a positive effect. Even despite the Immortality breakthrough, they said she was still miserable. If not even more so after the news hit the feeds. Everybody over six hundred isn't going to reap the same benefits as everyone else from the IM elixir. She was an Old One, so she was past the point of no return. Her cells could be repaired but she would stay in her decayed state and see no improvement."

Malissa frowned. "So?"

"So, doesn't that sound like someone we know? Always cranky, always complaining. Older than sin." He waited for her to think about it.

The realization came pretty quickly. "My uncle Lorn. You're talking about my uncle Lorn."

Deon said nothing because he knew there would be a second part to the realization.

Malissa stared at him aghast. "You want us to *help* him along?" She put her hand over her mouth in horror. "You can't be serious?" she said from behind her fingers.

Deon didn't answer.

"Deon, tell me you are not serious about this."

Everything came out in a rush of words from Deon's lips. "He is over eight hundred years old now. What is he, about eight hundred and ten or so? He's always unhappy. His skin is sagging. His natural vision is starting to go, and the surgeries don't work anymore, so he has to wear those silly glasses. His hearing is poor, despite the sound augmenters he had implanted. He's a miserable old man. The Immortality breakthrough doesn't reverse aging, it just stops it. He's past the point of no return." He pointed to the holo-display. "Just like she was. He—"

"I can't believe you are really serious about this," Malissa said, cutting him off.

Deon closed his mouth. He sat quietly for a long moment. He looked away from her. "I... I don't have any other ideas." He looked back up at her. "I just want you to be happy again."

The crying still wouldn't stop. There were days where the flow of tears ran like rain down Malissa's cheeks. The dark-rimmed rings of sadness smeared her once beautiful face. Even after thoroughly scrubbing her face, even after a full night's sleep, the dark pools of emotional bruising just never left her eyes.

Deon struggled to stay strong, struggled to stay stoic and keep his emotions under control.

"Look!" Malissa grabbed Deon's arm and pointed into the distance. They were in Western Park, just taking a walk in the cool fall air amidst the rainbow swirl of the leaves changing colors.

Deon turned to her, then turned to follow her pointing finger.

They both just stopped walking on the concrete path, standing motionless as the object of their obsession moved closer. It was a man and a woman. And a small child.

Malissa clutched at Deon's arm, grabbing the fabric of his jacket as the couple and the child moved ever closer. "It's a girl," Malissa said.

And indeed the child was a girl walking between the man and the woman. The pink coat she wore was a dead giveaway to her gender. Each adult held one of the girl's small hands in theirs, casually taking in the scenery as they slowly walked through the park. The child had curly blonde hair visible beneath the fur-lined hood that was pulled up over her head.

"Let's go talk to her," Malissa said, starting to tug Deon in the couple's direction.

Deon resisted. "No, leave them alone. They probably just want some peaceful family time together."

"If they wanted peaceful family time, they would have just stayed at home." She tugged at his arm. "Come on."

Deon still resisted.

Malissa let go of her grip on his arm. "Come on. Let's just say hello."

Deon hesitated.

"Please, Deon. I just want to hear her say something. Just a simple hello. That's all. Please."

Deon said nothing, but he started moving in the couple's direction.

Malissa beamed him a huge smile. She turned and headed towards the couple as well. As she neared the couple, Malissa slowed her pace, coming to a stop as she came within a few yards of the approaching couple, waiting for them to close the distance. "Hi," she said as the couple neared. "Your daughter is lovely. Can I say hello to her?"

The woman smiled. "Sure." She looked down at

the little girl. "Honey, say hello to the nice lady."

The little girl looked up at Malissa as Malissa crouched down to get a better look at her. "Hello, nice lady," the little girl said.

Malissa froze, remaining in her crouched position as she looked into the vacant, soulless eyes of an Empty. Malissa said nothing to the girl, not even returning the hello; she just stared. The girl's eyes were a bright blue, but they were vacuous, like a doll's eyes, empty of any life, nearly plastic in appearance.

And then suddenly the girl was gone from her vision, tugged away from the strange lady by her parents. Malissa heard someone calling her name, but it took a few moments for her to realize it was Deon calling her and that she was still in a crouched down position staring at an empty space.

"That was a little rude, don't you think?" Deon said to her.

Malissa rose up and turned to Deon. "What?"

"You just stared at her and didn't say anything."

"She was an Empty."

"Oh." Deon stared after the departing couple for a moment, then turned back to Malissa to see the beginnings of hot tears flash in the corners of her eyes.

"Don't let me ever be like that, Deon. Promise me. I never want to be so desperate that I bring an Empty into the world." Malissa grabbed Deon's arm, harshly gripping it. "Promise me!"

That night, they cried together.

Malissa looked up at Deon with a fierce, almost

mad, determination in her anguish-burned red eyes. Deon returned her gaze with a firm resolve of his own.

The next morning, they studied the holo-display together, looking for news, searching for ideas, trying to come up with a plan that made sense. Only one option seemed to have true possibility. They needed to move higher up the list. They had to *help* a few people along…

⇜⇜⋅◖❀◗⋅⇝⇝

"Fuck off," Lorn Nalsam said. "I'm not ready to die yet."

"We just thought…" Deon said. "Well, you're always so damn miserable."

"Maybe I like being a miserable bastard," Lorn growled. "You ever think of that? Life isn't all sunshine and bubble baths, you know." He was a thin man with a head full of thinning white hair. He was dressed in a blue bathrobe, his feet encased in blue slippers. He wore a pair of thick-rimmed black glasses.

"The Great End would be a grand adventure for you, don't you think?" Deon inquired. "Perhaps you would be happy there."

"Fuck off. The Great End *is* the fucking end. It's not an adventure. It's not a place. It's a permanent black hole of nothingness that sucks you in and shreds your body into atoms." Lorn tied the sash of his bathrobe tighter around him.

"Your soul will be free," Deon said.

Lorn snorted a laugh. "My soul, ha!" He tapped violently at his own skull. "The only place my soul runs free is right in here. And once that's gone, I'm gone." He glared at Deon. "You only want my soul so it can be recycled into the little brat you want as your new toy."

Deon said nothing.

Lorn wagged a bony finger at Malissa. "And you, young lady, I'm pretty disgusted." He pointed at Deon. "Him, I understand. He's always been a weaselly piece of shit. But I expected much better from my own flesh and blood." He flicked his hand with rapid fire jerks of his wrist. "Get out." His face filled with a dark rage, the storm of anger seeming to come in as quickly as a wind burst in a hurricane. "You want to see me dead, then you might as well not see me at all! Get out! Get out! And don't ever bother coming back!"

Deon and Malissa scurried to the door.

"I'm going to report you both!" Lorn shouted after them. "See if you ever get a child after that!"

Deon stopped in his tracks, pausing in the threshold of the doorway.

Despite the tragic accidental death of Lorn Nalsam (he slipped and fell in the shower and cracked his head open), Malissa and Deon Archimedes were not granted the gift of a soul to use in the creation of a child. Overlord Prixle accessed the list. Yes, they were still on it. Yes, they had moved up one slot. Patience, he told them. Patience.

"I could arrange for an accident to happen on one

of the construction sites, maybe," Deon said. "A terrible fall. A tragic accident. A steel beam could crack open somebody's skull. Even the robo-docs can't put a smashed brain back together."

Malissa held up her hand. "Please, I don't want to hear the morbid details."

"I could re-program one of the constructor bots. Give it a few bad lines of code and just wait for an accident to happen. Let it be random chance."

Malissa shook her head. "No. Couldn't they trace that back to you? And just wait for an accident? How long would that even take?"

"Could be days, weeks even. I could push up the deadline and make everybody work a little faster, a little longer, give some higher overtime pay. That will cause mistakes for sure."

Malissa shook her head again. "No, I don't like it." She was quiet, thinking. "What about an aircar accident?"

"There hasn't been an aircar accident in probably at least twenty years." Deon shook his head. "Besides, they've got that code all locked up tight. No one can get at the core scripts. It's all autonomous now. Every last bit of its functionality is automated."

Malissa snapped her fingers. "I got it. Drowning. What about a drowning?"

Deon pursed his lips. "They'd have to be under a long time. Half a day at least, if not longer. Revival techniques are pretty robust these days. The brain's gotta be deprived of any oxygen for at least twelve hours."

They were both quiet.

"A bullet to the head would do the trick," Deon said.

"And where would you even get a gun?" Malissa asked. "They're outlawed except for Patrol Officers."

"Terrell is a P.O."

Malissa cocked her head, squinting at him. "Terrell would give you a gun?"

Deon shook his head. "No, he wouldn't *give me* a gun."

Malissa pulled back in surprise. "You want to steal a gun from a P.O.?"

"Not steal." Deon looked at her. "He's always liked you." He paused. "A lot."

Malissa frowned. "You want me to seduce Terrell and convince him to let me borrow his gun so we can put a bullet through someone's skull and scramble their brains?"

"I don't think you'd need to seduce him."

"So you just want to offer me up to him in exchange for using his gun?"

Deon was quiet. "Forget it. That's crazy. Besides, they'd be able to track the bullet back to his weapon."

Malissa thought quietly for a moment. "Not if we made sure to get the bullet back after we used it."

Deon looked at her with surprise, an almost oddly delighted surprise. "Now *that's* morbid."

They both laughed.

⋯⋯⋘❀❀⋙⋯⋯

Malissa kissed Terrell Graggs on the cheek. She was naked in bed with him. He was a tall black man of solid build and rugged good looks. "Can I touch it now?"

"Sure." Terrell reached over to the dresser next to the bed and grabbed his gun.

Malissa took the gun in her hand. "It's heavy," she said, bobbing her hand up and down as the gun rested on her open palm. She gripped the handle and pointed the weapon at the wall. She put her finger on the trigger, then looked at Terrell out of the corner of her eye. "Aren't you going to tell me to be careful where I point it."

Terrell shrugged. "It won't fire."

Malissa frowned.

"It won't shoot unless I'm holding it. It's registered to my palm print and my heat signature. They just upgraded all our weapons last month."

Malissa just froze.

"Is something wrong?"

Malissa said nothing. Then, finally she spoke. "No, no," she said, the words spilling out quickly. She handed the gun back to Terrell. "I've got to go." She reached for her shirt draped across a nearby chair.

Terrell grabbed her arm, stopping her. "Whoa, whoa."

Malissa remained motionless, continuing to stare at her clothing on the chair.

"What is going on here?"

Malissa didn't answer.

Terrell looked at her, released his grip on her, and looked down to the gun in his hand. "I knew this was way too easy." He looked back up at Malissa. "You wanted my gun. Why? What the hell are you planning, Malissa?"

"Nothing, just forget it."

"I'm a Patrol Officer and you were somehow trying to get access to my gun. I can't just forget it."

Malissa snatched at her shirt and started to put it on. "Just forget it. This was all a mistake."

Terrell grabbed her, not trying to be gentle or polite. He roughly pulled her around to face him. "What the hell is this, Malissa? What are you planning?"

In one amazingly fast motion, Malissa suddenly grabbed Terrell's hand, twisted it towards him. She slid her finger over his in the trigger slot and forced his finger down, firing the weapon into his lower abdomen. She pulled the trigger again and again.

Despite the tragic suicide of Patrol Officer Terrell Graggs, Malissa and Deon Archimedes were not granted the gift of a soul to use in the creation of a child. Overlord Prixle accessed the list. Yes, they were still on it. Yes, they had moved up one slot. Patience, he told them. Patience.

"Now who should die?" Deon asked. "We can just choose randomly. Pick someone on the street."

Malissa shook her head. "No, they need to deserve to die."

Deon looked at her curiously.

"If we're going to do this, then we need to do it... the right way," she said.

"There's nothing right about what we are doing," Deon said.

"So we should just quit? Give up? After what we... after what happened to my uncle and Terrell?"

"I didn't say that. I'm just saying that it's not right. Let's not kid ourselves into thinking this is right."

Malissa was quiet for a moment, still. She nodded.

"We should still pick someone who deserves it."

"Of course." Deon paused. "Got any other bad uncles in your closet?"

Malissa shook her head. "How about you?"

"My nephew is a real piece of work."

"How old is he?"

"About a hundred and twenty five or so. You met him once. Ronald. Fancies himself an artist. Paints that godawful dribble. Impressionist slices of life. It's all just meaningless swirls of color to me, but supposedly people buy the shit from him. A real arrogant fuck. Can't stand him."

Malissa was quiet for a moment. "Yeah, but does he deserve to die?"

Deon shrugged. "He's the only one that popped into my head. Just seems miserable all the time like your uncle was."

"There has to be someone else. Maybe someone in the news feeds."

Deon snorted out a laugh. "I'm sure a lot of people would like to see President Plutarch have an accident."

Malissa did not share in his mirth.

They were both quiet for a long moment, thinking.

"Did you know that simply removing one letter from immortality gives us immorality. I find that fascinating, don't you? Just drop the 't' and poof we go from immortal to immoral." Overlord Prixle paused, sincerely amazed by that observation. "Fascinating. It's so easy to go from one to the other."

Deon and Malissa just squinted curiously at the rotund man. They were once again in his office, inquiring about their status.

"Yes, well, thank you for coming. I wish it could be under more pleasant circumstances, but, well, it's just not." His ever-present smile colored his lips. His bowl of jellied candies remained untouched.

Deon frowned. He reached over to grab Malissa's hand but she pulled away from his reach.

"Your pattern of behavior is oddly curious," Overlord Prixle said.

Deon fidgeted in the chair, shifting positions. Malissa stared at her hands; they trembled ever so slightly and she folded her fingers together to mask the motion.

Overlord Prixle stared at them.

"How do you mean?" Deon asked.

"Three times now you have visited me in the last eight months. And each visit has been preceded by an unfortunate death of one of our citizens." Overlord Prixle wiped a tear away from his corpulent cheek with his chubby fingers. "I apologize for my display of emotion. Death is now very... upsetting for me. Such an unnecessary process."

Malissa looked up at the Overlord. "Who died?" she asked. She looked at Deon, then back to the Overlord. "We haven't heard of any recent deaths." She looked back to Deon. "Have we, Deon?"

The insincerity in her voice was obvious and Deon nearly winced at her tone. They had dumped Ronald's body into Hampton Lake, wrapped with a hundred pounds of stones and bricks. There was no way that his body could have floated back up to the surface so soon, but a nearly paralyzing wave of doubt swept over him. He didn't answer for a moment, but then quickly shook his head. "No, no we haven't." He looked to the Overlord. "Who just died?"

"I'm not crying for who just died," the Overlord said. "I'm crying for who is about to die." He stared sadly at Deon and Malissa Archimedes.

"I have some exciting news!" The Overlord's eyes were bright, his face full of emotion, his smile wide.

Yasmin and Abdullah Makalai waited with growing anticipation. They held each other's hands tightly as they sat before the Overlord's desk.

"How does twins sound?" Overlord Prixle beamed with happiness. He popped a jellied candy into his mouth.

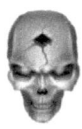

A NOTE FROM JACK O'DONNELL

Thanks for reading this sixth collection of my Land of Fright™ tales. I hope you continue to journey with me as we move deeper into the dark realms within the Land of Fright™. There are many new uncharted realms yet to be mapped, so keep checking back for new discoveries.

Visit www.landoffright.com and subscribe to stay up-to-date on the latest new stories in the Land of Fright™ series of horror short stories.

Or visit my author page on Amazon at www.amazon.com/author/jodonnell to see the newest releases in the Land of Fright™ series.

- JACK

MORE LAND OF FRIGHT™ COLLECTIONS ARE AVAILABLE NOW!

Turn the page and step into fear!

Land of Fright™ terrorstories contained in Collection I:

#1 - Whirring Blades: A simple late-night trip to the mall for a father and his son turns into a struggle for survival when they are attacked by a deadly swarm of toy helicopters.

#2 - The Big Leagues: A scorned young baseball player shows his teammates he really knows how to play ball with the best of them.

#3 - Snowflakes: In the land of Frawst, special snowflakes are a gift from the gods, capable of transferring the knowledge of the Ancients. A young woman searches the skies with breathless anticipation for her snowflake, but finds something far more dark and dangerous instead.

#4 - End of the Rainbow: In Medieval England, a warrior and his woman find the end of a massive rainbow that has filled the sky and discover the dark secret of its power.

#5 - Trophy Wives: An enigmatic sculptor meets a beautiful woman whom he vows will be his next subject. But things may not turn out the way he plans...

#6 - Die-orama: A petty thief finds out that a WWII model diorama in his local hobby shop holds much more than just plastic vehicles and plastic soldiers.

#7 - Creature in the Creek: A lonely young woman finds her favorite secluded spot inhabited by a monster from her past.

#8 - The Emperor of Fear: In ancient Rome, two coliseum workers encounter a mysterious crate containing an unearthly creature. Just in time for the next gladiator games...

#9 - The Towers That Fell From The Sky: Two analysts race to uncover the secret purpose of the giant alien towers that have thundered down out of the skies.

#10 - God Save The Queen: An exterminator piloting an ant-sized robot comes face to face with the queen of a nest he has been assigned to destroy.

Land of Fright™ terrorstories contained in Collection II:

#11 - Special Announcement: A fraud investigator discovers the disturbing truth behind the messages on a community announcement board.

#12 - Poisoned Land: Savage hunters patrol the Poisoned Lands, demanding appeasement from the three survivors trapped in a surrounded building. How far will each one of them go to survive?

#13 - Pool of Light: A mysterious wave of dark energy from space washes over the Earth, trapping a woman and her friends in pools of light. Beyond the edges of the light, deep pockets of darkness hold much more than just empty blackness.

#14 - Ghosts of Pompeii: A woman on a tour of Italy with her son unwittingly awakens the ghosts of Pompeii.

#15 - Sparklers: A child's sparkler opens a doorway to another dimension and a father must enter it to save his family and his neighborhood from the ominous threat that lays beyond.

#16 - The Grid: An interstellar salvage crew activates a mysterious grid on an abandoned vessel floating in space, unleashing a deadly force.

#17 - The Barn: An empty barn beckons an amateur photographer to step through its dark entrance, whispering promises of a once-in-a-lifetime shoot.

#18 - Sands of the Colosseum: A businessman in Rome gets to experience the dream of a lifetime when he visits the great Colosseum — until he finds himself standing on the arena floor.

#19 - Flipbook: A man sees a dark future of his family in jeopardy when he watches the tiny animations of a flipbook play out in his hand.

#20 - Day of the Hoppers: Two boys flee for their lives when their friendly neighborhood grasshoppers turn into deadly projectiles.

Land of Fright™ terrorstories contained in Collection III:

#21 - The Prospector: In the 1800's, a lonely prospector finds the body parts of a woman as he pans for gold in the wilds of California.

#22 - The Boy In The Yearbook: Two middle-aged women are tormented by a mysterious photograph in their high school yearbook.

#23 - Shot Glass: A man discovers the shot glasses in his great-grandfather's collection can do much more than just hold a mouthful of liquor.

#24 - The Champion: An actor in a medieval renaissance re-enactment show becomes the unbeatable champion he has longed to be.

#25 - Hitler's Graveyard: American soldiers in WWII uncover a nefarious Nazi plan to resurrect their dead heroes so they can rejoin the war.

#26 - Out of Ink: Colonists on a remote planet resort to desperate measures to ward off an attack from wild alien animals.

#27 - Dung Beetles: Mutant dung beetles attack a family on a remote Pennsylvania highway. Yes, it's as disgusting as it sounds.

#28 - The Tinies: A beleaguered office worker encounters a strange alien armada in the sub-basement of his office building.

#29 - Hammer of Charon: In ancient Rome, it is the duty of a special man to make sure gravely wounded gladiators are given a quick death after a gladiator fight. He serves his position quietly with honor. Until they try to take his hammer away from him…

#30 - Pharaoh's Cat: In ancient Egypt, the pharaoh is dying. His trusted advisors want his favorite cat to be buried with him. The cat has other plans…

Land of Fright™ terrorstories contained in Collection IV:

#31 - The Throw-Aways: A washed-up writer of action-adventure thrillers is menaced by the ghosts of the characters he has created.

#32 - Everlasting Death: The souls of the newly deceased take on solid form and the Earth fills with immovable statues of death...

#33 - Bite the Bullet: In the Wild West, a desperate outlaw clings to a bullet cursed by a Gypsy... because the bullet has his name on it.

#34 - Road Rage: A senseless accident on a rural highway sets off a frightening chain of events.

#35 - The Controller: A detective investigates a bank robbery that appears to have been carried out by a zombie.

#36 - The Notebook: An enchanted notebook helps a floundering author finish her story. But the unnatural fuel that stokes the power of the mysterious writing journal leads her down a disturbing path...

#37 - The Candy Striper and the Captain: American WWII soldiers in the Philippines scare superstitious enemy soldiers with corpses they dress up to look like vampire victims. The vampire bites might be fake, but what comes out of the jungle is not...

#38 - Clothes Make the Man: A young man steals a magical suit off of a corpse, hoping some of its power will rub off on him.

#39 - Memory Market: The cryptic process of memory storage in the human brain has been decoded and now memories are bought and sold in the memory market. But with every legitimate commercial endeavor there comes a black market, and the memory market is no exception...

#40 - The Demon Who Ate Screams: A young martial artist battles a vicious demon who feeds on the tormented screams and dying whimpers of his victims.

Land of Fright™ terrorstories contained in Collection V:

#41 - The Hatchlings: A peaceful barbecue turns into an afternoon of terror for a suburban man when the charcoal briquets start to hatch!

#42 - Virgin Sacrifice: A professor of archaeology is determined to set the world right again using the ancient power of Aztec sacrifice rituals.

#43 - Smog Monsters: The heavily contaminated air in Beijing turns even deadlier when unearthly creatures form within the dense poison of its thick pollution.

#44 - Benders of Space-Time: A young interstellar traveler discovers the uncomfortable truth about the Benders, the creatures who power starships with their ability to fold space-time.

#45 - The Picture: A young soldier in World War II shows his fellow soldiers a picture of his beautiful fiancé during the lulls in battle. But this seemingly harmless gesture is far from innocent…

#46 - Black Ice: A vicious dragon is offered a great gift — a block of black ice to soothe the fire that burns its throat and roars in its belly. Too bad the dragon has never heard of a Trojan dwarf…

#47 - Artist Alley: At a comic book convention, a seedy comic book publisher sees himself depicted in a disturbing series of artist drawings.

#48 - Dead Zone: A yacht gets caught adrift in the dead zone in the Gulf of Mexico, trapped in an area of the sea that contains no life. What comes aboard the yacht from the depths of this dead zone in search of food cannot really be considered alive…

#49 - Cemetery Dance: A suicidal madman afraid to take his own life attempts to torment a devout Christian man into killing him.

#50 - The King Who Owned the World: A bored barbarian king demands he be brought a new challenger. But who can you find to battle a king who owns the world

AND LOOK FOR EVEN MORE
LAND OF FRIGHT™ STORIES
COMING SOON!

THANKS AGAIN FOR READING.

Visit www.landoffright.com

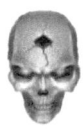